The 40 mm warhead slammed into the tread of the tank

Mack Bolan lifted the M-16 into target acquisition and squeezed off a series of 3-round bursts that caught the tank's machine gunner across the chest and face.

The ground trembled under the Executioner's driving legs as he sprinted for the disabled tank. He ripped a frag grenade from his combat harness, tossed the lever and pulled the pin, counting down the numbers. With three seconds left, he dropped the grenade down the hatch and backpedaled.

The world came apart around Bolan as shells inside the tank blew up. Moving in a solid sheet of force, the concussion lifted the big warrior from his feet and hurled him forward.

His breath exploded from his lungs as he hit the ground, and for a moment he thought he'd lost his weapon. Then he felt the pistol grip snug in his fingers. He reloaded the M-16 and began to advance.

The battle had been joined sooner than expected, but his men had come to fight, stirred on by a patriotic fervor and an edge that they hadn't expected to carry into battle.

The warrior only hoped it was enough to win the day.

DON PENDLETON'S

THE EXECUTIONER®

FEATURING

MACK BOLAN®

BATTLE FORCE

A GOLD EAGLE BOOK FROM

W RLDWIDE®

TORONTO • NEW YORK • LONDON
AMSTERDAM • PARIS • SYDNEY • HAMBURG
STOCKHOLM • ATHENS • TOKYO • MILAN
MADRID • WARSAW • BUDAPEST • AUCKLAND

First edition August 1993

ISBN 0-373-61432-2

Special thanks and acknowledgment to
Mel Odom for his contribution to this work.

BATTLE FORCE

... no cause is left but the most ancient of all, the one, in fact, that from the beginning of our history has determined the very existence of politics, the cause of freedom versus tyranny.

—Hannah Arendt
On Revolution, 1963

Freedom has never been won cheaply. It's something that revolutionaries take for themselves at immense cost, then give to their children with great love.

—Mack Bolan

CHAPTER ONE

Buckled into the passenger seat of the HMMWV M-998, Mack Bolan divided his attention between the night-darkened Baltic forest and the radioed communications feeding back to him from the various South Haakovian forces under his direction. The static over the radio frequencies popped and crackled, masking the whooshing thrust the rocket must have made as it exploded from the launcher.

The Executioner caught the threat in the periphery of his vision, saw the trail of sparks and gray fog splashing out in the missile's wake as it sped for the left side of the M-998. "Rocket!" he growled as he reached for the steering wheel. He yanked hard right, away from the rocket, but knew he wasn't quick enough to completely clear the round.

The shell slammed into the Hummer's left fender, the explosion shuddering through the vehicle. With a groan of tortured metal, wrapped in a wreath of crackling flames that hugged the fender, the M-998 jerked over onto its back.

Bolan's ears rang from the detonation as he hung upside down. He tried the seat belt, found it was jammed and wouldn't release. The raw smell of gasoline was cloying in his nostrils. He raked the Cold Steel Tanto combat knife from its harness sheath across his chest and checked the men with him.

The driver's head lolled to one side. Blood streamed from a long cut on his jaw and dripped in ragged splatters across the impacted roof of the military vehicle. His thready pulse beat in the dark hollow of his throat.

Both men in the back were scrambling to regain their bearings.

"Get out," Bolan ordered.

It was possible that the covert North Haakovian force that had attacked them knew that they'd had the acting commander of the South Haakovian army in their sights. Janyte Varkaus's confirmation as the Baltic country's political leader after her husband's assassination hadn't gone uncontested, and the snakes were still continuing to crawl out of the woodwork as Franzen Stensvik reached more deeply into the sister country.

"But Colonel Pollock," one of the men protested.

Pollock was the cover name Bolan was using while acting as a U.S. military adviser to South Haakovia. "Out," the warrior repeated. "Now."

"Yes, sir." The man reached up, popped the latch on the Hummer's rear door and got out on the side opposite the fender struck by the rocket. The other man followed, moving groggily.

Bullets whined off the M-998. The fire on the fender had established itself, was eating into the rubber tire and filling the air with thick, acrid smoke.

Bolan slashed the seat restraints with the combat knife and reached for the driver. It took two passes with the keen-edged knife to get the unconscious man loose. The driver rolled into a boneless heap.

The first of the North Haakovian soldiers came into view, cautiously taking cover in the brush. The brown field uniform almost blended in with the night, but there was no mistaking the barrel of the AK-47 cradled in his arms.

The attack on Larsborg, the capital of South Haako-via, was only hours in the past. Despite the southern army's preparations, losses had been considerable. And they had lost even more while driving the invading army back to the Inge River forming the natural boundary of the two countries. The Executioner had seen a lot of good men die, men he'd worked hard and trained with over the past handful of weeks while acting at the U.S. President's request to be in-country. Even when they'd routed Sten-svik's forces, Bolan had known some of them hadn't rushed back to the North, and were waiting to chip away at the southern offensive as it gathered to retaliate.

It was something the Executioner would have done himself. Tonight's maneuvers were designed to flush out the stragglers, clear the way for the tank platoons marching for the border. Operating on Janyte Varkaus's permission, Bolan had designed a combat scenario that would hopefully propel the South into a stance that would allow them to deal from a position of power. There was no longer any doubt that war existed between the two countries, only the question of how long it would last.

The North Haakovian soldier broke cover, kept low and advanced on the Hummer.

Bolan tugged the Desert Eagle .44 Magnum pistol from his hip holster. Dropping the big gun into target acquisition, he thrust it through the shattered window and took up the slack on the trigger. He fired two shots, and the sudden noise boomed in the black heart of the forest.

Both 240-grain rounds caught the approaching North Haakovian in the chest, punching him backward several steps before death robbed him of his balance.

Autofire rattled off the sides of the Hummer with renewed enthusiasm, but it was quickly discouraged by the

3-round bursts from the M-16A2s wielded by the two South Haakovians.

Shifting, Bolan slung his assault rifle, then fisted the driver's shirt collar. He had to kick the door open to get out. Muscles ached in his back and shoulders as he pulled the unconscious man from the vehicle. Heat washed over him from the twisting spiral of fire stabbing up from the tires. Knowing the glare would allow his attackers to find him now that he was exposed, he dropped to one knee, shrugged the driver's weight over his shoulder, pushed up and ran for the shelter offered by the forest.

Bullets chased him, cutting leaves from the trees and bushes around and beside him. He made sure the driver's injuries weren't life-threatening and covered him with brush as makeshift camouflage. Provided he and his team made it out of the confrontation intact, he'd see the man got medical attention.

Bolan scanned the forest. Within seconds he spotted three North Haakovian soldiers making a circle on the positions held by him and his men.

He took up his M-16 and flicked off the safety. Taking the walkie-talkie from his pocket, he shrugged off the coat and tossed it aside. He slipped the walkie-talkie into the leather harness designed for it on his left shoulder, keyed it into operation and attached the ear-throat headset. He checked to make sure it was set for the South Haakovian infantry frequency. "Stone Hammer team," he said softly, "this is Stone Hammer Leader. Over."

"Yes, Stone Hammer Leader."

Bolan reached into the equipment bag belted at his waist and took out an infrared night scope for the M-16, locking it into place. He uncapped it, dropped the caps into the bag and looked through the scope. Through the lenses, the forest turned a montage of greens. He slid the fire selector to single-shot. Recognizing the speaker's voice as Jurgis, the older of the two men left able-bodied, the Executioner said, "You're Stone Hammer One."

"Yes, sir."

"Come in, Stone Hammer Two," Bolan called.

There was only a small hesitation before the second man came onto the frequency. "Stone Hammer Two reads you, Stone Hammer Leader."

"Roger that," Bolan said. He rose, staying within the dark shadows of the forest, and moved toward the approaching enemy. "You two stay put, and be advised that you're going to have a friendly down there."

"But, sir—"

"That's an order, soldier. Over and out." Bolan bracketed a North Haakovian less than a hundred yards away, peering out from behind a tree. The warrior shouldered the assault rifle, put the cross hairs on his target and squeezed the trigger. The single report sounded sharp and flat.

The 5.56 mm round caught the soldier flat-footed, shattered his temple and yanked his head back. The corpse stumbled back into the brush, dead before it vanished.

A brief volley of rifle fire smashed into the brush the Executioner had used for cover, but by that time he was already gone.

Canting his rifle against a tree, Bolan stripped out of the unmarked South Haakovian cammies. The skintight blacksuit he wore beneath was as much a weapon to him as the M-16. A tube of combat cosmetics from his equipment bag masked his features and hands. Satisfied, he picked up his weapon and padded toward the remnants of the North Haakovian contingent that had hunted him down. But now, he was more predatory than they were. They worked with the night, used it as a tool. The Executioner was in his element.

He hit the transmit button on the headset. "Stone Hammer Leader to Stone Hammer team. Over."

"Stone Hammer Leader, you have One."

"And you have Two, Leader."

"How many do you count?"

"Three," Stone Hammer Two answered.

"Four," Jurgis replied.

"Acknowledged. Out." Bolan went on. Years of jungle warfare in Vietnam and in the violent hot spots of the worlds had prepared him for the action between the two Baltic countries.

The fire on the Hummer had finally reached the gas tank. The resulting explosion lighted up the night for a prolonged instant.

One of the North Haakovian soldiers pulled out of position less than thirty yards from Bolan, startled by the noise and sudden spray of flames.

The Executioner fired two rounds, catching the man in the throat with the first one, just below the nose with the second. Whatever noise the man might have made before he died was lost in the roaring whoosh surrounding the burning Hummer.

The warrior had counted four enemy soldiers. Now there were three.

Franzen Stensvik had surrounded himself with the last of the Communist forces as the old Soviet Union was crumbling. Most of those forces were the dregs of the Russian populace and political machine. And greed wasn't in the same league as freedom as a motivator. The North Haakovian dictator and his army had found that out earlier in the day when their assault ran aground on the South's defensive perimeters. But now it was time to take the torch back to the milling cannibals.

He eased the Beretta 93-R from shoulder leather when he found the next man. The guy sat nervously hunkered behind a gnarled oak tree. Some primeval instinct must have alerted him to Bolan's presence, because the big soldier was sure the man never heard him coming. The man whirled, tried to bring the AK-47 around.

The man didn't have a chance, dying with his finger on the trigger, the AK-47's burst cutting a ragged swath through the leafy canopy overhead.

Bolan broke left, angled away from the burning M-998. He tried to put the last two North Haakovian survivors between himself and the flames, hoping to skyline them against the night.

Voices called out but weren't answered. Autofire scarred the oak tree where the soldier had been hiding. Evidently his companions had already assumed the worst.

The headset buzzed in Bolan's ear. "Go," he whispered, still on the move.

"Emergency message coming in over Alpha Prime from Mockingbird," Jurgis said.

"Copy," Bolan replied. He reached over his shoulder, switched freqs on the walkie-talkie. Janyte Varkaus had already gone missing this night, and he'd had the impression that that bit of news wasn't going to be the last of the bad. Mockingbird was Special Forces Lieutenant-Colonel Neal R. Lansdale, the American adviser Bolan had left in charge of the infantry units. "Mockingbird, you have Stone Hammer Leader. You're calling me in a tight, mister."

"Understood, sir. Got a bit of intel you needed, though."

"The lady?" Bolan asked, thinking of Janyte Varkaus. There was still some guilt associated with her. Maybe if he hadn't pushed her so hard to take an aggressive stance, she wouldn't be in the situation she was in now. But it wasn't just him pushing. The whole damn war had been threatening to erupt since he'd been in-country. If anything, he'd allowed her to cut some of the country's losses with an offensive posture.

"Still unaccounted for, Stone Hammer Leader," Lansdale replied. "But I've got recon teams out beating the bushes for her now. If I get anything, I'll give you a shout. It also appears that the president's kidnapping wasn't the only treachery General Markus planned. I've got heavy armor dropping in place everywhere. Apparently the general rewrote some of the orders you cut this afternoon. He rerouted the gas-supply trucks, placed them miles from the rendezvous points. The whole advance has stalled out."

The Executioner turned the possibilities over in his mind. He'd led in the infantry units himself, preparatory to shoring up the offensive with the tanks. Without the heavy armor, the ground teams were going to be left conspicuously unprotected if Stensvik decided to go for a rout. And the air-support teams would be hard-pressed to cover all the soft areas left open. "Where are they?" He continued through the brush, his voice little more than a whisper.

Lansdale called out the four coordinates.

"Four areas?" Bolan asked as he placed the locations on his mental map of the country.

"Roger, Stone Hammer Leader."

Suspicion twisted in Bolan's stomach. "Get them out of there now," the warrior ordered. "Markus set them up."

"Acknowledged, Stone Hammer Leader. Mockingbird, out."

The headset clicked in Bolan's ear at the same time a branch crunched under a boot only a few feet away. He spun, felt the wind of a bullet pass by his face and saw the

North Haakovian soldier trying to line up his next shot. The Executioner's right hand dropped to the Desert Eagle, tugged the big pistol free. He brought it to his waist, fired from the hip, rode out the recoil and brought the gun up.

A second bullet from the AK-47 dug into the tree bole beside the warrior, kicking splinters into his face.

Four rounds from the Israeli-made hand cannon spilled the corpse backward. Bolan holstered the weapon and moved on, looking for the last man.

A frightened voice called out someone's name but went unanswered.

The Executioner homed in on the voice, heard the guy take flight a few seconds later. The N.H. soldier crashed through the brush like a startled wild beast. Vectoring in on the noise, the warrior closed the distance, navigating the shadows until he confronted the man.

The soldier didn't know whether to shoot or to run, and by the time he made up his mind it was too late.

Bolan lifted the M-16 and snap-fired a 5.56 mm round that cored through the man's heart and dropped him to the ground. After making sure the man was dead, he walked back toward the burning Hummer, using it as a point of reference. He adjusted the walkie-talkie's frequency again and tapped the transmit button. The com net they'd spread out from Larsborg would allow him to bootleg into the capital city where the South Haakovian air force was kept and maintained. "Stone Hammer Leader calling G-Force. Come in G-Force."

"Stone Hammer Leader, you have G-Force. Over." G-Force was Jack Grimaldi, Stony Man Farm's ace pilot and one of the closest friends Bolan had ever had. Between them they'd racked up a lot of years in war mileage.

Thunder crackled in the skies overhead. When Bolan looked up he could almost make out what he was sure were Russian MiGs streaking from North Haakovia. He didn't have to be psychic to guess what their targets were. In terse sentences he gave Jack Grimaldi and his team their orders.

MOVING AT A FLAT-OUT RUN from the hangar area, Jack Grimaldi finished zipping up his flight suit and adjusted the ear-throat mike that connected him to the rest of the team. Eagle One was a Navy pilot from the Top Gun program. Eagle Two and Eagle Three were domestic pilots. Both of them were good jet jockeys but hadn't had any real combat experience. He felt a pang of guilt about taking them up into the sky with him on the mission. The Navy pilot, Ted Paulsen, had been involved in the Gulf War missions against Iraq. He was already blooded.

"Look alive, gents," Grimaldi said in a calm voice. "This is definitely not going to be a milk run." His support officer steadied the ladder leading into the F-15 Eagle's cockpit. The pilot went up the rungs quickly, sat down and started to buckle himself in.

The support officer shoved a Colt Cobra in his shoulder holster. "Never know, sir," the young man said. "You end up losing the plane, could be a long walk back through occupied territory."

"I'll keep that in mind, son," Grimaldi replied dryly. "I wasn't looking at the positive side of this thing."

The guy grinned. "Yes, sir." He helped Grimaldi on with his helmet, then clapped it to signify that he was clear.

The cockpit dropped into place, locked down tight.

Grimaldi keyed the engines, got them up to cold idle. "Okay, girls," he said in a confident voice, "your basic diamond pattern. I'm in the lead."

The three other pilots quickly confirmed that they'd heard him.

"Give me clearance, Tower," Grimaldi called out over the tower freq.

"Clearance is yours, G-Force," the tower responded. "Have a safe trip."

"I doubt it," Grimaldi muttered under his breath as he took the yoke in hand. He powered the jets up, left the ground in a long scream, then heeled over in a roll that came out with him headed north, toward the quadrants Bolan had given him. With the ground beneath him and the air under his wings, some of the unease left him, unknotted from his shoulders.

So far the whole night had been one long snafu. The Stony Man teams seemed to be striking out across the board. And the stakes had never been higher. Stensvik was playing hard, and the man was playing for keeps. With the Soviet nuclear and bacteriological arsenal he had, the whole world wasn't going to be safe until the man was taken down. Part of the problem stemmed from the fact that the rest of the world didn't really believe that.

He glanced at the radar, picking up the MiGs as they came on-screen. He keyed his mike. "Okay, Eagle team," he said, "we have contact."

"Roger, G-Force," Paulsen replied.

The other two pilots radioed back as well.

"I count six," Grimaldi said.

"Six," Paulsen agreed.

Gauging his speed and the time elapsed, Grimaldi knew they had to be somewhere over the areas where the gas-supply trucks had been rerouted under General Markus's faked orders.

"They got one away," Paulsen called out calmly.

Grimaldi scanned the sky using the F-15's instrumentation. He tracked the pair of air-to-air missiles as they jetted free of the lead enemy aircraft's underbelly. "Brake hard left on my signal, Eagle team," he said. He watched the distance flip down to ground zero on the monitors. "Now!"

He glanced over his shoulder as the g-force increased and threw him back to one side of the seat. The three other fighter jets were at his heels.

The missile slid harmlessly by.

Glancing back at the two wing formations streaking toward them, he recognized the hard lines of the aircraft as MiG-29s. As he watched, the rear two jets broke out of formation and dropped altitude in screaming dives.

"Eagle One," Grimaldi said.

"Go," Paulsen replied.

"Take Eagle Two with you and intercept those guys."

"Roger."

The jet peeled off to his right, dropped into an attack path that would bring it on a level with the North Haakovian war birds. The second F-15 was slightly out of sync but was kicking in the afterburners.

Grimaldi turned his attention to the other four attacking aircraft. "Eagle Three."

"Go, G-Force."

"On my mark as I call it," Grimaldi said. "Let's see if we can stay alive here on the high deck."

"Yes, sir."

Grimaldi called out their response, kicked out hard right to avoid another pair of missiles, came out of a roll and fired two of his own air-to-air missiles. He felt them cut loose from the wings, the vibrations rippling back through the cockpit. Their twin streamers curved slightly as they picked up the heat trail of their target. A heartbeat later the Russian craft exploded.

"All right," Grimaldi congratulated himself quietly. He yanked the yoke, calling out instructions to his wingman. They broke, came up on deck again and went back for another pass. He monitored Paulsen's transmissions to his own wingman. He knew things weren't going so well below. Eagle Two had been shot down, but the pilot had safely made the silk.

One of the MiGs had gone down under Paulsen's guns, but the other managed to drop its payload on the tankers struggling to find safe haven below. Roiling clouds of fire lighted up the night, letting Grimaldi know the North Haakovians were using fuel-air explosives.

"Son of a bitch," Grimaldi muttered when he glanced out the side of the cockpit at the damage. It looked like an ocean of bloodred fire had spread across the forest below.

The tanker trucks were important to the operation Bolan had set up, and Grimaldi knew it. So had Markus and Stensvik. While the North was well stocked in military hardware, the South had had to depend on U.S. shipments to defend itself. Every piece of equipment was dear to the war effort, and it would take too damn long to replace the lost fuel.

He led another pass through the Russian warplanes, missed with his missiles and felt machine-gun fire rattle along the fuselage of his plane.

"I'm hit!" Eagle Three screamed.

Slipping the yoke comfortably in his hand, Grimaldi jockeyed around until he could see his wingman.

The F-15 was history. He could tell that immediately. Smoke streamed out of the body of the jet, and one of the engines had obviously blown out.

Grimaldi hit the transmit button on his mike. "Eject, dammit!"

There was no response. The American fighter jet shot toward the earth nose-first.

"Eagle Three, Eagle Three!" Grimaldi hated the helpless feeling that filled him. Orange tracer fire sped across his bow, hammered his cowling with a too-familiar tattoo of destruction.

The F-15 fell like a broken-backed bird.

"Eject!" Grimaldi yelled as he broke hard to escape the tracer fire.

The MiG followed him, kicked an air-to-air missile loose as soon as missile lock was achieved.

Grimaldi pulled back on the yoke and shot up, pulling as many g's as he could. Perspiration leaked down his face inside the mask. The oxygen tasted tainted, too thin to survive on. Then his instruments showed that the missile had cleared him. He heeled over, let the altitude drop away and came down behind the attacking craft, already noting the second one advancing on him from the rear. He triggered the machine guns, heard their muted roar as they kicked to life. Tracers cut through the Plexiglas of the cockpit.

The MiG fell away, the pilot obviously unable to control his craft anymore.

Heeling over, Grimaldi dropped more altitude. He glanced over his shoulder, making sure the pursuing MiG was still on him. He hit the transmit button. "Eagle One."

"Go." Paulsen's voice sounded harried.

Grimaldi couldn't find the pilot in the confusion below. "Do you see Eagle Three?"

"He didn't make it."

The Stony Man pilot cursed silently. He forced his attention back to the Russian jet burning up his backtrail.

Without warning, it turned away from him, streaking for the hard deck. "Look alive, Eagle One. Those MiGs have just decided that the tankers are more important than either of us."

"Roger, G-Force. I'm on this bad boy down here."

The fire had spread from the mushroom blasts of the fuel-air explosives and the trapped fuel in the tanker trucks to the surrounding forest. It would take a concerted effort on someone's part to extinguish the blaze before it claimed a large section of the trees and brush.

Altering his speed and direction, Grimaldi rolled off and exchanged roles with the Russian, became the pursuer instead of the pursued. Even mustering up every bit of speed the F-15 had, he didn't know if he was going to be on time.

The ground came rushing up at him, painted in austere blacks and grays under the quarter moon. The MiG was a silver shadow hurtling by only a few hundred feet above the ground, flying as straight and as true as if wire-guided. The second survivor from the top deck was a handful of plane lengths ahead of it, at almost the same height.

Grimaldi recognized the terrain from aerial recon patrols. Markus had chosen his false fuel sites with care. The trucks had to have had a hard time getting that far through the brush, and there was no damn way they could escape in any kind of a hurry.

They crossed the first line of fuel-air explosives, the smoke partially obscuring the twisted and broken wreckage that had been tanker trucks. Grimaldi was glad they were passing through so quickly he couldn't discern any of the bodies he was sure had to be down there. The defiles leading out of the low mountains flanking the Inge River in South Haakovia had become a valley of death. And the two Russian MiGs were the vultures come to pick over the bones.

He added power, coasted along the slipstream of the Russian war bird and closed the distance. The instrumentation bleeped and chattered at him as it tracked onto missile lock. "C'mon, c'mon," he said. A few hundred yards ahead of them he saw the last of the tankers struggling to make the grade. Even as he watched, one of them lost traction. The tractor's big tires flailed helplessly for a moment, then lost it entirely. It jackknifed, folded in on itself, then tumbled down the incline.

The F-15's attack computer showed missile lock.

Grimaldi's thumb closed over the launch button. Two air-to-air missiles cut loose from his wings and shot through the twisting smoke left over from the earlier strike.

But even then he could see that it was too late.

Dark pods flipped from the belly of the MiG, becoming a solid cloud that poured out over the fleeing tanker trucks.

"Dammit," Grimaldi shouted as he pulled back on the yoke to gain altitude.

The explosions came like a chain of firecrackers, throwing flames dozens of feet into the air as the oxygen itself caught fire.

Grimaldi rode the concussive wave, dimly aware that the MiG-29 had exploded somewhere under him. Regaining control over his craft, he heeled over and gained some altitude, then hit the transmit button. "Eagle One."

"I read you, G-Force."

"The other MiG?"

"Down. Too late."

Grimaldi looked out over the carnage. "I know the feeling. Kick it in the ass on the way home. There's nothing we can do here. G-Force out."

Paulsen streaked into the night.

Lingering for just a moment, Grimaldi made a final circle over the battleground, trying not to think about the casualties. You weren't always on time. He knew that. Hell, sometimes he could even accept that. It had happened in Nam, and it had happened since then. In every war there were losses, and every damned one of them hurt.

He shrugged his shoulders, tried to work the tension out of them, then changed radio freqs. "Stone Hammer Leader, this is G-Force. Over."

"Go, G-Force."

Grimaldi could tell by the tone in Bolan's voice that the hellfire warrior already knew the outcome of the rescue mission. Judging from the size of the fiery destruction shooting out below him, it was probably visible from where Bolan was. "Negative results on the scrub. I lost one, plus the ground troops. They lost six men and machines."

"Roger," Bolan replied. "See if you can arrange some air transport for me. I want to take a look at the situation from a different perspective."

"Acknowledged. G-Force, out." Grimaldi banked for Larsborg. It had been a long day, and it was promising to be an even longer night. Everything the South Haakovian army tried to put together seemed to turn to shit. Stensvik had plotted too well, found too many greedy people within the South's military ranks. Hell, the North Haakovian dictator had even managed to buy the finest general the country had turned out.

But the Baltic countries had never witnessed anything like Mack Bolan. The big warrior was the best fighting machine Grimaldi had ever seen, had the sharpest mind for the military arts the pilot had ever met, and the big guy only fought when he truly believed in what he was fighting for.

And in South Haakovia, there was a hell of a lot worth fighting for.

CHAPTER TWO

Hal Brognola walked on the President's left as the White House entourage passed down the hallway to the United Nations General Assembly. Secret Service men and uniformed UN security people flanked them on both sides. They'd left the majority of reporters and cameramen outside the building, but some of them still pursued relentlessly. Someone shoved a microphone in front of him, and he batted it away reflexively with enough force that the guy holding on to it dropped it on the floor.

The newsman went from asking questions to hurling invective. The other media people seemed to think that was newsworthy and instantly shifted focus.

Brognola figured that would just be frosting on the cake. The Man was already here to deliver bad news and an ultimatum. A top dog in the Justice Department manhandling an uncouth reporter wouldn't draw that much attention. He hoped. He sighed, reached a hand into his coat pocket and took out a roll of antacid tablets that had already been opened. Practice allowed him to shake out two of them with no more than cursory attention to the mechanics.

The President said something quietly.

"Sir?" Brognola said, ducking in close so their words wouldn't carry to the media.

The President waited outside the door leading to the General Assembly while the Secret Service teams checked everything out. The assassination attempts on the South

Haakovian ambassadors had caused security to be beefed up, and anxieties were still running high. The President's decision to visit that afternoon had met with resistance and a few well-founded fears.

"I said, 'milk,'" the Man said. He pointed to the roll of antacid tablets in Brognola's hand. "If you keep chewing those things, you're never going to get any better. Drink some warm milk. It'll help relax you."

"I'm sure it would," the head Fed replied. The Man was nervous and was choosing the topic of antacids to calm himself before giving his presentation to the assembled nations of the world. As liaison for the most top secret antiterrorist groups in the country, there weren't many opportunities for Brognola to relax. Especially not in the middle of a mission.

The President adjusted his tie. "Do I look okay?"

"You look fine," Brognola said. Actually he hadn't seen the Man look that bad since the previous year's riot in L.A.

"It's hard to say what's going to go down in there after I say what I've come to say," the President told him.

Brognola nodded. There was nothing he could respond with. The situation in the Haakovias was up in the air, and the rest of the world hung on every motion. Some of the countries represented inside would support the position the United States was taking on the issue of freedom for South Haakovia and against Franzen Stensvik's unspoken threats to use the Soviet arsenal in his possession. With the way the nuclear warheads had been parceled out after the dissolution of communism in the Soviet Union, it hadn't taken much guesswork to see that some kind of world blackmail would eventually take place. What remained to be seen was what people would be willing to do about it once they were threatened.

"We're clear here," the acting leader of the Secret Service team said.

The President nodded, grabbed the bottom of his jacket to straighten it briefly, then walked through the door. By the time the Man reached the other side of the door, his quiet, calm smile—the one he used to reassure the voting populace that everything was progressing as it should in the nation, and that all they had to do was stay the course—was in place.

Brognola scanned the crowd. One hundred fifty-eight countries were represented inside the immense room. The problems of the world were hashed out here, and attempts were made to mete out justice on an international scale and keep the peace.

It was also where Carl Lyons had stopped an assassination attempt only a few days ago, then run into more hit men in the hallway immediately afterward that linked the Colombian cartels to what was taking place in North Haakovia. Brognola had seen the videotaped footage. It had been a close call, and Lyons had almost been left at the starting gate.

"I'll see you in a few minutes," the President said to Brognola as a preselected escort cut him out of the group that had brought him in. "Let me know how you think they receive it."

Brognola wished him luck, then walked down to the visitors' section and took a seat that had been reserved for him. He flashed his Justice ID at the big UN security man, and the guy backed off with a short nod.

The visitors' section was filled to capacity with media people and interested observers. During the previous times Brognola had been inside the building, most of the spectators had seemed to be visiting school bodies or a loose collection of people who had nothing better to do with their time.

Voices began to die down as the assembled dignitaries and news people realized the President of the United States had entered the room. Usually the White House sent another representative or the Secretary of State if it didn't use its ambassadors. With the Man himself there, the onlookers knew he didn't want the message delivered by anyone else.

The President walked with a confident stride toward the stage and climbed the stairs to the lectern.

Brognola couldn't get out of his mind what one person with a rifle could accomplish in the space of a heartbeat. The back of his neck burned in unwilling anticipation.

The secretary-general and assembly president sat together on the raised dais near the lectern, talking quietly between themselves as the Man took his place. The coil of microphones running up over the lectern looked like a snarl of poisonous metallic vipers waiting to strike.

"Good afternoon, ladies and gentlemen," the President said.

An expectant hush settled over the crowd, although the representatives of China, Vietnam, Colombia and Cuba made rude conversation that could be heard several feet away. The assembly president fixed them with an icy stare that brought the noise to a more acceptable level.

"I come here," the President went on, "at a very troubled time for all of us. You are all aware of the events unfolding in the Haakovias. Much of that struggle seems to have taken place in these very halls. We've lost friends and family to assassins' bullets."

Camera flashes arced across the distance as the steady spray of video recorder lights washed over the lectern area.

"And despite everything we've done, that struggle continues." He paused. "During recent years we've all seen the world come closer. We're united with our neighbors these days, whether we want to be or not, and we're going to have to learn to live together. Walls have fallen, political societies and ideologies have crumbled. We don't have time to sort through the debris for sentimental issues. Our future depends on our making the right decisions *now,* based on what we see. And we have to see it. We can no longer ignore truths that we find unpleasant. They have to be dealt with."

"The way the American military is dealing with the domestic problems in North and South Haakovia?" The challenging voice rang throughout the chamber, drawing the attention of several media personnel.

Brognola glanced over at the representatives' tables and saw that the speaker was from Vietnam.

"We're seeking to right an injustice there," the President responded.

"The United States seems to find injustice lurking in every closet these days," the Vietnamese ambassador said. "It appears to have become a popular American hobby."

"Franzen Stensvik," the President replied, "is well on his way to becoming a real threat to the whole world. His actions in his own country, as well as what he has done in South Haakovia, are deplorable."

"By your standards, Mr. President," one of the Cuban representatives said.

"By anyone's standards."

"Personally, after having seen some of your predecessors in action," the Cuban went on, "I have to worry that the American interest in the Haakovias isn't just a knee-jerk reflex to surviving communism. Perhaps you would like to see us all give up our way of life and embrace the ruthless barbarism of capitalism."

The President took a deep breath. "I'm not here to debate political issues."

"You'll address them, but you won't debate them." The Cuban nodded as if he understood.

"The issues I'm concerned with in the Haakovias are not political ones," the President said. "They're moral issues. North Haakovia is being run by a madman with the ability to kill an untold number of people. We have to join together to take that ability away from him."

"So you say," the Chinese delegate scoffed. He stood, turned to address the rest of his peers and shrugged expansively. "However, I see only a country fraught with domestic perils, and an American president who once more wants to flex his muscles and display America's military might. We've all seen that before. Panama. Iraq. You say you stand for law and order, for a fair balance in the world. Yet you cannot even keep the peace in your own country. We are all aware of the strife caused in Los Angeles, California, last year. Those people were protesting the justice handed down by your own courts. But still you believe you know how the Haakovias should be governed." He shook his head. "As for myself and the political body I represent, we see only that you and your American generals are trying to continue your war on communism. Other countries may have knuckled under to your oppressive capitalist siege, but there still remains those of us who will never give up our way of life."

Brognola glanced at the Russian delegate, noted that the man had blanched with anger but kept quiet. President Niklai Tachek had already made his position clear to the Man behind closed doors. With the firepower Stensvik had at his disposal, the Commonwealth watched carefully where it trod these days. And then there was the matter of the phone relay systems and communications networks that were integral to daily Russian business. If push came to shove, the head Fed had no doubts where the Russian military machine would set up camp.

"I'm not attacking the Communist Party or its doctrines," the President said. "I'm speaking out against this man." He pointed at the big-screen television set up to the left of the dais. Turning to someone just offstage, he said, "Roll the tapes, please."

Other big-screen televisions had been set up throughout the room. They all came on at the same time as the lights in the General Assembly dimmed slightly. The Secret Service contingent shrank in on the President.

"This man," the President repeated.

The screens cleared instantly, focusing on a file photograph of Franzen Stensvik. The man was dressed in the brown uniform of the North Haakovian army. His general's stars gleamed, offset by a line of medals that seemed more of a decoration than any attempt at being officious. Stensvik was a tall man, and carried a lot of weight on what was a rather narrow frame. His hooded eyes looked belligerent, and the mustache he wore was scraggly. When communism failed and the coup attempt in Moscow couldn't hold things together, Stensvik had already been in a position to effectively seize control of North Haakovia. He'd been a soldier and a bandit, and now he painted himself to be a patriot.

"Franzen Stensvik is an animal," the President said, "and he'll stop at nothing to get whatever he wants."

Angry voices erupted immediately from the Communist nations represented in the General Assembly. The Cuban jumped to his feet. "You'd say the same of any loyal party member. For years the American CIA has tried to assassinate Castro. Do you not find any guilt in that?''

The President held up his hands. "I'm not here to debate those issues."

"'Those are as viable as any you would propose here today."

Taking the remote control an aide handed him, the President flicked it at a switch relay junction. Stensvik's picture melted from the television screens, replaced by Edvaard Varkaus. The man looked resplendent and powerful and seemed to ooze confidence.

Brognola knew he was looking at a dead man.

"The former South Haakovian president," the Man said. "Edvaard Varkaus was assassinated in the presidential castle a few days ago, in front of his wife and his closest friends."

The tape rolled, showing the marksman's cross hairs that had been digitized by computer over the actual news interview. Pandemonium erupted in the castle, but without the sound the scene was eerie. It ended abruptly when Varkaus's head was snapped back by a bullet. Blood streamered over the man's face as he crumpled.

"And the killing didn't stop there," the President stated.

Brognola recognized most of the following news footage as belonging to CNN. Some of the footage actually caught the action between the two sets of diplomats. In the early edition, Carl Lyons and Able Team had figured in prominently. None of those scenes had hit the airwaves. Barbara Price had worked out an arrangement with the news producers to edit Lyons, Blancanales and Schwarz from the shots in exchange for more information on Bin Chou and the Red Chinese hit men who had been put down earlier in the day. Until Stony Man Farm had shunted the intel to the network, no one had known who the Chinese agent was.

The President clicked the remote control. Immediately the television screens divided into three separate windows that depicted dead men of obvious South American heritage. The Man named each corpse in turn. "These men, ladies and gentlemen, were assassins working for the Medellín cartel."

"Lies," the Cuban delegate said, shoving himself to his feet.

The President fixed the man with a penetrating stare, then shifted his focus. "Would you care to elaborate on what I have just said, Mr. Godofredo?"

Obviously reluctant about his part in the proceedings, the Colombian representative stood and addressed the crowd. "What he says is true. I have had the identities of these men verified through my embassy. They did work for the cartels."

A murmur of apprehension moved through the crowd like a blast of arctic air.

The assembly president banged his gavel for order.

"You can imagine how concerned we were," the President went on, "and how puzzled. We couldn't put the pieces together. Then we received more reports from the North Haakovian resistance group via our military advisers stationed in South Haakovia."

Brognola knew that wasn't quite true. Mack Bolan had made the trip into North Haakovia himself and linked up with the freedom fighters.

"A freighter carrying cocaine into Sturegorsk was spotted by the resistance group and tagged with an electronic bug."

A feeling of satisfaction glowed inside Brognola when he noticed the Cuban representative loosening his collar.

"A transfer was made at sea," the President continued. "The mystery shipment was loaded onto a nuclear-powered Russian sub, then transferred in Harmony Cove in Key West to a cargo plane."

The television screens cleared on an aerial view of a blue-green ocean. Brognola would have known from the water and his own experience that it was from somewhere in the Caribbean.

"The cargo plane was brought down through the efforts of a Delta Force team here," the President said. "During the recovery operation, they were attacked by Cuban navy frogmen. A number of those men were killed in the sortie."

"Those men were probably pirates," the Cuban representative said. "Your people probably overreacted, stretched whatever the truth really was in that confrontation, the same way you're doing with what is going on in South Haakovia."

"I don't think so," the President replied in a hard voice. He clicked the remote control.

A series of close-ups flipped across the televisions. More than a dozen men were shown floating in a handful of rubber rafts, all dead and all wearing scuba gear.

"These men were identified as Cuban sailors," the President said.

"Not by my government," the representative replied haughtily.

"No," the President agreed. "Publicly Castro has admitted to nothing. But he is involved."

"Prove it," the dignitary snarled.

The Man eyed him with his steely gaze. "If we have to, Mr. Ambassador, we surely will."

"I've listened to enough insults," the Cuban said. He excused himself roughly, brushed by the people sitting beside him and strode out of the room. Several of the television cameras followed him.

One down, Brognola thought.

"The shipment," the President said in a more sedate voice, "contained sarin and soman."

A few voices started up a concerned murmur, and spread as others ingested the information supplied by those in the know.

"For those of you who are unaware of what sarin and soman are," the President said, "they're biochemical agents. They're old, maybe been around for years and are particularly hard to disperse once they've been unleashed. The American agents operating down there had to be extremely careful, but they recovered the shipment without losing any of the canisters."

"But why?" the Canadian representative asked.

"We think it's for blackmail purposes," the President said.

Brognola knew the Man's innate honesty had caught a number of the ambassadors by surprise. For those who chose to disbelieve, it was one more thing to ignore from Americans who seemed to be addicted to war of late. The big Fed glanced around at the representatives from the Communist countries. For those who were involved, they knew how damning the discovery could possibly be. And they knew the United States wasn't going to back down from the challenge.

"After accessing the records the Drug Enforcement Administration has on drug shipments throughout Europe and cross-referencing them with other international drug-enforcement organizations," the President went on, "my intelligence people, and myself included, have to believe that Colombia is shipping cocaine to North Haakovia and Stensvik to be sold across Eastern Europe."

"For what purpose, Mr. President?" a reporter in the first row asked.

"To finance the war he's been planning against the South." The President swept his hard gaze across the crowd. "You're all aware of Edvaard Varkaus's assassination. I've shown it to you here today. We've ascertained the man behind the hit was a terrorist named Dag Vaino."

The television screens projected Vaino's image. He was dressed in North Haakovian army fatigues and sat astride one of Stensvik's Soviet T-62 tanks. It was obviously a shot meant to show off the hardware, but Aaron Kurtzman had found the picture while leafing through news stills shot after the coup failed in Moscow and strife had ripped through the Balkans. Vaino was tall and good-looking in a roguish sort of way. His deadpan features, though, disavowed any intimacy.

"Vaino was trained by the KGB," the President said. "He's very good at what he does, and he's working with Stensvik."

"Where is he now?" the French ambassador asked.

"We don't know."

The Finnish delegate stood with quiet authority. "We know where Vaino was less than twenty-four hours ago. The man was in Finland, where he headed up the execution of Riso Kalle."

The Man flicked the remote control again. "Right." The television screens moved on to a series of stills showing Kalle addressing the Finnish people at the Helsinki city hall. The bullet hole in his forehead appeared suddenly, and the images moved fast enough that his fall appeared to be liquid stop-motion.

Kalle had been the leading voice in Finland wanting to return the two Haakovias to the mother country they had been carved from after World War II. There were factions in both the North and the South who were willing to accept the reannexation, but they were in the minority.

The whole thing, Brognola knew, revolved around greed over the oil fields in South Haakovia. In the time of economic hardships spreading around the globe, those fields could make or break some nations.

The televisions moved on, swept into actual live footage of the North Haakovian attack on South Haakovia during the funeral services for Edvaard Varkaus. The film was grainy and jumped often, but it captured the awesome might of the Soviet-made armor and attack planes raining death and destruction on Larsborg.

"You're already aware of Stensvik's attack on the South's capital city," the President said, "but I'm here to spread some more news. None of it's very pleasant. Earlier, the South Haakovian diplomats were taken hostage by Chinese terrorists. Those men were led by Bin Chou."

Chou's photograph appeared on the televisions. Quietly the Chinese diplomat excused himself and retreated from the room.

Two, Brognola told himself.

The journalists noted the exit, and some of them peeled off after the man.

"Chou worked as an espionage agent," the Man said, "for a number of years."

"He was KGB-trained, wasn't he?" the delegate from Great Britain asked.

"Yes," the President replied.

"So, your contention is that Chou was hired by Stensvik?"

"No. We have evidence that the Chinese government has made arrangements with Stensvik regarding setting up a military base in North Haakovia. Chou was their representative in these clandestine matters."

"And the Chinese government wanted the base in North Haakovia?"

"We're assuming," the President replied.

Brognola knew the Briton had been specially prepared to ask those questions. With Hong Kong being returned to the Chinese in a few years, despite what the British wanted to do, England was prepared to do a little propagandizing of its own against Chinese interests.

"I see," the Briton said in a way that indicated everyone else in the room should as well. He sat.

"I would have liked to ask Mr. Liang," the President said, "but it appears that he had pressing business elsewhere." He punched the remote control again. "Also, this news hasn't been released before."

Instantly a hush dropped over the crowd as they gave him their full attention.

"I've just received word that Janyte Varkaus, who is acting president of South Haakovia, has just been kidnapped. Apparently General Gustaf Markus was involved in her betrayal. At present the South Haakovian military is shoring up its defenses and is trying to find her." The President paused. "I hope you people will remember her in your prayers tonight, and God keep her safe."

A moment of silence hung over the General Assembly.

"An impassioned speech, Mr. President," the Russian delegate said.

The Man faced the speaker.

Brognola sat forward in his chair. The Russian ambassadors hadn't had too much to say so far during the conflict.

"But I have to ask myself," the ambassador went on, "if Janyte Varkaus is no longer there to say what her country will and will not do, and General Markus really is a traitor, then whose hand guides the South Haakovian military?''

"An American adviser named Rance Pollock. He was placed in charge of the South Haakovian defenses by President Varkaus."

"The wife, not the husband?"

"Correct."

"And she is grieving for her dead mate?"

The President was caught off stride for a heartbeat. Brognola figured most people might not have even noticed it. But he did. "Yes," the Man replied.

"I suppose Colonel Pollock cuts a dashing figure to a grieving widow."

"I don't see what that has to do with anything."

"Perhaps you are no romantic, Mr. President," the Russian stated. He spread his hands expressively. "However, as I see it, you have a young woman suddenly bereft of her husband, on whose shoulders the fate of an entire nation has ultimately dropped—and you have a hero waiting in the wings. It would not be a great stretch of the imagination to think that perhaps Mrs. Varkaus would want someone to bear those burdens with her. Maybe she could even have the good fortune that your Colonel Pollock would volunteer to share them with her."

The journalists sat in rapt attention, pencils poised and microcassette recorders at the ready.

Brognola hated to even guess at what the supermarket tabloids would make of the Russian diplomat's suggested scenario.

Surprisingly the Man smiled.

The head Fed knew it was a strained one however.

"Mr. Maksimka, you astound me. You've embraced capitalism with far more fervor than I would have imagined. What you've just stated is clearly the plot to a movie of the week."

Polite laughter rumbled throughout the auditorium.

Bright spots of color appeared in the Russian's face.

"You're to be commended for your imagination," the President went on. "However, the business we're dealing with here is deadly serious. People are dying even as we meet here. You have my assurances that Colonel Pollock is every inch the gentleman, and his interests in Mrs. Varkaus are purely for the betterment of her country."

"But what will he do about the South Haakovian president," the Russian persisted, "if, in fact, she has been kidnapped as you say?"

"Even now we're working on plans to get her back," the President replied. "Stensvik isn't going to be allowed to ride roughshod over the people of that nation."

"And where will you draw the line?"

The President paused and walked from behind the lectern, staying close enough that his voice was still picked up by the microphones. "It's not a matter of America drawing the line. It's a matter of what lines South Haakovia chooses to step over in her bid for continued freedom. Tell me who the players are in this affair for sure, Mr. Maksimka, and I can give you a more informed answer."

The Russian sat down.

"We've got evidence," the President said, "that Colombia is actively involved in drug trade that financially benefits North Haakovia and Stensvik's army. We know that the Chinese are interested in establishing a military base to help keep the emerging capitalist Commonwealth of Independent States at bay because they've already had their domestic democratic problems. Cuba is definitely looking for someone to shore up Castro. Finland wants to jump in and take both Haakovias." He paused. "Maybe it would be easier for you to give me a list of the nations *not* involved in this.''

A pregnant pause drifted over the collection of international thinkers.

''I'm not going to defend the position of the United States in these matters,'' the President added. ''We were asked to take part in South Haakovia's struggle for continued independence. I won't make any apologies for accepting. Those are a brave, strong people fighting for their very lives against a madman who would rape and kill them, then burn their houses to the ground. If I didn't move to aid them, then I'd feel I owed you people an apology. The only thing I want to see out of this is that South Haakovian flag still flying when the smoke clears.''

A number of the Third World countries' delegates and some of the European representatives got to their feet and started clapping in agreement.

''And if it takes war, Mr. President?'' the Russian diplomat asked.

''The American soldiers over there won't turn away from it. And I'm sure the South Haakovian fighting men feel the same way. I won't rest until I'm sure Franzen Stensvik is no longer a threat to any of us.''

''Even if it means killing him?''

''That,'' the President said with conviction, ''is up to Stensvik.''

Without another word the Russian got up from his seat and walked away. A number of journalists set out in hot pursuit.

The President opened the floor up to questions from the press and from the other member nations.

Satisfied that he'd seen the main show and that all others would pale by comparison, Brognola eased himself out of his seat and walked out of the room. It was easy to guess that the President's decision to pour more American troops into South Haakovia in the coming weeks wouldn't be met with enthusiasm. And it wasn't hard to figure which way the Russians would jump when the scenario was presented. Stensvik was a necessary blight until they were able to gain control of the phone exchanges in North Haakovian boundaries. And any "accidents" that took place at ground zero in the Haakovias would sweep across the Commonwealth.

The big Fed didn't blame their reticence a bit. He wouldn't have trusted them to be able to handle a job that would touch his country either.

And now Janyte Varkaus was among the missing.

He sighed, then thought about his troops.

Able Team had been shunted back to Stony Man Farm after the incident involving the Chinese, waiting for something else to break on the domestic horizon. It was a safe bet that it wouldn't be long.

Somewhere in Finland, Phoenix Force was waiting to break free of Finnish patrols and move back to the main action.

And Striker and Grimaldi were stuck working through the treacheries left by General Gustaf Markus in the no-man's-land South Haakovia was becoming. The Executioner had been in some tough spots before. Hell, Brognola had been guilty of putting the big man in a lot of them. It was the same with Phoenix and Able. No matter what he'd asked them to do, he'd never doubted their willingness to get the job done, nor had he ever questioned whether they were the best men for that job.

But he said a prayer for them because he cared and because they were in foreign lands—most of them—fighting an enemy who was able to make up the rules as he went along.

And, yeah, the Man was right about one thing. With Janyte Varkaus in enemy hands, the situation in the Haakovias would advance to full-scale war. Striker wouldn't back off now until he had the lady safely returned, or had her avenged.

CHAPTER THREE

Night had closed over Helsinki, Finland, hours ago, and a chill black breeze pushed the fog in off the South Harbor. Yakov Katzenelenbogen blew in with the fog, dressed in black night clothes and a beret. His side arm was leathered at his left hip, and an Uzi machine pistol was hidden under the loose folds of his black coat. Camou paint striped his face, taking away some of the sheen of his features. A glove covered his hand, his prosthesis having been confiscated by the Finnish police.

He tapped the transmit button on the ear-throat headset he wore. "Phoenix One to Phoenix Five. Over."

"Go, One. You have Five." Calvin James's voice sounded confident. The black ex-SEAL was the youngest member of the team and was given to exuberance when things were going well.

Katz paused by the dock and looked out over the harbor. Squat, powerfully built tugboats were laboring in the dark waters, the chugging of their diesel engines creating a cacophony that echoed over the ocean surface. Specially fitted prows crunched through the huge islands of ice drifting in from the sea in an effort to keep the harbor clear. Helsinki was open only a few months before winter closed it off from the sea.

"You sound better," Katz commented.

"Warmer," James replied. "I even found one with a working heater."

"I was beginning to wonder," Katz said. "It was taking some time."

"Hot-wiring this baby was no problem," James said. "You got to remember, I come from the badlands of Chicago. Kids learn how to boost cars before they make double-digit birthdays."

"I feel better already," Katz said dryly.

Out in the harbor a tugboat rushed into an ice floe like an American football linebacker smashing down a halfback. The sound of the ice splitting penetrated the normal din. Surprisingly the prow held.

James evidently chose to ignore the dig. "Reason it took so long was the Finnish soldiers out wandering the streets tonight. Last thing we need right now is for me to get caught stealing this puppy."

"Agreed," Katz said. "How soon will you be here?"

"Better give me ten minutes. These roads are already a bitch. Thank God I'm not going to have to drive them in the morning rush-hour traffic. Five, clear."

A plane thundered overhead.

Katz watched, recognizing it as a military fighter jet used by the country. Evidently the Finnish war machine remained geared up for any hostile action Franzen Stensvik might take—or stayed ready in case the chance presented itself for them to go on the offensive. Finnish pride had been injured some time ago after being on the wrong side of World War II and losing the land to Russia that had become North and South Haakovia. Reacquiring either or both countries would give them more ports, as well as the economic wealth contained in the South.

He drifted away from the dock, legged it slowly around the tarp-covered shipments of paper, pulp and furniture that were already parceled out for early-morning pickup. He longed for a Camel, but left the cigarette pack untouched in his shirt pocket. With his hand in his coat pocket he tried to stay warm. It was difficult. Phoenix Force hadn't been allowed much recovery time since they'd penetrated the Finnish defense lines.

And the time spent in-country had been used up chasing Dag Vaino, a man who'd turned out to be about as substantial as a will-o'-the-wisp. Vaino had had no problems taking out Risto Kalle and leaving Phoenix caught in the middle of Finnish army members who suspected them of masterminding the assassination. The time they'd spent waking up the Finnish political bodies to their own vulnerabilities seemed like a waste, looking back now, but it had caused the nation's war hawks to take stock of the situation.

Katz looked up at the residence of the president of Finland. The collection of three-story buildings overlooking the harbor were undecorated and plain. In the moonlight the brickwork looked the color of ash. Several lights burned in the windows. Across the boulevard that curved away from the harbor and headed downtown was a large, Gothic-style church covered with gingerbread trimming. The cross at the domed top was lost in the flurries of snow that had started less than an hour ago.

A military half-track trundled down the street in front of the presidential buildings, the tarp pulled over the rear section of the vehicle whipping in the bitter wind.

Katz ran a quick eye over the men inside, trying not to draw attention to himself. Staring too long, or not staring at all, either would have been a giveaway. He stared just long enough, then turned away. He felt sorry for the young soldiers in the back. They didn't look comfortable huddled up to the mounted .50-caliber machine guns. He shivered in sympathy and turned up his collar.

The half-track continued on, either on patrol or returning from one.

The Israeli felt a little better when the vehicle's tail-lights faded in the distance. Acting under the guidelines handed down to Brognola by the President, then on to Stony Man Farm, Phoenix Force wasn't allowed to use deadly force against the Finnish soldiers. Katz wouldn't have wanted to at any rate, but it was definitely an uncomfortable position to be in. He'd decided hours ago that he'd be glad to be hitting the front lines in South Haakovia with Striker.

It only made things a little sweeter when he thought it was probably logical that Dag Vaino would return to his master now that his jobs in Finland had been completed. Katz only hoped that he'd catch up to the assassin there.

He walked toward the street, aware of the military personnel guarding the presidential buildings. Helsinki had fallen under a period of martial law, but the Finnish president hadn't been able to keep a lid on the local activity as much as he'd wanted. Journalists from several countries had still found a haven in the city, and were able to make quick hops across the four hundred miles separating the city from the Haakovias. The threat to security, while trying to make a case for the restoration of the Baltic countries to Finland, had to be taxing.

His face almost numb from the exposure to the cold, the Israeli waited patiently at the roadside. He tapped the transmit button on his radio. "Phoenix One to Phoenix Two. Over."

"Go, mate," David McCarter's laconic voice answered immediately. He sounded distant, as if miles away, but Katz knew it was only the radio skip battling the weather.

"Do we fly?" Katz asked. "Or do we paddle? From the looks of things out in the harbor, it would be easier to thread a camel through the eye of a needle than take a boat out tonight.''

''Depends on whether it's filtered or unfiltered,'' the Briton cracked dryly.

Katz didn't bother to reply. McCarter was a good man, an ex-SAS commando and dangerous whether on the ground or in the air. However, his warped sense of humor seemed to kick into overdrive whenever an operation had turned into a busted play and was running at its most ragged. During those times the Israeli never encouraged the insanity, for his own peace of mind. The only people he'd ever seen that were worse than McCarter were Pol Blancanales and Gadgets Schwarz of Able Team. Occasionally his heart went out to Carl Lyons, but he would never tell the big man so.

''David...''

''We fly. But we'd better be bloody well ready to fly quick.''

''Whereaway?''

''The military airfield. Just like you called it. These jokers know it's a temporary base, and it's a cold night. The guards are spending more time inside then outside.''

''Can you commandeer the plane by the time we get there?''

''Maybe. But I don't know how quiet I can be. Right now I'm by my lonesome. Three and Four are rounding up supplies that are supposed to help us make a bloodless exit.''

''Do you know their ETA?''

''Nope. Three was being secretive, but he promised a pyrotechnic delight.''

Phoenix Three was Gary Manning, the Canadian of the group, a big outdoorsman with a gift for explosives.

Rafael Encizo was Phoenix Four, a master of several forms of death on land, on water and under it. The little Cuban had been through hell before joining the covert team, having survived both the Bay of Pigs and El Principe prison.

"Understand, Two. Wait for your backup. Five and I are pulling the periphery in and putting ourselves in your hands."

"Not to worry, mate," McCarter replied. "You'll be safe as houses. Two, out."

Though having learned to trust the Briton's flying skills scores of missions ago, Katz still knew McCarter was going to be hard-pressed to fly out of the country without being shot down. There was no question of being able to fight back against any Finnish fighters that were able to take up pursuit.

The only other option had been to somehow make their way out into the ocean and try to arrange an aerial linkup with whatever Barbara Price could arrange. And with the storm blowing in from the sea, Katz had elected not to take that route. Stealing a military jet from the temporary landing field outside Helsinki seemed much easier. Plus it put their fates squarely on their own abilities to survive, which was where the ex-Mossad agent preferred to have his destiny.

A red Saab sports car pulled out of the line of traffic toward the curb, washing a wave of slush over Katz's already-wet pant legs. The engine idled as the passenger window rolled down.

"Hop in," Calvin James said from behind the steering wheel. "You can tell me how great it looks later. Right now I don't want to lose the heat."

"Red?" Katz slid into the passenger seat, pausing to shake the slush from his pants. Only when he felt the hot air of the heater flowing over his legs did he realize how cold his lower limbs were.

"Yeah," James said with noticeable pride. "Me and you, Katz, we're going to blow this pop stand in style." He tucked the gearshift lever into first and let out the clutch as the Israeli closed the door. The wheels ground through the ice and slush, slipping a couple of times before gaining traction.

"Maybe they can put that on your headstone," Katz said.

James laughed and batted the fuzzy white dice with black spots hanging from the rearview mirror. They swung back and forth. "Live fast, love hard, die young and leave a good-looking corpse." He tapped the brake, avoided a sedan that suddenly slithered out of control and went up over a curb. "Where to?"

"The airport."

"McCarter scored?"

"Yes."

"Can't wait to get out of this burg," James said with real feeling. "We've been a day late and a dollar short ever since we've been here. 'Bout time I started feeling like I was earning my keep again."

Katz noticed the thermos between the bucket seats. "Coffee?"

"Yeah. Stopped and picked it up at an all-night diner before I boosted the wheels." James raised his eyebrows. "Like I said, Katz, style." He reached toward the radio and punched in a CD. Music filled the interior of the car, issued from a quad system. "Listen to that. Aretha's new album. It's been so long since I got any R&R stateside that I didn't even know it was out."

"I'm thrilled," Katz said. He poured the dark coffee into one of the foam cups from the paper bag by the thermos and inhaled the aroma with deep appreciation.

James looked in the rearview mirror and said, "Shit."

Lambent blue light lanced into the Saab's interior.

Craning his neck to look behind them, Katz saw the police car fall into their backtrail. The blue cherry mounted on top whirled like a dervish. He tried a sip of coffee, succeeding only in burning his tongue. He dumped the cup's contents back into the thermos and capped it.

"At the next side road," the Israeli directed, "turn right. Slowly. You don't want to give him the impression you're trying to run."

James nodded, punched the CD out of the player, said, "Sorry, lady," and put both hands on the steering wheel.

Katz reached under his long coat and freed the silenced Uzi machine pistol.

Slowing and turning easily, James negotiated the next turn.

"Park at the curb." Katz laid the Uzi in his lap long enough to work the door latch, then took up the wicked little weapon again.

Under James's steady hand, the Saab slid to a stop against the curb. "I didn't figure they'd have made a stolen vehicle this soon," he said in disgust, keeping his eyes on the rearview mirror.

Katz peered through the back windshield. The police car pulled in behind them, the light from the whirling blue cherry cutting through the back window and glaring over the sports car's interior. The Israeli reached up and took the dome light bulb out.

On the other side of the glass the two policemen started to get out. They were dressed in heavy parkas, their side arms pronounced on their hips.

"Now," Katz said softly, "pull back onto the street. Let them know it's coming."

James dropped the Saab in gear and popped the clutch. The car shivered, hunted traction like a big cat, and sprayed slush and ice over the police cruiser.

Immediately the two cops raced back for their vehicle. One of them fell hard against the side of the car, then regained his balance.

"Slower," Katz called. "Make them think you've lost it on the ice."

James complied, twisted the wheel violently and sent the Saab into a controlled skid. The nose drifted sickeningly.

Once the two policemen were inside their car they took up pursuit. The cruiser was front-wheel drive, which made getting around on the icy roads a little easier. They were making speed in short order, and the keening cry of the siren started up a moment later.

Katz pushed the door open and leaned out with the Uzi held tightly in his fist. He emptied the clip in a sweeping burst that cut through both front tires.

Out of control, the police cruiser left the road and smashed into one of the wooden light poles lining the street. The front end of the car crumpled, lost on the sheet of ice, and drowned out the siren.

"Stop and go back," Katz ordered.

James tapped the brake, upshifted to lessen the power supply to the drive train, double-clutched, and brought the back end of the sports car around easily. The headlights played over the wrecked police car. Both men were moving inside.

Katz slipped a fresh clip into the Uzi. "Here."

Already prepared, James tapped the brake again and slewed the Saab around to a skidding halt only a few feet from the police vehicle.

"Quickly," Katz said, "before they are able to contact anyone, and without hurting them more than is necessary."

James unlimbered the Beretta from his shoulder holster and threw himself in a sliding dive across the hood of the Saab. He landed on his feet running.

Moving at a trot, Katz closed on the police cruiser, keeping the Uzi in plain sight to dissuade any heroic attempts on part of the cops. It didn't work. The driver had his pistol out and was trying to secure a two-handed grip on it. Katz swept the revolver out of the man's hands with the butt of his Uzi. Something cracked in the man's wrist and he fell back inside the car.

The other policeman was digging for his own weapon when Katz froze him in place with the snout of the Uzi.

"No," the Israeli said in a soft, authoritative voice. It was the same tone he used when instructing the young soldiers of his adopted country, the tone a caring drill instructor used to those still young enough to make very bad mistakes.

The cop hesitated for just a moment, blood trickling down his brow from a small cut just below his hairline, then took his hand away from the holstered revolver.

"Good," Katz said. "Take the weapon with your thumb and forefinger only, and pitch it out the window. No one has to get hurt here."

"He doesn't have English," the driver said, finding the words difficult himself.

"Translate," Katz ordered. "If I'd wanted you dead, you would be by now."

The driver nodded, speaking quickly in Finnish. A tense moment later, the other man pitched his pistol through the window and it plunged out of sight into a pile of dirty snow.

Katz caught James's attention with a look.

"Yeah," the ex-SEAL replied.

"Decommission the horn, siren and radio."

"You got it." James slipped a Randall survival knife from under his pant leg and approached the cruiser. Reaching inside, he cut the microphone from the radio, then popped the hood. Within seconds wires were strewn across the street. "Done and done."

Katz motioned with the Uzi. "Your handcuffs, please."

Taking care not to jar his injured wrist, the driver produced the cuffs.

"Secure yourself and your partner through the steering wheel," the Israeli instructed.

Neither man appeared happy about the situation, but they didn't offer any resistance. The cuffs clicked together with metallic pings.

Raising the Uzi, Katz put a burst through the whirling blue cherry. Bits of plastic and glass flew backward, sucked into the slipstream of the chill breeze. The light died, leaving the neighborhood unlighted except for the Saab's twin beams.

"Why did you stop us?" James asked as he came around from closing the hood.

It was a question Katz wanted an answer to as well. It was possible with all the scouting around and preparations Phoenix Force had had to do in the city tonight that they'd been compromised in some way.

"Your car," the cop said weakly.

"The car?" James echoed.

"Yes." The cop nodded. "Kosti and I were jealous."

"Jealous."

"Yes." The cop shrugged helplessly. "The car was so stylish-looking, we wanted to know what it was."

"Stylish."

"Yes."

A humorless smile twisted James's lips as he holstered the Beretta. "Terrific."

Katz concealed the Uzi under the folds of his coat, aware that the clock was counting down precious seconds. He led the way to the Saab. "Maybe next time," he said quietly, "you could settle for something a little less stylish."

"A Ford LTD," James promised as he slid behind the steering wheel. "Now there's a car that's not stylish."

OCCUPYING THE PASSENGER seat of the OH-58 Bell helicopter, Mack Bolan surveyed the broken forest land below with a pair of night-vision goggles that took away the night. He was still outfitted in the blacksuit, with the *shrapka* once more in place. The headset was locked onto the main frequency used by the South Haakovian forces. Reports, staggered and just now beginning to slow, continued to come in regarding various sorties still being fought as the South's light armor ran into North Haakovian ambushes. The losses weren't high, but it would have a telling effect on morale if it kept on.

As the helicopter topped a treed ridge, the golden glow that had been building like a rising sun ahead of them became a pit of flames.

The warrior lowered the night-vision goggles because their effectiveness was suddenly gone.

Fire twisted and ravaged the broken backs of the tanker trucks, danced over them in wild abandon like some kind of elemental spirit celebrating a savage victory. Gray-hued smoke strands coiled and writhed like restless serpents trying to sink their fangs into the slice of moon. Every now and then a secondary explosion would go off, hurling comets of fire into the surrounding brush and trees.

South Haakovia soldiers worked as if possessed, striving to pull wounded from the flames before any more were lost, and struggling to create a firebreak by felling trees back in on the fire. There was no hope of extinguishing the blaze soon. It would have to burn itself out.

Other helicopters hovered around the area in defensive and support positions. Half a dozen AH-64 Apaches beat the treetops down with rotor wash as they scanned for North Haakovian ground troops that might have gathered in the area.

Fat-bodied Huey UH-1D helicopters hovered in place within safe distances of the burning tankers. Rescue crews carried stretchers out to waiting gurneys to be winched up into the choppers and relayed to the Larsborg medical facilities. The dead were stacked in places like cordwood for later retrieval.

Bolan glanced at the corpses, made himself accept them for what they were, then moved his gaze on. There were no acceptable losses when a soldier was dealing in human lives. There were only losses that were unavoidable and could only be avenged.

"FUBAR," Jack Grimaldi said from the pilot's seat as his head swiveled back and forth, staring through the helicopter's Plexiglas nose. "Fucked-up beyond all repair."

Bolan silently agreed.

A brace of F-16s rocketed by overhead, settling into the protective perimeters the warrior had established around the exfiltration maneuver. Somewhere in the darkness below were a scattered dozen M-1 Abrams Main Battle Tanks running on fumes.

From the air, the losses looked total.

Bolan tried to work through a dozen different scenarios he'd come up with to alleviate the fuel shortage and maintain the offensive stance he wanted for the South Haakovian army. Only one plan made any sense and allowed for a margin of success, and it was the most daring strategy he could have devised. The only thing that could take some of the danger and uncertainty out of the mission was information from Stony Man Farm. He'd already put the call out to Barbara Price and Aaron Kurtzman to get an uplink ready to transmit intel.

He switched freqs, settled on the band assigned to the mop-up operation below and keyed the transmit button. "Fireman Leader, this is Stone Hammer Leader. Over."

"Go, Stone Hammer Leader. You have Fireman Leader." The voice belonged to Lieutenant Konrad Ludis, a career soldier in the South Haakovia army whose career had been found to be impeccable even under Barbara Price's scrutiny.

Grimaldi pulled the Bell copter into position to one side of the roaring flames. When the winds shifted, the heat washed over the craft and made the cabin suddenly too warm.

"Does it look as bad from down there as it does from up here?"

"Worse, I'm afraid, sir." Ludis sounded tired. "Everything always looks worse when you find yourself right in the middle of it."

It was a familiar tone Bolan was hearing from all his officers. They'd suffered a tremendous beating during the North Haakovian attack after Edvaard Varkaus's funeral, and they were all aware of Janyte Varkaus's kidnapping under their very noses, as well as General Markus's betrayal of the country. More than anything else, the Executioner realized, the South Haakovian army needed a win. And he thought he had a way to give it to them.

"Everything you see there before you is a waste. There'll be no salvaging any of the fuel in those tankers."

"Understood, Fireman Leader. You people have done everything you could."

"Precious little in the long run, I'm afraid. And we've taken some wounded in achieving that. But we have managed to save some of the tractors."

Bolan watched as a tractor rig jerked forward, trailing flames from the passenger side and from the trailer mounting. The tires on the driver's side were flat and smoking as well. Once it cleared the deadly ring of fire, a handful of men dressed in silver fire suits and carrying fire extinguishers rushed forward and hosed the big rig down. White foam splashed over the truck's blistered hide as it loped to a stop like a mortally wounded animal.

"How high are the casualties running?" Bolan asked.

"At last count, we lost thirty-seven men in the attack."

"Christ," Grimaldi said softly. "I hope Markus burns in hell for this. Those guys down there never had a chance."

"What about the losses in fuel supplies?" Bolan asked.

"Checked that out with Mockingbird," Ludis replied. "Counting the reserves they have in Larsborg, we could manage to refuel maybe twenty percent of the heavy armored units. And transportation to those units would be a problem even then."

"Understood. Stay with the hell zone down there, Fireman Leader, and let me know if there is anything I can do for you. Stone Hammer Leader out." Bolan reached into a thigh pocket of the blacksuit and took out his map case.

Grimaldi passed over a plastic mug of coffee with a convenience cap.

Bolan accepted it with a nod of thanks.

"Where to, Sarge?" the ace flyer asked.

"Field headquarters," Bolan replied as he scanned the topographical map depicting the joint Haakovian borders. "I've got a suicide scenario I have to present, and I haven't figured out any kind of happy face to slap on it to make it more palatable."

"Think they'll be ready to hear it?" Grimaldi gained altitude, turned south-southeast as he homed in on his target through a preset beacon.

"Yeah. But I don't think they'll like it." The warrior used his protractor, marking distances between the last known advances made by the North Haakovian ground units. He speculated on where they might have gone on to since the last contact and made those notes as well. He scouted the Inge River, sought a jumping-off point for the plan he'd come up with, kept in mind that the whole operation would have to remain low-slung and career like an amusement park roller coaster once in motion.

"Stone Hammer Leader, this is Mockingbird. Over." Lansdale's voice sounded concerned.

"Go, Mockingbird."

Men's voices could be heard as excited murmurs at the other end of the transmission.

"Your present position is under attack, Stone Hammer Leader. Our satellite recon shows three Scud missiles launched from a position less than ten miles north of the Inge River. Ground radar has confirmed those launches. Patriots have been launched and are away, but you people are going to experience some fallout there."

Bolan glanced at Grimaldi, saw the pilot was already relaying the intel to Fireman Leader. "Acknowledged, Mockingbird. Have you got a lock on the Scud base?"

"That's affirmative."

Taking another map from his case, Bolan asked for the coordinates triangulated by the satellite recon and the ground-based radar. Lansdale quickly supplied them. Cross-indexing the entries he'd made in his war book for the present mission, the warrior found the strike team he was looking for. He cleared with Mockingbird, accessing the new frequency.

Below, the rescue teams on the ground were sprinting for cover. The Hueys and the Apache gunships had kicked their rotors around and were clearing out of the compromised airspace.

Without warning, three stars went nova against the sable backdrop of the night. The sudden flares were already starting to die away as the noise reached the Bell helicopter, followed quickly by the concussive force.

Grimaldi flexed the yoke and heeled the light copter around in spite of the gusting wind. He brought the nose of the Bell into the unseen force and leveled out. Once he had it under control again, he resumed his heading.

"Warthog Beta Unit," Bolan said, "this is Stone Hammer Leader. Over."

"Acknowledged, Stone Hammer Leader, you have Warthog Beta Unit."

"I've got a strike mission for your people. How soon can you get planes into the air?"

"How many?"

"Two."

"They're taxiing down the runaway now, Stone Hammer Leader."

"Here are your coordinates." Bolan gave them. "Tell your people they're looking for the Scud unit that just launched the three missiles across the river."

"Yes, sir."

"Fast strike," Bolan said. "I want your people in and out in one piece. They take the Scud down as retaliatory and preventive action. If they miss it, I want them back—

no foul. If they succeed, we give Stensvik's troops reason to be cautious. If it's a scrub, it's okay. I don't want to lose any more men or hardware."

"Affirmative. Warthog Beta Unit clear."

Bolan cleared the channel. The Warthog units were comprised of Fairchild Republic A-10A Thunderbolt IIs armed with Maverick air-to-surface precision-guided tactical missiles. They'd been inserted only hours ago, left under camou netting and were operational along runways that had been cleared by civilian bulldozers hauled into place by CH-47 Chinook helicopters. They'd been strategically placed to keep the North Haakovian tank units and mobile Scud launchers from becoming overly confident.

"I got radio contact with Stony Man Farm," Grimaldi called.

Bolan changed freqs. As he glanced behind the Bell helicopter, he saw the rescue and defensive units moving back into place over the blazing wreckage of the tankers. "Stony Base, this is Stony One. Over."

"Go, Stony One." Barbara Price's voice sounded perky and alert, but the warrior knew instinctively part of her attention was diverted to other areas.

Bolan smiled and felt some of the tension drain from his body. The beautiful Stony Man Farm mission controller held a special place in his heart. It wasn't love. The warrior had allowed himself an intimate love only once, and that had been April Rose, who had later fallen before enemy guns. There had been other women in his life, Price included, but there would never again be one that deep. His life, and the missions he believed in, didn't allow for that. But it felt just fine knowing there was someone out there who cared when things seemed darkest.

"Things have heated up out here on the frontier," the big warrior said. "How's the Bear's eye in the sky?"

"Claims he's just as good as Pinkerton's." Price's voice held a warm smile. "Says he never sleeps."

"Must be bloodshot all to hell by now," Grimaldi cut in.

"Physical attraction isn't everything," Aaron Kurtzman's gruff voice said. "What do you need?"

"A little information," Bolan said, "and a little luck." In clear, concise sentences he relayed the latest setback engineered by Markus's betrayals and laid out his ideas for what he was planning.

When he was finished, Kurtzman said, "Striker, for that to come off, you're going to have to be just shot-in-the-ass plumb full of luck."

Bolan exchanged grins with Grimaldi. "Bear, you just make sure the intel's on the money. Out here, we'll make our own luck. Stony One, clear."

CHAPTER FOUR

"Laddie buck," David McCarter said in his most deadly voice, "if you don't speak English, we're both screwed here." He pressed the barrel of his Browning Hi-Power into the back of the man's neck.

The Finnish pilot froze, his left foot still propped on the sink in the barracks bathroom, the shoelace left untied. He was young, early twenties, with a softly serious face that took the Briton back years and wars.

"I understand English."

"Good," McCarter replied. "Then we're halfway home. Raise your hands, slowly, and clasp them behind your neck. I don't want to kill you if I don't have to because this pistol doesn't have a silencer. It would be damned inconvenient for both of us."

The pilot nodded and complied.

"Ahead of me, quietly," McCarter ordered. "I want to find a more solitary place."

"Where?" the young pilot asked.

"Someplace warm. I need your clothes."

A hard gleam fired through the Finn's china-blue eyes.

"Don't bloody well try to be a hero, mate," McCarter said with real feeling. "You do it, and I'll be obliged to break something to prove that I'm serious about this business. And anything I break will take weeks to heal. You don't want to be grounded that long."

"No."

"There's a good lad. Now let's be about finding some privacy." McCarter let the pilot lead. He'd already scouted out the terrain so he would know if the guy tried to lead him astray.

The soldiers had been housed in a small motel only a couple blocks away from an airstrip that had been laid in response to the North Haakovian threat. The first two floors were taken up with deployment personnel and supply officers in the daylight hours. The third, fourth and fifth floors were released to officers. Pilots were restricted to the top two floors. The very top floor had been converted from a gym area complete with men's and women's saunas to no-frills sleeping quarters.

They took the stairs.

"Where are we going?" McCarter asked.

"There's a maintenance building...."

"On the east side of the roof. I know. I've seen it." He remembered it from his earlier recon.

The pilot nodded. "It'll be warm there."

"Good thinking." He followed the pilot out onto the roof and grimaced against the cold wind and snow flurries.

And he wasn't surprised at all that the young pilot's machismo finally got the better of his common sense when the door of the maintenance building came into view. McCarter let the ill-timed blow go past his face by ducking to one side, then rabbit-punched his prisoner in the side and elbowed him in the face.

The pilot went down like a poleaxed steer. Blood glistened from the cut beside his eye, and seeped from his nose.

"You satisfied, mate?" McCarter asked, standing just out of reach. "I'd rather not get any more blood on that flight suit than I have to."

The pilot grumbled something in his native tongue that the Phoenix Force member took to be a fairly impressive amount of invective, judging from the emotional intensity behind the words. But he nodded and got unsteadily to his feet.

Inside, with the meager light bulb switched on, the maintenance shed was bereft of personal accoutrements. The scent of machine oil and air-conditioning coolant was pronounced, trapped inside the small room. Tools hung neatly arranged on a wallboard. A narrow and scarred gray locker held half a dozen uniforms with the base's name stiched on them.

"Take off the flight suit," McCarter demanded.

The pilot hesitated.

"Either way, lad," he said in that soft, easy voice SAS interrogators had taught him to use, "your way or my way, but I'll be having those clothes."

Face dark with suppressed fury, the pilot stripped out of the flight suit. McCarter let him keep the insulated underwear.

"Now grab the wall," the Briton ordered, "and keep your palms flat against it." When the man moved into position, McCarter stripped out of his own clothes and dropped them into a pile at his feet. He shrugged into the flight suit, then snugged his shoulder leather over it and covered the whole thing with his coat. He slipped the pilot's ID into a pocket, memorizing the last name. "Put those clothes on."

For a moment it seemed the pilot was going to try resisting again.

"Come on, lad, wise up," McCarter said congenially. "It's going to be bloody cold out here and you might well need the extra clothing. Pride will only get the arse frozen off you. You're going to have a hell of a shiner and some other bruises to let your commanding officers know you didn't go willingly. No sense in you catching your death of something out here before someone finds you."

Without another word the pilot pulled the clothes on.

"Sit," McCarter said, indicating the narrow bench in front of the worktable. He took a roll of gray duct tape from his coat pocket and taped the man's hands together at the wrists, made sure the circulation was left intact, then taped his feet together at the ankles. When he was finished, he took a small radio from his coat pocket and handed it to the pilot. "Peace offering. That way you'll have something to do while you're here. Picks up stations pretty good, but sounds a little tinny. Still, it'll beat hell out of listening to the wind whistle around this building until someone comes looking for you."

"Thank you," the pilot said.

McCarter grinned. "Think nothing of it. Professional courtesy." He let himself out.

Five minutes later he was at ground level. Ten minutes after that, moving at a distance-eating jog, he was at the outer perimeters of the airfield.

He watched with interest, as the trucks hosed deicer onto the runways, their whirling yellow caution lights throwing warped shadows over the piles of dirty ice and snow pushed to both sides of the runway. Wheels squeaked as moisture tried to freeze up in unprotected bearings.

Even without the threat of the Finnish air force and army dropping on them with both feet at any moment, McCarter knew getting a plane up in this type of weather was going to be tricky.

He tapped the transmit button on his headset. "Phoenix Two to Phoenix One. Over."

"Go, Phoenix Two," Katz replied.

The way the Israeli's voice was breaking up over the frequency let McCarter know Katz and James were still en route. He glanced at his watch and saw that it was a quarter to midnight. "I take it you haven't made the airfield yet."

"Affirmative. You can take that issue up with Five when you see him. He's being particularly style-conscious tonight."

"This isn't a time to be stylishly late, mate," McCarter growled. "Granted, the top brass around this place isn't exactly top-notch, but they'll notice when one of their planes doesn't take to the air on time."

"We'll be there."

Despite the calm in Katz's voice, McCarter knew the man well enough to know the Israeli was concerned about the timetable as well. The Briton was sure every one of the team was ready to quit Finland and get to someplace where the rules were simpler. "I'll see you when I see you, mate. Two, out."

He unzipped his coat and freed the Browning in its shoulder leather, then strode toward the aircraft hangars. The flight suit, recognizable even under the coat, would keep a lot of regular enlisted men away from him. Officers were expected to know what they were doing at all times. He wouldn't be questioned until someone noticed him doing something he wasn't supposed to be doing. And he realized that would be pretty bloody quick.

Hunching his shoulders against the wind and pulling the hood of his coat up as he walked toward the gate, he fished the ID out of his pocket and flashed it at the armed guard keeping watch. The man didn't even bother to check the ID against his face. Then McCarter was inside the airfield, moving on borrowed time.

His target was the AC-130-H Spectre transport gunship chocked near the main hangar. The pilot whose clothes he'd borrowed was supposed to be at a preflight check on a fighter jet patrolling Finland's southeastern borders in a few minutes.

The Spectre was just under ninety-eight feet long, with a wingspan over one hundred thirty feet. The propellers were twice as tall as most men, and it stood thirty-eight feet in height. With the four Allison turboprops, the Lockheed craft was going to be a slow-moving duck compared to the Finnish jet fighters. This particular version, however, was armed with a side-firing cannon, which would earn them some respect as well as running room. The weather would help shut down his heat signature for air-to-air heat-seekers.

The snow came down harder, obscuring most of his surroundings and muting the flashing lights of the tower relay station that had been slapped together to direct air traffic.

McCarter tapped the headset. "Three, this is Two. Where the bloody hell are you, mate?"

"At your heels," Gary Manning called back. "Keep your shorts on."

"I'm knocking on the door of the bus now," McCarter said. "Once I get those props kicked over, you'd better be waiting with ticket in hand."

"Understood. We're parking our special delivery now. After we get it into place, there shouldn't be any worries about pursuit."

"I'm going to hold you to that. Two, out." McCarter closed on the big plane. Despite the cold surrounding him, he wanted a Coke and the time to fire up a Player's cigarette. Either would have served to relax him. Both would have been a few moments of bliss. He felt jaded, worn down by the broken-field running that had been made necessary in Finland. He was a professional soldier, a believer in fighting the good fight. But their enemy wasn't here—at least not now.

He reached for the Spectre's door and found it locked. That only stopped him for a moment. Getting through locked doors had been something he'd learned in extracurricular activity in Sandhurst Academy, and a necessary survival skill for a young British pilot who'd enjoyed the nightlife.

He let himself into the big plane and closed the door behind him. "Hello, you big ungainly brute," he said quietly to the aircraft as he made his way to the cockpit. The cargo area was cavernous, and his voice echoed. "Me and you, we got the impossible set before us tonight." He grinned. "Or at best, only the nearly impossible."

Seated in the pilot's seat, he went through his own preflight check, quickly satisfying himself that everything was as it should be.

Snow had caked the windows. He activated the deicer sprayers and watched the ice melt away as he brought the navigation systems on-line.

A canvas-covered jeep made its cautious way toward the Spectre. McCarter watched it closely, slipped the Browning free of its shoulder leather and laid it on the console before him. When the jeep came to a stop, he recognized Manning at once, then saw Encizo climb out from behind the steering wheel.

"Nice to have the pleasure of your company," McCarter said dryly as he continued with his preflight checks.

"Wouldn't miss it for the world," Encizo replied. He retreated to the rear of the jeep and started helping Manning with what looked like long tangles of ropes.

"Is that a net?" McCarter asked.

"Yeah," Manning replied. "A few of them. We salvaged them from the dock area earlier after we came up with our idea for taking out the runway. Custom-designed. Hell, Calvin Klein would think this was righteous."

"I'll take your word for it, mate, and breathlessly await the unveiling. Over."

McCarter cleared the channel and glanced out over the airfield. Some of the field-workers were starting to take notice of the activity around the Spectre. He knew it wouldn't take more than a few minutes before someone would question their actions.

"Hey, Two," Encizo called. "We caught their attention."

"Knew it was too good to last," Manning griped.

Out of the periphery of his vision, McCarter saw the security vehicle slowly approach the jeep. Encizo slipped a cut-down shotgun from under his coat, out of view of the people in the airfield security car.

"They're going to ask questions I can't answer," Manning said. The big Canadian stood between the jeep and the car as the security personnel clambered out, taking time to button their coats and pull their hats down around their ears. "Can you get the rear ramp down so I get these nets aboard?"

"Sure," McCarter replied.

One of the security people started asking questions and waving imperiously. The Briton could hear the conversation over the open mike. Even though he couldn't understand the language, the tone was familiar.

"Sorry, buddy," Manning said, "I don't understand a word you're saying."

The security people went for their holstered pistols.

Moving with an economy of motion, Encizo stepped around the jeep and leveled the combat pumpgun. The slamming booms of the rounds being touched off penetrated the Plexiglas panels of the cockpit.

"Bloody hell," McCarter said as he saw the Finnish security men go flying backward as both were caught in the chest. They crumpled to the ice-covered tarmac and writhed in agony.

"Not to worry," Encizo said calmly as he jacked a fresh round into the shotgun's breech. "Those were PVC baton rounds. Take the fight out of them for a few minutes, but they won't have any permanent damage. Especially through those thick coats."

Manning jumped behind the wheel of the jeep and roared around the back of the Spectre.

After tripping the release switch, McCarter felt the plane vibrate as the ramp was lowered. He scanned the airfield. Emergency lights flickered on. He keyed the ignition on the four turboprops and the big propellers started their rotations with a blat of power.

"Dammit, Katz," the Briton muttered. "We can't wait for you."

BUCKLED into the passenger seat of the Saab, Katz placed his hand firmly against the dashboard as the fence surrounding the Finnish air base came into view. Two soldiers were already swinging the gates closed.

"Go through," Katz said grimly.

James nodded curtly, then trod harder on the accelerator. The sports car shuddered, lost traction for a moment, then sped for the closing gate like a fiery red arrow. "Don't know if this thing's built to take that kind of punishment."

"Well, it won't be long before you do."

"Right."

Then the car was on top of the gate, the two soldiers scattering an instant before the impact.

Katz felt the vibration run the entire length of the car when it slammed into the double gates. Pieces of fiberglass came away in hunks, making the nose of the Saab look like it had been run under a chain saw.

James cut the wheel hard, slewed out of control for a moment, then recovered.

A burst of autofire took out the back window, blowing glass fragments over the interior of the car. A stray round exploded one of the fuzzy dice, then cored through the windshield, leaving a fist-size hole.

Glancing around the airfield, Katz saw indecision in the body language of the troops racing onto the tarmac. Muzzle-flashes popped intermittently as the broad beams of kleig lights swept over the parked aircraft. The Israeli tapped the transmit button on his headset. "Two, this is One. What's your location? Over."

"Hey, One, thought you'd never get here," McCarter said with real relief in his voice. "That's me in the idling Spectre at two o'clock from your current bearing."

Katz saw the big AC-130-H throwing a spray of snow behind the turboprops. "Roger, Two. We have you in sight. Where are Three and Four?"

"With me, mate."

Katz watched a jeep trundle up the loading ramp leading into the Spectre's spacious interior. Encizo brought up the rear.

"Got him," James said, cutting the wheel toward the big plane. He glanced over his shoulder. "But it looks like everybody else is going to get him, too."

When he looked back at the hangar area, Katz saw almost a dozen vehicles in motion, plowing across the snow and ice in their attempt to close in on the AC-130-H. He hit the transmit button. "Begin your takeoff, Two."

"Can't leave without you," McCarter argued. "I got a rule that says I go home with the ones that brought me to the dance."

"That's an order."

"Yes, sir."

"And leave the cargo ramp down," Katz said. "We'll be along. One, out." He turned to James. "It's your show, Calvin."

The ex-SEAL nodded, focusing his concentration on closing the gap between the Saab and the Spectre.

More snow clouds exploded behind the big turboprops, whipping around like shimmering wraiths. The aircraft moved for the main runway. Before it pulled onto the concourse a string of explosions rocked the hangar area.

Rather than going up all at once, the detonations were spaced for maximum effect, creating a rolling thunder that filled the night with hollow booms. Checking on the destruction, Katz saw that most of the damage was limited to the perimeter buildings and areas that were normally deserted at this time of night.

But the personnel of the Finnish air base didn't know that. Most of the soldiers hit the ground and covered their heads.

"How about that for an opening act?" Manning asked.

"Way to fire," McCarter said.

Katz reached down and released the seat belt as James stepped harder on the accelerator.

The nose of the Saab was only a few yards from the dragging ramp of the airplane. It beat against the ice-covered tarmac, kicking up chips and fist-size clods that impacted against the car's windshield. James shifted into a higher gear, lost traction for a moment, then gained

ground. The front wheels jerked and jumped as they settled onto the ramp, then the Saab slid smoothly up. It took
a lot of brake to come to a stop once it gained the traction
available inside the plane, and it thudded up against the
rear bumper of the jeep. James cut the engine.

Katz slid out of the car at once and saw Encizo and
Manning standing braced on either side of the ramp with
what looked like fishing nets in their hands. When he
glanced back out the opening, he saw that two base security cars had tracked onto their backtrail. "Calvin."

"Yeah."

"Jettison the car. I don't think we'll be needing it any
further."

James reached inside the sports car and released the
handbrake. Once he had the transmission in neutral, he
and Katz were able to get it started down the ramp. It
gained speed and exited the plane before the fast-
approaching security cars could see what was happening.

"Bombs away," James called out cheerfully.

The Saab took out the lead vehicle and went whirling
away, lost on the ice. The other security car tried to juke
left, but the driver lost control and slammed into a fighter
jet, crippling the craft and bringing it crashing down onto
the car.

"How long before we reach the runway?" Manning
asked.

"You're on it now, mate," McCarter replied. "Whatever you blokes have planned, now's the time to be doing
it."

Outside the ramp, the tarmac gave way to a deiced section. Metal grated loudly against the concrete.

"On three," Manning called out to Encizo, then counted
down.

Together they heaved the net down the ramp. The hemp strands looked like an unfolding spiderweb when it struck the ground and began paying out of the parked jeep. And it was, as Katz had initially thought, a bunch of fishing nets that had been laced together. He looked questioningly at Manning, who had a big grin on his face and a remote-control device in one huge hand.

"Nets," Manning said agreeably. "Figured if we took out the runway, we could cut down on the amount of gunners looking for us later."

"The nets have a special C-4 weave," Encizo explained.

Katz looked more closely at the nets and saw the clumps of hand-molded white plastic explosive threaded in with the hemp as it uncoiled from the rear of the jeep and unfurled along the runaway.

The Spectre rattled with power as the wheels started to clear the tarmac.

"I need the cargo ramp closed," McCarter said over his headset, "if I'm going to get full cooperation from this unacrobatic beast."

"Give it another minute," Manning said.

Abruptly the end of the nets ripped through the ramp opening and dropped like a dying snake on the runway. Near the hangars fighter jets were already falling into formation to begin pursuit.

"Say goodbye to the nice runway," Manning said with glee, his thumb hitting the remote-control button.

It looked like a minefield had gone off in the middle of the airfield runway. The explosions weren't large, but Katz was certain they were big enough to do the job Manning had designed them to do.

"Instant chug holes," Manning said. "I'd like to see them get anything in the air off that surface."

The Spectre left the ground, and the air base dropped away beneath them.

"Okay," Katz said, "you can pull up the ramp now."

Hydraulic motors growled as they winched in the loading ramp.

The Israeli made his way through the belly of the big plane to the cockpit and took the copilot's chair. Whirling white madness slammed into the windshield as they flew into the approaching snowstorm.

"Be a gent and keep an eye on that radar screen," McCarter said. "I've been checking it and I haven't seen anything, but you can bet the call has gone out from the tower to whatever teams are on patrol."

Katz turned so he could keep watch on the device, then reached for the radio communications gear. "The way I estimated it, we have about four hundred thirty-seven miles to the North Haakovian coast, then the jump to the rendezvous point with Striker."

McCarter nodded. "That's about the size of it, mate. I'd say an hour and a half, maybe two given the weather conditions, and we'll find us a nice civil war to enter. Myself, I was sick to death creeping around trying to do a job nobody wanted us to do."

"Do we have enough fuel to make the distance?"

"Oh, yeah. This ugly beast will make twenty-four hundred miles with a full payload. We're running basically empty. I'll lose a little fuel juking around below radar so the Finns can't get a fix on us, but we'll make it just fine."

"Good enough, David." Katz dialed the frequency tuner, found the special band Stony Man Farm was monitoring and put the call through. He gazed through the window, saw the black sea below and felt a chill. So many things could be passing by under that calm surface. He reined in his imagination for the time, took out his map packet and turned his mind to the business at hand. Before they even made the link to Striker and the South Haakovian army, there were miles of North Haakovian airspace to negotiate. One thing was certain: the flight wasn't going to be a restful one.

CHAPTER FIVE

Franzen Stensvik paced the length of the den restlessly. His army uniform was crisp and clean, perfectly pressed, but already there were perspiration stains at his armpits. Every time he passed the mirrored wall behind the full-size bar tucked in one corner of the room, he couldn't help glancing at them. And the more he glanced at them, the angrier he got. The news media had already been quick to point out the wet spots.

He paused at the bar, freshened his drink, and glimpsed at the stains in the mirror. Even though he was freshly shaved, a five-o'clock shadow peeked out from under his skin. "I'm getting too soft, Niklavs," he said to the old man sitting on one of the expensive couches near the center of the room. He stroked his chin thoughtfully. "There was a time when my skin did not look so pallid, and this weight was not such a problem to get off."

Niklavs laughed, a harsh barking sound made in a two-pack-a-day smoker's throat. "My president," the aide said, "I knew you back when we had only one horse and a dream of conquest between us. And throughout all that time, I have never seen you cut a finer figure of a man. You are meant to control these countries. It shows in the way you carry yourself." He finished the unfiltered cigarette down to the very last nub, pinched it out and dropped it in the ceramic ashtray on the polished walnut coffee table in front of him.

The old man reminded Stensvik of the maiden aunt who had raised him after his parents' deaths. He'd left the aunt when he was thirteen, stole into Sturegorsk and set about learning how to survive on his own. He would never think of leaving Niklavs—unless the man tried to steal from him or somehow betray him, and with his background he never ruled that out completely. People were jealous of others who could become larger than life.

Stensvik sipped his drink. "Those days were much simpler, my friend. Then, when we pointed a gun at someone's head, they knew we had them. In these more enlightened times, in dealing with political figures instead of people whose very lives are on the line, they do not believe."

"They will."

"When?"

Niklavs shrugged. "When you make them. That is all I know."

There was a knock at the door.

"Enter," Stensvik called.

A presidential guard stepped into the room. "I was sent to let you know Colonel Vaino has returned with the Varkaus woman."

"President Varkaus," Stensvik snarled. "She is a head of state. You would do well to remember that."

The soldier snapped to attention, a blush staining his features. "Yes, sir."

"Inform the colonel I will be along shortly."

"Yes, sir." The soldier executed a one-eighty and marched back through the door.

Stensvik examined the opulence of the room. There were rugs from the Middle East, wines from the vineyards of South France and expensive vases and paintings from places that at one time he hadn't even known existed. The room was a far cry from the shack he'd been brought up in. And he'd never willingly go back to that kind of life—not when he had the means to take everything he'd ever wanted from the people striving to keep it from him. There was a greatness to his life. He'd known it from the day he'd first fisted a pistol and took another man's life. And he wouldn't be denied that destiny.

He finished his drink, placed the empty glass on the bar and picked up his gun belt from a nearby stool. As he snugged it around him, he watched the CNN replay of the American President addressing the United Nations.

"That man," he said, leveling a blunt forefinger, "is a fool. He doesn't think I'll use the weapons at my disposal."

"Perhaps he is only wanting to force your hand," Niklavs suggested. "Once you have committed yourself and the first nuclear warhead strikes its target, the other countries may stop demanding the United States stay out of an active part of the conflict."

"They already are taking an active part."

"Military advisers," Niklavs said. "It's not the same thing."

"Those military advisers are out there taking the lives of my soldiers." Stensvik picked up his hat, popped it sharply across his arm, then placed it gently on his head.

"Not for much longer, Franzen," the older man said coyly. "Now you have their Madam President. It could be that by morning they will lose heart for the fight."

"I would rather break their spirits myself." Stensvik led the way to the door, turned right and followed the hall down to the private elevator. Niklavs joined him. "And I want to see their precious Colonel Pollock's head on a pike." He hit the button for the fourth floor, then lifted the red phone in the recessed area.

"Yes, President Stensvik," the operator said.

"My call to the United States?"

"I'm assured that it will be put through in the next seven minutes."

"Let me know immediately."

"Yes, sir."

Stensvik hung up the phone and took the computer-coded card from inside the calfskin wallet he carried. He ran it through the reader slot, watched the locking lights go from red to green and waited for the doors to open.

Two armed guards waiting on the other side immediately stepped back when they recognized him.

The room was huge, taking up two stories inside the presidential building. Like the lower floor, there were no windows. Behind the brick walls, buried under the functional interiors, was enough armor plating to withstand a low-yield nuclear attack. The building had been expensive, and most of the money he'd garnered from the Japanese and profited from the Colombian cocaine had gone into its construction. But in order to achieve the goals he'd set for himself, he'd needed a fortress from which to operate. He'd never thought it money ill-spent.

Inside the large room was the complex assembly of offensive and defensive computer hardware, created from Russian, German and Japanese technologies, wired into American satellites. Four giant screens lighted up the main viewing wall, holding at different times radar intel and information being downloaded from satellites.

Stensvik ascended the metal catwalk that led to the observation post suspended over the banks of computers and technicians. He noted with satisfaction that the duty officer kept rotating within the ranks of his men. Nearly all of the computer hardware below was a mystery to him. He didn't claim to be intelligent about such matters. There were men who understood such things, and they worked for him, helped him shape *his* dreams.

Leaning on the railing with one hand, he picked up the phone mounted in front of him and watched the duty officer quickly scramble to pick up the phone below before its second strident ring sounded. "Yes, President Stensvik?"

"Where is the South Haakovian army?"

The duty officer stretched the long cord as he hustled over to a computer console and began giving orders to the technician seated there. "There, sir. Screen three."

Stensvik looked and saw the big screen waver as the previous image dissolved and became an obviously computer-generated image of the North and South Haakovian borders and the Inge River. Bright sapphire blips lighted up in quick succession, clustered just a few miles short of the riverbank. "Their fuel supplies?"

"Destroyed, sir. If you'll move your attention to screen two, you can see actual footage taken from one of the fighter-bombers we sent to take them out."

Turning his head slightly, Stensvik looked at the screen. Images blurred, carved out of the shadow of night by the bright explosions that leaped from the erupting tanker trucks. "Very good. What about the American colonel? Pollock."

"Unknown at this time, sir. We still have strike teams working within the South Haakovian borders. It's possible that the man is already dead. They know President Varkaus has been abducted through Markus's betrayal."

"Is it on their media?"

"Not yet."

"See that it is."

"Yes, sir."

"Once they find out they are a nation fighting blind, with only an American at the helm, they may break easier."

"Yes, sir."

"Where are our troops?" Stensvik asked.

"Here, sir."

More blips, this time colored a jack-o'lantern orange, dotted the North Haakovian border.

The duty officer said, "They are massed and ready, sir, awaiting your orders."

"Make sure the air strike commanders remember their six-o'clock meeting with me in the morning. How certain are we that the fuel supplies won't be renewed before noon tomorrow?"

"According to calculations, sir, eighty percent—possibly more—of the South Haakovian fuel stores were destryed in the surprise raid. Our tacticians put it at a ninety-eight-percent probability that the South will not be able to arrange transport from Larsborg in time to mount a defensive line that will stop our armor from grinding them down tomorrow afternoon."

"Good." Stensvik hung up the phone and gazed with fondness at the staggered orange dots—his army, a force to be reckoned with. It destroyed whom and when he willed it. It was a long way from killing a man just to take his horse, then eating that horse because there was nothing else to be found.

"Things seem to be going well," Niklavs commented.

"Of course," Stensvik replied. "My men have their missions, and their fear of me will not allow them to think of failing. The South is going to fall tomorrow after the main offensive is launched."

"Do not be so quick to write those people off," Niklavs advised. "They are fighting for their homes and families, for their very lives. You have backed them up against the wall. Even a dying rat will fight against the flashing talons and beak of a bird of prey when it is cornered.''

"Their armor is mired as surely as an insect on flypaper. The only thing they can do is delay the inevitable. I predict that when the first air strikes reach the South Haakovian front lines, they will have a major troop withdrawal. The fighter jets will be shooting paper targets left unable to defend themselves.''

Niklavs hesitated, as if choosing his words and wondering if they might be better left unsaid. Then he forged ahead. "You're forgetting patriotism.''

"Patriotism?''

"Yes.''

"You call that soft, ragtag collection of military misfits patriots?''

"You're providing the crucible that can make them more than what they are. A delaying war, perhaps in time they would have deserted, could possibly have become persuaded that the South Haakovian government was an American puppet interested only in maintaining an egress for the United States. With the pressure you are putting on them, you are forcing them to become a staunch enemy.''

"They will buckle,'' Stensvik said harshly, "and they will break. By this time tomorrow, I will start handing you the pieces.''

Niklavs pursed his lips and said no more.

Stensvik returned his attention to the flickering screens set on the wall. South Haakovia couldn't continue to stand against him—not with the massed firepower he had at his command. The American President was playing a fool's game by thinking he wouldn't use the weapons at his disposal. And he would find that out in short order. While it was true that much of the secret caches he'd planned to have in place by now were not there, enough of them had been succesfully hidden in the United States to cause grievous damage.

It still chafed him that he wouldn't be able to announce his victory on the floor of the United Nations. But it was possible that Cuba or Vietnam or China would be able to get him an audience for that time. Eastern Europe had been seduced by the capitalist culture of the Western world, but those nations were going to find out it wasn't so easy to duck out on the Communist influence. Under the current capitalist regime in the Commonwealth of Independent States, the breadlines had never been longer. It was a sad state of affairs that the television news reports were filled with donations given by American religious orders or philanthropists. Soon there would be no pride left for Russians at all.

In time the Russian people would recognize Stensvik for the hero he was. His efforts in the Haakovias would show them the error of their ways. When all else failed, and they saw through the seduction of the Western powers, those people would return to the way of thinking that had seen them through hard times before. And they would need a leader. He intended to be that leader, and intended to go down in the history books as being as great an influence on the Communist way of thinking as Lenin or Stalin.

The phone rang, startling him out of his reverie. He needed to sleep, but the anxious energy that always filled him at the culmination of a goal wouldn't allow it. Later, after the battles were won, the bleak depression would fill him for days. Until then he would live his life on the edge of his excitements.

He picked up the phone and said hello.

"President Stensvik," the male operator said, "I have your call to the United States on the line."

"Put me through."

The connection clicked.

"Greetings, President Stensvik," the heavily accented voice said. "How is the war treating you?"

"I am winning," Stensvik replied with a confident grin. "How could it be treating me any other way?"

"Then let me be the first to congratulate you."

"I've already congratulated myself."

"Oh." Hector Osmundo sounded nonplussed.

"But your thoughts are appreciated," Stensvik went on.

"Of course. What can I do for you?"

"The diversion we planned for Los Angeles, California. How long before that can be put into operation?"

"Within the hour."

"And how soon will the effects be noticed by the American President?"

"This early in the month, there are a lot of people on the streets looking to score. I'd say maybe a handful of hours and hospitals would start taking on casualties. With the current attention the federal agencies are giving domestic situations out of the ordinary, I'd say he would know in a matter of minutes after the first or second case."

"Good. See that it gets done as soon as we have finished this conversation."

"President Stensvik, might I remind you that when we agreed to this scenario, it was understood that it would be used only in the event of an emergency." Osmundo hesitated. "Is this an emergency? My backers will ask."

"Tell them yes."

"The site that we planned to use is a highly productive one to us. We've invested in it for a long time, and the profits are exceeding our expectations. Once we start the infected stuff onto the streets, we're going to lose that."

Stensvik snorted angrily. He was learning to hate dealing with capitalists more and more every hour. All they ever thought about was their bottom line profits at any given moment, from the Wall Street brokers to the cocaine dealers. They seemed ignorant of the wisdom of long-range planning. "My friend, don't the cartel people appreciate the avenues I have opened up for them in Eastern Europe and the other satellite countries?"

"Of course, President Stensvik. You should never question our appreciation over—"

"And you," Stensvik said, "should never question my judgment. I am here, in control of this war, bringing it to an end within a matter of hours now, and I don't want to have to immediately step into another one with the United States. The American President is already beating his chest and crying out 'Woe is me for I have to defend the free world.' Before the American people rally behind that cry as they have in the past, I want to show them the cost of their involvement."

"I see."

"Don't just see. Get it done. The American intelligence circles are already aware of the cartel's involvement in the civil war between the Haakovias. They're probably only a step away from shooting holes in the pipelines you've sunk into this country."

"The cartel is going to be concerned about the losses."

"Tell your bosses I'll offer an intial start-up fee for a similar operation wherever they want to put it," Stensvik said. It was possible he could leverage more money from the Japanese corporations he'd negotiated with for the exclusive rights to work the South Haakovian oil fields once they were within his grasp.

"That will help," Osmundo conceded.

"Do it. Do it now, or I'll start cutting off those drug pipelines myself." He hung up before the Colombian could reply. "Damned capitalist civilian," he snarled.

He turned on his heel, breathed out through his nose and concentrated on the pleasant task that lay ahead of him. It was tiring work to run a country bordering on the successful conclusion of taking over another nation. Getting the chance to work with his hands again was something he looked forward to.

Entering the elevator again, he got out on the second floor beneath ground level. Guards lined the hallways every few feet. He pointed to three of them. "You, you and you, follow me."

The men fell in behind Niklavs at once, their AK-47s canted across their chests.

A sentry guarding the door the president approached came to attention.

"Is Colonel Vaino inside, soldier?" Stensvik asked.

"Yes, sir."

"Open the door and announce us then."

"Yes, sir." The soldier turned sharply, passed through the door and held it open. He raised his voice to command the attention of everyone in the room. "Presenting President Franzen Stensvik, commanding officer of the North Haakovian armies, and his aide-de-camp, Colonel Tymek Niklavs. Attention!"

Stensvik noted with irritation that Dag Vaino was slow to get to his feet. The sniper-assassin wasn't getting with the program as quickly as Stensvik had wished. Chain of command was everything in an army, and even more so in a bandit brigade, which was how Stensvik viewed the North Haakovian military machine he'd put together. Maybe the uniforms and popular support had given the army a legitimacy, but at heart every man in this room was a robber or a thief.

Nine of his other commanding officers were in the room. Even the carefully tailored and crisply starched uniforms couldn't blunt the edges they'd acquired in the streets and in the rough forest lands as they'd crawled into their present positions of power. Stensvik felt kinship with these men, even Vaino to a degree, because he knew the roots of each and everyone. Vaino was a bit different, though, because under the tutelage of the KGB and other espionage agencies, he'd acquired a smattering of etiquette. And the sniper was the best-looking man in the room.

A scattered handful of chairs and couches formed a semicircle around a false fireplace that had been artfully contrived to look more real than the genuine article. Fake flames lapped at a trio of artificial logs. Expensive carpet covered the floor.

Vaino stood near the long wet bar where two female bartenders with long blond hair and negligible clothing busily worked with shot glasses. Although the liquor was provided and the appetites of the men in the room were voracious, Stensvik had made certain each man knew that getting caught drunk while on duty was an offense punishable by death.

Through with his preliminary inspection of the room's occupants, he turned his attention to the two who most interested him.

Gustaf Markus, former general and commanding officer of the South Haakovian army, stood in front of an easy chair, a smile on his face and a martini in his hand. "President Stensvik," Markus said with a small, old-world bow that Stensvik found nauseating.

"General Markus," Stensvik replied with a curt nod.

Markus grinned, as if believing the form of address had conferred on him the same military status as he'd enjoyed in his previous army. At present he was dressed in formal clothes, a tuxedo with a yellow cummerbund.

Janyte Varkaus sat in tight-lipped silence on a plush couch where she'd been sandwiched between two officers. A small bruise showed on her left cheek, but it didn't detract from her beauty. Her black hair touched her bare shoulders, which the expensive chiffon evening gown didn't conceal. Her eyes were the bluest ice. Her features were exquisite, enhanced by the small scar on her chin.

One of the scantily clad bartenders hurried over and gave Stensvik a drink. Every man in the room watched the woman walk back to the bar with a hip-swaying stride designed to catch their attention.

Stensvik walked over to Janyte and raised his glass in a toast. "Madam President, you're ravishing. So much more than I'd expected from the news footage I've seen of you."

"And you're disgusting," Janyte said bravely, not showing any fear at all, "in many of the same ways that I'd always thought you would be."

The room became very silent, to the point that the audiotapes of burning logs could be heard.

When Stensvik broke out laughing in honest amusement, he could tell from Janyte's masked expression that it was the last thing she'd expected. "Hell, I've had bar whores who were more insulting over a low tip than you're capable of being."

A scarlet flush washed over Janyte's features. She broke eye contact with him.

"Do you have a drink?" Stensvik asked.

"No."

"What would you like?"

"Nothing."

"I'd hoped we could be more civil about this," Stensvik said. "After all we are both heads of state."

"You," Janyte said in a clear voice, "are a thief and a murderer."

Stensvik closed on her and lowered his voice. "At this moment, lady, I'm also the only man who can predict your future. You might want to keep that in mind."

Whatever retort she thought to make died on her lips.

Catching the attention of the bartenders, Stensvik said, "Put some music on, and bring Madam President a piña colada." He turned back to the assembled officers. "Everyone else relax. This is not a formal affair. Enjoy yourself, for tomorrow we make war the like of which has never been seen in these countries."

Within moments a drink had been placed on the coffee table before Janyte and Elvis Presley was singing "Heartbreak Hotel" in the background.

Vaino lounged easily at the bar, exchanging small talk with the bartenders as they replenished drinks.

Stensvik remained standing, his attention riveted on South Haakovia's political leader. The nervous energy that filled him cried out hungrily, and he felt lust banging at his temples and loins. "It would be better," he suggested, "if you didn't act like you hated being here so much."

"But it would be a lie."

Stensvik shrugged. "We all lie on occasion."

"Not me. Not about this."

Grinning, knowing he held the attention of every eye in the room, Stensvik put his drink down, walked over to Markus and dropped an arm over the smaller man's shoulders. He playfully tugged Markus over in front of the woman. "How well do you know me?" he asked Janyte.

"Not much," she replied. "And I certainly don't want the opportunity to add to what I do know."

Stensvik hugged Markus fiercely with one arm, felt the man try to draw away at first, then give himself over to Stensvik's control. "Do you know why you are here tonight?"

Janyte turned her cold gaze on Markus.

Stensvik felt the man squirm uncomfortably in his grip.

"I was betrayed by the worst traitor I have ever had the misfortune to meet," Janyte said in a cool voice.

"See?" Stensvik said with the biggest smile he could muster. "Already we have found something we have in common. We both despise traitors." He shook his free arm, triggered the release on the hideaway knife strapped to his forearm and grabbed the handle as it dropped into his waiting hand.

Markus looked at him in perplexion, trying to take a step back.

Stensvik tightened his grip, keeping the man close. The blade flashed as it came up in his fist. With a practiced economy of motion he stabbed it into Markus's neck just below the man's left ear, then drew it in a fluid movement across his throat.

Blood erupted from the smooth edges of the wounds, splashed across the coffee table, stained the collection of drinks sitting there and spotted Janyte's legs.

Stumbling, hands flailing uselessly to stem the arterial flow, Markus tried to scream but couldn't. In only a few seconds, he collapsed to the floor, shivered out his death throes and lay still.

Stensvik reached down and pulled the cummerbund from around Markus's waist. He took his time cleaning the hideout knife and noticed the thin grin on Vaino's face.

Janyte's features, though composed, held the sudden realization of exactly what kind of man held her at his mercy. Cold horror etched her jawline, put a frightened sheen in her eyes.

"I don't like traitors, either," Stensvik said in a casual voice. "They're loose cannons, and you can never truly depend on them." He glanced at the dead man. "But you have to admit—they do have their uses."

CHAPTER SIX

The room was like another world, jammed with state-of-the-art technology and hardware, spinning out information and intelligence on cybernetic programs that were only now beginning to leave their true mark on the rest of progressive thinking. All the equipment in that room provided a lightning-quick connection to the rest of the physical world that had always existed, yet could give springboards into worlds that were tucked uncomfortably between imagination and reality. A guy working the distance between those two realms had to create his own signposts.

Seated at the U-shaped desk on the raised dais overlooking the pit area of the three other main programming areas, Aaron Kurtzman knew he loved those worlds.

But it wasn't always a search using applied theory. There was a lot of ball-busting legwork to do at times. This, he knew, was one of those times.

He tapped the keyboard and watched the main monitor in front of him as he searched different quadrants of the North Haakovian topography. "Akira."

"Yeah." Akira Tokaido was one of the brightest computer hackers Kurtzman had ever had the chance to work with. Where most people the Bear collaborated with used applied science to their computer skills, Tokaido seemed to find his way through the bits and bytes of computer programming by a cybernetic sixth sense. As usual, Tokaido sat at his workstation chewing bubble gum, earphone tucked in one ear while he listened to mind-jarring heavy metal from the CD player strapped in gunslinger fashion to his right thigh.

"We've only got a few minutes on this flyby," Kurtzman said. "The next one's not due for hours. If I know Striker, he'll want to be up and running long before that. I want to get as much out of this as I can."

"You find it," Tokaido promised, "and I'll get it filed."

Kurtzman nodded, opened a window near the center of the screen and started to track the weather satellite's progress as it sped by thousands of miles out in space. "Now," he said as he tripped the programming he'd created. The weather satellite was one of several used by the CIA. The Bear had broken in through their codes years ago and used them at his leisure. Stony Man Farm had also financed a few satellites of their own over the years, disguised as domestic business investments. Each of those satellites were used in gathering intel from around the world.

The computer image of the program's clock ticked away seconds and finally came up 0:00:00.

"Okay," Kurtzman said, "we're out of there. Collate that data and get back to me as soon as you have it."

"Right."

Kurtzman skimmed over the information himself, zoomed in on sections and tried to decipher what Striker planned to do with it.

"Stumped?"

Looking up, Kurtzman saw Barbara Price approaching from the small cubicle of an office she maintained to one side of the computer room. While the Bear lived up to his nickname even in the wheelchair, looking something like a village blacksmith or a professional wrestler, Price was a honey blonde and put together with curves more dangerous than a single-lane highway coming down off a Rocky Mountain peak.

"Puzzled," Kurtzman admitted.

"How so?" Price stopped at the iced trays containing cans of orange juice and iced tea. She picked up a can of juice, shook it and popped the tab.

"Striker's current need-to-know. The way I know him, at this point I wouldn't expect anything but a wild-card play."

"It's the hand he's been dealt," Price stated as she scanned the three computer screens at the other end of the room.

"Over the years I've seen him draw them more than anybody I know. This one, I think, is going to take the cake. I just get itchy thinking about it and wondering."

"I know. So do I. And Hal's wondering what the hell is going to happen now that Markus's treachery has stalled out the South Haakovian armored units."

"No luck on sending any additional American forces into the area?"

"No. Russia and China are standing adamant in the United Nations. If the President tries sending any more troops or supplies into South Haakovia, everyone's afraid the Russians and the Chinese are going to step in."

"All this for two little countries that didn't have a pot to piss in between them only a few years ago."

Price sipped her orange juice. "Times have changed over there. So many countries are in a state of flux, and economies are teetering on the edge of disaster. The raw resources that have been uncovered in South Haakovia could mean salvation for a lot of people. And the arsenal Stensvik has his hands on needs to be negated."

"But nobody else wants to take the chance."

"Yeah."

Kurtzman sighed. "Don't you ever once in awhile—when nobody's looking—just think about what it might be like to lead a normal life. You know, getting up in the morning on Saturday wondering if your husband's still home or if you're going to find a note on the refrigerator telling you he's gone fishing?"

Price smiled at him, patted his arm. "No, I don't. Somebody's got to do our jobs, and I'm just damned thankful we're big enough to carry the load."

"Aaron," Carmen Delahunt called. She was old-line FBI, and Kurtzman had counted it a coup the day he recruited her from Quantico. Red-headed and fiesty, she was currently putting the last of her three children through college in Maryland.

"What's up?" Kurtzman asked.

"I've got Striker on radio up-link."

Kurtzman nodded and reached for the headset plugged into his desk. Price scooped up her own and slipped it over her head.

"Stony One, you have Stony Base. Over," Price said.

Mack Bolan's voice sounded as clear and as concise as ever, but Kurtzman could hear the fatigue behind the words. "Roger, Stony Base. It's good to hear a friendly voice."

"Heard you've had your share of misfortune," Price said casually.

"A chain's only as strong as its weakest link," the big warrior said. "We didn't have a chance to shake out all the weak links. Have you heard anything about the lady?"

Kurtzman looked over at the third workstation where Huntington Wethers kept diligently plugging away at media reports and intelligence briefs stemming from the Baltic countries, Eastern Europe and the various espionage agencies who had their ears to the ground in that area. His

ebony face looked downcast, but the Bear knew that was
a usual expression for the man and had thought seriously
about nicknaming him Gloomy.

Wethers looked up and shook his head, then went back
to work. For an ex-professor of cybernetics at Berkeley,
Hunt Wethers had shown a remarkable aptitude for behind the scenes skullduggery.

"No, Stony One," Kurtzman replied. "We're still
drawing a blank on that end."

"How are things there?" Price asked.

"Tight," the Executioner replied. "Our armored units
are scattered to hell and gone. We're unable to move them
without leaving most of them stranded. At night we can
bury up, not leave much of a heat signature for fighter
bombers and attack planes set up for infrared. But come
the daylight hours, they're going to be easy pickings for
Stensvik's vulture patrols even if we try to defend them
with the air force."

"What about writing the heavy armor off as a loss,
Stony One?"

"Can't," Bolan replied tersely. "I need those units up
and rolling to break the back of the North's military machine. This is going to be a ground-based war. Stensvik's
got too much we don't know about to go in on successive
air raids. And we don't have the support to maintain the
kind of air offensive we'd need to pull it off. This is going
to be pure grunt work once we enter hostile territory.
Trench mentality. We'll go in, establish a beachhead, then
leapfrog over it to get to a new position. Once we make a
line, it's going to take everything we've got to hold it."

"You talk like you're still going in," Price said.

"That's affirmative, Stony Base," Bolan said. "There's
no way back, and we can't stay here. That leaves nowhere
to go but onward. What's the situation with Phoenix?"

"They're en route, Stony One," Price replied. "I've been waiting for you to call to figure out a rendezvous point."

"What's their ETA?"

Price looked at Kurtzman.

The big man hit the keyboard and brought up the active files on Phoenix Force. He scanned the information and cross-referenced the digitally created maps and images he'd constructed of their planned flight path. "Near dawn as best as I can figure it, Stony One."

"That might work right in based on the intel you're able to get me concerning North Haakovia's recent troop movements."

"That's all coming," Kurtzman said. "You'll get it soonest."

"You might give them a call, Stony Base," the Executioner said, "and ask if they feel like working on a Robin Hood scenario. Over."

Kurtzman swapped looks with Price. She didn't appear to be any more enlightened than he was. Once Bolan explained what he had in mind, Kurtzman wasn't sure if he felt any better knowing. One thing he was sure of: he'd be on pins and needles until the initial stages of the mission were over. Then he'd get down to some serious worrying.

"JUMP POINT COMING UP," the pilot's voice crackled over the C-130 Hercules's interior speaker setup. "T-minus three minutes."

Clad in warm clothing for the high-altitude, low opening parachute drop, Mack Bolan nodded for the payload crew to open the cargo door of the big transport plane.

The tail section opened electronically, giving the big warrior the feeling that he was in the belly of a gigantic alligator about to spit him out into the night. Wind whistled by outside, and the heat that had grudgingly built up in the transport area was quickly sucked away.

Bolan pulled his gloves on more tightly, then checked his gear one last time. In addition to the two parachute packs and an oxygen tank, he carried the Desert Eagle on his hip and the Beretta in shoulder leather. Under the bulky jacket that would keep him warm during the descent, he wore the blacksuit and combat harness with extra clips and an assortment of grenades. His lead weapon was a Heckler & Koch MP-5 SD-3. A Cold Steel Tanto combat knife was sheathed in his boot.

He tapped the headset he wore under his jump helmet. "Okay, Scarlet Team, count off."

The ten handpicked men counted off in quick succession as they lined up for the jump.

"T-minus one minute," the pilot said calmly.

Bolan walked to the edge of the open cargo door and peered down. From thirty thousand feet, there wasn't much to see. Despite that, he knew they were over North Haakovia. He could feel it. The mission they were on this night was the linchpin that allowed the morning's plan to have even a slim chance of success. If they failed here and things didn't go as planned, the South Haakovian cav units wouldn't stand a chance when the dawn came.

"You are over our target zone," the pilot announced. "Good luck, gentlemen."

Bolan glanced back at his second. Sergeant Mark Smith was 82nd Airborne, and a veteran of the Gulf War. Short and stocky, with greasepaint clouding his features, he looked nothing short of barbaric. "Sergeant."

"Yes, sir," Smith responded.

"See you on the ground."

"Yes, sir." Smith took the downward slant of the open cargo hatch at a dead run and threw himself into the night, headed for the ground almost six miles below.

The rest of the team showed no hesitation, tumbling out the back of the Hercules like stacked dominoes.

Bolan slipped his protective face mask into place, thumbed on the oxygen and jogged out after the last man. He hurled himself from the lip of the hatch like a diver, drifted out of the big transport plane's slipstream and assumed the classic starfish pattern as he took control over his descent.

Despite the warm outerwear, the altitude and the rushing wind were bitingly cold. His face mask iced up. The C-130 headed back for safe airspace, but continued to guide the parachutists' descent by instrumentation.

Long minutes later the target area came into sight. To the south the Inge River was a wet black snake that twisted among the broken forestland through solid walls of trees. The trees thinned out slightly in the other three directions of the compass, leaving the bald rocky knob where the North Haakovian tracking station was located.

Bolan took a small pair of binoculars from his chest pocket and scanned the scrub-covered ridge. The building had been designed to have most of the angles blunted by the natural rock formations. It was constructed of concrete block and wood, probably overnight, and set up with all the electronic surveillance equipment necessary to watch over that section of the country. He saw the two satellite dishes marking their side-to-side sweeps like metronomes to the north and the west.

The ground came up fast.

The area was too thick with trees to expect to come down gracefully. Unable to do anything about it, Bolan came crashing down through the limbs of a big elm. Blunt tree

fingers stabbed for his eyes but were deflected by the thick
plastic face mask. Other branches whipped into him hard
enough to bruise. He was left stranded almost fifteen feet
from the ground hanging by the snarled chute strands.
Unbuckling the chute pack, he shrugged free, climbed
down to the lowest height possible by the nylon, dumped
his heavier equipment to the leaf-covered forest floor, then
dropped after it.

His boots sank into the soft loam, and he automatically
went into a roll to lessen the impact, then came to his feet
a moment later. Tapping the headset, he called, "Scarlet
Leader to Scarlet Squad. Report in."

"Scarlet Two," Smith radioed back immediately. "Op-
erative."

The others followed in quick succession. Seven had suffered a broken arm, and Bolan assigned the team's medic
to get the man mobile.

Arranging his gear, the Executioner jogged out of the
forest and took up a position along the perimeter. The
others vectored in on him, hunkered down in the brush by
the trees as he scoped out the surveillance post.

Bolan was grimly aware of the numbers clicking down
in his head. Time was burning at both ends on this maneuver. The surveillance post had to fall before any of the
other jockeying could begin.

From the initial intel on the outpost, eight to twelve men
were stationed there at any one time. The only problem the
big warrior could see was that they had to take the post
quietly.

He scanned the building for ten minutes. There were no
windows, and only two guards worked the outside perimeters.

"Sergeant," Bolan said, "give me your best stalker."

Smith nodded, looked at his team and said, "Madden, you're with the colonel."

"Yes, sir." A young American soldier crept forward, a serious look on his unlined face.

Bolan rearranged his gear, making sure it wouldn't come loose until he was ready for it. He looked at the soldier. "We go in as quietly and as quickly as possible, and take out those two guys without anyone being the wiser."

"Yes, sir."

"Have you ever killed anyone like this before?"

"Yes, sir. Twice."

"Any problems with taking them out before they know you're there?"

"I grew up on reruns of the Lone Ranger and Roy Rogers. Doesn't mean I feel terrible when I don't just shoot the gun out of the bad guy's hand."

A ghost of a smile tugged at Bolan's lips in spite of the seriousness of the situation. "Fair enough. I've got the one on the east. You've got the one on the west. Do you see him?"

"Yes, sir."

"No radio contact once we're out there unless I initiate it."

Madden nodded.

"Sergeant, you and your people don't move in unless I tell you to."

"Yes, sir." Smith sat hunkered back on his heels, watching the outpost. He waved, splitting the group into halves that faded one by one along the brush line.

Bolan turned to Madden. "Let's get it done."

The soldier headed out at once, melting into the shadows.

As he moved away from the covert group, the Executioner reached out for the night and became a part of it.

He'd first learned his trade in the jungles of Vietnam with Pen-Team Able, but he'd spent the years since perfecting it.

He slid the Cold Steel Tanto combat knife free of its sheath as he got within twenty yards of the guard. The man never heard him coming. Bolan stepped out of the darkness, looped an arm around the guy's neck as he slipped a palm over the man's mouth, then shoved the knife between the third and fourth ribs. He held on while the man struggled and life left him, then lowered the body to the brush. After cleaning the knife on the grass he went on.

The Executioner unslung the H&K MP-5, slipped the safety and closed on the building. He hit the transmit button on his headset. "Scarlet Five?"

"Yes, sir," Madden came back, his voice tighter than it had been.

"Your target?"

"No longer a factor in this equation, sir."

"And you?"

"Fully functional, sir."

The Executioner came up against the wood-and-concrete-block exterior of the outpost, heard the vibration of men's voices inside, but couldn't understand the conversations going on. He activated the headset again. "Scarlet Two."

"Yes, sir."

"Bring in the troops. We're going to take this building."

"Yes, sir."

Up close now, Bolan saw the building was larger than he'd first guessed. It was at least forty feet in length, by fifteen feet wide, staggered in sections as it followed the broken decline of the terrain. There were doors at the north, south and east walls, so that when they were opened, they formed a throat that ran through the guts of the surveillance post.

Soft footsteps approached from behind the Executioner. He looked over his shoulder and saw Smith padding quietly toward the building.

"Team's in place," the sergeant said.

"Get the door."

Smith slung his H&K MP-5, knelt by the door and affixed a line of plastic explosives, stabbing a timer in the center of it. "Door's ready."

Bolan nodded and tapped the transmit button on the headset. "On my go, gentlemen, just the way we talked about. No more gunfire than necessary, and no damage to the hardware inside." He took a deep breath—charging his lungs with oxygen—closed his hand around the subgun's pistol grip and told Smith to activate the timer.

Thirty seconds later, the C-4 went off like a small cannon. The sound echoed through the forest, startling birds into the air.

Bolan moved into the smoky haze left by the explosion, leveling the H&K. He raised a leg and kicked out. The door shuddered and came off its hinges. He followed it inside, squinting his eyes against the sudden bright light inside.

The main room took up the first twenty-five feet of the outpost. Computer hardware lined the walls, carved into working niches by unpainted plywood rectangles. Maps covered the walls, decorated with pushpins marking troop and mechanized-unit movement.

The Executioner took it all in at a glance, targeting the first North Haakovian soldier as the guy brought his side arm into target acquisition. He squeezed the trigger, loosing a 3-round burst that stitched the man from sternum to shoulder.

That soldier fell back, his eyes already glazing in death.

Another man tried to swivel around in the chair in front of the radio communications base unit. The muzzle of an AK-47 dropped to the top of the plywood partition.

Still on the move, Bolan swung up the H&K, chopping a burst through the plywood. The subsonic 9 mm Parabellum rounds cored easily through the wood, then slammed the communications officer back against the wall.

One North Haakovian soldier tried to take cover behind a filing cabinet at the end of the room.

Switching to single-fire, the Executioner placed a bullet between the man's eyes. The corpse slumped to the floor, his weapon sliding from his nerveless fingers.

"Pavils," Bolan called out.

"Sir." The man came forward at once.

"The radio."

"Yes, sir." Pavils yanked the corpse of the communications officer out of the way and slipped on the headset.

Bolan moved on, feeding a fresh clip into the subgun.

He found two men in the barracks room just beyond the outpost's nerve center. The warrior pulled the first man from his rack before the guy had really woken up. Bolan slammed the guy to the hardwood floor, put a knee in his back and dropped the H&K long enough to bind the man's hands behind his back with a pair of the disposable plastic handcuffs the team carried.

Smith had the other man up against the wall, kicking the soldier's feet apart and jamming the snout of the subgun into the guy's cheek to keep his head in contact with the wall.

Bolan continued the search, trailed by two other members of the squad. The next door they came to was locked. A 9 mm Parabellum shattered the locking mechanism.

Subgun at the ready, the Executioner crossed the threshold into darkness.

Nothing moved in the shadows, and chemical smells filled the air.

"I've got a light switch," someone said.

"Use it," Bolan replied.

A heartbeat later illumination filled the room and revealed the long shelves of the storage room. Boxes of canned and packaged goods vied for space with computer and electronic components. There was no one in the room.

"Secure this room," Bolan ordered.

One of the men fell into position.

"Get me a list together in five minutes. Besides those gas cans, let me know if there's anything else we can salvage from here to take back with us."

"Yes, Colonel."

Leaving the supply room, Bolan tapped the headset's transmit button. "Pavils."

"Yes, sir."

"The communications lines?"

"Weren't open, sir. They were neither sending nor receiving. No one knows we're here."

"Good. Madden?"

"Everything's fine here, sir."

"Anyone get out of the building?"

"Two, sir," the man replied. "But they didn't get far."

"Good job, son."

"Yes, sir."

Smith met him as he entered the nerve center. "We're in control here." He jerked a thumb over his shoulder at a man working on the computer circuitry. "Jussi's finishing up slaving the master motherboard to the system your friends preprogrammed."

Bolan nodded. He shouldered the subgun and turned to Pavils, reciting a frequency from memory. "Open up a channel and get Electron Rider for me."

The communications officer acknowledged the order with a snappy salute, then set about the task.

Squatting in front of the computer mainframe, Jussi worked quickly and confidently with a series of screwdrivers, wire cutters, and a battery-powered soldering iron. The odor of burning metal filled the room, overpowering the throat-burning sensation of leftover cordite hanging in the air.

Two members of the squad dragged the bodies of the dead North Haakovia soldiers from the outpost and brought in dirt and grass to scatter over the bloodstains to reduce the chance of slipping.

"Colonel Pollock."

Bolan turned to the communications officer.

"I've got Electron Rider for you."

"Put it on the speakerphone."

"Yes, sir." Pavils made the necessary adjustments and the speakerphone whistled as it came on-line.

"Electron Rider," Bolan said, "this is Stony One. Glad to have you here with us." He knew Kurtzman would catch the reference to the other listeners in the room. The reason for leaving the communication open to the squad was because of the grapevine he knew existed in every army. By morning, when the South Haakovian Special Forces were gearing up to go into battle on the daylight raid he'd planned, every man in that army would know the outpost had been neutered. It would give each man an edge of confidence, those who went out to meet the enemy early, and those who had to wait behind to see the success or failure of their comrades that could spell life or death for many of them. There had been no problem with desertion yet, but General Markus's betrayal had to have left some deep scars in the minds of the domestic fighting men. In some small way this would restore a portion of their pride.

"How are your people?" Kurtzman asked.

"Intact," Bolan replied. "So far it's been by the numbers."

"The motherboard?"

Jussi held up a handful of fingers, then returned his attention to his work.

"Five minutes," Bolan said. "Has Stony Base reached Phoenix?"

"That's affirmative, Stony One. Despite the prospects of being dropped into enemy territory before they've even sat down to a warm meal, they're champing at the bit to do their part. And we've worked out the timetables. They'll be there when you are."

Not quite five minutes later, Jussi backed away from the computer and wiped his hands on a red rag. "She's in place, sir."

Bolan nodded. "Okay, Electron Rider, you have the green."

"Roger, Stony One. Let's see what we have."

Bolan walked to the radar screen and watched the sweep of the lambent green arm as it walked around its cycle. The screen's green glow lighted up the faces of the curious men as they lined up around and behind him.

"We control the horizontal," Kurtzman said, "and we control the vertical. There's a signpost up ahead. The next stop...the Twilight Zone."

A grin crossed Mark Smith's face as he folded his arms over his chest. "Your buddy has a sense of humor, but can he produce?"

"I heard that," Kurtzman said. "And yeah, I'm a hell of a lot more than just bad television clichés."

Abruptly the radar arm froze like clock hands pointing at midnight.

"Don't worry," Kurtzman said. "In Sturegorsk, they're still receiving the same radar transmissions they've been receiving all day. I preprogrammed a ten-hour cycle so there wouldn't be a repetition that might red-flag your operation to some alert data jockey. You'll be covered in the morning, on your way in and on your way out until Stensvik's troops recover the outpost."

"There's no chance of that," Bolan replied. "Once the exfiltration begins tomorrow morning, this outpost is going to be one of the first casualties."

"Now, while Stensvik's intelligence is satisfied that nothing is going on here," Kurtzman continued, "I can do anything I want with the hardware there."

Color drained from the radar screen, followed last by the frozen radar arm. Then a new image exploded into the circle. It showed a woman dressed in black with a beehive hairdo sporting heavy black eyeliner and impressive cleavage.

"Hey," one of the Americans in the squad said suddenly, pushing forward and pointing, "that's Elvira, Mistress of the Dark."

"One of my personal favorites," Kurtzman said.

On-screen the late-night horror-show hostess winked at her audience, then fluttered her fingers. Then the screen cleared and returned to the radar image.

"You've proved yourself by me," Smith stated.

"Was there anything else, Stony One?" Kurtzman asked.

"Negative, Electron Rider. I appreciate the assistance."

"You stay hard out there, Stony One. Electron Rider clear."

Bolan glanced at the communications officer. "Pavils, open a line to G-Force."

"Yes, sir." A moment later the South Haakovian corporal said, "He's on-line now, sir."

"G-Force, this is Scarlet Leader. Over."

"Roger, Scarlet Leader. G-Force reads you five-by-five."

"The prelim bout is over," Bolan said. "You've got clear skies coming in."

"Acknowledged, buddy. The bus will be there in a short. G-Force, clear."

Bolan passed the mike back to Pavils and gave Smith orders to regroup his men. They were moving out. The opening bid had been played successfully, but they were nowhere near the main objective.

CHAPTER SEVEN

"Hey, Carl," Hermann Schwarz called from the back seat of the spacious Cadillac, "me and the Politician were wondering something."

As he hung up the mobile phone and put his hand back on the steering wheel of the big luxury car, Carl Lyons glanced in the rearview mirror at his teammates. The saying about idle hands was true, and Schwarz and Rosario Blancanales were living proof of it. When in the heat of a battle, there was no one the big ex-LAPD cop would rather have at his side. And they'd worked enough together over the past few years that they'd learned to function together without words. But when they had nothing to occupy their minds they could be worse than two precocious five-year-old boys with a penchant for aggravation.

Schwarz was trim and athletic, and looked like an aging outfielder dressed in a navy ball cap, a black T-shirt and jeans. A Houston Astros windbreaker covered his shoulder rig, which carried a Beretta Model 92-S. Years in Vietnam, working as a private investigator specializing in surveillance, and the past years with Able Team had made Schwarz a master of any and all things electronic. Nicknamed Gadgets, he was the only man Lyons knew who could take a regular two-slice toaster and make it a deadly weapon.

Seated next to him, Rosario Blancanales was a study in contrasts. His attire was considerably upgraded for one thing, and he wore the dark slacks and open-throated dress shirt with a casual air. The sports coat was cut to conceal the Beretta slung in custom-made hip leather. Dark sunglasses covered his eyes. With the salt-and-pepper hair and his stocky build, Blancanales could pass ten years either way on his age, and come across as anything from a pimp to a major player on Wall Street. A gold chain glinted at his throat, and the diamond-studded watch easily went into four figures. His gift with people, coupled with his ability to be whatever anyone wanted to believe he was, had earned him the sobriquet of Politician. But when the time for words and negotiations was over, he was a deadly adversary.

"Wondering what?" Lyons asked, returning to the conversation. There was no way to be cautious about it.

"Whether you had a phone in your bathroom at home," Schwarz said.

"No." Lyons took a right at the streetlight, powering the Cadillac deeper into the urban blight sprawled across the inner city of Washington, D.C.

"Good," Schwarz went on. "Then Pol and I know what to get you for Christmas."

Blancanales leaned forward. "It was either that or one of those CONTROL shoe phones Maxwell Smart carries around."

"Much as you've been on the phone since we got back to the Farm, we figured it's just a fetish of yours that we previously hadn't known about."

"Yeah," Blancanales added. "We've only really covered the annoying ones, not ones of truly disgusting stature."

"But we're waiting," Schwarz said enthusiastically, "with bated breath."

"I thought I smelled something," Lyons said. "Now I know."

"Ouch," Schwarz said. "I walked into that one with both eyes closed."

"It's okay," the Politician said. "I've been keeping tabs. Lately the only thing Carl's been scoring with are the easy ones."

Lyons sighed and looked at Leo Turrin, sitting in the passenger seat.

"Don't look at me. They're your friends."

"Your moral support is overwhelming," Lyons said.

"Don't mention it." The stocky Fed flashed him a quick grin. "Besides, I'm perfectly content for them to practice their witticisms on you." Leo Turrin had spent years as an undercover Justice agent in the Mafia, had been in on the ground-breaking campaigns of the Executioner as had Lyons, had even been—in the earliest days—in the warrior's sights for a time. These days he divided his time between being semiretired from the Mafia, and working undercover for the Justice Department again as Leonard Justice.

"Maybe we could even go so far as to come up with some kind of prosthetic implant," Blancanales suggested.

"Could be kind of tricky, though," Schwarz replied. "Get some crossed wires in there, it might not just be Ironman's garage door that goes up when the phone rings."

Blancanales cracked up.

Lyons picked up the mobile phone receiver and shook it at the pair. "For your information, guys, the phone is a good cop's best friend. Saves you shoe leather, time and aggravation. In this case, two out of three ain't bad."

"The Bear's computers probably would have found out the same information in less time," Schwarz suggested.

"Wrong, Bated Breath," Lyons said. "The people I talked to this afternoon don't owe Kurtzman's computers any favors. Kurtzman's little cybernetic marvels might do long division quicker than I can, but they can't get a closemouthed cop to cough up a pet theory he's been playing with for months or years, or go out on a limb to give you an educated guess.''

"You want to tell us what you got?'' Blancanales asked.

"So *now* you want to know,'' Lyons replied.

Schwarz and Blancanales looked at each other, then said, "Yeah.''

"Remember a Washington detective by the name of Maurloe? He helped us out with the Hezbollah attack way back when.''

"That wasn't that long ago,'' Schwarz said.

Lyons shrugged. "Anyway, I kept playing off the Colombian angle we uncovered at the United Nations. Figured Gonzales, López and Guttierez had to have been somewhere before Aaron turned them up on the airline records. Rather than cooling our heels, I thought we might check out the tip Maurloe gave me.''

"Tip?'' Blancanales said. "You told Barb it was a substantial lead.''

Lyons waved the admonishment away. "Why quibble over the detail work?''

"You lied,'' Schwarz said, "and brought us out here on this wild-goose chase.''

"It was a trade-off. Barb's no dummy. She knew I was lying, and she knew I knew she knew.'' He pulled the car to a stop in front of a tavern called the Dew Drop Inn and killed the engine. He swiveled around to look over the seat. "We're here to find a guy named Teodoro Hughon. He's of Colombian extraction, but he's making his way through the murky middle ground between the cops and the dealers. Somebody steals somebody else's coke shipment, the traffickers get in touch with Hughon. Our guy checks around a little, finds out who's suddenly living in the lap of luxury and the Colombians lay out a few new clients for the funeral homes. Hughon keeps his hands clean for the most part, and he rolls over information for the local cops when he has to—nothing big, but something for the hungry guys working vice or homicide. Maurloe said that Hughon's making noises like he knows some of what's in the air between the cartel and North Haakovia."

"So why hasn't Maurloe busted the guy and brought him in?" Schwarz asked.

"Hughon's not moving any product," Turrin said.

"Right," Lyons agreed. "And without a lever, Maurloe can't lean on the guy. At the same time, it's been bothering him that nobody's even checking Hughon out. He phoned the CIA, but they told him not to tell them how to run their business. He was relieved when I called, even though he doesn't know who I really work for."

Blancanales squinted up at the side of the seven-story building. "And Hughon's inside?"

"That's the word Maurloe gave me."

"Where?"

"Top floor. Supposed to have an apartment at the back."

"Anybody running interference?" Turrin asked.

"He keeps a few gorillas around to take care of the light work," Lyons said.

"So, are we going to do this, or are we going to just sit and talk about it?" Schwarz asked.

"I got the front door," Lyons replied.

"You turn around real sudden, remember that I got your back," Turrin said.

"Me and Pol, we'll take the scenic route and cover the fire escape," Schwarz said as he popped the door handle and threw a leg out.

Blancanales folded down a section of the rear seat, reached into the dark cavity and brought out two Ingram MAC-10s with extra clips. He kept one for himself and handed the other to Schwarz.

"Let's do it," Lyons said. Reaching under the seat, he pulled out a sliding rack and took up a SPAS-12 assault shotgun with a folding stock.

"That gun," Turrin said as he got out of the car, "is bulldog ugly."

Slipping a pair of mirrored sunglasses into place, Lyons nodded. "Damned intimidating. That's half its job." He took the lead with Turrin close behind. The big ex-cop was dressed in jeans, joggers, sweatshirt and a black duster. He carried his Colt Python .357 Magnum in shoulder leather, and extra speedloaders tucked in the pockets of his jacket. The SPAS-12, with the butt stock folded, was partially concealed behind his leg and under the loose tail of the duster.

Inside the heater pushed away the last of the late-spring chill. The tavern was small and dark, cloudy with heavy wreaths of cigar and cigarette smoke. A jukebox occupied one corner, belting out an old Steppenwolf tune.

The bar's patrons consisted of a dozen people divided into small groups around wobbly tables and chairs that had definitely seen better days. A quiet fell over them as their eyes focused on Lyons.

The big Able Team warrior knew they could smell the cop scent on him as surely as he smelled the faded odor of marijuana coming from the bathroom in the back. He gave them a hard look back, letting them know he was no stranger to the dangers of the street.

The bartender continued to polish shot glasses behind the bar, slowly sidled toward the cash register at the end of the counter. He was a big man, muscle going to flab and straining at the buttons of his shirt. His blond hair was pulled back in a ponytail, and an attempt had been made to make it look dandyish.

Lyons walked down the three steps to the floor and headed straight for the bartender. He trusted Turrin to cover his back, and never shifted his eyes away from the big man on the other side of the counter.

"Something I can help you with?" the bartender asked.

"Yeah," Lyons said as he came to a stop with his free hand on top of the scarred bar. He pushed an overflowing ashtray away. "I want to see Teodoro Hughon."

The bartender shook his head. "Sorry. Never heard of the guy."

"Bullshit." Lyons turned around and addressed the patrons. "This asshole is bullshitting me. Tells me he doesn't know Teodoro Hughon, the guy who lives on the top floor. Apartment D. You know the guy I'm talking about. Now, does anyone in here want to come forward with some information? Some of you would be performing your civic duty for maybe the first time in your lives."

Most of them sat wooden-faced, but some of them weren't so intimidated and let their displeasure show.

It was all part of the act Lyons felt was necessary to convince Hughon to come clean when they took him for questioning. The easiest thing would have been to apprehend the man in his apartment and walk off with him. But it would have been hard to get answers out of him without generating some kind of fear. Lyons was betting that news of the action going down in the tavern would reach the Colombian before they did. He was depending on Schwarz and Blancanales to cut off any escape routes before Hughon pulled a fast fade.

"Hey, man," the bartender said, "you got no call to come in here rousting my customers like that. Who the fuck do you think you are?"

Lyons turned slowly, letting the smile he felt show on his face. After spending the past few days playing pat-a-cake with UN diplomats that he had absolutely no control over, being back in street action was a breeze. "Take a good look at me, pal," he said in a cold voice. "You *know* who I am."

The bartender set his glass and bar towel on the counter and dropped a hand out of sight under the cash register. "Show me some tin or get the hell out of my place of business."

"How about some black mat finish instead, Eagle-eye?" Lyons thumped the muzzle of the combat shotgun on the counter and jacked a round into the chamber. "And I better see that hand come up empty, or I'm going to amputate it with my first shot."

"Hey, brother, no sweat. You got it." The bartender lifted his hand and held it at shoulder-level while it shook.

"Now drag your ass from around that counter and find a seat out here. I want you comfortable."

"You bet." The bartender walked around the bar and took a seat at the first table.

"Is Hughon in?" Lyons asked.

The bartender glanced over his shoulder at a swarthy man seated two tables away. "I don't know. Ask Luis."

"Fuck you, Gannon."

"Hey, man, you make the big bucks hustling Hughon's problems. I just pull the tap levers around here."

"Shut up," Lyons roared. He switched his attention to Luis. "What about it? Is the man upstairs?"

"Man," the Hispanic said with real feeling, "you're stepping off in deep shit now. You'd better back off before you lose sight of shore."

Breaking glass punctuated the man's statement. A hail of autofire ripped splinters from the wall and chopped up the framed black-and-white pictures of boxing matches hanging there.

Lyons whirled, barely spotting the sedan rolling by the tavern. There was also a handful of people on foot sporting assault rifles. When he turned back to check Luis, he saw the man standing behind his table, his hand already coming out from under his jacket.

Firing from the hip, the big ex-cop caught the man full in the chest with a load of double-aught buckshot. The corpse flipped over the chair and shuddered to a halt against the wall.

"Holy shit," the bartender yelled as he fell to the floor and covered his head with his arms.

"Hope ol' Luis wasn't running a tab," Lyons commented as he hunkered down and watched the front door. He fumbled in his jacket pocket and came out with the ear-throat headset.

Turrin was only a few feet away, his hammerless Airweight Bodyguard clenched in both fists like a gunfighter from an old Western movie. But when a guy burst through the front door carrying an Uzi and the stocky little Fed burned him down with three rounds to the chest and face, it broke the illusion for Lyons. In the movies the bad guy caught one bullet in an unspecified section of the chest, pirouetted neatly and fell down dead. The .38-caliber Glaser Safety Slugs Turrin was using tore the hell out of whatever they hit. When the gunner fell on the floor and spilled inside the doorway, the guy was a torn and bloody mess.

Lyons tapped the transmit button on the headset. "Pol?"

"Go."

"Gadgets?"

"Here."

"I take it you guys are aware of what's going on down here."

"Oh, yeah," Blancanales said. "They had a couple snipers out there too. Cut us off at the fifth floor. I hadn't been wearing Second Chance armor, I'd be looking for a new kidney right now. As it is, I'll be pissing blood for weeks until the bruising goes away."

"Cover me," Turrin called as he snapped the cylinder closed on the .38.

Lyons nodded.

The stocky little Fed stayed low as he crossed the floor and started going through the dead man's pockets.

"What about Hughon?" Lyons asked.

"We're on him," Blancanales replied. "If we find out something, you'll be the first person we call."

"Stay in touch."

"Affirmative, amigo. You do the same."

The headset squealed in Lyons's ear as Blancanales cleared the frequency.

A shadow filled the doorway, then advanced cautiously. A dark face peered intently around the corner.

Dispassionately Lyons shouldered the SPAS-12 and pulled the trigger. The spread took out the corner of the door frame and the man's head, shoving the corpse back out into the street.

"It's a suck," Turrin said when he returned to Lyons's side. He handed over a few blood-smeared black-and-white photographs.

Flipping through them, Lyons discovered they were of Able Team, shots of some of the aftermath of the attempted assassinations of the North and South Haakovian diplomats.

"They were looking for you guys," Turrin said. "Hughon was bait."

Lyons threw the pictures onto the floor. "Well, let's hope the slimy son of a bitch really knows something. This stands a real good chance of just pissing the hell out of me."

A baseball-shaped object crashed through the broken front window, bounced and came to a rest against the jukebox.

Recognizing it, Lyons yelled, "Grenade!" and grabbed Turrin by the jacket. He moved the smaller man easily, shoving them both through the side door into the hallway.

The concussive force slapped them to the ground.

"Ironman?" Schwarz sounded worried.

"Mobile."

"Leo?"

"With me." Lyons helped Turrin to his feet and started moving for the stairway. Behind them the screams of the wounded filled the tavern. "Hughon?"

"Not there yet."

"Get it done or I'm going to be there before you are." Lyons slammed into the stairway door, grabbed the railing and started up the stairs two at a time.

"Seven flights of stairs," Turrin said behind him. "You've got to be kidding. I smoke."

"Six," Lyons corrected. "Save your breath for running. You fall behind and you're on your own until I can come back for you."

Gunfire erupted from up the stairs, urging the Able Team warrior on to greater effort.

Turrin began to lose it on the fourth floor, his lungs heaving like bellows pumps.

Lyons hesitated.

"Go on," the stocky little Fed yelled. "I'll be along as soon as my legs stop turning to jelly."

Lyons pressed on. A door on the seventh floor opened overhead and Blancanales and Schwarz came through, herding a heavyset Hispanic man between them. Bullet holes over Blancanales's left hip showed the gleam of the Second Chance armor beneath the material.

"Got him," Schwarz called down. "Guy even seemed happy to see us." He shoved Hughon down the stairs, carrying his MAC-10 canted over his shoulder at the ready. Blancanales brought up the rear.

Before the trio reached the sixth-floor landing, two gunners burst through the door on the seventh floor.

Lyons leaned over the railing, flipped the SPAS-12's fire selector to full-auto and held the trigger. The remaining seven rounds cycled through in seconds, pumping a storm of double-aught death that raked the two gunners from the landing. Reaching inside his jacket pocket, he freed a smoke grenade, popped the ring and lobbed it up in front of the bullet-scarred door.

It detonated with a loud snap, spewing a bilious cloud of dark smoke that quickly filled the upper portion of the stairwell.

Reloading on the run, Lyons took the point position of the flying wedge with Hughon in the center. Turrin picked them up and matched their pace as they descended.

"You know who these people are?" Lyons asked Hughon.

"*Sí.* Cartel. Cartel guns."

"Do you know why they're after you?"

"No." The man tripped, would have fallen if Schwarz hadn't reached forward to steady him.

"They knew about us," Lyons said.

"You have a price on your heads," Hughon replied.

"Who put it there?"

"The cartel."

"Their doing, or Stensvik's?"

"I don't know. Right now it doesn't matter. For the moment they are one and the same."

At the first floor Lyons avoided the door he and Turrin had entered through. He turned left, doubling back under the stairwell.

"Side door lets out onto an alley," Blancanales said. "Gadgets and I checked it out on the way up."

"Alley gives us two ways to move," Lyons pointed out. He had to shoot the lock off the door and unwrap the chain before he could lead them out. "If they got them both blocked, we still have the cover the building affords."

He peered around the corner, found it clear and led the way out. Schwarz was next, his hand wrapped in the collar of Hughon's coat as he hustled the guy forward. Turrin and Blancanales brought up the rear.

Two Hispanic men rounded the corner, spotted the entourage and dropped to their knees as they brought up their Uzis.

Lyons dived for the ground, knowing the trash cans they took cover behind were only pitiful protection against the sudden onslaught of 9 mm bursts. Before he could lift the SPAS-12 to return fire, a stripped-down sedan came skidding around the alley, then powered up and shot forward, knocking the Colombian gunners away like tenpins. When both bodies came to rolling stops in the middle of the alley near Lyons, there wasn't much life left in either of them.

Glancing up, the first thing Lyons noted about the car was the magnetic cherry haphazardly stuck on the driver's side. The next was the blocky form of Washington, D.C. police detective Rollie Maurloe seated behind the wheel. Now that he was listening, Lyons also heard the whoop-whoop-whoop of police sirens screaming into the neighborhood.

Detective Sergeant Maurloe drove forward, coming to a stop beside Lyons with a sour grin plastered across his black face. A sharp-creased fedora shadowed his features, making him look like something out of an old Broderick Crawford movie. "Hello, son." His hand automatically closed around the Remington Model 870 pumpgun canted forward against the dashboard and held in restraining clips.

"Hey, Rollie. You make a hell of a cavalry."

"Got your boy?"

"Yeah. You got here fast."

"I was here before you and your gang of pirates arrived. Knew after I gave you the skinny on this guy there'd be fireworks. Figured I'd come on down and see how many pieces I could pick up when no one was looking."

"Don't know about any pieces," Turrin said, "but that was a hell of a spare back there."

"These days sometimes I'm faster on the accelerator than I am at pulling my pistol. Besides, you wrap a bumper around some shithead, you don't have to show up for a shooting-board dog-and-pony show. You boys gonna get in, or are you gonna try to fuck up my amazing and timely rescue?"

Lyons opened the rear door, then slid into the passenger seat while the rest of the team crawled in with Hughon.

Gunfire cracked out on the street, but Lyons knew the pace was definitely dying down.

Maurloe dropped the tranny in drive and burned rubber. He didn't even spare a pained grimace when he drove over one of the downed Colombians. "Fucking traffickers are getting thick as cockroaches here. Always bumping into them."

"Or over them," Lyons agreed as the rear wheels rocked over the corpse.

Maurloe laughed. "Now that's a fact." He steered carefully, shooting out of the alley onto the street.

Six police cruisers were staggered across the four-lane street. One of them was in flames, but the uniforms seemed to be in control of the situation. The front of the Dew Drop Inn now looked like it belonged in Lebanon or some other continual war zone. Most of the glass was gone from the windows, and the walls were covered with bullet scars.

A couple of the uniforms started to block Maurloe's car, then appeared to recognize who the detective was. They stepped back and waved him through.

Maurloe took the next corner, turned hard left and narrowly avoided a head-on collision with a news van owned by a local station. The van driver honked indignantly. The detective hooked an arm out the window and flipped the driver the bird.

"I like the working arrangement you have with the media," Lyons commented as he held on to the overhead strap.

"Way I see it," Maurloe said, "fuck 'em if they can't take a joke." He whipped the steering wheel again and blew through a red light without crossing bumpers with the traffic just beginning to surge forward from either side.

"Jesus," Schwarz said. "Do all cops drive as bad as this?"

"No," Maurloe and Lyons said at the same time. "It takes years of experience."

Lyons shook his head and exchanged grins with the big cop.

"Hey, son," Maurloe said, "can you still do that magic trick with your ID? You know, wave it around and there's no such thing as red tape for you and your people?"

"Oh, yeah," Lyons replied, thinking of the clout Barbara Price maintained as mission controller at Stony Man Farm. "Got enough on this one to make Hughon disappear with me."

"You on your way out of town after this?"

"Yes."

"Then let me drive you," Maurloe said. "The sooner I get you out of my city, the sooner the local raping, looting and pillaging returns to a level I can almost handle."

CHAPTER EIGHT

"It's being called Operation Fast Break," Mack Bolan told the men assembled in the tent being used as tactical command headquarters. "And it goes into play an hour after we close up shop here."

He was dressed in a South Haakovian army uniform bare of rank or insignia. The Desert Eagle was holstered on his hip in a military holster. For the moment, his boots were spit-shined. Appearance meant a lot toward confidence, he knew, which was why he'd made every officer in the camp come to the debrief ready for inspection.

As the twenty men in the room faced him, they looked like career soldiers. Hell, even more than that, they looked like men who had something to fight for.

Bolan was there to tell them not only how they were going to fight, but how they were going to win as well. "I'll take questions as we go along. I don't want anyone leaving this tent when we're finished unable to go out and answer any question men under him might ask."

They looked at him, American advisers and South Haakovian military brass, with the same doubts in their eyes, but behind those doubts was a desire to believe.

"Sir," an American major spoke up from the back, "you know that our fuel reserves have been destroyed."

"Yes," Bolan said. "I saw what was left of the trucks and tankers firsthand."

"Then we were able to salvage more than I'd heard?"

"No. Almost ninety percent of that fuel was destroyed."

"That leaves our cav units stranded," a South Haakovian lieutenant said. "They'll be easy targets when Stensvik launches his next offensive."

"We're not going to give him the chance to launch another offensive," Bolan said in a hard voice. He stepped around the table holding the topographical maps and satellite pictures Kurtzman and Price had faxed to him, getting closer to them. "Gentlemen, we're taking this war into our hands. We didn't start out this mission to try to beat Stensvik at his own game. As of this moment we're throwing out the board and drawing up our own rules. Too many good people have died to get us this far. Their sacrifices are going to count. You have my word on that."

A moment of silence fell over the group, and a handful crossed themselves in quiet prayers.

"Then where do we get the fuel supplies?" a major asked.

"From the North Haakovian army."

A surprised rumble passed through the room.

"Jack," Bolan called out to Grimaldi, "would you get the lights?"

The pilot reached over to the switch hurriedly mounted on one of the tent poles with screws, and the tent went dark.

Reaching over to the heads-up display projector at the end of the table, Bolan flipped the machine on, took the first of the colored transparencies Kurtzman had generated with his computers, and laid it on the illuminated rectangle.

The image was thrown onto the white movie screen pulled down behind him. Splashed in various shades of greens, it was a replica of the topographical maps he knew all of the officers were familiar with.

"You all have copies of these in the packets you'll be given when we break up here," Bolan said. "They're marked individually for each of you as they're needed." He glanced at the screen as he slid his finger onto the lighted surface and tracked along the transparency. He crossed the Inge River, tapping the spot where the earlier HALO jump had taken place. "At 0230 hours this morning, I took a small insertion group into North Haakovian air and ground space for a mission most of you didn't know about until now."

"For what reasons?" an officer asked.

"To neutralize the command post the North Haakovian army had emplaced there." Bolan switched transparencies, using one of those Kurtzman had digitized from actual aerial photos. This one showed the bare outlines of the command post. "From what we'd been able to ascertain, the post covered this area." He traced the suspect area with his forefinger.

"But if you took the command post out," a lieutenant said, "won't that let Stensvik know you're planning something there?"

"We didn't take it down." Bolan exchanged transparencies again, using one of the pictures the insertion team had taken of the outpost at ground level. "We set up our own programs to spoof their systems. Right now their main intelligence units are receiving only information we're broadcasting to them." He looked at the officers. "And I can assure you, they won't see us coming."

"Who's going over there?" another officer asked.

"Special Forces teams under my direction," Bolan replied.

"With what? You barely have enough fuel left in the armored troops to maneuver them together and hope to salvage some of them."

"Hey," Bolan said in a graveyard whisper that caught the attention of every man in the room. "Markus's defection hurt us. He got some people killed on the way out. And hell yes, we've been bloodied, but we're not out of this by a long shot."

They looked at him.

He gave them confidence just by being himself, by believing in the words he spoke to them. "We've got a job to do here, and we all believe that it needs doing. All we needed was a way to get it done. I'm here to tell you how we're going to do just that."

"Yes, sir," the man said.

Bolan returned his attention to the projector, switching transparencies again. This one showed a valley tucked between a trio of low-slung hills. Ribbons that might have been roads tracked over them. Forest and foliage was at a minimum. "Tell me what you see." He put on another transparency, this one showing the same shot but cropped closer, the details a little clearer.

"Tasenka Valley," someone said.

"Right," the big warrior replied. He sorted through the pile of transparencies available to him and found the one he wanted. He put it on the screen.

The topographical map emphasized the area between South Haakovia and the Tasenka Valley.

"Ninety klicks in and out," Bolan said. "With the command post out of the way, the infiltration will be almost unquestionably successful. The only problem we're going to have is getting back out again. But there are ways we can cut down on the resistance. We'll go into those as we get down to the specifics of this thing."

"But why would we want to go there with a small force?" someone asked. "If we're going to try subterfuge like this, couldn't we go ahead and make the attempt on Stensvik himself?"

"Organizing a surgical strike against Stensvik and his generals would take too much time," Bolan answered. "Plus we don't have the intel we need. Yet." He switched transparencies and knew this one would take their questions about the mission objective away.

He glanced at the screen behind him, silently congratulating Kurtzman and his people on the job they'd done. There, separated out of the shadows by computer digitation and special camera lenses the passing weather satellite had, was a convoy of gasoline tanker trucks.

"The North Haakovian fuel depot," a major said.

"One of them, yeah." The Executioner tapped the picture of the trucks for emphasis. "Stensvik was up against the same problems of having to supply cav troops so far away from the source."

"So your Special Forces teams are going in to destroy his fuel dump?"

Bolan shook his head. "No. We're going to liberate it. His cavalry is already gassed up and waiting for his signal to begin the onslaught. Even if we destroyed his supplies, he has enough on hand to roll into this country and break us. I don't want that. You don't want that. When we go in tomorrow, the North Haakovian military machine is going to be a bitter memory. As we withdraw, we're going to bring the gasoline with us to refuel our own troops."

"Son of a bitch," an American lieutenant-colonel said. "That might just work."

"It *will* work," Bolan stated. "We're going to make it work."

"Stensvik will not be expecting this," a South Haakovian captain said. "With the treachery General Markus has done to us, he will be thinking we are waiting like sheep to be slaughtered."

"Yeah," Bolan replied, "and we're going to give him some more to worry about tonight."

"The only problem I can think of," the American lieutenant-colonel said, "is that we're not going to be able to spread the armor out as we'd planned with the refueling we'll have to do."

"You're right. I've had to look at the tactical side of that and do some refiguring. But I think I've got it worked out. We'll divide the armored up over the night, pool our resources together and put them in two places. One will be the major assault force, and the other will be held back for a pincer attack behind the lines that is designed to fracture the North Haakovian front line."

Another transparency took the place of the previous one. This one had two places highlighted along the Inge River.

"We're going to cross here and here," Bolan said. He indicated the point upriver. "This is where we take the main attack force across. Here is the pincer movement." He regarded the group. "The pincer will be led by an Israeli commando code-named Phoenix One. That's all you'll be told about him, but rest assured the man knows what he's doing."

"Where is Phoenix One?" the lieutenant-colonel asked.

"En route," Bolan replied. "He and his specialist team will be joining us at Tasenka Valley.

"You can't take our armored division across either of those places," a South Haakovian armored officer said as he scratched the back of his neck nervously. "I don't mean to disagree."

"You're right," Bolan said.

"The pincer movement I can maybe see getting across.
It would be tricky, but it could be done. Slowly. If those
people were made before they could get across, chances are
you would lose a lot of them."

"They're not going to be discovered," Bolan said firmly.
"We're going to see to that. As far as getting across the
river at the main juncture, when the time comes, I've got
an angle figured out there, too." He nodded at Grimaldi
to switch the lights back on. After killing the projector, he
approached the table and the scattered maps. "Now, let's
get down to the nuts and bolts of Fast Break."

"THERE'S SOMETHING BIG going on in L.A.," Teodoro
Hughon said. His round face was covered with perspiration and droplets clung to his Zapata mustache.

Carl Lyons sat reversed in a straight-backed chair with
his arms folded across its back and watched Barbara Price
work.

They were in one of the interrogation rooms at Stony
Man Farm that doubled as a holding cell when necessary.
Hughon sat on the edge of the narrow bed with his head in
his hands. His jacket was in a crumpled heap beside him,
and his shirt was damp with sweat.

Standing in the middle of the floor with her arms folded
across her breasts, Price looked like a formidable oppo-
nent. "What?" she demanded.

"I don't know. Swear on my mother's eyes."

Lyons had heard the man say he didn't know for so long
he was really beginning to believe him. "But what you do
know is that the cartel isn't happy about some deal they
made with Stensvik?"

"Yes. That I am sure of. This deal, whatever it is, is
costing them some serious money."

"They're also making some serious money from the trafficking lanes Stensvik opened up in Eastern Europe," Price pointed out.

Hughon shrugged. "True. But these cartel people, you have to remember that they are in it for the money. It is the only thing that matters."

"And L.A. is the best you can do?" Price asked.

"Yes. Put me back on the street, maybe I can find you something more."

"They're hunting you," Lyons said. "They staked you out like a Judas goat, let you start ringing bells they figured might draw out me and my team. They knew enough to realize we might be hooked into the Washington, D.C. street scene. You really think they're going to let you walk away from this thing?"

"There are people I can contact," Hughon said, meeting the big Able Team warrior's hard gaze. "I can't do that from in here."

"If we turn you out," Price said, "how do we know you won't pull a fade the first chance you get?"

"I give you my word."

"Boy," Lyons said sarcastically, "I really feel better now."

"It is all I can offer."

Price exchanged looks with Lyons, but neither of them said anything. The Able Team leader knew what the mission controller was thinking. The fishing expedition in D.C. had netted something, but neither of them knew what.

"If you keep me here," Hughon asked, "what then? You have nothing to hold me on. No charges. No crimes. Nothing."

Lyons stood and glared at the smaller man. "Buddy, you're not in a place where you get checked in and out like a library book. You could disappear from here forever and nobody would be the wiser. You know what I'm talking about?''

Hughon nodded.

''This isn't cops and robbers like you're used to dicking around with, and you haven't got pockets deep enough to buy us off. If we do decide to put you out there again, I want you to know exactly what will happen to you if you try to jerk us around.''

''I understand.''

''Sure you do,'' Lyons said. ''Look, we'll get back to you. Could be we don't need you as much as we thought we did.'' He headed for the door with Price at his heels. He opened it, held it until Price passed through, then closed it and locked it. The door was plain, without any markings. The people who lived and worked there knew what those rooms were for.

Two black-uniformed Stony Man security people stood on each side of the door.

They took the stairs down.

''So what do we do with this guy?'' Lyons asked.

''Sweat him a few more hours,'' Price replied. ''Let him think he might be on the list to become dog food. Then cut him loose. It's possible he'll be more good to us loose and running than held here.''

They rounded the corner, heading toward Kurtzman's computer lab. Lyons paused in the spacious farm-style kitchen, helping himself to three oranges from the large fruit bowl centered on the red-and-white-checked tablecloth. ''Want one?''

Price accepted the fruit and they continued on their way. ''Worst-case scenario,'' she said, peeling the orange, ''is that somebody will whack him while he's out there trying to earn his keep. I'm going to keep some people on him. He won't know they're there."

Lyons nodded, popping several sections of orange into his mouth.

"Even if someone does succeed in whacking Hughon," Price continued, "it might tell us something when we track the shooter back to his roots."

"You're frosty at heart, Barb."

Price raised an arched brow as they paused at the door to the computer lab.

"But that's okay," Lyons said quickly. "I happen to like that in a woman." He broke the eye contact and held the door while she entered.

Kurtzman was still at his desk.

"Hey, Barb," Kurtzman said in a tired voice, "I think maybe I can shed some light on the L.A. angle our guest was talking about." His hands flexed across the computer keyboard.

Lyons sat on a corner of the big work space and glanced at the array of monitors in front of the Bear.

"I set up a program that filters through police, deputy sheriff, emergency and media reports and stories being filed. Established parameters for the search-and-find function to only single out those incidences that were out of the ordinary."

"In L.A.?" Lyons said. "That's California craziness at its finest. How do you plan to separate the regular insanity from the stuff you're looking for?"

"It was long and arduous work, believe me."

"You ruled out psychic experiences with Elvis?"

"Yeah."

"Pregnancies consummated by extraterrestrials?"

"Yeah."

"Bigfoot sightings?"

"Yeah."

"What did you come up with?" Price asked.

"Hospital reports," Kurtzman said. He brought them up on-screen.

Lyons scooted closer and read them, wondering what the hell he was supposed to be seeing. Both reports concerned male victims. Both victims were dead. "Tell me what I'm looking at."

"Cause of death," Kurtzman replied.

"Diphtheria." Lyons read it out loud. "Hell, I don't even know what that is."

"It's an infectious disease," Price said. Her face was taut with interest. "How sure are they about the cause of death?"

"Proof positive," Kurtzman answered. "I raided their medical-arts lab to make sure."

"You think because you got two cases of a disease here that you've figured out what's going on in L.A.?" Lyons asked.

"Diphtheria is rare in the United States," Price said. "It's a bacteria. Most people are immunized against it while they're kids."

"So what we have here are two people who weren't immunized against it?"

"One of them," Kurtzman said, "was definitely vaccinated. I ran them both through the NCIC computers. Both of them had records." One of the monitors filled with side-by-side mug shots of the two men. "Stan Barry, the first man, was in the Marines for six years. Spent time in the Philippines and Okinawa. You can bet he was immunized. The other guy I'm not sure about."

Lyons finished his orange slices, his mind captured by the detail work as the cop machine went to work inside his head. "You have a disease where a disease shouldn't be."

"Yeah." Kurtzman shifted the monitor back to the hospital reports, dropped the one on Barry and blew up the incident report on Ken Taylor. It continued to blow up section by section until the duty nurse's comments were legible. "Take a look at this."

"It says that Taylor was only complaining about throat pain a few hours before he died in the hospital," Price said.

"Right." Kurtzman stroked the keyboard again. The monitor cleared, showing clumps of rod-shaped particles. "The average time it takes diphtheria to kill someone, if that's what it's going to do, is days. And that's only if it goes untreated. The doctors' reports say that they saw marked spreading of the diphtheria membrane across the throats of both individuals even while they were treating them. Both of these men literally choked to death while the emergency-room staff was working on them."

"Were they in the same hospital?" Price asked.

"No," Kurtzman said.

"But they both had police records."

"Yeah. In the L.A. area. Cocaine possession. Intent to distribute."

"There's a chance they knew each other?"

"I'd say so. But what the hell that might mean, I have no idea."

"What am I looking at here?" Lyons pointed at the little rod shapes. A cold feeling crawled up his spine and vibrated there like the purring of a contented cat.

"Diphtheria bacillus," Kurtzman said. "In the human body it's characterized by patches of gray membrane on the tonsils and in the throat. It also produces a toxin that damages the heart and nervous system. It's nasty stuff, Ironman. Before the anti-diphtheria toxoid was invented that practically eradicated it in this country, there were a lot of deaths—especially small children.''

''What's the incubation period?'' Price asked.

''Two to five days,'' Kurtzman said. ''I've done my homework.''

Price nodded. ''It shows. How's it passed?''

''Exposure to an individual who has the disease. Or exposure to discharges by that individual.''

''These guys worked the coke circles,'' Lyons said. ''If they did any mainlining, you could be talking about a lot of dirty needles here. You could have a damn outbreak all the way across the state in a heartbeat.'' He glanced up at Price. ''You know anybody at the Centers for Disease Control?''

She nodded.

''You might want to nudge somebody, get them to send somebody down there to take a look at this.''

''Hey, Aaron.''

Lyons looked up and saw Hunt Wethers at his workstation waving for attention.

''Yeah,'' Kurtzman responded.

''I turned up another four cases of diphtheria at L.A. hospitals. And at Mercy, where one of the dead men showed up, one of the emergency-room doctors just succumbed to the disease.''

Lyons glanced back at the computerized picture of the diphtheria bacillus and wondered how the hell he was supposed to fight a disease.

''Carl,'' Price said, ''I want Able Team in L.A. as soon as possible. Aaron and I will put together cover packets by the time you touch down at LAX.'' She looked at the representation of the disease as well. ''I'm thinking we're seeing the first of Stensvik's bacteriological arsenal surfacing. As soon as I'm able, I'll arrange for a special team from the Disease Control people to meet you there. Let me know if there's anything else you need."

Lyons nodded and headed for the door to get Blancanales and Schwarz ready for the jump. He could already picture their reactions. There was something decidedly different about taking on bacteria instead of bullets. At least you knew when the bullets were coming, and when you'd been mortally wounded.

"THEY DIDN'T ASK about Janyte Varkaus," Jack Grimaldi said as he watched Mack Bolan clear the table of the maps and other paraphernalia he'd used.

The big warrior dumped them into a wastepaper can, dropped in a few ounces of lighter fluid, then threw a match on the contents. Flames whooshed up at once. "No," he agreed, "but you can bet she was in their minds."

"So what do we do about her?" Grimaldi asked.

Bolan watched the fire. "For now there's nothing we can do, Jack. If this country rolls over and plays dead, Stensvik will never let it regain its feet. Thousands of innocent people will die. Janyte wouldn't want that. And neither do I." He took a cup of water from the two-liter dispenser in the corner of the tent, dumped it in the wastepaper can and stirred the wet, charred contents with a pencil. When he was satisfied, he left it and headed outside.

The air was cool. The morning dew would be ice flakes in a few hours' time.

He watched the activity filling the campsite. Everyone had been rousted out of bed to prepare for the next day's offensive. Men walked quickly everywhere they went, flashlights lighting the way.

The motor pool was north of the camp, and the sound of engines drifted over the tents. The movement of tanks and armored personnel carriers shook the ground like tiny earthquakes. Other groups were taking down the tents they'd worked so hard only a few hours earlier to erect.

"You got some time before we kick off Fast Break," Grimaldi said. "Think maybe you should try to get some shut-eye? You could curl up in the jeep for a while."

Bolan shook his head. "Let's get a helicopter and take a last look around before we move on this thing."

Within five minutes they'd drawn an AH-1W Super-Cobra gunship from the airfield and turned north. The Executioner sat in the passenger seat and gazed down at the forested lands below. Even in the weak moonlight he could see the line of tanks headed west toward the Sergiusz mountain range fronting the Inge River.

Across the black ribbon of river, the forested lands continued into North Haakovian territory, sprouting out from the foothills of the Sergiusz Mountains.

The promontory Bolan had chosen for the second part of the offensive was a fairly broad area reasonably free of trees. Brush and grass covered it, but nothing that would really slow the tanks and heavy armor.

The main problem was the fact that the crest of the low mountains towered almost a hundred feet above the river. Although the riverside wasn't sheer, it also wasn't navigable by the tanks.

Grimaldi took the helicopter down and flew alongside the mountainside. An open rock face looked back at them, covered by a few straggling roots and bushes that poked out haphazardly.

"Think Manning can do it?" the pilot asked.

"If anybody can," Bolan replied.

"Once the armored cav gets up on that cliff, they're going to be all out of options."

"Yeah. Well, the thing of it is, we're already out of options. Wars aren't always won because of planning and equipment, Jack. Luck plays a big part, so does overconfidence, or lack of confidence. But the thing that really helps the guy who wants to win is that thin edge of desperation that stops just short of insanity."

"We're going over the edge on this one, Sarge."

Bolan nodded. "We will be tomorrow. That's for sure." He studied the mountain range, tried to see past the exterior to the heart of nature's architecture.

The landscape had been there as it was for decades, perhaps hundreds of years or more, and it had revealed none of its flaws until Kurtzman's computers had rooted them out.

The big warrior glanced at his watch, saw that the final numbers for the operation were tumbling through now. He told Grimaldi to head back.

The pilot nodded and swung the tail rotor around, and aimed the SuperCobra back at the camp.

SEATED ON THE PLUSH COUCH, Janyte Varkaus watched Franzen Stensvik rant and rave as he paced the floor of the reception room. She tried not to let her fear show, because she knew the man well enough to realize he would try to find some way to use it against her.

Still clad in the chiffon dress, she felt incredibly naked and vulnerable. So far Stensvik's advances had been clumsy and relentless, slowed only by his attempts at a class he could never possess.

Her gaze roved over the room, looking for anything she might use as a weapon. This room was far smaller than the previous one he'd entertained his officers in. It was meant to be personal, show some of the warmth of the owner, but instead it came across as a showplace of conquests. All the objects in the room had impressive intrinsic value, but they were arranged carelessly, revealing that the owner placed no value on the pieces themselves.

Janyte shivered, tried to make herself stop, but shivered again. When she looked back at Stensvik, she knew the man had caught her. His smile was totally devoid of warmth, and his eyes moved to her breasts. She resisted the impulse to cover them with her arms, denying him the satisfaction of making her squirm. But she couldn't hold back the hot blush that covered her bosom and her face. She made herself meet his lust-filled eyes without looking away.

"Look," Stensvik roared into the telephone receiver he carried as he paced, "I want no excuses. You are my intelligence officer. Do your damned job or I'll find someone who can. If there has been troop movement along the border, it is your responsibility to find out what it means. I don't want guesswork." He reached the end of the long cord, turned and paced back the other way, toward the bar where Dag Vaino lounged.

Vaino sat on a stool, his back to the bar, and his elbows up on the counter. A soft, cruel smile touched his lips. The .45 automatic on his hip had drawn Janyte's attention, and she'd planned out scenarios on how she could get close to the man and get it before he could stop her. Visions of what she could do with the weapon once she had her hands on it had danced in her head. Even if Vaino overpowered her and killed her, it would be worth it to bring Stensvik down—for Edvaard, and for her adopted people. When she thought of the losses South Haakovia had already suffered, she believed her heart would break.

Maybe it would have been better, she told herself, if she hadn't done as Colonel Pollock had asked and took a more aggressive stance against Stensvik. When she thought of the American fighting man, his blue eyes ablaze with the passions that propelled him through his violent world, she asked herself if she'd allowed herself to become too easily swayed.

But when she looked at Stensvik, she knew that wasn't true. Pollock had only made her face the inevitable. Stensvik and the Communist powers running North Haakovia would never rest until her country was overrun and blood covered the streets.

Nightmares had often filled her head with stark images of the North Haakovian tanks invading Larsborg. Even though her love for Edvaard had cooled over the years as he was drawn more and more into the responsibility of running their nation, her love for her adopted country had soared. She remembered the parks filled with families, and she remembered wanting to have children of her own. But Edvaard had insisted they wait, until they could assure those children a safe and promising future.

Now, she knew, they had waited too long. And she wondered if she would ever know the love and pride of her baby's first kiss. Thinking of the North Haakovian tanks wreaking carnage through those parks hurt her. She stiffened her resolve, rested her gaze briefly again on the .45 at Vaino's side. She worked hard to make herself forget that the man had been directly responsible for her husband's death, steeled herself for what she was going to attempt.

With another threat and a snarled curse, Stensvik hung up on the man and cradled the phone on the wall by the bar.

Vaino swiveled his head to face his commanding officer. "I thought the South Haakovians were running on gas fumes."

"They are," Stensvik snapped. "Unless Markus lied to us about the fuel stores."

"I doubt that," Vaino said. "He wanted to be part of the winning team too much. Madam President—" he inclined his head in Janyte's direction "—offended his male pride too much when she insisted the American colonel take over control of the South Haakovia army."

Stensvik freshened his drink generously. "I'd already been in contact with him before Varkaus's assassination."

Janyte returned the man's level, taunting gaze without flinching. Coolly she reached for the glass of wine sitting on the low table before her and took a sip. She didn't even notice the taste over the bile that had risen in her throat. She forced it back down.

"Markus had been thinking of coming into our camp for some time," Stensvik continued.

"Where are the tanks and the armored forces heading?" Vaino asked.

Stensvik crossed the room to a pull-down map mounted on the wall. He hooked a blunt finger in the ring and yanked. The retractor gears whined as it slid.

Janyte studied the map over their shoulders, wishing there was some way she could get word to her people that the North Haakovia military already knew what they were doing before they could do it. She couldn't help wondering how many lives were going to be lost while she sat trapped and unable to aid them.

"They're pulling away from the border," Stensvik said as he moved his forefinger over the topographical map.

"Sinking back in on themselves to make a stronger line?" Vaino asked.

The big North Haakovian dictator shrugged. "Perhaps."

"It could mean they're expecting your offensive tomorrow."

"That's fine. There's nothing they can do about it at this point. And even if they don't know about it for sure, they have to be expecting it."

Vaino studied the map a moment longer, then asked, "Where is your armor?"

Stensvik pointed out the front lines.

"For you to cover their new positions, you're going to have to move your armored divisions."

"Yes," Stensvik grinned evilly. "But that is no problem, you see, because I have the fuel to do it with."

"It will also give them a chance to scout you out better."

"So what? Without the fuel supplies, they don't stand a chance. It would be like you going after an armed target mired in quicksand. The man might be able to shoot back, so you would have to be careful, but he can't run anywhere, can he?"

Vaino touched the map. "But here—" he tapped the area "—here, you leave yourself open to a flanking maneuver."

"Those are the Serguisz Mountains," Stensvik said. "There's no place to cross the river at that point. And besides, their armor isn't moving in that direction. They're moving to the east. My thinking is that they are trying to form a holding position to brunt our offensive from Larsborg." He sipped his drink. "But it will do them no good. They are only delaying what is foreordained. The city will fall to us by early afternoon tomorrow."

"Have you confirmed the troop movement?" Vaino asked.

"Only by radar and other instrumentation."

"No physical sightings?"

"No. I lost six jets destroying the fuel supplies. Jets do not come cheaply."

"True," Vaino said, "but it might be worth the investment to make sure all your high-priced intelligence hardware is really doing its job."

Janyte could tell Stensvik found offense at the suggestion.

"I'll take it into consideration," Stensvik said. He jerked the bottom of the map and it whirled back up inside its container. "In the meantime, I want you to go to the United States."

"For what?"

"The first bacterial weapon is being unleashed in Los Angeles," Stensvik said. "The first casualties have already hit the streets. The body count will continue to rise. Your mission will be to secure the second. You will be given instructions in a later debrief regarding how and when it is to be deployed."

"When do I leave?"

"In the morning."

Vaino smiled and raised his glass in a toast. "Then we still have the night to celebrate, eh, Comrade?"

Stensvik raised his own glass, then drained it in a single swallow.

Steeling herself for what she had to do, having recognized the animosity lurking beneath the surface of the two men, Janyte stood and slowly approached the bar.

Both men turned to watch her.

She felt like a fool and thought they would surely see right through her subterfuge. She made herself recall the times she'd acted as the very proper wife of Edvaard Varkaus at political functions she hadn't wanted to be a part of. It had taken skill and determination, and she'd never had more motivation in her life. The struggle to keep her eyes off the pistol holstered at Vaino's side was intense.

"Would you like more to drink?" Stensvik asked.

"No." She remained cold and aloof, knew the man would take it for the challenge she intended.

"Something else, perhaps? We have a broad selection." He waved at the shelves behind the bar.

"No. I'd like to return to my room. I'm very tired."

Humor sparkled in Vaino's eyes, but it never touched his face.

The smile drooped on Stensvik's mouth. He looked away from her hard gaze, stared at the bare shoulder closest to him. "You know," he said softly, "you have the power to stop some of the death and destruction that's going to take place in your country tomorrow."

"As you've told me many times since I've been here, General Stensvik, the fate of South Haakovia resides solely in your hands. I am only a woman, completely out of her depth running that country."

"Perhaps I was too harsh," Stensvik said, his eyes meeting hers briefly again for a moment. "As a woman you also have many charms. I have the feeling that you can be most . . . persuasive, should you choose to do so."

She waited him out, knew he couldn't leave it at that. Men like Stensvik, she'd learned in her early years as a girl and as a young woman, let their animal passions control them.

"Maybe," he said, raising his hand and stroking her bare shoulder, "you should consider trying to be persuasive at this point. Think of the lives you could possibly save."

His skin against hers felt burning hot. She restrained the impulse to be sick, was surprised at the effort it took even though she'd been prepared for him to touch her. "Even if you gave your word," she said coldly, "which I would have no reason to trust, I could never be a woman for such a man as yourself. I find you ugly and unappealing."

Stensvik's face purpled.

For a moment she thought he was going to lose his temper. Making herself move, she closed on Vaino and pressed her body suggestively to the man's. Her left arm draped over Vaino's heavily muscled shoulder and her hand curled around the back of his neck. She looked up at him and smiled. "However, this man, I think he knows how to pleasure a woman without taking too much only for himself. And he has a nice look about him." She raised her free hand toward the holstered pistol as she lifted her face toward Vaino's. Her hand trailed seductively along his jaw.

Vaino grinned.

Nausea threatened to overwhelm Janyte. This was the man who had taken Edvaard's life so coldly, and he was experiencing pleasure at her touch. Her hand was only inches from the holstered gun. She felt the terrorist's breath warm against her cheek. For a moment she didn't think she could make herself shoot Stensvik no matter how much of a threat he posed to her people.

"And this," Stensvik said sarcastically, "is the grieving widow the media people have painted as being such a martyr for her country. Stripped to her baser instincts, she is nothing more than a whore."

Janyte used the anger that fired her, let it push her hesitation and indecision out of her mind. Her hand closed around the gun butt and tugged the pistol free of the holster. Before she could move away, however, Vaino dropped a big hand over hers, trapping her hand there. His other hand caught up in her hair and pulled her head up and against him. His lips crushed hers in a harsh kiss.

Flailing against him, Janyte released the pistol and pulled herself away from the assassin. Hot tears burned the back of her eyes but she didn't let them come.

Vaino burst out laughing.

Lights of amusement gleamed in Stensvik's eyes, letting her know that he had been aware of her ploy as well.

Before either man could move, she threw herself at the bar, grabbed the neck of the whiskey bottle Stensvik was serving himself from and smashed it against the corner. Glass crumbled away. Liquid poured down her arm and drops stained the chiffon dress. Small cuts on her hand and arm burned when the whiskey got into them. She turned as quickly as she could, slashing at Stensvik with the jagged shards that remained in her fist.

Moving faster than she would have believed possible, Stensvik blocked her arm, then slapped her in the face with the full force of his weight behind the blow.

Janyte lost her footing, tasted blood in her mouth when she hit the floor and lost her breath.

Stensvik moved forward and put a heavy boot on the wrist of the hand still holding the broken bottle. "Let it go," he commanded, "or I'll break your damn arm and shoot you through the head."

She had to focus her double vision to see the pistol aimed at her. The barrel looked massive. Weakly she let the bottle neck roll from her grip.

"Get up," Stensvik ordered.

It took her two attempts, but she managed to get on her feet. She wiped at her mouth and saw the blood come away on her hand. Fear filled her, not knowing what Stensvik would do next. Images of the way he'd so coldly cut Markus's throat were stark in her mind. And the most troubling thought was that if he killed her now, her people wouldn't know, and Stensvik could continue to use her as a hostage.

"I'm surprised," Stensvik said. "You've still got some fire left." He licked his lips. "I'm going to enjoy taming you, woman."

The door buzzed.

Janyte stood uncertainly, not knowing what to do.

"Come in," Stensvik said.

The door opened and a guard walked in looking flustered. "I'm sorry, sir, but I couldn't dissuade him from—"

An angry-looking Japanese man in a black suit stepped around the guard, pushing his glasses up his nose with a forefinger. "President Stensvik-san," he began imperiously, "I have been instructed by my corporate chairman to speak to you concerning your planned invasion of South Haakovia."

Stensvik stared at the man as if he were a bothersome fly.

"We feel that you are unnecessarily endangering the oil fields. You must stop. Our corporation has invested heavily in your war efforts and trusted you to follow through on your end of the bargain. I've been told to tell you that the board of directors, including Mr. Sasamori-san, is very displeased."

Drawing his side arm with slow deliberation, Stensvik shot the Japanese representative through the head. The bullet passed through, punching a fist-size hole in the wall beyond. The dead man fell to the floor, spasmed twice and lay still. Blood pooled out and covered the carpet.

Holstering his pistol, Stensvik spit on the corpse. "Damned capitalist pig." He glanced at the frightened guard. "Well, don't just stand there, man, clean that up."

"Yes, sir." The guard bent down, grabbed two fistfuls of the Japanese's jacket and dragged the body from the room. It left a long red smear behind.

"And soldier," Stensvik said.

The guard looked up, and the realization of how vulnerable he was in his present position made his face go gray. "Yes, sir."

"The next time you allow someone to interrupt me, bring someone with you to clean up the mess you leave behind."

"Yes, sir." He hurried on through the door.

Stensvik walked to the wall where the telephone was mounted, lifted the receiver and dialed. "Svoboda. Get in touch with the Hagakure Corporation and tell them they need to get a new chief negotiator in here. The last one didn't work out at all." He hung up.

Cold certainty filled Janyte as she watched the North Haakovian dictator pour himself a fresh drink. All hope of getting out of the present situation was gone. She only hoped the big American could think of something to save her country from the invading hordes.

CHAPTER NINE

"Stone Hammer Leader, this is Fast Break Base. Over."

Mack Bolan tapped the transmit button on the headset. "Go, Base, you've got Stone Hammer Leader." He scanned the assembled mobile ranks scattered out across the remnants of the temporary base camp. Twenty Hummers were accompanied by ten of the deadly little assault buggies first used by the SEALs in the Gulf War. The Hummers were there to carry crews to bring the North Haakovian fuel tanks back across the Inge River while the buggies ran blocker action. Half of the Hummers were armed with TOW missile launchers and two 7.62 mm machine guns, aft and forward. The other half carried MK-19 grenade launchers with the same machine guns. The assault buggies were equipped with .50-caliber machine guns, LAWs and whatever personal weapons the two-man teams wanted to carry. The engines of all the vehicles rattled around in the depression, making hearing difficult.

"I've got three bogies approaching from two o'clock," the base operator said. "The bogies will arrive at your position in forty seconds with their present speed. Looks like a slow flyby. Two of our Apache gunships are closing in, but they're going to be too late to intercept. Over."

"Understood, Base. Stone Hammer Leader, out." Bolan switched freqs, clambered up from the passenger seat of the assault buggy he was using as a command vehicle and looked out over the Fast Break troops. "Stone Hammer Leader to Fast Break crews. Break ranks *now*. We'll rendezvous at our first coordinates. Clear."

Dirt sprayed out from the rear wheels of the assault buggies as the drivers engaged the transmissions and released the clutches. The Hummers dug in and bounced away quickly, looking like ungainly bears as they disappeared into the forest.

Bolan tapped his driver on the helmet. "Let's go, Larkin. Find a place nearby to bury this rig for a moment." He dropped into the passenger seat but didn't bother with the seat belt in case he had to maneuver around. Taking a pair of night-vision glasses from the chest pouch of his BDU, he fitted them to his eyes and searched the approach path where the operator had pegged the bogies.

Larkin put his foot down, and the assault buggy roared forward.

The dash-mounted radio that tied the ground forces of Fast Break to their aerial support crackled and beeped for attention. "G-Force to Stone Hammer Leader. Over."

Bolan picked up the mike and made out the lead Russian jet only a heartbeat later. "Go, G-Force."

"Be there in a short, guy."

"I'll be looking for you," Bolan said. "Clear."

Larkin pulled the assault buggy into the brush and killed the engine.

Following the flight path of the approaching aircraft, Bolan knew they'd see the line of tanks and APCs headed for the Sergiusz Mountains. Once the MiG pilots radioed the information back to the North Haakovian Intelligence unit, the surprise attack the soldier had planned for shortly after dawn would be all over. Much of what they had in mind depended on Stensvik having to wheel around his heavy armor at the last moment.

Bolan reached into the organized pile of equipment in the back of the buggy and pulled out a Stinger missile launcher. He flipped the arming switches and got it ready to fire. He reached for the mike again, calling for Grimaldi.

"Go, Stone Hammer Leader, you have G-Force. Over."

"The bogies have to be brought down immediately," Bolan said. "If they get the chance to send off communications regarding our troop movement, Fast Break could be history from the outset."

"Understood. G-Force, clear."

Bolan stood in the seat and settled the Stinger comfortably over his shoulder. He took up slack on the trigger, aiming one hundred eighty degrees from the flyby path. Once the missile was fired, it would lock on to the heat signature of the MiG. By firing after the jet had passed, the rocket would be able to achieve lock sooner and have a straighter course to its target.

He heard the thunder of the approaching aircraft, and the sound reverberated in the trees.

Then the MiGs were overhead, gone a heartbeat later.

Bolan fired the Stinger, felt it push against his shoulder, heard the whoosh as the rocket shoved it through the tube and saw the gray cloud spread out against the night. He lost the rocket immediately.

Before he could drop the empty Stinger into the back of the buggy, the warhead zoomed up into one of the MiG's engines and blew the wing off. Out of control, the fighter jet flipped, then headed straight for the ground. When it hit, an orange-and-black fiery mushroom lighted up the night.

The warrior tapped the transmit button, then fitted himself behind the big .50-cal mounted at the rear of the assault buggy. "Stone Hammer Leader to Longshot. Over."

"Longshot here."

Longshot was the antiaircraft unit Bolan had deployed to cover the base camp while it was there. It was the last unit to be pulled from the area. Armed with three 23 mm guns, he knew it could be an impressive force against the MiGs.

"Longshot, have you confirmed the bogies?" Bolan asked.

"That's affirmative. We count two, repeat, two bogies."

"Roger, Longshot. You have two bogies. Bogie Three has been downed. Are the remaining two within your sights?"

"If we get lucky, Stone Hammer Leader."

"Hold your fire for the moment, Longshot. Over." Bolan lifted the microphone from the dashboard radio. "G-Force, come in."

"Go, Stone Hammer Leader."

"What's your heading?"

Grimaldi told him.

"Alter that, G-Force." Bolan gave him the new heading. "They'll pick you up on their radar screens any second. When they do, they'll probably decide to cut and run. Moving away from your current heading will take them within range of the Longshot unit."

"Roger that. G-Force, clear."

Bolan watched the jets heel around in a tight circle far away, still hugging the ground. He squeezed the .50-cal's trigger and fired at them, knowing his chances of hitting them were negligible. But they would be able to spot the orange tracer fire as the rounds streaked through the night sky.

Thunder cracked in the night as the MiGs came around. Obviously the pilots were worried about the presence of more Stingers, but they were willing to take out a target that presented itself.

Bolan let the .50-cal run dry, all hundred rounds expended.

The MiGs lost altitude and came in lower, silver birds of prey against the star-studded shadows draped across the night sky.

The Executioner tapped the headset. "Longshot, do you have them within your parameters?"

"No, sir."

"Hold your fire. I don't want them to know about you until it's too late."

"Roger, Stone Hammer Leader. Over."

"Stone Hammer Leader, this is G-Force." Grimaldi sounded loose and relaxed, but there was tension in his words. "We have them on-screen, so they must have us. I'm firing a Hellfire across their bows just to let them know we mean business. They're thinking they can hit your position, then be gone before these choppers arrive. They don't know we're equipped with long-range strike capabilities."

"Affirmative, G-Force. Stone Hammer Leader, clear." Bolan reached down, hooked another belt into the .50-cal and waited with his finger on the trigger.

Abruptly the jets shied away. At least one of the pilots dumped a load of flares into the sky as the Hellfire missile tracked on to them. When the explosive went off after contacting one of the flares, it seemed like a miniature sun had dawned.

Blinking away the spots that danced suddenly in front of his eyes, Bolan saw the jets streak on their new heading, apparently forgetting about the easy target they thought they'd spotted. He tapped the transmit button. "Come in, Longshot."

"You have Longshot."

"Are they within your range?"

"That's a big affirmative."

"Take them down," Bolan said. "Stone Hammer Leader, clear."

The bright orange flares of the 23 mm guns splattered against the sky around the two fleeing MiGs. Less than fifteen seconds later, the two fighter jets were broken into pieces by the dozens of rounds the antiaircraft guns fired. They trickled to the ground in flaming chunks.

"Good shooting, Longshot," Bolan congratulated. "Stone Hammer Leader, clear."

"Thank you, sir," the artillery man radioed back. "You guys have a safe trip out there, and come back home to us. Longshot, clear."

"Okay, soldier," Bolan told his driver, "let's go. We're wasting time sitting here."

Larkin nodded and keyed the ignition. The assault buggy rocked down the awkward incline toward the Inge River, scattering loose stones and dirt in its wake. When they topped the ridge, the other vehicles of Fast Break could be seen rolling toward a low point of the river where they could safely cross without miring up. Tanks and the APCs would never have made it.

Glancing at his watch, Bolan heard the falling numbers of the operation tumble through his mind. It was less than two hours to the fuel dump, time enough for a lot of things to become unraveled.

"PUT THOSE ON," the morgue attendant said.

Carl Lyons accepted the plastic gloves, passing the extra pairs to Schwarz and Blancanales. They didn't look happy about getting them. The big ex-LAPD detective was suffering from jet lag from the jump out from Stony Man Farm. Once the team had unloaded at LAX, a helicopter had been waiting to ferry them to the coroner's office.

"Mr. Leiter."

Finished pulling the second glove on, Lyons suddenly realized *he* was Mr. Leiter. In fact, he was Mr. Chet Leiter, a representative of the National Centers for Disease Control, out of Atlanta. "Yeah."

"Have you and your people recently been inoculated against diphtheria?" The assistant medical examiner was young, probably barely out of college, and had a serious demeanor that revealed none of the black humor people in his trade were normally known for. He was long, lean and lantern-jawed, and already going bald on top. His pale gray eyes rarely blinked behind the black-rimmed glasses he wore.

"Only a couple hours ago," Lyons replied. "We were given booster shots." His bicep was still sore from the needle.

"They also told you when you were given the inoculation that we weren't sure if it would help prevent you from getting infected with the disease?"

"Yeah." Lyons took the face mask from his pocket and slipped it on.

Able Team followed the assistant into the hallway, where he pushed through a swing door. Lyons came to a stop beside him, looking around at the stainless-steel-and-ceramic interior. One wall was nothing but drawers labeled with case file numbers. It seemed like the temperature had dropped twenty degrees since they'd entered the room.

"Who did you want to see?" the assistant asked.

"You pick one," Lyons said. "One of the first ones, probably. Somebody who'll give me a good idea of what we're looking at here."

"Okay." The assistant consulted a logbook on a small metal desk, then crossed the room to the vault wall and pulled out a drawer.

Under the loose folds of the white sheet, the body looked small and thin. They usually did, no matter how big the guy had been in life, and Lyons knew that from experience.

The young assistant pulled the sheet off the body in a practiced maneuver.

The corpse looked early thirties, with dark curly hair and a week's growth of beard. Knife scars twisted into the pallid flesh at his left shoulder and left rib cage, both of them looking years old. Acne had left pocked ridges across his nose and on both cheeks.

"Who is he?" Lyons asked.

"Harold Bender," the assistant said after checking the clipboard tucked beside the body. "He succumbed pretty quick to the infection as I recall. Would you like to see the disease?"

Lyons didn't really want to, but his cover demanded it. And he needed to know as much about what he was dealing with as he could. He nodded, feeling his throat go dry and tight. It was one thing to see bodies shot, stabbed, or after an accidental death by violence, and quite another to see someone who'd wasted away from a disease.

Leaning over the body, the assistant grabbed the man's lower face, pried the jaws open with his fingers and opened the mouth. He turned the head so Lyons could see in. Rigor was starting to set in so, he had some trouble getting it positioned the way he wanted.

"Here," the young guy said. He pointed at the furry gray patches staining the man's throat and tonsils. More was spread across the corpse's tongue.

"It doesn't usually spread to the tongue, does it?" Lyons asked.

"Not in most diphtheria cases." The assistant shoved his glasses back up his nose again. "Of course, these are the first actual cases I've ever seen. But I'm starting to do some extensive research on the subject. Dr. Phillips and I have discovered that this particular strain of the diphtheria bacillus is far more greatly spread than what we've been trained to expect."

"Did you run any tests to find out if this guy was a habitual drug abuser?"

"No." The assistant referenced the clipboard again.

"Were there any drugs in his system at the time he was admitted to the hospital emergency room?"

"Cocaine," the guy said with a nod. "I see an observation here by the doctor of record that Bender was obviously high when he was checked in. Later they determined that it was cocaine."

"Can you tell me if the guy was a regular user?"

The assistant closed the dead man's mouth, knelt and fished a small penlight from his smock pocket. He flicked it on, pinched the corpse's nostrils and peered inside. "Lots of scarring," he said. "I'd say he's been using heavy for some time now."

"I'm through with him," Lyons said.

The assistant nodded and pushed the drawer back into its niche in the wall.

"Do you have any facts or figures on how many of the diphtheria victims were drug users?"

"No, but it won't take too long for me to get that information for you."

"I'd appreciate it."

"Can I call you?"

Lyons pulled out one of the freshly minted business cards that had come in his ID packet. "The number that's on the card is the L.A. County Sheriff's Department. If you call, ask for Jerry Mitchell. He's working as the liaison between the sheriff's office and our group."

"I can save you some time," a voice said.

Lyons turned to look at the speaker.

The man was tall and broad-shouldered with a swimmer's build. Dark curly hair ran rampant over his head and dropped almost to his shoulders in a ducktail, giving him an American Indian look with the beachcomber's tan. Black sunglasses covered his eyes. The beard and mustache were worn short and neatly trimmed, but hadn't been taken care of for a couple of days. He wore a purple tank top with bright orange bands, knee-length khaki shorts with snap pockets on the thighs, running shoes without socks and a bright lime-green fanny pack that was a little on the heavy side.

"You shouldn't be in here without a mask and gloves," the assistant medical examiner said.

"It's okay, Doc." The beachcomber waved away the warning. "I'm an adrenaline addict." He switched his gaze to Lyons. "You're in from Atlanta?"

"Yeah."

"And you want to know what kind of drugs these people used?"

There was no avoiding the direct question. Lyons nodded.

"Kind of an unusual interest for a guy in your field, isn't it? Aren't you guys usually more interested in water supplies, foods, that kind of thing?"

"I'm an unusual-interest addict," Lyons replied.

There was a moment of silence, then the beachcomber's lips peeled back and revealed a boyish white smile. "Good for a man to have a hobby."

"Keeps the mind limber."

"Right."

"Who is this joker?" Blancanales asked.

Lyons knew his teammate was worried that the guy might be a reporter. In order to work effectively, Able Team had to run a low profile for a short time. "He's a cop."

"Right," the beachcomber agreed. He walked the wall of vaults and pointed out individual doors. "Harold 'Screaming Harry' Bender, busted for cocaine twice. William 'Billy the Kid' Newton, cocaine dealer. Rita Sanders, street prostitute with a big cocaine habit to support. Dave Markham, burglar who stole anything that wasn't tied down to support his habit." He smiled. "Markham stole an artificial prosthesis once and tried to pawn it. Went down for two years on that rap. Even a pawnshop owner with a professionally hazy memory about details can remember somebody who tried to sell him a fake leg. Sally Jestro, small-time dealer making enough to get herself through a really miserable life." He turned around at the end of the vaults.

"He's a vice cop," Lyons stated.

"Right," the guy said with the broad smile again. "I'm a cop and you're not with Disease Control."

Lyons didn't say anything, wondering where the man was coming from.

The vice cop crossed his arms over his tanned, muscular chest. "C'mon, dudes, I spotted the weight you were carrying when I first laid eyes on you. What the hell do you need with that cannon on your hip if you're just here to study bacteria?"

Lyons gave him a stony look. "It's for the really big germs."

There was a pause, then the vice cop started to laugh. It sounded forced, strained. Then, "My shield's out in the car if you want a positive ID."

Lyons waved it away. Some cops wore their badges like another skin. For the guy to pull off undercover work, the big Able Team warrior knew he had to be a good actor when the time was right. But he also knew there sometimes wasn't much difference between a good street hustler and a good street cop. They both moved in the same circles, and the stakes were always against a sudden and violent death.

"My name's Ethan. J. D. Ethan." He waved toward the wall of dead. "You seen enough here?"

"Yeah," Lyons said.

"Then let's blow this pop stand."

"We're supposed to be meeting somebody from the sheriff's office here," Schwarz said.

"No prob. You want to stay, stay. But I can tell you now they're going to be sending you a John Wayne type who hasn't seen anything but that uniform and a Sam Browne belt. He won't know these streets like I do." Ethan glanced at Lyons. "And the way I got it figured, you guys aren't packing test tubes and shit, and you're not here to log new entries at the morgue. Me, I look at it, I see a lot of people that are known movers in the cocaine circles dropping dead, and I got a Disease people team here that aren't what they say they are. Made me ask myself what we could accomplish if we worked together on this thing."

Lyons studied the man and knew there was a ragged edge to the vice cop that he didn't understand.

"The way I figure it," Ethan said, "you guys got some stuff I don't know about. I got the street connections you need to get your job done. One hand washes the other. And if we don't deal, I'll be hanging on to your coattails anyway till I figure out if you've got something worth knowing."

"You could be a real pain in the ass," Lyons said.

"Count on it. People have told me I can be damned childish when I don't get my way."

"It's your call, Ironman," Blancanales said.

Lyons nodded. "I've always been a backdoor man myself. You get the red-carpet treatment, sometimes you lose the detail work that you need the most."

"Great." Ethan led the way out of the building and to a Ford Econoline van with a faded surfing mural painted on the sides, which was parked out back.

Lyons, Blancanales and Schwarz paused only long enough to pick up the equipment cases that had been dropped off by the helicopter, and dispose of the morgue clothing. They could pick up a rental car later when it was necessary. Twilight had colored the smoggy skies while they'd been inside the building. True night was only a few minutes away.

Ethan clambered behind the steering wheel as Lyons took the shotgun seat and Blancanales and Schwarz made themselves comfortable on the made-to-fit bed in the back.

A Blazer with deputy sheriff's markings and a light bar across the top pulled to a stop and killed its lights in the parking lot as Ethan was trying to back out. The uniformed deputy who got out looked like he could have played linebacker for the Raiders.

"That's Garvey," Ethan said as he headed the van for the street. "You guys should feel honored. He wore his good hat."

"So where are we going?" Lyons asked as they eased into traffic.

"To knock on a few doors," Ethan replied. "See if something comes out of the woodwork when we bang on some walls."

"Okay." That suited the big Able Team warrior just fine. Sometimes that was the only game plan in town. And he remembered a lot about L.A., especially the types that came out after the night shift went on.

CHAPTER TEN

Out of habit, Hal Brognola logged the call in at 11:47 p.m. He was with the President in the Oval Office. They hadn't talked much in the past hour, as they sat watching the CNN broadcasts coming from North and South Haakovia. As eager and as daring as the journalists had been, however, they hadn't been allowed out of Larsborg to pursue Bolan's army.

Although he agreed with Striker's assessment of the current situation regarding the vulnerability of the South, and of the fact that Stensvik stood poised and willing to swoop across the border with his troops on the coming day, the head Fed knew the chances Striker was taking. They were long ones, based on solid concepts with an eye toward breaking the North's military might early on. But things were going to be dicey. However, no one else had any other answers. Freedom and independence were going to rise and fall with the ragtag army Mack Bolan was leading into battle. And that was only if it didn't die an early death if Operation Fast Break failed.

"Mr. President?" The intercom made the secretary's voice sound tinny and far away.

The Man blinked his eyes, moving them away from the television mounted in the wall across the room. He sat forward, stuck a finger in his coffee and grimaced. "Yes."

"I've got an incoming audio and video transmission from North Haakovia."

"Who is it?" the Man asked.

"An aide to President Stensvik, sir. He wouldn't give his name."

"And we've traced the transmission back?"

"Yes, Mr. President. It's connected by satellite relay to Sturegorsk, North Haakovia."

"What's the nature of the call?" The President got up from behind the desk, approached the coffee service table and poured himself a fresh cup. He glanced at Brognola inquiringly.

The big Fed nodded, pushed up from the chair and realized he ached all over from being so sedentary these past few days. He longed for the time when he could see Helen again, spend time working in their garden together, not really talking, but just being there for each other. By the time he reached the President's side, the Man already had the coffee fixed.

"He won't tell me that either, sir. But he says that you should take it."

"Dammit," the President said. He stared at the television screen.

Footage from yesterday's battle scenes from around the presidential palace played there, depicting the atrocities and the carnage.

"If I start dealing with this son of a bitch now," the President said, "it may weaken my case if I have to start playing hardball with him later."

"Doesn't matter what he thinks," Brognola said. "Stensvik is going to believe he's dealing from a position of power no matter what you do or say. He has to. At least if you talk to him, we stand a chance of learning something, or at least diverting his attention from Striker and his people."

"Sir?" the secretary said. "The aide is getting restless and abusive."

"Put him through," the President replied, squaring his shoulders and facing the video camera wired into the return line, "and initiate audio and video feedback."

"Yes, sir."

Brognola brushed at the shoulders of his jacket and stood slightly behind the executive officer.

The face that materialized on the television was grainy and of Slavic origins. The North Haakovian captain's uniform was crisp, the bars polished to a high gleam. "The president doesn't like to be kept waiting," he said in a stern voice. "You are lucky he even bothers communicating with you at all."

"I'll count my blessings later," the President muttered.

"What?" the aide demanded.

"If I'm going to talk to the man," the President said in an authoritative voice, "trot him out here and let's talk. I don't need to waste my time worrying about your ego too."

"You need to be respectful of President Stensvik and of me. The chance he is giving you—"

"How do you think your precious general would feel toward you if I got tired of listening to a petty bureaucrat with a confidence problem and hung up?"

A shocked look filled the man's face.

Brognola had to restrain a tight-lipped grin. The Man might feel like he was placing himself in a position where less negotiation was possible later, but he was racking up some points along the way.

"A moment," the aide said frostily, "and I'll have President Stensvik for you."

The screen cleared and was replaced immediately by a file photo of the flag of North Haakovia fluttering over the presidential building.

The President shrugged his shoulders in an effort to loosen them, then sipped his coffee and perched on the edge of his desk in a relaxed fashion. He looked at Brognola expectantly. "Do I look relaxed?"

"No," the head Fed said truthfully, "but you don't look like you're ready to swallow his line of bull either."

"That'll do," the Man said. "If things had happened differently for Stensvik, he wouldn't have a pot to piss in." He smiled wryly. "That would be about the extent of the modern technology he'd be prepared to handle. Thinking about those nuclear arms and those other weapons under his control still puts knots in my stomach."

The television buzzed, then filled with Franzen Stensvik's face. He clasped his hands before him and smiled, his eyes almost disappearing in folds of flesh. "My aide was given the impression that you didn't wish to speak to me." His English was rough and a little slow.

"I'd thought," the President replied, "that it was somewhat stronger than just an impression."

The smile vanished as a hate-filled scowl took its place. "You're a fool," he said. "You Americans. You think your money allows you to push us around, to make monkeys of us. But you should know by now that the weapons I have in my possession make us equals. More than equals. I will not hesitate to use mine as you will."

"That remains to be seen," the President said. "It could be that that whole Baltic coastline will be reshaped before this is over."

"Idle threats do not become you."

"What do you want?" the Man asked in a low, tight voice.

"I want you to back off," Stensvik replied. "Your showmanship in the United Nations has made a number of my associates nervous. For now they don't like being put into the public eye."

"Maybe," the President suggested, "they never will."

"You *will* do as I say, or the events that are going on in Los Angeles, California, will be spread all across your nation."

Butterflies with icicle wings fluttered inside Brognola's stomach. At the last count he'd seen on Headline News, there had been more than forty-seven deaths related to the new strain of diphtheria bacillus.

"You're responsible for that insanity?" the President demanded.

Stensvik didn't hesitate. "Of course. Do you think a new disease simply created itself and started spreading to the degree it has all by itself?"

"You callous bastard."

Brognola forced himself to stay stone-faced. The havoc that Stensvik was capable of didn't surprise him. He'd seen too many examples of it since the Haakovian mission had started.

"And that's only the beginning," Stensvik promised. "if you don't pull the American forces out of South Haakovia, what is going on in Los Angeles will be only the taste of what is to come. Think about it, then get back to me."

"Wait," the President said.

Stensvik eyed him in silence. "Yes?"

"What about President Varkaus?"

"At present she's enjoying my company." Stensvik paused melodramatically. "Of course, that could change at any moment, too."

The picture wavered, turned grainy for an instant, then faded away.

"Hal," the President said as he turned to peer out the bulletproof windows behind the desk.

"Yeah."

"Tell me everything's going to be all right."

"I could," Brognola said. "But I wouldn't believe it, either."

"Everything hinges on Mack at this moment, doesn't it?"

"In the Haakovias? Yeah. That's the way I see it. But there's not another man I'd want to trust with the responsibility."

"I know. That's the way I feel, too. I just wish we could pour some more troops or hardware into that area without running afoul of UN dictates."

"Well," Brognola said, "there is one thing."

The Man looked at him.

"Stensvik just gave you an ace to play." The head Fed pointed at the television. "I assume that transmission was taped."

"Yes."

"He just publicly admitted he's responsible for the diphtheria outbreak in L.A. That should win us some support from the UN."

The President rubbed his jaw. "True. But Stensvik could always insist that we dubbed the whole thing and faked it."

"I was a cop for a lot of years, Mr. President," Brognola said. "All that time I never stepped over the line, but I skated close a few times."

"The same way we have this arm's-length alliance with Striker."

"Exactly. See, when we had a tough case and knew we were going to have trouble making it work in the courtroom because of public sentiment or ignorance, certain information was leaked to the press. Those cases got a lot of coverage as a result because the press was there while we were doing some of the ground-breaking. While the judge instructed the jury not to give heed to news reports on television or the papers, you know most people don't live life in a vacuum."

"And they were educated through the media."

"Yeah."

"So your suggestion?"

"Don't try to sit on that tape. Disseminate it. Every news agency worth its salt has a Deep Throat somewhere in this town. I'm sure you either know who those people are, or you know people who do. Let them have the tape, but don't let them know you're just giving it to them."

"I like that. And when I walk back into the United Nations General Assembly tomorrow, some of my case will already be made for me."

"Hopefully," Brognola pointed out. "Sometimes this kind of thing can blow up in your face."

"At this juncture," the Man said as he thumbed the intercom, "I'm willing to take that gamble. Stensvik's going down, and I want to be part of the team that puts him there."

FOR A WHILE David McCarter thought he was going to stay ahead of the snowstorm, but the extra time that was eaten up coming down the western coastline of Northern Haakovia allowed it to catch up.

He sat at the controls and felt stiff and lethargic, his eyes roving restlessly over the instrument panel. So far they'd successfully avoided North Haakovian radar.

Katz occupied the passenger seat and worked by the light of the small overhead bulb. His pencil alternately tapped against the maps he studied, and made marks on them. Contrary to his usual appearance, gray stubble darkened the Israeli's jowls.

Unconsciously McCarter put a hand to his own face, feeling the rough growth there. On Katz the growth served to soften the blunt and tanned features into something grandchildren could love. McCarter, on the other hand, knew the whiskers on his own fox-face made him look like one of those bleeding punks in leather jackets a bloke could find in the East End of London. Of course, without the body-piercing paraphernalia they sported he knew he looked like the generic version.

"What are you thinking, David?" Katz asked without looking up from the maps. He made more notations.

"That all work and no play makes Jack a dull boy."

"Getting tired of piloting the bus?"

"It has been a tad boring these past couple of hours. If we'd hurried things along, we could be with Striker and his merry little band of ruffians by now."

"True, but then he wouldn't have anyone to help instill confusion in the North Haakovian forces."

"Did you notice the way Barb and Striker assumed that we would be the best decoy for the confusion part?"

Katz looked up, a smile pulling at his lips. "Yes, but I didn't take it personally."

McCarter sighed. "Ah, bugger it. Probably just having Coke withdrawal. Do you know how long it's been since I've had one?"

"No."

"Want to hear me bitch about it?"

"No."

"I didn't think so. You're not very bloody entertaining at the moment."

"No."

"Terrific. I'm doing a monologue, and you're doing a monotone."

"I'm looking over Striker's plans for setting up the North Haakovian armor."

"And?"

"And it looks good. This is a chance for Gary to really excel at his trade."

"Do you think he can do it?"

"I think Gary has a talent for destruction."

"Was he excited when you told him about it?" Price had relayed Bolan's plans earlier.

"Yes."

"Christ," McCarter grumbled, "now I'm beginning to feel like the straight man for a talk-show host. So how bloody excited was he?"

"He was so excited that you'd think this was his first bang." Katz's pale blue eyes twinkled.

McCarter groaned. "I'll shut up. I promise. The last thing I need while we're cooling our heels out here is to listen to a string of bad puns."

Katz returned his attention to the maps.

"Ninety klicks in for the fuel supplies," McCarter said, "taking them away from a hostile army, then making that same ninety-klick run back across the border. In the dead of night."

"Near dawn."

"That's when patients who've been struggling usually give up the ghost."

"Those people aren't prepared to give up. Not yet. And if Striker's successful, they'll have the supplies and the heart to go on."

"Still, it's a sticky bit of business."

"It'll work. Stensvik won't be expecting it."

"How could he?"

The sharp ping of the radar alarm going off sounded like a gunshot in the quiet of the cockpit.

Katz pushed the maps away and swiveled in his chair to take in the navigator's station. "Two blips, closing fast."

"Whereaway?"

"Six o'clock. Coming in from behind and above."

McCarter flicked on the headset and transmitted along the frequency monitored inside the AC-130-H Spectre. "Hey, mates, we just picked up a tail. In our present location, need I mention that they probably aren't going to be chums?"

"I'm on it," Gary Manning said.

The Briton moved the yoke, pulling the big plane into a slow, lazy circle that would put him back on track with the two approaching bogies. "We're going on a flyby. Maybe we can out-finesse this one. They can't be too sure of us, either. We're flying too low to be picked up by the coastal radar, so they must have made us on their own systems. Since we're not making an aggressive move into North Haakovia, they won't be overly anxious to fire without finding out who we are." He paused. "At least that's what I think. Bloody bastards could prove me wrong."

Katz evacuated the copilot's seat and moved back into the weapons officer's station. They'd already verified that everything was in working condition. Besides the .50-cal tail gun that Manning would now be hunkered behind, the Spectre was outfitted with two 20 mm Vulcan cannons, a 105 mm howitzer and a 40 mm cannon The big transport plane was an aerial juggernaut, but no way in any speed class with a fighter jet.

Straining his eyes against the whirling panorama presented by the snowstorm, McCarter searched for the approaching planes against the sky. They were mere specks when he first saw them. His brain kicked into gear, flipping through the mental catalog he had of all the aircraft he'd ever encountered or read or heard about.

It didn't take long. They were a very familiar design.

"MiGs," McCarter radioed.

A heartbeat later both jets flashed by.

He pulled on the yoke, headed back out to the Gulf of Finland to give himself some maneuvering room. The radar showed the two MiGs sweeping around to track back onto him. He searched for the radio frequency the MiG pilots were using and found it. When the North Haakovian dialect scratched through the headphone, he knew there was no way they could run a bluff.

"Katz," he said as he skimmed low over the black water, "you need to get Barb on the phone and find out how she wants us to handle this." And he was praying they'd have the time.

"BARBARA?"

The Stony Man mission controller glanced over at Carmen Delahunt's workstation and nodded.

"It's Jerry Mitchell, with the L.A. sheriff's department."

"I'm busy," Price replied.

Delahunt nodded and turned back to the mouthpiece on her headset.

Price massaged her temples, hoping that the headache would abate on its own and that she wouldn't have to resort to analgesics. She had a low tolerance to them, and she wouldn't be able to perform up to snuff.

"Blame it on Ironman," Kurtzman said as he poked halfheartedly at his computer keyboard. "He's the one that made that wild-card call about the vice cop."

"It's his call to make," Price replied. "I make the assignments, facilitate matters when I can and be there when I'm able."

"And go crazy when it looks like things aren't going according to Hoyle."

Price gave the big cybernetics expert a pat on the shoulder and a wan smile. "Hell, Bear, that's a fringe benefit.

Why would I gripe about that? If things didn't occasionally drive us crazy around here we'd never get vacations.''

Kurtzman's rumbling laughter sounded good to her. ''The L.A. sheriff's office isn't too happy about Able not being there.''

''That's because they thought they were helping out an FBI-sponsored investigation by the National Centers for Disease Control.''

''Could be trouble later.''

''If it is, I'll deal with it then.''

The radio buzzed for attention and Price scooped it up. Katz's voice came through, calm and unhurried. ''Stony Base, this is Phoenix One. Over.''

''Go, Phoenix One. You have Stony Base.''

''There are two MiGs bearing down on our plane. We are unable to identify ourselves as friend or foe because of language differences. At this point we have two options. We can dump the plane in the water and take our chances getting to shore and staying out of the action. Or we can attempt to take down the unfriendlies here and make our way into North Haakovia early. We need to know if Stony One's timetable is flexible enough to handle that.''

''Hold on, Phoenix One, and I'll get that answer for you.'' Price covered the mouthpiece on the headset and looked at Kurtzman. ''Patch me through to Striker.''

Kurtzman nodded and went to work on the keyboard.

Price stared at the digital-clock readout in a window opened up on one of the computer monitors. Thirteen minutes and forty-one seconds remained before Phoenix was supposed to begin penetration.

''Go, Stony Base,'' Mack Bolan's strong voice said. ''You have Stony One.''

In terse, clear sentences, Price outlined Phoenix Force's situation.

"Tell them to bring it on," Bolan said. "I need Phoenix One running the flanker action with his team during the next stage of this mission. And we're not going to push them out into the cold and let them fend for themselves. If things run tight here, we'll find or make the flex we need to make it work."

"Understood," Price said. "Stony Base will relay your message. Stony Base, clear."

Bolan clicked off the line.

"Phoenix One, this is Stony Base."

"Go, Stony Base."

"Stony One says you are to proceed with the plan. He's moving his timetable forward to cover you."

"Acknowledged, Stony Base. See you on the other side. Phoenix One, out."

Just before the mike went dead, Price could hear the sound of explosions in the background. She suddenly realized that her headache was gone, washed away by the flood of sudden worry.

CHAPTER ELEVEN

Leaving the assault buggy parked with Larkin at the wheel two klicks south of the North Haakovian fuel depot, Mack Bolan stayed with the sparse forest and moved at a steady, distance-eating jog. He was dressed in South Haakovian night cammies, complete with a watch cap that served a dual purpose of keeping his head warm and making him blend with the night.

The sliver of moon had vanished some time ago, blocked out by the snow clouds that had rolled in from the sea. Snowflakes, as big as plums, fell to the ground as far as the eye could see.

The big warrior paused at a tree line and looked up the final slope that led to the waiting trucks. The snow was already starting to stick, which was going to cause problems for the covert team as far as concealment went. The trees and brush would help some, but the overall effect of the night was being blunted by every fraction of an inch of snow that piled up.

He glanced over his shoulder, studying the movement of his troops through the night-vision goggles he wore. Gray clouds streamed out from the mouths of the few men he saw. With the ground not really frozen and some of the snow melting when it hit, the going was getting tougher. It would make a difference when they moved the tanks in the morning, too.

He turned his mind from projecting what the next day might bring. He had his hands full dealing with this, and it wasn't finished yet. He pushed himself back into motion. With having to move things along faster because of Phoenix Force's problems, the slack time he'd built into this part of the operation had suddenly evaporated. The fuel depot was only thirty miles in from the coast. It was conceivable that the central intelligence post might radio them to confirm the presence of enemy aircraft. And Phoenix's run in-country would bring extra defenders from the coastline. Of course, the up side was that it could prove to make things even more confusing for the North Haakovians.

Carrying a full pack and wearing a Kevlar vest made climbing the hill at a near run even harder. The Desert Eagle rode at his hip, while the Beretta 93-R occupied its usual shoulder leather in his military webbing. Grenades, extra clips and garrotes lined his pockets, pouches and harness. For the close-in work necessitated by capturing the tanker trucks with as little damage done to the big rigs as possible, his choice of lead weapons was a 12-gauge Mossberg Model 500 Bullpup.

At the top of the ridge he hunkered next to an oak tree and took out the night glasses. The tanker trucks were parked in formation, all facing the southeast, away from the bitingly cold wind coming in with the storm. The tractor rigs were painted North Haakovian brown.

A few minutes passed as the Executioner picked out the security teams maintaining a loose perimeter around the site. None of them took pains to be hidden. The warrior knew that would work against his covert force to a degree because the soldiers would be more apt to notice someone's disappearance if they weren't hiding from everyone else. When the numbers started to fall on this part of the operation, they were going to fall damn fast.

He scanned the tractor rigs again and found that most of them were older models that lacked locking transmissions or locking steering wheels. It removed the added trouble of trying to find the keys. When the South Haakovian forces took over the trucks they could easily hot-wire them. Grimaldi and Bolan had spent the time back at the transitory base camp training the men who hadn't known how to do it.

He tapped the transmit button on the headset and talked quietly. "Stone Hammer Leader to Fox Group. Count in, by the numbers. Over."

In a matter of seconds all ten men had counted in, logged on as ready to proceed.

"Do it," Bolan said. "Clear." He picked up the Mossberg Bullpup and headed out, staying with the terrain as he went down the incline, using it for cover. Eight other men, he knew, were on their way down with him. Two snipers were left to pick off North Haakovian soldiers once the covert action went ballistic.

When he was a few feet away from the pair of guards separating him from the first of the tanker trucks, one of the soldiers lighted up a cigarette, trapping Bolan in the circle of illumination. The guy's eyes widened as he spotted the Executioner. He dropped the cigarette and the lighter, and flailed for his weapon.

Smoothly Bolan drew the silenced Beretta and squeezed the trigger. A 3-round burst of 9 mm Parabellums caught the man in the collarbone and drilled their way up to his chin. The corpse dropped back into the brush.

The second man whirled, already bringing up his AK-47.

Bolan stood and fired from the point, putting another 3-round burst into the soldier's face. The guy was dead before he hit the ground. Working swiftly, the Executioner tucked the bodies deeper into the brush so they wouldn't be easily found.

Squaring his shoulders, he left the shadows and stepped into the open space leading to the first of the trucks. He dropped his chin to his chest, giving the appearance of a tired soldier just trying to keep warm. He kept the Beretta in his fist, tucked under his left arm. Using his peripheral vision, he avoided contact with other North Haakovian regulars drifting between the trucks.

His destination was the communications building at the northeast quadrant behind the vehicles. Each tractor was equipped with a shortwave radio, but the communications building tied the unit to North Haakovian Intelligence. It was imperative to knock it out before word could be sent about the confiscation of the fuel supplies.

Someone called out to him.

He looked up and saw a bored driver sitting in a tractor cab to his left as he walked between the rigs. After having been a soldier as long as he had, Bolan felt sure he knew what the guy wanted without understanding the language. He nodded, reached into his pocket and came out with a pack of cigarettes. Approaching the truck, knowing the guy was going to recognize the South Haakovian cammies any moment, the big warrior flipped the cigarettes at the other man and kept on slowly closing the distance.

The truck driver caught the pack, started to shake one out, then saw Bolan more clearly. Dropping the cigarettes, he opened his mouth to shout a warning as he clawed for the assault rifle canted against the windshield beside him.

Bolan raised the 93-R and put a single round through the man's open mouth that silenced the guy forever. The bullet cored through the windshield with a sharp thwack and sailed harmlessly off into the forest.

Head snapping back from the impact of the 9 mm round, the truck driver sprawled bonelessly across the seat and started to slide out.

Moving quickly without appearing hurried, Bolan put a foot onto the steps leading into the cab and swung himself up. He leathered the Beretta and grabbed the dead man by the belt before he could fall to the ground. It was hard lifting the deadweight, but he got it shifted back inside the truck cab and clear of the driver's seat and gear stick.

He had his 9 mm pistol back in his hand, hidden along his leg, when he climbed back out. He closed the truck door without attracting attention and started back for the communications building.

A sudden blast from an AK-47 woke up the fuel site to the fact that wolves were among them.

Slipping the Beretta into shoulder leather, Bolan brought up the Mossberg Bullpup and ran for the target building. He tapped the transmit button on the headset. "Stone Hammer Leader to Fox Two, Three and Five. Over."

The three men responded immediately.

"Get those flares up, *now!* Fox One, Fox Nine."

"Here, sir."

"Ready, sir."

Bolan threw himself up against the communications building. "You have the field. Pick your targets and take them down. Nobody gets out of here alive. Stone Hammer Leader, clear."

With all the gunfire erupting around the trucks, it was impossible to hear the pops of the three flare guns when they were used. But their projectiles sped skyward, painting gray streamers against the black of night and the falling swirl of snow. A heartbeat later they exploded, becoming crimson novas illuminating the scene below. Wildly shaped, elongated shadows danced around the trucks and over the fallen bodies of men. The heavy reports of the Barrett Model 82A1 .50-caliber sniper rifles was heard above the din of autofire. The flares also served to bring up the assault-buggy attack force, flanked by the Hummers ferrying the drivers in.

The communications-building door opened inward to Bolan's right. He whirled, lifted the Mossberg and fired point-blank into the chest of the man starting to run through the door, the double-aught charge knocking the guy backward. The Executioner turned sideways and kicked out, slamming the door open. He yanked a grenade from his combat harness, flipped it into the room, then broke into a run down the side of the building. At the first window he came to, he fired another round from the shotgun and took out the thin wooden slats of the closed window. He shoved another grenade through, catching a momentary glimpse of a radio dispatcher slipping on a headset.

Counting down the time on the first grenade, Bolan leaned around the window frame and rattled through the remaining six rounds in the clip, putting them into the radio equipment and the operator.

Knowing the numbers had run out, Bolan pushed off the side of the building and ran, aware of the bullets that scored the wooden wall where he'd just been. The explosions came a couple seconds apart, created a ripple with the first one, then became a concussive wave with the second. Evidently other explosives or fuel cans had been stored inside.

Bolan was plucked from his feet, slammed into the air and came down twisting and off balance as a nearby North Haakovian soldier leveled his AK-47.

"WE'RE GOING TO TRY to take the bloody beggar down, mate."

"I'm on it," Gary Manning radioed back to McCarter. The Canadian sighted down the barrel of the .50-caliber tail gun, hunkered uncomfortably into the gunner's port. He watched the approaching MiG streak up behind the transport plane and kept it within the .50-cal's sights. So far the two fighter jets didn't know there was an enemy in their midst.

"On my mark as you have it," McCarter said. "We'll try to go two for two. When you take out the first man up, I'm going to roll out and try for the second. You get the first guy, my target should instinctively break for the upper deck and leave his belly open to me. You miss, we could be in for a real squeaker."

Manning smiled grimly. "I'm glad there's no pressure on this."

The MiG blazed into the Spectre's backwash, drawing closer.

"You got him?" McCarter asked.

"Yeah."

"Then take him."

Manning squeezed the .50-cal's trigger, feeling the big gun rock solidly into his shoulder despite the mounting brackets. Green tracers flared out in a wavering stream as the Canadian adjusted his aim.

The MiG pilot was caught flat-footed as the .50-caliber whip flicked out and made contact. The slugs hammered into the cowling and across the Plexiglas cockpit. Veering away sharply, the jet streaked for the dark waters below.

"He's down!" Manning yelled. "Go for your guy."

The Spectre heeled to port violently.

Manning's last view of the other MiG was of it breaking its flight pattern and rising into the air. He pushed himself out of the gunport, using every surface he could cling to while he made his way back to the belly of the transport ship.

Calvin James and Rafael Encizo held on to the jeep they'd brought with them from Helsinki. The vehicle had been strapped down with restraining ties mounted into the Spectre's flooring. It shivered and shook with every twist and turn McCarter followed, but it held its ground.

Releasing the railing he was presently holding on to, Manning flung himself at the jeep, grabbed onto the rear section and steadied himself. His boots slipped out from under him when the main howitzer went off and caused the AC-130-H to shudder like a dog shaking off water. He busted his lip against the jeep's body and tasted blood. The howitzer went off twice more.

Then the Spectre angled down in a gliding descent that left Manning's stomach spinning sickly.

"Okay, mates," McCarter said in a cocky voice, "we've done all the damage we can do here. Now let's see about the rest of this pleasant little country. We'll start out with a low-level scenic tour of the environs."

"And if they have antiaircraft guns?" Encizo asked.

"It'll be a short trip," McCarter replied. "But according to Barb and the Bear, we should have smooth sailing here. Regular little alley ahead of us if we play it right."

Katz's transmission was hot on the heels of McCarter's. "Do you have the jeep ready to be dropped?"

James reached out and slapped the cargo parachute nestled in the rear deck of the jeep and attached to the bumper. "We're all set here, Katz."

Taking the parachute Encizo handed him, Manning shrugged into it and quickly fastened the straps. He checked his pockets, making sure the notes he'd made regarding the Sergiusz Mountains were still there. In spite of the situation and the uncertainty of the next few moments, he grinned at the Cuban. "You know, Rafe, I've never killed a whole frigging mountain before."

"If anyone can do it, I'm sure it's you."

Manning grinned, then reflected that his teammate might not have intended the compliment as a totally good thing. Before he could ask about the motivation behind the comment, McCarter broke in over the intercom.

"Let's look lively, mates. Drop site coming up in three minutes."

"Cut the jeep loose," James said as he worked to free his side of the vehicle.

"Parking brake set?" Encizo asked.

"Yeah."

Manning unbolted the jeep's front wheel as the Cuban worked on the rear tire. He decided not to let Encizo's words bother him. He *was* excited, dammit. If he pulled off Striker's plan, it would be one of the biggest and most complicated projects of his life. He could hardly wait.

"Free," Encizo said.

Manning echoed the same.

"Me, too," James said.

"Drop site in two minutes, lads, and it looks like Striker and his people have already hit some rough spots." McCarter's voice was enthusiastic. "And we've attracted some extra attention.

The vibration of cannon fire shook the Spectre.

"Get the cargo door open," Katz called out.

James hit the cargo-door release button and the ramp opened with a metallic groan. Cold air whistled in, the eerie hissing sounds broken by the booms of the cannon fire pursuing them.

Pulling his coat tighter, Manning could tell the Spectre was dropping altitude again by the increased pressure on his ears. He ran his hands over his gear and checked it against his mental inventory. The Beretta 92-S was in shoulder leather over the Kevlar vest he wore under his coat. A Crain battle dagger was strapped to his left shin under his pant leg. His M-16/M-240 assault rifle and grenade launcher combo was slung over his shoulder, tied to his combat harness so he wouldn't lose it during the drop. Other deadly devices draped his body in pouches, pockets and combat webbing.

The other members of Phoenix Force were similarly outfitted.

"Put your arm bands on," Katz ordered.

Manning reached into a coat pocket and pulled out the canary yellow scarf that would identify the team to the South Haakovian Special Forces below. He used his teeth and free hand to tie it securely around his left bicep.

Before he could get stabilized again, a barrage of cannon fire exploded just outside the open cargo ramp, threw sparks against the metal incline and buffeted the big transport plane into an awkward roll.

With a groan of metal the jeep rolled forward, aimed at the forward bulkheads.

"Oh, shit," James cried out. He'd been thrown against the side wall and was struggling to get free.

Without hesitation Manning pushed himself to his feet and went in pursuit of the loose jeep.

"Everyone out," Katz called.

The Spectre was still in a dive, pursued by the enemy aircraft. Manning couldn't pull the jeep back toward the cargo ramp. Cursing softly, he ran around and clambered inside. Keying the ignition, he slammed the stick into reverse, released the parking brake and backed toward the open ramp.

There was a sickening twist in his stomach when he ran out of solid ground. The jeep dropped like a rock and fell through the night. Manning saw two of the North Haakovian aircraft dogging the big plane. Then he pulled himself free of the steering wheel and threw himself out into open space. The automatic chute deployment would kick in at any second, and he didn't want to get tangled up in the shroud lines.

He fell free, checked his wrist altimeter and found he was still seven thousand feet up. There was no rush for the parachute he wore. As long as he kept the jeep in sight, he had plenty of time.

A couple seconds later the cargo chute deployed. The chute billowed up, became a black mushroom that floated against the snow and yanked the jeep into a nosedive toward the ground.

"Gary?" It was Encizo.

"Yo," Manning called back. He glanced up at the Spectre and saw three bodies come tumbling out the cargo hatch.

"Are you okay?"

"Yeah. Who's missing?"

"David has elected to stay with the plane for the moment," Katz replied calmly. "He'll be joining us later. He's persuaded me that the transport plane can still be used effectively.

Manning wished his teammate luck, then turned his gaze up to find the jeep hanging like a fat fruit under the canopy of the open parachute. Not wanting the vehicle to get away from him, knowing it could drift a mile in the winds before it touched down after he'd already landed, he yanked the rip cord. His chute unfurled, harness tightening around him like a giant fist, and yanked him into the sky. When he glanced at the spread out clumps of ground fire, he knew they'd all need luck once they reached ground zero.

THE SKY RAINED FIRE, sending it streaming down in fiery cinders and flaming clumps.

Still off balance from the concussive blast that had leveled the communications building and erupted the burning wreckage into the air, Mack Bolan pulled the Mossberg into target acquisition on the North Haakovian soldier gunning for him.

The AK-47 hammered out a long, continuous blast that ripped chunks of black earth from the ground and spit them out over the carpet of fresh fallen snow. The line was tracking directly onto the Executioner.

Firing from instinct, breaking his fall with his free arm while he shot the shotgun one-handed, Bolan put three rounds in the gunner's general direction. Two charges of buckshot hit their target, hammering into the North Haakovian soldier's midsection and knocking him backward.

When the warrior glanced back at the communications building, all that remained was a blazing inferno licking at the foundation. He thumbed fresh cartridges into the Mossberg on the run and advanced on the parked trucks.

A soldier stepped out in front of him unexpectedly. Bolan cut the man down, started at knee-level with the first shot, then unloaded the second into his face. The corpse went down without a sound.

He ran around the nose of the tractor rig, ducked when a sudden spray of 7.62 mm rounds cored through and sparked off the grillwork. Leaning around the truck at bumper level, he blistered three rounds that shoved the North Haakovian soldier from partial cover behind a set of tires, then blew him to the ground.

He thumbed the headset button. "Stone Hammer Leader to G-Force. Over."

"Go, Stone Hammer Leader." Grimaldi sounded tense and alert.

"Begin your first stage."

"Acknowledged. G-Force and Nighthawk squad moving in. Clear."

Looking to the south, Bolan saw the first of the assault buggies come barreling over the ridge. With the fog lights flaring at the front, sides and top of the metal roll cage, they looked like insectoid aliens from an old science-fiction movie. They hurtled without hesitation down the incline at the confused knots of North Haakovian soldiers. Their fat tires slipped, slid, then regained traction as the drivers fought the snow.

Abruptly the fuel-supply crews were fighting agressors on two fronts.

Bolan went through them at a run, firing the Mossberg dry, then unlimbered the Desert Eagle and emptied the clip. He made no effort to communicate with the rest of his team. They knew their jobs, made certain of it before they'd left base. Here in the killing ground life was reduced to a matter of survival, with only a heartbeat separating the quick from the dead.

He took cover behind a rig momentarily to reload, shoving fresh magazines into the .44 and the combat shotgun. A North Haakovian soldier fleeing from the circling menace of a pursuing assault buggy ran into his sights just as he took up the Mossberg. A single charge of buckshot cleared the deck.

The Hummers were up next, rolling down the ridge and stopping at the outer perimeters. Two men leaped from each vehicle, their rifles held across their chests. They closed on the trucks.

Thirty feet away a North Haakovian gunner who'd been steadily firing from concealment suddenly jerked out into the open, both hands pressed to his bleeding face. Before he could take more than a couple stumbling steps, his head came apart in his hands and his corpse slumped to the ground. The Fox sniper unit was still making its presence felt.

Bolan grabbed the metal railing of the nearest tractor rig and pulled himself inside. He fell into the seat behind the steering wheel, tossed the Mossberg into the passenger seat and unsheathed the Cold Steel Tanto. The blade flickered in the moonlight, then sliced neatly through the plastic coating the ignition wires. The warrior pressed them together, ignoring the brief unpleasant sensation of being shocked as sparks flared out.

The diesel engine turned over. He pressed the accelerator a couple times and it caught, rumbling like an angry lion deep within the bowels of a cave.

Hands appeared on the passenger-side door, pulling a North Haakovian soldier's head level with the window as Bolan shoved the stick into first gear and let out the clutch. Before the enemy soldier could move, the Executioner drew the Beretta, knowing the detonation of the .44 inside the enclosed space might have ruptured his eardrums, and placed a round between the wide, staring eyes. The dead man dropped away as the truck jerked into motion.

Cutting the wheels hard left, Bolan shifted again, gaining speed to make the attempt on the incline. At least two bullets smashed through the windshield on the passenger side and showered glass over the seat. He switched on the lights and caught the North Haakovian gunner in the high-intensity beams. Seconds later the big rig ran over the man.

Checking out the rest of the site, Bolan saw that other trucks were underway now, headed in the same general direction that he was. Only three of them seemed to be losses so far. They sat alone, wreathed in flames, black smoke washing from their melting tires.

The truck had some trouble negotiating the snow-covered incline, sliding haphazardly for a moment. Then he downshifted, let the weight settle to dig the wheels into the mud and accelerated again. It crept up the hill, crested the ridge and kept going.

When Bolan glanced in both side mirrors, he saw the fuel trucks come scrambling up out of the valley. He punched the transmit button on the headset. "Stone Hammer Leader to Designated Driver One. Over."

"Go, Stone Hammer Leader."

"How's your unit, One?"

"Intact, sir." The man's voice sounded jubilant. "Hell, just look at those trucks, sir, and tell me what you think."

"One," Bolan said as he shifted gears again, "it looks like we've got a regular convoy."

"Yes, sir. Clear."

Somebody cut loose with a rebel yell that echoed over the frequency. Then air horns were blaring, blasting sound out over the battlefield.

For good measure, Bolan reached up and tugged his own. Then he put his foot down harder on the pedal. They'd enjoyed a success, but there were still a lot of miles to go before they were clear.

WORKING THE STICK of the AH-64 Apache attack chopper, Jack Grimaldi cut a low profile across the rolling forest north of the valley where the South Haakovian ground forces were enmeshed with the North Haakovian army. He kept his head swiveling, having to work to keep his peripheral vision operational through the night-vision goggles.

Besides the fuel dump, Kurtzman's satellite eyes had discovered three sentry squads of tanks. The armor was stacked in conventional three-bys with a leader and two wings. The Soviet T-55s were armed with 100 mm main guns capable of lobbing rounds out to a range of over a thousand yards. Built for the uneven terrain and able to travel at roughly thirty miles an hour, the tanks would pose a threat to the fleeing fuel trucks before they were able to gain a main road headed for the South Haakovian rendezvous points.

Grimaldi and his team were there to neutralize that threat. By the time other tank teams mobilized to take up pursuit, the trucks would have enough of a head start to only have to worry about North Haakovian aircraft and guards stationed along the roadway.

He hit the radio. "G-Force to Nighthawks. We're coming up on the target areas now. Look alive, ladies. We're playing for keeps, and we're playing on the heartbeat. Over."

The Nighthawks reported in quickly signifying each pilot's readiness.

There were six Apaches in the group, two assigned to each tank squad. Equipped with the heavy Hellfire missiles, Bolan and Grimaldi both figured they had enough firepower for overkill on that leg of Fast Break.

"G-Force, this is Spotter One. Over." The Spotter team was three OH-58 Kiowa scout helicopters assigned to pinpoint the tanks with laser beams the Hellfire missiles would follow to their targets.

"Go, Spotter One."

"I have lock, sir. Fire at will."

"Roger, One." Grimaldi brought the Apache to hover mode above a thick copse of trees. Somewhere on the other side of them was his group of tanks. "Spotter Two, Three?"

"This is Two. Lock achieved."

"Three here, sir. We have lock."

Grimaldi armed the Hellfire missiles and punched up the laser guidance systems. "Fire." He thumbed the release button, emptying a whole pod of four Hellfires from the stubby wing to his left.

A moment later the dark horizon was briefly lighted by explosions.

"Spotter teams, report," Grimaldi said.

"Spotter One, your target is downed."

"Spotter Two, same-same, guys."

"Spotter Three, your target has been destroyed. Over."

Grimaldi moved the stick, pulling the helicopter into a forward ascension that took it over his target area. Less than a minute later he was over the smoldering remains of three T-55s. Satisfied, he hit the transmit button. "Spotter teams, you're freed to search for new targets. Keep within the perimeters we established. Over."

They radioed back their acknowledgments.

"G-Force to Buster group. Over."

"Go, G-Force, you have Buster Leader."

"Proceed to second phase of your missions, Buster Leader. You have the green."

"Acknowledged. Buster Leader, clear."

Knowing where to look because he'd laid in the flight path, Grimaldi watched the F-111F fighter bombers descend from the black heavens and start dropping their bombs. The payloads were 500-pound cluster bombs filled with trackbuster mines. Two of those bombs could cover an area of a thousand yards by one hundred yards. Each of the four F-111Fs carried twelve bombs, and their instructions were to create an overlapping half-moon ahead of the valley where the fuel supply trucks had been. It wouldn't completely halt the North Haakovian armor and ground forces, but it would give them pause.

The cluster bombs exploded in rapid succession as they struck the ground.

"Stone Hammer Leader, this is Tracker Prime. Over."

"Go, Tracker Prime, this is Stone Hammer Leader."

Through the headset, Grimaldi could hear Bolan's voice muffled inside the truck's cab, and the echo of air horns.

Tracker Prime was the satellite relay based in Larsborg that was overseeing Operation Fast Break. "Our screens show a squadron of planes approaching from Sturegorsk airfields."

"Acknowledged, Tracker Prime. Stone Hammer Leader to G-Force. Over."

Grimaldi keyed the mike. "Roger, Stone Hammer Leader."

"Can you assist?"

"On my way buddy. G-Force, out."

"OH, BLOODY HELL, mate, what have you let yourself in for?" McCarter grimly hung on to the Spectre's controls. The transport plane was already starting to feel sluggish, going from sleek aircraft to a balloon. He flicked through the rudder and ailerons. Everything was mushy but operable.

He glanced out the cockpit and saw the remaining MiG go speeding by, unable to keep the slow pace the AC-130-H held. McCarter had knocked the other North Haakovian fighter from the sky, but now the cannon and the howitzer were empty. The only things left were the machine guns with perhaps five hundred rounds between them, and to use them effectively he'd need more control over his plane.

He monitored the ground, saw the blazing pyre where Striker and his forces had removed the fuel trucks from the valley. South of that were the lines of rolling metal navigating toward the highway Fast Break was using to get back home. There wasn't anyplace to put down the transport ship safely.

Releasing a pent-up breath, McCarter started to reconsider his decision to keep the plane afloat as a diversion that would allow the rest of the Phoenix Force to make a safe landing. He hadn't exactly planned on stepping from the frying pan into the fire.

The MiG flipped over and looped back toward the Spectre, coming in at an angle for the nose of the transport plane.

McCarter knew then that the enemy pilot was aware that the Spectre's big guns were no longer working. He slid his thumb over the firing button for the machine guns.

"Come on, you old cow," he said to the plane as he fought with the controls to keep it level.

Tracer fire streaked out from the MiG's wings, hammered into the side of the transport plane, then blew patches of Plexiglas from the cockpit.

McCarter returned fire instinctively, held his thumb down and heard the machine guns blow dry. He knew he'd never touched the fighter jet with any of the rounds.

Cold air rushed in through the jagged rips in the Plexiglas. A glance at the instruments showed the Briton that a number of them had been smashed by the flying bullets. Any landing he made would have to be made by gut instinct. He searched to the west and saw the thin ribbon of highway that the truck convoy was heading for. He nosed the plane down, settling into a glide path that would take him to the road.

He didn't need radar to tell him that the pursuing MiG was already breathing hard on his backtrail again. He could feel it.

Radio static burst in his ear, then he heard Striker's voice. "G-Force, this is Stone Hammer Leader. Over."

"Go," Grimaldi radioed back.

"I've got a heavy armored roadblock ahead. Can you or your team do anything about it? I don't want to lose any of the Hummers or the buggies if I can help it because we're going to need as many of them as we can get to dispense the fuel supplies."

McCarter scanned the highway, saw the cluster of tanks sitting in the middle of the road. He grabbed the mike. "Stone Hammer Leader, this is Phoenix Two. Over."

"Go, Phoenix Two."

"Let me take a run at that roadblock for you, mate. If G-Force or his boys take them out, you're going to lose a lot of that road surface."

"Have you got a better idea?"

McCarter grinned thinly. "Don't know that it's any better, but it's surely something different."

"Get it done. Stone Hammer Leader out."

Moving the yoke, listening to the MiG hammer a metallic tattoo on the rear of the Spectre, McCarter angled for a straight approach to the roadblock. He left the landing gear up, set the autopilot for the degree of descent and fisted the straps of his equipment bag. With the degree of descent, knowing the time for this dicey little maneuver was cut thin to begin with, the Briton ran for the side door. He hastily pulled on a parachute, negotiated the door locks and shoved it open. The wind screamed at him and ra-

zored tears from his eyes before he slid down his goggles
to protect them.

Throwing his equipment bag over his shoulder, he
launched himself into the sky like a swimmer leaping from
the high dive. His altimeter showed him that he was at two
thousand feet. He pulled the rip cord immediately, heard
the crack of silk above his head as the parachute belled out.
He was yanked upward, felt the heavy kick of the equipment bag as it twirled and tried to resist the drag of the
chute.

He moved the parachute, searched the sky, found and
tracked the AC-130-H as it plummeted earthward.

The MiG was pursuing it with tongues of orange tracer
fire. Smoke was streaming out from the inside starboard
engine.

With the low, flat angle McCarter had programmed into
the autopilot, the fifty feet or so that it hit in front of
where he'd planned didn't really matter. With the landing
gear up, the big plane thudded into the highway and threw
a wave of sparks before it as it skidded toward the line of
tanks.

The men standing in a hard line in front of the armored
vehicles scattered as soon as they realized the transport
plane was coming at them.

It wasn't going to hit exactly true, McCarter realized.
Already the nose was listing to the left, bringing the plane
about in a broadside that would spread out the impact. But
as a sliding fifty-ton wall coming in at considerable speed,
that spread wouldn't matter much.

The Spectre hit the tanks like a broom taking out a dust
bunny, scattered the three T-55s and wrapped them in an
explosion a moment later.

Debris came flying up faster than McCarter would have
believed. Jagged shards of metal punched holes in his

chute. Then something hot and hard struck his head and everything went black.

"GO THROUGH!" Bolan yelled to his driver.

"Yes, sir," Larkin responded, then put his foot on the accelerator and aimed the assault buggy at the flaming hole left between the debris of the tanks and the big airplane.

The Executioner reached into the back of the vehicle and freed up the M-16/M-203. He dropped an ammo bandolier for the grenade launcher over his shoulder and fed a 40 mm round into the M-203.

Flames reached out for the buggy almost close enough to touch as it went roaring through the carnage left by the tanks and the AC-130-H.

Bolan keyed the transmit button on the headset. "Stone Hammer Leader to Designated Driver One. Over."

"You've got One."

"Bring your people through," Bolan said. "Don't stop for anything."

"Understood, sir. One, clear."

Bolan pointed at the outskirts of the fiery perimeter. "Pull it over there."

"Yes, sir." Larkin cut the wheel.

Clambering out of the buggy, Bolan surveyed the wreckage. There were no doubts in his mind that there were some survivors. He thumbed the transmit button. "Fox Unit, this is Stone Hammer Leader. Over."

"Go."

"Secure the outer perimeters. I want teams searching through the debris for any stragglers who might attempt to stop the convoy, and I want teams posted with the Stinger missile launchers to take out any North Haakovian aircraft that might show an interest in us. Clear."

Bolan ran, kept the M-16/M-203 across his chest in both hands. He stayed low, searching the dancing shadows for his prey, aware that some of the rounds inside the tanks could start to go off.

"Stone Hammer Leader, this is Fox Four. Be advised that we have unfriendlies in the area in jeeps. Over."

"Roger, Four." Bolan barely heard the gunning engine over the whoosh and crackle of the flames. The jeep that came around the corner of an overturned tank bore North Haakovian military markings and had three soldiers inside. One of them sat behind the mounted .50-cal on the rear deck.

Bringing the rifle to his shoulder, the Executioner squeezed the trigger of the grenade launcher. The 40 mm warhead jumped from the mouth of the M-203 and impacted just above the left front tire. The explosion turned the jeep turtle, set it spinning on the roll bar until the windshield dug into the ground enough to bring it to a stop.

A soldier came up out of the jeep with his AK-47 blazing. Bolan fired a burst of 5.56 mm tumblers that zipped the guy from hip to clavicle. The soldier stumbled and sat down sightlessly against the jeep. After a brief inspection, the warrior found out the other two men hadn't made it.

Another soldier burst from hiding behind the broken fuselage of the Spectre.

Bolan wheeled around and cut the man's legs out from under him with a sustained burst, then finished him off with a single round to the temple. He put a fresh magazine into the M-16, fed another grenade to the launcher, then keyed the headset. "Stone Hammer Leader to G-Force. Over."

"Go, Stone Hammer Leader."

"You've got cleanup at the fuel site."

"Roger," Grimaldi replied, "and I've got myself pegged for taking care of that other loose end. Over."

Bolan knew the pilot was talking about the communications outpost the Special Forces team had taken over earlier that morning. "Get it done and get home, buddy. Clear."

Less than three minutes later, the last of the trucks had blown by the fiery debris left from the collision. The Hummers were running fore and rear guard. Overhead an assortment of Apaches, A-10 Warthogs and F-111Fs formed a layered phalanx of aerial coverage for the departing convoy.

"Phoenix One to Stone Hammer Leader." Katz sounded tired and a little anxious.

"Go, Phoenix One." Bolan exchanged hand signals with the Fox unit commandos and found out the area was now clear of North Haakovian troops.

"Have you heard from Phoenix Two?"

"Not since he ditched the plane."

"Excuse me, sir, this is Fox Eight. I saw your man hit the silk. He was coming down close to the collision area when I saw him, on the southwest side. After that I lost him."

"Acknowledged, Eight. I want you men to mount up and let's get him found. Nobody gets left behind in this operation. Clear." Bolan trotted back to his assault buggy and gave Larkin directions.

The ten vehicles crawled over the snow-covered terrain looking like praying mantises with head beams. It took Bolan five minutes before he found McCarter buried under the loose folds of the white parachute, almost blending in with the snow.

Bolan pushed himself out of the buggy and sprinted across the intervening distance. A sheen of blood covered the Briton's forehead and face. The Executioner threw himself down beside McCarter and searched for injuries.

Other than the long, jagged cut on the left side of McCarter's face, there didn't seem to be any other damage—at least not on the outside. Bolan was grimly aware that the gutsy pilot's brains might be torn up. He put a hand against the Briton's neck and found a pulse that was good and strong.

A jeep bearing Finnish military insignia came to a rocking stop near the Executioner, covering him and McCarter with the headlights.

"David?" Katz asked as he unfolded himself from the passenger seat. His face was set in grim lines.

Bolan recognized the pain in the Phoenix commander's eyes. Katz and his team had already experienced the loss of one member. And the Excutioner was no stranger to losing good friends and comrades himself. "He's alive," the warrior said. "Pulse feels good."

McCarter stirred in Bolan's arms. "Like they say, mate, any landing you can walk away from ..."

Manning came forward, slinging his rifle over his shoulder. "Yeah, walk, it looks like you're going to be carried away from this one." He stooped and picked up McCarter, then turned to face Bolan. "He's out again. We'll take care of him from here on."

Bolan nodded. The Phoenix members were a close-knit unit and he respected that.

"Put him up here." Calvin James, the group's medic, was already preparing a field dressing.

"How soon can you move him?"

"Five minutes," James answered.

"You might not have five minutes," Bolan pointed out. "You can safely figure there's an armada of North Haakovian aircraft headed this way. I can't spread the withdrawal too thin."

"We understand," Katz said, "but we're going to take our five minutes. Go on ahead. We'll catch up."

Bolan looked at the Phoenix commander. "I'm counting on you to lead the pincer movement."

"I'll be there."

The Executioner nodded. "Take care of your man. I'll see you when I see you."

"Soon," Katz promised.

James was already applying the dressing.

Bolan turned on his heel, assigned Fox Nine and Ten to run flanker for Phoenix and levered himself back into the assault buggy. "Step on it, Corporal," he said to Larkin. "We're supposed to be leading this action, and all I see are taillights."

"Yes, sir." The assault buggy's tires spun for an instant, then found traction, sending them bouncing up onto the highway.

At the fuel storage site, Grimaldi's air forces were dumping bombs over the trucks that hadn't made it out or that Fast Break didn't have drivers for. It would create some confusion for later troops trying to ascertain everything that had happened and how much fuel had actually been taken.

Reaching outside the assault buggy, Bolan flipped the small flagpole with a forefinger. Springing back from the tension, the flexible rod shot free of its moorings and locked into position standing straight up. A small replica of the South Haakovian flag fluttered in the slipstream.

Bolan watched it wave, then glanced at the fuel trucks as Larkin increased speed and caught up to them. They'd risked a lot in this night's raid, but once they made it back, they'd have a chance. And that, he knew, was all a professional fighting man could ask of any situation.

CHAPTER TWELVE

Carl Lyons took up a position at the side of the apartment door opposite J. D. Ethan. The L.A. vice cop slid a Delta Elite 10 mm from his fanny pack and pressed his back against the wall. Lyons's own Colt Government Model .45 was in his hands.

Weak single-fixture bulbs ran the length of the narrow apartment breezeway. Only half of them were working. Television noises and canned laugh tracks echoed the length of the building. Occasionally real human voices would rise above the music and television programs.

Schwarz and Blancanales were posted at either end of the hallway to keep bystanders out of the way.

"Ready?" Ethan asked.

"Oh, yeah," Lyons replied.

Ethan grinned. "You look like a guy used to going through doors."

"I watch a lot of cop movies."

"Me, too. Doesn't make it any easier. My kids like those horror movies, the ones where the victims obligingly go into those rooms so the latest demented crazy can chop them up into fish flakes. I want to yell at the assholes, tell them not to go into that damn room. That's how I feel every time I have to go up against a door."

"And here you are."

"And here I am."

Despite the tension of the moment and his uncertainty concerning Able Team's impromptu liaison, Lyons couldn't help but smile. Hell, he even liked the guy. He held up a fist. "On three," he said. "You want odd or even?"

"Odd."

Lyons shook his fist in time with Ethan's, then stuck out three fingers.

Ethan produced two of his own, bringing the total to five. "You got the door big guy."

Nodding, the Able Team leader stepped away from the wall, held the .45 in both hands and cocked his leg.

"Jefferies will have a lot of locks on that door," Ethan said. "You kick it in, you're going to have to kick like you're the Jolly Green Giant."

"I hear you."

"You going high or low?" Ethan asked.

"Low," Lyons replied.

"I got your back."

"I'll hold you to that. You ready?"

"No, but let's do it anyway."

Lyons drove his foot into the door just above the lock. Wood splintered, but the door remained solid. Excited voices sounded on the other side. Going back with the rebound, Lyons took a running start at the door and slammed his shoulder into it with bruising force.

Metal shrieked as wood cracked and gave way.

Going with the flow of his motion, Lyons sprawled inside the room, groaning loudly as he fell on his stomach with his hands in front of him tracking the Colt Government Model onto his first target.

A guy built like a post in a rail fence tried to push his glasses up on his face while he pointed a large-caliber wheelgun at the door.

Lyons triggered the .45, putting two hollowpoint rounds into the gunner's chest. The guy staggered back and fell over the couch, his revolver falling from nerveless fingers.

A woman dropped the razor blade she'd been using to cut out lines of coke on a flat mirror lying on a coffee table in front of the couch, covered her face with her hands and started to scream.

Ethan's 10 mm pistol banged loudly, and the bullet spun another armed man out of the chair he'd been sitting in near the balcony window. "Police!" the vice cop yelled. "Everybody chill!"

"Oh *shit,*" a man sitting on the couch yelled. He was heavyset and dressed in overalls, and a flannel shirt with the sleeves hacked off. He raised his hands and exposed hairy armpits.

A fourth man tried for a pistol tucked under the cushion of the recliner.

Firing from a one-handed push-up position, Lyons put a round through the man's shoulder and knocked him back in the chair. "The next one," the Able Team warrior warned, "kills."

Pain etched the man's face as he clapped a meaty hand over the wound.

Lyons got to his feet. "I got the kitchen."

"It's yours," Ethan said as he fished a pair of handcuffs from his fanny pack. "All right scum and scumettes, down on your faces. You know the drill. Most of you learned it back in kindergarten."

Lyons moved through the kitchen, hallway, both bedrooms and the bathroom without encountering anyone else. By the time he got back to the living room, Ethan had handcuffed everybody and left them lying on their stomachs.

"Look at this," the vice cop said. "Wall-to-wall scum. Now *this* is entertainment." His grin was feral and held no humor.

"Hey, man, I'm bleeding to death over here," the wounded man said.

Ethan ripped two hand-sized sections from the man's shirttails, put his knee in the man's back, then plugged the entry and exit wounds. The man yelled the whole time before he slumped into unconsciousness.

"Hey," the fat man in the coveralls complained, "you can't do that."

Ethan whirled on the man, deliberately stepping on the man's bent elbow, then hunkered down and tapped the guy's nose with the muzzle of the Delta Elite. "Don't try to tell me what I can and can't do, fat boy. Right now I own your ugly ass."

The big man's eyes got round as silver dollars.

Lyons saw the anger burning bright in Ethan's gaze, and wondered for a moment if he was going to have to step in to prevent anything worse from happening.

Then Ethan got visible control of himself and backed off. He used the barrel of the Delta Elite to push himself up. "The rest of the apartment?"

"Clean," Lyons said.

Blancanales and Schwarz guarded the front door of the apartment, keeping the dozen spectators at bay by brandishing their weapons without being directly menacing.

"Get up, Jefferies," Ethan ordered, nudging the fat man with his foot.

"I got nothing to say to you, cop." Jefferies spit, but it landed on the carpet inches away from Ethan's foot.

"You got plenty to say, you countrified turd," Ethan said. "What you don't have is a lot of time to say it." He reached down and yanked the big man to his feet, using the cuff chain.

Jefferies yelped in pain but got to his feet.

Pushing in behind the man, Ethan rested the barrel of his pistol between his shoulder blades and shoved him into the kitchen.

Lyons caught Blancanales's eye and nodded toward the people handcuffed on the floor. Then the big ex-cop stepped into the kitchen, not knowing what to expect.

"Meet Ronald Jefferies," Ethan said as he herded his captive toward the stove. Pots and pans cluttered the burners, smelling like they'd been there more than a couple days. "One of L.A.'s lower life-forms. Newton and Markham back at the morgue were two of his clients. They sold for Jefferies to support their own habits. Isn't that right, lardass?"

"I don't know what you're talking about."

Ethan cuffed the back of the man's head with his open palm. "If I want any shit out of you, I'll squeeze your head." He opened the oven door and switched it on.

The smell of natural gas filtered into the room.

"What I do want out of you," Ethan said, "is the name of the guy you buy your dope from."

"Man, I got my rights. You can't violate my rights."

"Human beings have rights," Ethan corrected. "You're pond scum. Pond scum doesn't have any rights. It rates somewhere on the evolutionary scale just above a cow pie."

"I want my lawyer."

"And I want that name, asshole. One of us is going to leave this room happy, one way or another. I've been watching you for weeks. Whoever's supplying you is slick. I've seen drops, I've seen exchanges, but I don't know where the main source is. I want to know that in the next sixty seconds."

"Screw you, Ethan, you can't do this to me."

"You stupid son of a bitch." The vice cop yanked the man around to face him. "They got a new disease running rampant in the streets, and most of the dead people turning up are men and women with a jones for your product. Are you getting the two-plus-two thing here, or am I going to have to slow down for you?"

"Bullshit." But Jefferies no longer looked convinced.

Ethan jerked a thumb toward Lyons. "This guy's from the disease control board in Atlanta."

Jefferies shook his head doubtfully. "He's a cop. I smelled it on him as soon as he came through the door."

Without looking, Ethan said, "Show this backwoods bozo your ID."

Lyons took the fake ID from his shirt pocket and gave it a workout. He had to hold it longer than he figured because Jefferies's lips moved silently while the guy worked through it.

"There's bad product out there, man," Ethan said with passion, "and you're helping move it."

"Not me. I don't know anything about no bad dope."

"They wouldn't tell you," Ethan pointed out. "How the hell would you sell nickel and dime bags, knowing the customers you sold them to weren't going to be back next week for more of the same? Hell, it'd fuck up your financial portfolio. And besides that, you could already be infected yourself. Is that dope in there on the table old stuff, or some of the new?"

Lyons could tell from the blanched features and the nervous tic of Jefferies's right eye that the cocaine was new.

"Give me a name," Ethan demanded.

"Get me a lawyer."

Without warning, Ethan slammed a fist into the big man's stomach and doubled him over. While he was bent over, the vice cop shoved his head into the oven. The smell of gas was intense. "Give me the name."

Jefferies struggled to pull his head out of the oven but didn't have the necessary leverage. "Hey, I'm gonna choke in here."

"Give me the name," Ethan said, "or I'm going to kick your fat ass in after you."

Grunting in fear, Jefferies tried to shove himself out of the oven.

Ethan stuck the Delta Elite in beside the fat man's head, screwing it into his ear. "You want to guess what's going to happen if I slip and accidentally pull the trigger with all that gas trapped in there?"

Jefferies quieted.

"Yeah. I'd get my hand burned some, but that stove will probably blow your head right through your asshole. Now give me a name and address."

"Vasquez," Jefferies said in a strained voice. He coughed, sounding as if he were going to hack up a lung. "Rudy Vasquez."

"I know him," Ethan said. "The vice squad's been busting their humps to get some dirt on him."

"I can give you the place he deals."

"So give it."

"The Springer Apartments over in Watts."

Lyons could tell from the expression on Ethan's face that the address meant something to the vice cop.

"What apartment?" Ethan asked.

"No apartment." Jefferies went through another bout of coughing. Ethan eased him out of the oven a little, reached up and turned the gas off. "Vasquez runs the whole damn apartment complex."

Without another word, Ethan herded Jefferies back into the living room, then put him down on the floor. He returned to the kitchen and opened the window to let the gas out. "We've been working on the Springer Apartments for two months, following up on a lot of unsubstantiated rumors. Got three people inside—damn good cops, all of them—and they all turned up dead. We thought the management might be involved, but we never figured on everybody in there being part of this."

"Money," Lyons said, "can buy a lot these days." He led the way back into the living room and out into the breezeway.

"We got company," Schwarz announced.

Looking at the stairway that led up into the breezeway, Lyons saw the first of the uniforms cresting the ridge of the stairs.

Ethan stepped forward and palmed his shield. "J. D. Ethan. Vice."

The uniforms proceeded carefully in spite of the introduction, their hands keeping their weapons at the ready. "Ethan, huh?" a grizzled man wearing sergeant's stripes asked.

"Yeah."

"I got orders to take you downtown. Your captain wants to see you. Now. I'll take your weapon."

Ethan shook his head. "You'll take my weapon after you kick my ass, maybe." He didn't move.

"Back off, Johnson," another sergeant said as he approached.

Johnson scowled and went to join the other men just beginning to circulate within the apartment. Inside Jefferies was already yelling about having his rights violated.

"Hey, Garrison," Ethan said with a crooked smile.

Lyons saw the tension in the uniformed sergeant and realized that Ethan wasn't happy about dealing with the man.

"You're gonna have to go down to the Hall of Justice, buddy," Garrison said. "Captain's orders."

"I got other things to do."

"Not anymore. Keller's about ready to pull the plug on you and tank you." There was no backup in the older cop. "You crossed the line, buddy. You need to see what you can salvage of your career. You got two choices—you can walk with me, or walk over me. What's it gonna be?"

"Ah, batshit. Do you want my piece, too?"

"Hell, no," Garrison replied with a grin. "Took me all these years to learn how to carry my own. Let's just go downtown together."

Lyons turned to his companions. "You guys cover this. I'm going with them. I want to see how deep Ethan's got himself in this mess. If I have a choice, I want to put my money on him to get us to the root of this."

"Sure," Blancanales said. "Just make sure whatever edge he's standing on, that he doesn't get the chance to pull you in after him."

Lyons nodded. Whatever Ethan's plight was, it registered a lot of old memories from when Lyons had been working the LAPD himself. He just hoped the guy was salvageable. He knew from experience that a vice guy who knew his way around the streets and still worked the job with a vengeance was worth his weight in gold. Ethan seemed to know a lot about Vasquez, but at the moment Lyons didn't know if that was a good thing or not.

"THAT WAS a very brave thing you did back there, Madam President, but it was also very foolish."

Janyte Varkaus kept herself from trembling with effort. They were in the quarters Stensvik had assigned for her shortly after she'd arrived. There were two rooms, the living room they were in now, and the bedroom to her right. She tried to keep her mind off the darkened doorway, but Stensvik glanced at it frequently. With each glance it was harder to repress the shudders that filled her. She'd changed from the chiffon dress into jeans and a loose blouse that concealed the curves of her body.

The North Haakovian dictator was close to being drunk. A dulled sheen had pooled across his eyes, and his shirt collar was pulled open, leaving his tie waving at half-mast. He carried a glass and a whiskey bottle with him as he paced the floor in front of her.

"Would you have killed me if you were able?" he asked.

"Yes."

Stensvik appeared to consider that, as if her reply had been more honest than he'd anticipated. "Have you ever killed a man before?"

"No."

Pouring himself a fresh drink, slopping it over the top to splash stains on the light gray carpet, Stensvik asked, "Have you ever thought about it before?"

"No."

"But you were prepared to shoot me?"

Janyte didn't say anything. She'd already answered that question. She sat in the room's plush recliner and switched her gaze to the darkened screen of the television set across the room.

The room was furnished elegantly. Expensive paintings complemented the overstuffed furniture and the thick carpet. But it was a gilded prison cell.

The painful throbbing in her mouth reminded her of that. When she'd checked in the bathroom mirror earlier, she'd seen that the dark stain of bruises were already creeping under her skin.

Stensvik sprawled on the couch, balancing his whiskey bottle on his knee as if afraid to release it. Janyte could smell the alcohol on his breath even across the room. "Have you asked yourself," he asked, "why you were prepared to kill me?"

"Because you don't deserve to live."

For a moment the dark glower that suffused Stensvik's features made her think she'd pushed him over his emotional edge. Then he laughed. "Would you have been killing me for your husband, or for the people of South Haakovia, Madam President?"

Janyte gave him a hard stare.

"Perhaps you don't even know yourself." Stensvik thumped his bottle and glass down on the low table in front of him. "You didn't love your husband," he said in a low voice. He studied her for a reaction.

She kept her face placid, didn't reveal the hurt his words had caused. Guilt and fear cycled within her like a raging fever.

"Remember," Stensvik said, "I had spies within the presidential castle. I heard many stories of the pretty young president's wife who went to bed several nights alone because her husband was more interested in his politics than in her sexuality." He paused. "It must have made for some long, painfully lonely nights." He reached out and drained his glass, slipped the tie from around his neck and toyed with it in his hands. "I've known several young women throughout my years. Known their love and their needs, seen how they could be filled with burning desire and not even know what to call it."

Janyte made her voice cold when she addressed him. "If you were a gentleman, General, you would recognize that you are drunk now, and you would graciously take your leave.''

"But I'm not a gentleman," Stensvik said as he got to his feet. "Nor am I so drunk that I don't notice your charms." He walked over to her chair and came to a stop, towering over her.

Janyte barely kept herself from flinching at his approach. Her heart hammered in her rib cage.

"I am more man than your husband ever thought about being," Stensvik said. "I've seen nights when I brought several women to full satisfaction. And I can see your need now, even if you can't."

"You're inventing something that isn't there."

"Am I? I don't think so." Before Janyte could move, he slipped the open noose of the tie over one of her wrists, quickly captured the other one and bound it with the first.

Janyte screamed in rage and fear, and kicked out at him with both her feet.

Stensvik effortlessly swept her feet aside with one arm, laughing at her as he yanked the tie. The sudden pressure bruised her wrists and pulled her from the chair. She landed hard against the carpet and tried to roll away from him, but he threw a leg on either side of her body and fell on top of her.

"Get off me, you son of a bitch!" Janyte screamed. She didn't know if her voice would carry past the door, but there were only Stensvik's guards waiting on the other side anyway. There was no one who could save her, and that thought had never really struck home until she could feel his maleness hard against her leg. She tried to strike him with her fists, but he pulled the tie and kept her arms pinned above her head. When she moved one of her legs to knee him, it only allowed him to slip a leg in between hers and compromise her defenses.

"Fight me, Madam President," Stensvik said in a low voice that was clearly intended to be seductive. "Fight me as hard as you can. It will only make the passion inside me stronger."

Struggling with her own fears, Janyte made herself go rigid and closed her eyes against Stensvik's face. She tried to retreat within herself, draw down into that core of existence that didn't allow for other things to intrude on her own thoughts. She failed.

Stensvik's breath was hot on her cheek. He ran a rough, callused hand across her blouse, groping painfully. Shifting his body, he forced himself into a more natural position. He kissed her neck.

Feeling nauseous, Janyte opened her eyes and spit on him.

He backhanded her, a painful blow that sent shooting stars rocketing inside her skull.

Half-blinded by tears, she looked up and found him glaring down at her as he wiped the spittle from his cheek.

"Stupid bitch. You and I, we could unite these two countries without all the bloodshed. A marriage of convenience, something symbolic that would take away the need to fight."

"The only thing it would symbolize," Janyte said in a breaking voice, "is the rape of South Haakovia by you and the Communist forces gathered here. You might take me, you might take South Haakovia, but none of us are going to make it easy for you." She bucked up against him, trying to dislodge his weight, but failed. He was too heavy and he had her pinned. Still, she didn't give up.

Someone knocked at the door.

"Enter," Stensvik yelled, straightening up but maintaining his kneeling stance over Janyte.

A soldier stepped into the room, saw what was going on and immediately fell into parade rest, his eyes focused on the wall beyond the events transpiring on the floor.

"What is it?" Stensvik demanded. "I told you to not interrupt me."

"There's a top-priority message from Colonel Petrov," the soldier said. "A contingent of South Haakovian forces broke through our lines less than an hour ago and stole several trucks transporting gasoline to be used by our forces."

"What!" Stensvik stood. "Tell Colonel Petrov to get back here immediately on the first helicopter he can find."

"Yes, sir." The soldier about-faced and walked quickly out of the room.

Stensvik made a show of putting his uniform into proper order, then glanced down at Janyte. "I'll be back, Madam President, and you can count on that." He walked away, not bothering to retrieve his tie.

Janyte waited until the door closed and locked, then slowly rolled into a sitting position. She had to use her teeth to pry the knotted tie free of her wrists.

Wrapping her arms around her knees, she let the tears come, crying silently until the fear and frustration she felt had abated and the trembling had mostly passed. On unsteady legs she walked into the bathroom and flipped on the light.

Her reflection in the mirror was wan, her hair disheveled. As always when she was really emotional or stressed, the small scar on her chin was pink. Her cheekbone was showing additional bruising in the shape of Stensvik's fingers that matched the ones that he'd already inflicted on her mouth.

She wiped her tears away as she faced herself and screwed up her resolve. From the very moment when Vaino and Markus had spirited her out of the presidential castle, she knew Stensvik would use her against her people. She was just another pawn in Stensvik's bid for control over the nation, but he would be playing her like she was the queen, thinking her fate could make or break the South Haakovian people.

She couldn't allow that to happen.

Her thoughts drifted briefly to the big American colonel, Rance Pollock. Then she shook her head. No, her life was in her hands. Despite her willingness to depend on the warrior, she had no one now but herself.

Memory of Stensvik's hands savaging her body stung in her mind, and Janyte made herself pick up the ceramic top from the toilet. Holding it in both hands she smashed the heavy ceramic top against the mirror.

Jagged pieces rained to the tiled floor.

After replacing the toilet lid, she carefully knelt and began sorting through the fragments. The one she liked the most was nearly ten inches long and curved to a point. At the thickest end she was still able to wrap her fingers comfortably around the shard. It wouldn't last, she knew, but it might be enough to make a difference.

She walked back to the living room, hid the shard under one of the couch cushions and sat to await Stensvik's return. While dreading the feel of his hands on her body again, she prayed that the man didn't stay away too long.

CHAPTER THIRTEEN

The Inge River looked black and insubstantial against the foothills of the Sergiusz Mountains. Larkin halted the assault buggy on the north side of the river at Bolan's command. Vaulting out of the vehicle, the Executioner immediately started coordinating the deployment of the fuel tankers as they came to stops with hisses from air brakes.

"Stone Hammer Leader to Horatio group. Over." The big warrior surveyed the south bank and saw the blocky outlines of the M-928 long-bed military trucks.

"Go, Stone Hammer Leader." Lance Corporal Eddie Wilson was a young soldier Bolan had rescued from the motor pool in the Larsborg military base. Despite the assignment, he had a can-do attitude, and the Executioner had recruited him for Fast Break for that reason.

"Head 'em up and move 'em out. Clear."

The diesel engines of the five-ton trucks caught with a roar of power that echoed along the riverbank. The first one pulled out, followed quickly by the others as they formed a single line. As they came out into the light of the approaching dawn, the metal plates mounted across the cabs and beds glinted bright steely reflections. The steel plates and the wooden beams had been transported from Larsborg via transport choppers, put together by Wilson's engineering crews.

Bolan hit the transmit button on the headset again. "Phoenix One? Over."

"Go, Stone Hammer Leader."

"How is Phoenix Two?"

"He has a headache and a sour disposition, but is otherwise intact. However, the headache is the only thing out of the ordinary."

Bolan grinned. They were soldiers, and they fought hard when the time came to put it all on the line, but they found times for play as well. Even Katzenelenbogen, as serious as the Israeli was, had to make time for that. "Understood, One. Per our conversations, your group is going across first. You have two hours, sixteen minutes to set up your crossing."

"We'll be there," Katz replied.

"I'm counting on it. Clear." He swung his attention to the line of five-tons, watching them dig into the mud of the riverbank and wade into the water.

The first five-ton went all the way across the river. Once it parked, a group of soldiers debarked and started pulling wooden ramps from the bed. Four trucks stopped in the water, parked nose to bumper. The river continued to flow under and around the stalled vehicles, but broke against the doors and bodies, almost spilling into the cab through the open windows despite the high clearance of the M-928s. The drivers clambered out and swam to either shore to assist with the ramps.

Bolan established contact with Grimaldi. "How far behind is our pursuit? Over."

The ace pilot's voice sounded tight and tense. "We got the armored held up, Sarge. They're barely making it through the field of trackbuster mines we dropped. Taking lots of casualties, and they're pretty confused about what to do next. But you've got a small jeep patrol that's burning up your backtrail. I just spotted them a minute ago and was going to call you. You don't have time to get your people across before they get there.''

"How about our airspace?"

"We're keeping it clean, but they're testing our resistance.''

"Keep your perimeters established, G-Force. You're providing a major smoke screen for Stensvik's intel groups.''

"Roger. But you're going to have to deal with the ground forces."

"We'll get it done. Give me the coordinates.'' After Grimaldi complied, Bolan turned to Larkin, said, "Let's go," and climbed back into the assault buggy. "Horatio, this is Stone Hammer Leader. Over.'' The warrior pointed back in the direction they'd just come.

Larkin nodded and let out the clutch, sending a spray of wet mud slinging out into the river.

The first of the fuel transport trucks was just beginning to creep across the line of five-tons. It looked uncertain and unsteady, but it made the other side reasonably well.

"This is Horatio," Wilson transmitted back.

"You've got the helm," Bolan said. "Get them across and making tracks as soon as possible."

"Yes, sir. Horatio, clear."

The next truck mounted the first wooden ramp, struggled up the incline and started across.

Bolan took out his map case and a penlight. He found the coordinates Grimaldi had given him, then moved from the main area map to another map showing more detail. Less than a minute later he found the spot he was looking for. He refolded the map, gave the driver instructions and settled down to wait the ten minutes it would take to intercept the approaching convoy.

He felt tired and bruised to the soul. He didn't even try to think of how many hours he'd been on the move with no sleep. The fate of a country hinged on the major offensive he'd planned to take place in only a little more than two hours. By midmorning the area would be a bloody no-man's-land.

The warrior turned his attention to the task at hand. Reaching back into the rear deck of the buggy, he opened a gun case and took out a Barrett Model 82 Light Fifty. He gave it a quick but thorough inspection, making sure nothing had jarred loose during the hop back from the fuel-depot raid.

"There," Bolan said.

Larkin cut the assault buggy's wheels and pulled into hiding behind an outcrop of trees.

Retrieving his night glasses from the kit under his seat, Bolan got out of the vehicle and trotted up the steep incline, keeping below the crest of the ridge so he couldn't be skylined. He crawled the last few feet, Larkin at his side.

A bowl-shaped depression was on the other side. The slopes were punctuated occasionally by stubby conifers. The sound of rumbling engines echoed in the trees. The snow had stopped almost forty minutes earlier, leaving a solid white carpet draped over the land.

Headlights drew Bolan's gaze. He targeted them with the binoculars, brought them in close with the high-power lenses.

There were eight vehicles, jeeps, trucks and a half-track, and they were making good time.

Raising the Barrett .50-cal to the crest, Bolan unfolded the bipod and settled into position behind the Leupold MI Ultra 10X telescope. "I figure that at about two miles," he said.

Larkin nodded. "Yes, sir. I'd say that's pretty close."

The warrior changed freqs on the radio, accessing the one used by Mockingbird at Larsborg. "Stone Hammer Leader to Mockingbird. Over."

"Go. You have Mockingbird." Lansdale sounded alert and primed.

"I want a fire strike in this area on my go." Bolan read off the coordinates. "Three Lance missiles on a tight spread, followed by another three. You'll be receiving coordinate adjustments after the first salvo."

"Roger, Stone Hammer Leader. Just give us the green. Mockingbird standing by."

Bolan stripped the headset off and pocketed it as he glanced at Larkin. "You're calling in the coordinate adjustments. I'm going to confuse them as much as possible, keep them in a tight group."

"Yes, sir." Larkin pulled his mouthpiece into position and took up Bolan's binoculars.

The Executioner snugged the big sniper rifle into his shoulder, mentally wedding himself to the scope and the expected recoil, becoming as much a part of the rifle as a machined piece. He blinked and drew the image in as he set the sights for one thousand yards. The rifle was capable of securing kills beyond that distance, but he figured he could get three rounds off before the North Haakovian soldiers heard the report of the first one.

He swung the scope across the military convoy, choosing his targets carefully. The lead jeep was an obvious target, followed by the two two-and-a-half-ton trucks riding in a loose wing formation out from the staggered line of vehicles.

Taking up the trigger slack, the warrior rested the sights over the heart of his first target. "Larkin."

"Yes, sir."

"Tell Mockingbird to fire the first salvo. Your course corrections should follow immediately, then the second salvo."

"Yes, sir." A moment later, Larkin said, "They're away, sir."

Figuring in the Mach 3 speed the Lances were capable of, Bolan counted down the numbers. When he reached his time envelope and the lead jeep hit the one-thousand-yard mark, he squeezed off the first round, moved on to his second target, squeezed and moved on again. Only after he'd fired the third round did he check his marksmanship.

The lead jeep had ground to a stop with a dead man at the helm, his body wrapped loosely over the steering wheel. On the port side, the deuce-and-a-half was still underway, swinging wildly back into the line of vehicles. Metal crunched as it slammed into the half-track and rebounded. The truck on the starboard side rolled to a stop against a snow-covered knoll that jutted up from the tall grass. Soldiers were falling out of the vehicles, racing for cover.

Bolan placed the remaining eight rounds in the clip with precision, seeking out flesh where he could find it, settling for unprotected tires and engine blocks when he couldn't. While he was reaching for the next .50-caliber clip, the Lance missiles fell fifty yards short of their intended targets.

Dirt and snow erupted in a series of explosions that dug gouges in the black earth. Trees blew over, pushed by the cyclonic winds.

Larkin was talking rapidly as the sounds of the explosions died away.

Bolan sighted down the barrel again. Some of the vehicles had been immobilized. The North Haakovian soldiers, realizing they were under fire by more than just a sniper or snipers, were running for the half-track and the operational jeeps. The Executioner swept the field from left to right, putting the bullets into man-shaped targets between the waist and shoulders. He didn't check the results.

A jeep got under way, speeding north in a looping one-eighty that tore up a sizable portion of the ground.

Locked in behind the measured sights, Bolan squeezed the trigger and fired the last two rounds into the driver. Just as it started to career wildly out of control, the second flurry of Lance missiles struck dead on target.

The jeeps and trucks went flying, turned into flaming wreckage. The half-track ended up on its side. Nothing was moving.

"Tell Mockingbird to relay to his people that that was a fine piece of shooting," Bolan said as he got to his feet.

Larkin nodded and did so.

Slipping his own headset back on, the warrior contacted Horatio. He continued watching the hell zone to reaffirm that nothing out there still lived. "Horatio, has everyone gotten across?"

"Yes, sir. We almost lost one truck, but we were able to winch it back on course."

"Fair enough. Head to base. I'll be along shortly."

"Yes, sir. Horatio, clear."

"Phoenix One?"

"Go, Stone Hammer Leader."

"Your people?"

"We're moving now. I'll radio you when we're in place."

"Where's Phoenix Three?"

"With your on-site second-in-command."

"Fine. You people stay hard out there, Phoenix One. We want everyone coming home when we're done here."

"Acknowledged, Stone Hammer Leader. Good hunting. Phoenix One, out."

"LOOK," BARBARA PRICE said sharply as she stood behind her desk and banged her hand on it for emphasis, "I don't give a rat's ass what orders the judge gave you. I need to talk to him. *Now*. In the morning is too goddamn late." Even though she knew the person on the other end of the speakerphone couldn't see her, she knew the effort wasn't wasted. As a secretary for a federal judge in the Justice Department, Mary Shores knew what the sound signified the moment she heard it. At the same time that she knew it created the effect she desired, Price hated having to use it. But attitude counted a lot when dealing with the nearly impossible. And it was nearly impossible to get a federal judge in the middle of the night.

"But Judge Harball specifically requested that he be left alone the next few days," the secretary said. "He's having some personal problems he has to work out."

Price knew through her own grapevine that sixty-one-year-old Judge Harball's personal problems related to a wife who didn't understand his current twenty-three-year-old girlfriend. "I need him tonight," she repeated, "and if I don't get him, you're going to be looking for another cushy job at 9:05 tomorrow morning."

There was some hesitation.

Price knew she'd caught the woman out of her element by calling her at home.

"Let me see if I can reach him," the secretary relented. "He left me a number."

"You've got fifteen minutes," Price said, glancing at her watch. "Either you or he will call me back within that time, or I'll have a D.C. cop banging on your door two minutes later." She hung up without giving the woman a chance to respond.

Walking out of her small office attached to the computer room, she found Aaron Kurtzman at his console watching various windows open on his computer. The radio buzzed for attention. Kurtzman snatched up his headset with one big hand, growled a response, then looked up at Price. "It's Striker."

Price slipped on her headset and plugged into the radio system. "Go, Stony One. You have Stony Base. How are things going there?"

"We've made the first leg of Fast Break, Stony Base," Bolan replied, "but we haven't taken our first shot at Stensvik's military machine yet."

"You have your requisitioned supplies in hand?"

"Yes. Losses were kept to a surprising minimum. Phoenix also touched down and made the hump with us. They're intact. How are things there?"

"Able Team has routed out one of the bacteriological weapons Stensvik was able to ferry over here with his Cuban and Colombian cohorts. So far we've got ninety-three dead, and the opportunity for more before the outbreak comes to a close is big."

"Have they shut it down?"

"We're in the process now. What can we do for you, Stony One?" Price could hear the weariness in the big warrior's voice. Most people wouldn't have noticed it, but she shared an intimate relationship with him when the occasion permitted.

"I need Stensvik's intelligence spoofed," Bolan said. "The communciations outpost we took over is still functioning, and will be until the Bear gets through playing with their systems."

"Roger," Kurtzman said. His fingers stroked the keyboard in rapid succession. "Collating the files now, Stony One." He hit a final button. "They're on their way. If this thing works the way it's supposed to, Stensvik and his people will be looking for you where you aren't."

"Have you heard anything about Janyte Varkaus?" Bolan asked.

Price answered, knowing the big man felt responsible for the South Haakovian president's current plight. "No. Chances are he might be waiting until morning there before unveiling her."

"However," Kurtzman added, "we do have a schematic on the presidential buildings in North Haakovia. I'm going to be faxing them to you at the command post."

"Where did you come up with those?" Bolan asked.

Price smiled thinly. "Apparently some of the loyal Communists Stensvik has surrounded himself with have developed a taste for larceny. A CIA section chief who owes me a long list of favors turned up a guy who was bribable. It cost, but we know what the inside of Stensvik's fortress looks like."

"Do you know where Janyte Varkaus is being held?"

"Yeah," Kurtzman said. The flickering cursor suddenly froze on the screen, signifying the program had finished running. "It's marked on the schematics you'll be getting. Apparently there are some retaining cells on the first underground floor. I also think I have a way inside the building for you."

"I'll get back to you if I have any questions."

"Your program's finished, Stony One," Kurtzman said, "and it appears that Stensvik's computers don't know the fake reports from the real ones."

"Thanks for the assist, Stony Base."

Price keyed the headset. "Our pleasure, Stony One. And good luck. Stony Base, out."

"It's in their hands now," Kurtzman said.

"Most of it, yeah," Price replied as she folded her arms across her breasts. "But I'm not about to let up on what we might be able to accomplish from here. If I find a lever, I'm going to use it."

Kurtzman grinned up at her. "I heard you in there with the judge's secretary. I'd say you were more in the mood for hammers. Big hammers."

"Those, too," Price agreed, "but at this point I'll take anything I can get."

"How solid is that lead on the diphtheria bacteria?"

"Solid enough for me. Hughon worked the D.C. streets and turned up the same name Able came up with."

"Is it solid enough for the judge to issue a writ?"

"It will be," Price said. "Do you know what's twenty-three years old and goes jiggle, jiggle in the dark?"

"No."

"Judge Harball does." Price explained about the girlfriend.

"You're going to blackmail a judge to produce a federal writ for Able Team?"

"Not blackmail," Price corrected. "But I'm definitely going to let him know I'm in the position to do some heavy lobbying."

The phone rang, lighting up Price's extension.

"I'm going to take that in my office." She crossed the room and ducked inside her room, picking up the phone receiver in one fluid movement. "Price."

Judge Harball sounded tired and wary. "Yes, Miss Price, I was told that this was some kind of emergency."

Price sat in her chair, content to let the dealing start. "It is," she said, and she opened with her hole card.

GRIMALDI TOUCHED the transmit button on his headset. "Go, Stone Hammer Leader. Over."

"Take down your secondary objective, G-Force," Bolan said. "Electron Rider has slipped the spoof in place."

"Roger," Grimaldi replied. "Give me three minutes here, then it's gone. G-Force, out." He cleared the channel, then switched back to the freq used by the air wing he was commanding that protected the withdrawing South Haakovian forces from the attacking MiGs.

With the night as black as it was, and the snow reflecting the moonlight in awkward places from the ground, the fighting was being conducted solely by instrumentation.

Responding to a threat picked up by the combat computer, Grimaldi rolled right and dived toward the ground. An air-to-air missile jumped through the night, just missing Grimaldi's Apache. He triggered a Hellfire missile in return, watched it cut through the air like a steel shark, then home in on the attacking MiG before it could get away.

A black-and-orange explosion enfolded a white sun, lowering the numbers of the aggressors by one more. So far the South Haakovian air squad had lost only two people, and both of those had landed unharmed. A rescue team from Bolan's attack-buggy unit was already en route to pick them up.

"G-Force to Blackbat Unit Leader," Grimaldi called out.

"Go, you have Blackbat Unit Leader."

"You're the sky marshal, buddy. Take care of 'em till I get back. G-Force, out." Grimaldi peeled away from the mixed bag of attack helicopters and F-15s.

He stayed low to the ground as he took up his new course bearing. His weapons officer stayed alert below him, working his night-vision goggles as much as Grimaldi did. Despite the increased vision during the darkness, wearing the goggles was dangerous because it cut down peripheral vision by forty percent.

"Target coming up," the weapons officer said.

"Got it." Grimaldi moved the stick, gaining altitude briefly to clear a copse of snow-frosted trees.

The communications outpost was much as he'd left it earlier.

"Lock on," Grimaldi instructed.

"It's there," the weapons officer answered.

Turning the nose of the Apache toward the communications outpost, Grimaldi kicked both the wing-mounted rocket launchers into full. Explosions racked the building, tore down the walls and dropped the fractured ceiling inside it. By the time he let up on the trigger, the outpost had been razed to the ground.

"G-Force to Stone Hammer Leader. Over."

"Go," Bolan replied.

"Your target's down."

"Okay. Come on home, G-Force, and let's get the next stage of this in motion. Stone Hammer Leader, out."

Grimaldi lifted the copter and took to the air. When he saw the Sergiusz Mountains in the distance, he couldn't help but wonder if Gary Manning was really going to be up to the task. Even if it worked, breaking the stranglehold the North Haakovian military had on the region was going to be tough.

He blinked his eyes against fatigue and the after-effects generated by exploding rockets, then figured if he managed to grab a cup of coffee and a sandwich before he went back up, he'd be ready to take the war to the enemy for a change. He grinned at the night when he realized he was ready for that change of pace.

PRESIDENT Franzen Stensvik strode into the North Haakovian command center burning with unslaked lust. He was still unsure why he hadn't gone ahead and taken Janyte Varkaus by force. The mere thought of it created a pressure in his crotch that bordered on pain.

Part of it, he knew, was due to the fact that he considered her a special trophy, one he was unwilling to defile before its proper time. And perhaps part of it was simply that he enjoyed holding her on the edge of her fate, knowing she could see what was coming, allowing her little glimpses of hope then snatching them away.

The security people inside the command center came to instant attention. He motioned to one of them.

"Yes, sir?"

"Go wake Niklavs, and tell him to prepare the reporters for an interview."

The soldier nodded and hustled off at double time.

Stensvik walked to the railing, leaned on it and looked down.

Lieutenant-Colonel Pavlo Gerik was on duty watch. He was young and sallow, a nervous man around superior officers even in the best of times.

Stensvik enjoyed seeing the younger man jump when he called him to the carpet for things he had done wrong, real and imagined. The Colonel was the product of Communist military academies, full of book smarts, but had little practical application.

Lifting the phone, Stensvik waited until the duty officer picked up his own receiver, then barked, "Tell me what happened."

"South Haakovian invaders," Gerik said. "They entered the country undetected and surprised our fuel depot at Tasenka Valley. There was a brief battle. Survivors tell us that the enemy forces must have been in the hundreds."

"Hundreds," Stensvik repeated in obvious disbelief.

"Yes, sir. They had planes, tanks and armored personnel carriers according to the people I have talked to."

"I don't believe that for an instant. If the South Haakovian forces had been able to land that many cavalry units on this side of the Inge River, they would have marched on until they reached Sturegorsk."

"Yes, sir." Gerik's shoulders visibly slumped. "I will check again."

"Show me the map," Stensvik ordered.

Gerik quickly conferred with one of the computer operators. "The central screen, sir."

The central screen lighted up, revealing a topography that Stensvik barely recognized. He didn't really remember where the fuel dump had been.

"The red dot denotes the location of the attack," Gerik said.

"How far in-country is that?"

"Ninety kilometers."

Stensvik nodded, realizing that the attack had taken place almost at the midway point to Sturegorsk from the Inge River. It sent a cold chill down his spine. "Can we replace those fuel supplies?"

"Yes, sir. I've spoken with Colonel Fomka. He assures me those supplies will be restocked in plenty of time for tomorrow's assault."

Stensvik considered that. His fuel resources were dwindling quickly. If the South did manage to put up some kind of fight, held the Northern armor by smashing the brunt of their attack in some unforeseen fashion, he might have a problem taking over the country by tomorrow as he intended.

Still, all those fuel supplies allowed the South to do was advance farther than he'd thought possible. In the end, there remained nowhere for them to hide or to run. They would stand and fight, and then they would die. The thought pleased him well enough that he smiled in spite of the circumstances.

"Where are the South Haakovian forces now?" Stensvik asked.

Gerik summoned a new map, shrinking the first until it fit into the upper left-hand corner of the present one. "Along here, sir." A green line drew itself along the southern bank of the river.

"How do we know this?"

"Our spy satellites confirmed it, President Stensvik."

"When?"

"Perhaps ten, fifteen minutes ago. About forty minutes after we suspect the attack took place on the fuel depot."

"How fordable is that section of the river?"

"Just a moment." Gerik pushed a computer operator out of his chair and manned the machine himself.

"It's not easily fordable, sir."

"Then they must have built a bridge," Stensvik mused. "Perhaps even one under the water." He studied the map. "There is enough forest in the area that the South Haakovian generals might be thinking of sneaking their forces across the border and mass an attack by early morning, or at the least establish a beachhead that the ground forces might be able to build on while protected by air support."

"Yes, sir."

The elevator door opened, disgorging the nine men who commanded the North Haakovian army with Stensvik. Most of them looked as if they'd just been wakened from sleep. Dag Vaino wasn't among them. He'd been flown out by military jet hours earlier to Colombia, then on to the United States via commercial flight. The terrorist's ultimate destination was Niagara Falls, New York, where the second of the biological units was to be activated.

Stensvik had Gerik bring the other men up to speed.

"Which communications outpost was supposed to be keeping the fuel depot under surveillance?" he asked when the duty officer was finished.

Gerik gave him an identification number that meant nothing to him, then pointed it out on the map.

"What have those people got to say about the invasion force?" Stensvik demanded.

"Nothing, sir," Gerik said. "That outpost was destroyed only a few moments ago. No one reported in, and so far the ground patrol I assigned to check on them hasn't radioed back."

Stensvik stared at the green representation of the South Haakovia forces. His gut twisted in indecision, then he remembered the American colonel running the South's defenses. Americans were fond of subterfuges. They loved to think their movements on battlefields were sleight-of-hand magic tricks. But this time, Stensvik knew, that misdirection wasn't going to work. He would be too clever for them. Even by directing the attention of his armored units toward the suspect area, they could still quickly mount an offensive against the original area they expected an attack to come from.

Besides which, Stensvik intended to be the one to attack. And he wouldn't back off until he'd won.

He folded his hands behind his back. "Give the order to move the armor toward the new South Haakovian position."

"But, sir," Colonel Stenya said in consternation, "if you move the armor, you open our flank to attack."

Stensvik glared at the man. "Look at that map. The only flank that is open is shielded by the Sergiusz Mountains. Even if the South Haakovian forces were able to reach those mountains undetected, how the hell would you expect them to attack? Armored units—as far as I know—do not fly."

"Yes, President Stensvik." Stenya moved back into the ranks of the other officers and kept his face clear of emotion.

"The time has come," Stensvik said, "for us to throw caution to the wind. We are jumping at shadows. It doesn't matter that they have stolen fuel. Those supplies will only let them advance a few hours longer. They still have nowhere to run." He closed his hand into a fist. "We have them. I won't be a coward and not take this victory when it is so clearly mine. And I won't let a soldier anywhere near me who chooses caution over courage."

A quick rumble of acknowledgment ran through their ranks.

"Stay here," Stensvik ordered. "Make sure that my commands are carried out." They responded quickly, and he paused to let them feel the weight of his glare, then moved to the elevator.

When he stepped out on the fifth floor above ground, he found four guardsmen waiting for him, fronted by Niklavs. As always, the old man was impeccably attired no matter the lateness of the hour.

"President Stensvik," Niklavs greeted.

"The news people are ready?" Stensvik asked. He marched toward the double doors at the end of the hallway leading to the large conference room.

"Yes. They are anxiously awaiting to hear what you have to say."

The four security people fell into step in standard two-by-two deployment.

"Do they know anything about the South Haakovian raid?" Stensvik asked.

"Our spies among them have heard nothing of that," Niklavs said. "However, there is some rumor that North Haakovia is behind the disease running rampant in Los Angeles, California."

"How many are dead?"

"One hundred and nine," Niklavs replied as he opened the door for Stensvik. "CNN has been very diligent about its coverage."

"Good. Then we can be sure of excellent coverage of the speech I am about to give." He walked into the room and strode down the hallway between rows of chairs that had been set up for the media people. Heads turned to look at him but he ignored them. Some of the reporters started to get up from their seats, but security people brandished pistols meaningfully and they sat back down.

The podium was on a raised dais at the front of the room, specially built so that he looked taller and leaner when he was behind it. As he climbed the steps, a hush fell over the crowd, encouraged by the soldiers moving within the ranks of the reporters.

When he grasped the edges of the podium and looked out over the dozens of people facing him, flashbulbs and video cameras flared with brilliance. It was hot under the lighting, and he felt droplets of perspiration begin to gather along his hairline. He silently cursed the fact that he sweated so easily, because it limited his time at the podium. There was no way he would allow himself to be photographed or filmed with perspiration dripping from his face like he was a nervous young girl on her wedding night.

Leaning forward into the cluster of microphones, he said, "There will be no questions tonight. I have come to deliver a message. It is a message concerning the miseries of war and their inevitable costs." He paused, watching the media people shift uncomfortably. He pointed dramatically. "And that cost is going to be leveled at you, Mr. President of the United States."

More flashbulbs popped.

Stensvik went on. "You and your Congress thought you could interfere in the politics of the Haakovias with impunity. Well, tonight that belief has been stripped away by the events taking place in Los Angeles, California. More than a hundred people have died, and it is on your head, Mr. President. How many more are going to have to die before you realize the folly of your actions?"

Hands went up during his pause, but he ignored all of them.

"I want your military people and your hardware out of these countries," Stensvik said. "Notify me of your decision, or the terror that is descending on Los Angeles will pale by comparison of what is to come. Your Bible speaks of years of plagues and pestilence. Are you prepared to weather years of that? Are your people? For a Baltic country no one gave a damn about only a few months ago?" He drew in a ragged breath and gripped the sides of the podium. "You have escalated this, Mr. President, escalated this from civil disorder into a full-scale war being fought in these countries. That is the guilt you will bear for the rest of your life. I hope it wears well over the years as you think of the dead and deformed that will be left inside the borders of your country. For now, though, think of the lives you might yet save." He turned and walked away from the podium.

Reporters screamed questions at him, and some of the security people had to forcibly restrain them. Curses and imprecations were wound in there as well. A man slipped free of the security people and ran at Stensvik with a microphone pointed out in front of him like a weapon.

With cold deliberation the North Haakovian president shot the man through the head, watched the body go in a disjointed tumble and land only a few feet from him. He checked to make sure none of the blood had spattered on his uniform, then stepped over the body, keeping his pistol in his fist.

The media people became much more docile.

CHAPTER FOURTEEN

Seated in the chair he'd occupied off and on for hours in the Oval Office, Hal Brognola watched the replay of Stensvik's unveiled threats again. Instead of the impact lessening with each repetition, it only seemed to get sharper, harder.

"That son of a bitch," the President said. He threw a pencil and it bounced away from his desk, coming to a stop on the carpet.

"We knew going in that it would probably come to this."

"Screw that, Hal," the Man said in obvious agitation. "We've got corpses scattered across half of L.A. County. I thought we'd be more on top of this than we evidently are. I thought your people would be more in control of this situation."

Brognola bit back a scathing retort out of respect for the Man and the office he held, and because he knew both of them were tired and emotionally frazzled. But it was hard. He'd been personally responsible for assigning those ten men to do the impossible.

The President sighed. "I'm sorry, Hal. I shouldn't have said that. The things that you and your group have done for this country that no one can ever know about should keep you above any reproach." He reached for the remote control, punched a button and froze Stensvik's image on the television. "Get with your people. Find out where they stand and let me know. I've got a meeting with the Joint

Chiefs of Staff in five minutes. God only knows what I'm going to tell them."

"And if Striker and his people are prepared to go on the offensive?"

"They maintain their positions until they are told otherwise." The President stood behind his desk, reached for his jacket, shook it out and slipped it on.

"Mr. President," Brognola said as he got to his feet also, "I respectfully point out that Striker and the South Haakovian forces are in a very tenuous position now. The offensive they're prepared to launch hinges on the secrecy they're able to maintain. Waiting might mean that they are compromised."

The President halted by the door, but didn't look at Brognola. "That's a chance we've got to take. If Stensvik does have more bacteriological weapons over here that's going to cause the kind of damage they're having in L.A., I've got to take that into consideration."

"If the American forces pull out now, South Haakovia will fall."

"I know." The President opened the door and stepped through. "God forbid it, but other countries who have depended on this nation at other times have fallen as well. If we can't get this over soon, there's no way we can hope to hold on to popular opinion. I won't see this country divided."

"Yes, sir." Brognola watched the door close and felt as alone then as he had at any time in his life. For a moment he gave in to the doubts, then forced them away and reached for the phone. There was only one way to deal with fears, and that was to confront them as squarely as possible. Whatever the outcome of the meeting the President had with the Joint Chiefs, Stony Man Farm was going to be ready.

EARLY-MORNING SUNLIGHT cascaded off the white-capped peaks of the Sergiusz Mountains, glistening from the wet surfaces as the snow started to melt.

Mack Bolan looked at the terrain through opposing viewpoints. As a man of peace, he could see the land plastered on a picture postcard. But he was there as a warrior, and that same terrain could prove treacherous.

Dressed in a fresh uniform and long coat, loaded down with gear, his head kept warm by a woolen cap, the Executioner walked through the snow to the edge of the mountains.

He'd taken time for a Marine bath and a quick shave because his appearance was critical to the morale of the men who were placing their lives on the line at his word today. They needed to believe in him in order to believe in themselves.

Small groups of men worked around the ridges of the mountains, setting up block-and-tackle equipment. Wheelbarrows filled with specially shaped explosive charges were nearby, and every once in awhile the men would pass some of them down. They were color-coded, with specific markings on them. Gary Manning had been working on the charges since his arrival at the base camp and had only started inserting them a half hour earlier, less than five minutes ahead of schedule. But they'd lost that five minutes because the ground was more frozen and more rocky than they'd expected.

Bolan knelt at the edge of the cliff and peered down. Ten men from the demolitions crew worked with Manning, hanging from ropes and rappeling gear. Battery-powered drills were tied to thongs secured to their belts, humming with power as they drilled through rock. The surface charges went relatively easy, but the deeper ones required more time and more care as extensions were added. Some of the charges, Manning had told the warrior, needed to be placed thirty feet deep in the unstable strata of the mountains.

More of Manning's handpicked crew worked the southern slope of the mountains. Drilling was easier there because the ground was softer, not filled with as much rock. The glaciers that had cut away the path for the Inge River three hundred feet below, leaving the sheer cliff face, had stripped away nearly all of the dirt and left only broken stone behind.

Bolan didn't bother the Phoenix warrior. There was nothing to say to make Manning work his crew or himself harder or faster. The big Canadian was giving it his all, and had been since he'd arrived.

Tapping the headset's transmit button, Bolan called for Grimaldi and got him. "How are things on the north forty?"

"Couldn't be better, although the North Haakovians reacted a little more quickly than we'd expected. They're massing along the designated strip, so evidently the Bear's little cybernetic charades were effective."

"How soon do you think they'll arrive?"

"Maybe a full half hour before we planned."

Bolan considered that. With the time frames built into Fast Break, it would be cutting the South Haakovian attack close to potential discovery. And the whole scenario was based on having the advantage of surprise. "Can you slow them down?"

"It could be dicey," Grimaldi admitted, "but the Blackbats and I have already been kicking some ideas around."

"I'll contact Mockingbird," Bolan replied. "Missiles from Larsborg can be directed from your point and should help give them reason to reconsider a running start at the position. It will also help convince them that we're massed there hoping to hold our own when they attack.''

"Roger, Stone Hammer Leader. We're on it. G-Force, clear.''

Bolan used the Alpha Prime freq to contact Lansdale to let the man know Grimaldi would be calling in with brief fire-strike missions. Satisfied with the progress Manning was making on the mountain, he walked back down to the waiting armor.

One hundred and two tanks, a mixed bag of M-1A1s and M-60A3s took cover under the carpet of trees, starting five hundred yards from the ridge. They sat pointed up the incline, looking like a herd of spiked and armored beetles waiting impatiently to go on a rampage.

The fuel tankers were parked behind them, waiting as crews continued to lug jerricans back and forth, filling up the South Haakovia cav units. According to reports from the refueling-group leaders, they'd be finished in twenty minutes.

Bolan's headset buzzed with an incoming transmission.

"Stone Hammer Leader, this is Com Net. Over.'' Com Net was the communications outpost connecting the various military arms of Fast Break.

The warrior keyed the transmit button. "Go, Com Net.''

"I've got a message incoming from Stony Base, sir.''

"Acknowledged. Relay it here. Stone Hammer Leader, out.'' Bolan switched freqs.

"Stony One, this is Stony Base. Over.''

"Go, Stony Base.'' Bolan continued to watch the preparations, aware that even with interference provided by Grimaldi and his fighter-jet squadrons, time was critical now. With the sun up, even with the denseness of the forest, the cav units were apt to be spotted by aerial survey.

"I've got some bad news, Stony One," Barbara Price announced. In her no-nonsense fashion she quickly related the events taking place in Los Angeles and Washington, D.C., since Stensvik had publicly admitted masterminding the viral infections in the city and had threatened more to come. "So for now, Stony One, you and your team are grounded. There can be no offensive until the President pulls off the yellow light. Do you understand?"

"Stony One understands," Bolan said, "but does the Man? Our position here is untenable."

"He understands," Price replied, "and he sends his regrets. But those are his orders."

Bolan cleared the channel and looked out over the army he commanded, wondering what the hell he was supposed to do with them since they could neither run nor fight.

EVEN CLOTHED in insulated gear, Yakov Katzenelenbogen felt the freezing chill of the Inge River as it swirled around him. He stood hip-deep in it, helping to pull tanker drivers from the water as they buried their rigs.

Katz grabbed the latest driver as another man passed him down the line, pushing him spluttering and cursing toward other men who would help him get to shore. With the depth they were working at, there was no way to avoid getting the drivers totally immersed in the river. By the time many of them had made shore they were already turning blue.

The tractor-trailer bubbled as it sank beneath the river. The empty fuel tanks tried to float away, but the steel cables holding it to the five-ton truck parked on the other shoreline kept it from doing so.

"Okay, back it up, mate," David McCarter yelled from the South Haakovian side of the Inge.

Another five-ton backed away. A set of steel cables attached to the front bumper took up slack and pulled taut. Grudgingly, in spite of the flowing water that slapped against the empty hull, the tanker pulled into line. Huge bubbles broke the surface as the open petcocks sucked the river into the empty cells.

The South Haakovian soldiers hurriedly slogged away from the sinking truck before they were caught in the undertow. Long minutes later it was completely submerged.

"That's the first one in the middle of the river," Calvin James said as he walked past Katz. The ex-SEAL was dressed in a neoprene wet suit designed for near-arctic conditions. He pulled a face mask down and took up the air tank mouthpiece. "I'm going under for a look."

"Be careful," Katz advised. He waved his hand, giving the signal for the people in the water to change places with those on the shore.

James flipped him a quick salute, then cleaved the water and disappeared from view.

After he'd waded to the near-frozen mud of the South Haakovian shore, Katz took out his cigarettes and lighted up. Now that the freezing waters weren't wrapped around him, he could feel the cold around the river.

A private with a flamethrower showered flames on a pile of rocks for nearly a minute. When he moved away, the stones were glowing a cherry red.

Katz moved forward, then held his hand out to the stones. He couldn't help but vocalize his pleasure at the sensation.

McCarter joined him. "Man could freeze his arse off out there, mates."

"It could," Encizo added as he stepped up, "freeze the balls off a brass billy goat."

While McCarter and Encizo got involved in a light discussion regarding the coldest places they'd ever been, Katz inspected the campsite with a fresh eye now that dawn was creeping over the mountains and driving the shadows away.

His attack squad consisted of one-fifth of all available South Haakovian tanks. At present they were parked under trees and staked under camou netting. One of Grimaldi's pilots had ascertained only a few minutes ago that the rising sun hadn't given them away. The tanks and APCs had been fueled before the hop to this section of the river, then topped up after arrival. They were as ready for battle as they could be.

The only obstacle was the river crossing.

Katz surveyed the physical results of the plan Bolan had concocted, and he had to admit it was a good one. A master strategist always made use of the things he had at hand, and used them again whenever possible.

A bridge hadn't been possible in the amount of time remaining before the attack, but Striker had come up with a tactic that bordered on genius.

Granted, the tanker trucks wouldn't normally support the weight of the APCs, let alone the tanks, but once they were filled with water to shore up the cell walls and disperse the weight evenly, it certainly appeared possible. And running two lines side by side, with the center of each tanker truck as track for the tank and APC treads, cut the weight by half again. The trick had been in securing the tankers side by side in the water without losing them. But the five-ton trucks equipped with come-alongs and steel cable were doing the job quite nicely.

James surfaced and swam to shore. Another driver pulled the next rig in line up to the river and drove in.

"Damn," the ex-SEAL said as he hunkered next to the heated rocks. "That is *cold* water."

McCarter passed him one of the few dry blankets the squad had while Encizo passed him a cup of coffee.

"How did it look?" Katz asked.

"In the center it still looks like we're about three feet too deep for the tanks to make it."

"If Manning's part of this comes through," Katz said, "that shouldn't be a problem. If he can't achieve his part of the operation, the last place this unit needs to be is on the other side of that river with no way back across."

"True," McCarter commented. "Striker's playing this one awfully close to the vest. Me, I'm glad that when the shit hits the fan I'm going to be up there with the birds."

"It's going to be something of a maelstrom up there too," Encizo commented.

Glancing at his watch, Katz saw that they would be finished with the mechanical part of the mission well ahead of the deadline. Then the headset buzzed in his ear and he heard Bolan's voice. He answered, then was told how and why Fast Break had been put on ice.

"There's no way this can be stopped," the Israeli said quietly into the mike as he walked away from his men. "It's come too far. One way or another, a lot of men are going to die today. If we try to hold our positions or fall back, the North Haakovians are going to slash us to pieces."

"Understood, Phoenix One," Bolan replied. "But for now we have our orders. The fate of this mission rests in the hands of Stony Base. Let's just hope she can make a hell of a pitch to the interested parties." Striker cleared the frequency.

Katz stripped out of the insulated outerwear, reached into a thigh pocket of his pants and took out his map case.

He sat down with it, studying the best points to fight a delaying war if it came down to that now, all the time praying that it wouldn't.

"YOU'VE GOT BAGS under your eyes," Barbara Price chided herself as she looked at her reflection in her office mirror. "How the hell can you expect to look competent when you're a mess?"

"Maybe," Aaron Kurtzman suggested from the doorway, "you need someone with an objective opinion."

She gave him a withering glance that was only partially playful. "Do you know someone like that?"

Kurtzman took the hint and looked away. "No, I don't." He rolled into the room and began to tinker with the keyboard on the desk.

"Sorry," Price said. She reached into her purse, produced a small jar of foundation and unscrewed the lid. "I hate being a bitch." She looked back at her reflection but monitored Kurtzman as well.

"It's okay. I love seeing an artist at work."

Price dabbed her finger into the foundation makeup and applied it to the puffy flesh beneath her eyes. A pretty face didn't always help, but it sure beat the hell out of looking like something the cat dragged in.

She glanced at the digital clock mounted on the wall above the video camera wired into the satellite transmissions systems. "Two minute warning."

"I'm ready." Kurtzman leaned back in his chair, giving the appearance of being totally relaxed. He reached out and flicked on the television set that rested on a corner of the desk.

Dragging her fingers through her hair one more time, Price checked her image in the television set and was almost satisfied. She was more interested in looking competent than beautiful. Beauty didn't fight wars. And win them, she added. She had to keep the right mental attitude.

Price reached for the phone, placed the call to the White House and heard Kurtzman's systems automatically shunt the communications relay into the audio and video pickups. She activated the speakerphone, hearing the receiver picked up on the third ring.

The television under the mounted video camera filled with the picture of the Oval Office. The President, looking dour and grim, sat behind his desk with a pencil tapping nervously between his fingers. Brognola was on his feet in one corner, his face showing no emotion at all.

"Ms. Price," the President greeted.

"Mr. President," Stony Man's mission controller replied. They'd had arguments before, none exactly out in the open, but the disagreements had been there just the same. A tacit respect had built up over the years of their acquaintance.

"So what do you have for me?" the Man asked bluntly.

"A war waiting to be fought," she said without preamble. "One we're prepared to win."

"I have no real doubts about Striker's abilities in the Baltic theater," the President said as he shifted in his chair, "but there is a lot of apprehension about the things Stensvik's capable of within the continental United States. The switchboard here has been lighted up like a Christmas tree since that bastard's announcements."

"Yes, sir."

"And the death toll in L.A. has reached one hundred twenty-one people."

"One hundred and twenty-three, sir," Price corrected. "We're wired directly into the hospitals in and around Los Angeles County."

"You're keeping informed."

"That's my job," she said, cutting him off before he could say something both of them would regret. "Able Team is prepared to take down a crack house that we believe is supplying cocaine laced with the diphtheria bacteria."

"How sure are you about that?"

Price counted off on her fingers. "One, Able traced the drugs back to the crack suppliers. Two, a man I cut a deal with—"she saw no reason to involve Lyons's neck on the block with hers on that call "—turned up the name Hector Osmundo on the streets of Washington, D.C. Three, using computer intel, we were able to track Osmundo back, learned that he was critical to the Colombian assassins being present in the United Nations. He's been out of the country a lot these past few months—using a visa he has to North Haakovia."

"And Osmundo?"

"Is the man behind the crack house in L.A."

"Where is he at this time?"

Price went out on a limb. "We have reason to believe that he is at the crack house now, overseeing the dispersal of the tainted cocaine." They had just as much concrete evidence that Osmundo was in Paris, France, or Paris, Texas. But from the NCIC information Kurtzman had dug up on the man, Osmundo was very hands-on with any operation he was involved with.

"How do you know the cocaine has been tampered with?"

"Considering the initial victims were known and unknown drug abusers, we considered that a natural medium. And there is the cartel connection Stensvik has cultivated. Plus, Able turned up some of the cocaine in a raid. When it was tested, it was found to contain the diphtheria bacteria." Price nodded at Kurtzman. "I'm sending you some hard copy on that now."

The President turned and looked at the fax machine suddenly spitting out sheets of paper at his elbow. He gathered them up and glanced through them. "So you think we can halt Stensvik's threats about bacteriological warfare before he can get it going good."

"Yes." A short answer, Price knew, was better if said with conviction, than a long one that could be confusing with too many supporting facts.

"What about Striker and Phoenix?"

"Poised and ready to go, sir," Price answered. "Every minute we delay on this is another minute toward potential disaster for the plans and preparations they have made."

"And they're satisfied they can break Stensvik's military dominance in North Haakovia?"

"Yes, sir. And so am I." She signaled Kurtzman, saw the television containing her own image fade and be replaced by a computer-generated map of the Haakovias.

Blue triangles lighted up the map near the Inge River.

"These are Stensvik's armored units. They represent the might of the North Haakovian army. They've been fed false information and believe they have cornered the South Haakovian forces along the river, giving them no escape." Price watched as red circles lighted up to the west of the blue triangles. "These are Striker's main troops, based in the Sergiusz Mountains. They are using a flanking action, coming in from the mountains in a way that Stensvik and his military personnel will never suspect."

The red circles blinked, came crashing down on the other side of the Inge River.

"Stensvik will automatically order his cavalry units to wheel and attack the South Haakovian forces. But it will take time and pull them even farther out of position."

As the blue triangles turned to face the red circles, a series of green diamonds jumped onto the screen behind the triangles.

"This will open them up to another, smaller armored cavalry marshaled by Phoenix Force that will attack them from behind, trapping them in a deadly cross fire. The way Striker has this figured, eighty to ninety percent of the North Haakovian armor will be destroyed on those steppes before they can fight their way into a withdrawal that can protect Sturegorsk."

The screen cleared and returned to Price.

"What's the worst-case scenario on this thing?" the President asked.

"That South Haakovia will establish a solid beachhead deep within North Haakovian territory. One that they can build on in the next few days."

"And the best case?"

"Sturegorsk could possibly fall to the South Haakovian forces by nightfall."

"What about Janyte Varkaus?"

"Striker's secondary mission, once penetration of the North Haakovian military arm has been established, is to rescue her. We've gotten our hands on some intel regarding the presidential buildings. And we think we have a way inside for our people."

"What are the chances of that?"

"We think they're good."

The President leaned forward. "That leaves the ICBM missiles Stensvik has in his possession."

"Given our access to the Strategic Defense Initiative systems," Price said, "we believe we can knock them down in space before anyone is hurt."

"That seems like a lot."

"Only because it is," Price agreed. "But it's what we're going to have to do if we're going to take Stensvik down. If we leave him in place, the threat he poses today will only crop up again."

"And he might have a better chance to cause more damage," the President said. He nodded. "I've talked with the Joint Chiefs of Staff, and we feel—along with congressional heads—that we have no choice at this point but to attempt to break Stensvik's stranglehold on those countries. Our course appears completely clear to me." He glanced at Brognola, then back at the video camera sending his image to Stony Man Farm. "You have your green light, Ms. Price. Get those men in there and get the job done."

"Yes, sir." She didn't permit herself a smile of satisfaction until after Kurtzman assured her they were no longer transmitting to the White House. She reached for the radio and started making calls.

CHAPTER FIFTEEN

"I don't know what the hell you idiots thought you were doing by invading those premises without a search warrant!" Captain Dwight Keller shouted.

Carl Lyons had to admit the guy had a certain sense of presence while breaking the decibel level. During his days as a cop, Lyons had been yelled at by some of the best, and Keller left a lot of them in the shade.

They were in the vice captain's office with the blinds shut, though Lyons was sure the detectives in the outer cubicles could hear every word that was being said. The walls held the traditional black-and-white pictures of academy days, honorable citations, and—of a more personal note—three Little League baseball trophies on a shelf that looked handmade.

"Rita Sanders," J. D. Ethan said to Lyons as they sat together on the couch by the water cooler.

Lyons looked at the man.

"She was my ex-wife. That's why I wanted to make this case so bad."

Lyons remembered the body in the morgue. "I'm sorry, man."

"What the hell are you two clowns talking about?" Keller demanded. "Aren't you listening to a goddamned word I'm saying here?"

Both Lyons and Ethan turned to the man and said no at the same time.

"You miserable son of a bitch," Keller yelled. He came around his desk and threw a forefinger in Ethan's face. "Do you know how much of a problem you might have created for this department with that little stunt?"

Ethan didn't say anything.

Keller got closer. "Look, I feel sorry for you. It's too bad about Rita, but there isn't anything you or I can do about it. And I can't cover you on this."

"You know," Ethan said quietly, "you're going to feel awfully funny when I rip that finger off and shove it up your ass."

"Goddammit, J.D., when Internal Affairs gets finished with you, you'll be lucky if all you lose is your badge. I'm going to get some air." Keller slammed the door behind him when he left.

"Not a really cheerful soul, is he?" Blancanales commented from the other side of the room.

Schwarz tugged at an ear and grinned. "And he's too unimaginative and pedantic to really be any good at verbal abuse." He pushed himself up out of his chair. "Come on, Pol, let's get some air, too. I saw a couple vice detectives rousting some uncooperative hookers. I bet after a few minutes go by out there, we'll see some real verbal abuse in action."

After they left, Ethan took out his cigarettes and lighted one. Lyons turned down the offer. "She was my ex-wife," the vice cop said in a pained voice. "I could bore you with the whole story of how a young hot-dog cop thought he could go out and save the world but couldn't even manage to save his own family."

"I know the story," Lyons said. "Scored a few refrains myself."

"Yeah. I knew you were a cop in a past life."

"Maybe even a couple."

"I feel the same way. Rita had a habit when I met her. I thought I had her off it. But two kids later, and the kinds of hours I started pulling when I got promoted to vice, took its toll. We started having trouble I didn't know how to fix. Then I came home one day, only I didn't live there anymore. Rita got back into dope, started dealing. Took me eighteen months to get custody of my boys. They live with me now, and my sister watches them while I work." Ethan's voice broke slightly. "And when I saw Rita lying on that goddamned slab today, I had to ask myself how the fuck I was going to go home and tell my kids that their mother finally killed herself." Tears slid unnoticed down the cop's face as he stared hard through a window looking out over the street.

Lyons waited, knowing from experience that that was all he could do.

"I had to do something," Ethan said. "Fucking pushers. You bust them, they're back out on the street in nothing flat. I saw you, knew you were more than what you were saying and I figured I had a chance."

"You do have a chance, buddy. And if you can't fade the heat down here, you give a guy named Harold Brognola a call in the Justice Department and tell him Iron man said to give him a call. Keep you in cop work. That's where you belong."

Ethan wiped his face. "Thanks. I'll keep that in mind. This is a pretty miserable excuse for a job some days, but I believe in it. You know?"

Lyons nodded. "I know."

Somebody rapped on the door, then followed it inside. "Is there a Leiter in here?" a young detective asked.

"Me," Lyons said.

The detective jerked a thumb over his shoulders. "Got a phone call. You can take it out here."

"Thanks." Lyons stood and clapped Ethan on the shoulder. "Maybe it's good news. I'll be right back."

"Sure."

The call was from Barbara Price, summing up the talk she'd had with the President. While Lyons was on the phone, he saw three nattily attired men with fresh shaves follow Keller into the vice captain's office. He knew from experience that they were Internal Affairs people. He had nothing against them, but sometimes that job really sucked and impeded the work good cops tried to do. When Price rang off, he waved to Blancanales and Schwarz. "We're on."

Both men nodded.

Lyons entered Keller's office without an invitation, which drew a dark glower from the three IA people and the vice captain.

"This is a private conversation, Mr. Leiter," one of the IA investigators said.

Lyons stopped in front of the desk and grinned at Ethan. The vice cop smiled back. "I know. You're giving him the old speech about how he's going to lose his shield, lose his ass, and never get to have lunch in this town again."

"Hey, mister," Keller barked, getting to his feet. "You're not exactly out of the fire here yourself. Once I contact your superiors, you might not be working for the control center anymore."

Lyons didn't even bother to correct the guy. He just fixed him with a stare. "Look, if you'll go look at the office fax machine, you'll see I just got a federal writ giving me permission to crash the premises that you're so concerned about. There's another writ in there about the Springer Apartments. We've got leave to go in there, too. Now if you think L.A.'s finest has got time to go make a hell of a drug bust with Detective Ethan and me instead of sitting around here wondering who's ass can be sacrificed, that's great. If not, I'll give the sheriff's department a call. Now, what's it going to be?''

"OKAY, PHOENIX THREE," Mack Bolan said via the radio headset, "the show's all yours."

Gary Manning shifted in the passenger seat of the OH-58 Bell helicopter and surveyed the section of Sergiusz Mountains he and his team had mined. The geographical maps Kurtzman had provided had given him a wealth of information to work from, but it was still his craftsmanship that was going to make the difference. Part of it was skill, part of it instinct. He'd been involved in demolitions for so long he could no longer tell where the overlap occurred.

"Take it down a little more," Manning told the pilot.

The guy complied, bringing the little helicopter to a hover about a third of the way down the cliffside.

"In closer," Manning said. "Sweep it, from one end to the other."

"Yes, sir." The guy was obviously nervous about flying so close to the cliff face. He glanced at the remote-control box in Manning's hands.

The big Canadian went inside his own mind as he surveyed the cliff, remembering the shaped charges, the feel of the drill squirming in his hands, the anticipatory satisfaction he felt when the last one had been placed. He'd blown up a number of things over his years in demolitions, but he'd never before taken out a mountain.

"Okay," Manning said, "take us back about five hundred yards."

The pilot glanced at him as he kicked the tail rotor around and flew north of the river. "Begging your pardon, sir, but shouldn't we be back further? When those charges blow, won't they throw rock everywhere?"

"Not those explosives," Manning said with confidence. "Those charges are going to do exactly what I tell them to. And they won't do it until I tell them to." He pulled out the antennas, switched on the battery power and watched the ready lights come up in the proper sequence. He keyed the headset. "Phoenix Three ready here, Stone Hammer Leader. Over."

"Your call, Three."

"Now." Manning shifted the toggle protector out of the way and flipped the switch.

At first glance the cliff face didn't seem to be disturbed. The white puffs of rock dust coughed out from different charge holes. A low rumble of thunder accompanied them, not sounding in any way dangerous.

Kurtzman had found the fault line inside the mountain, a scar made thousands of years ago when the land had been shaped by the glacier movement. Manning had scoped it out with surveyor's equipment, laid out the attack on the land with the skill of a neurosurgeon, put the first charges in place just to loosen things up a bit, then laid in the heavier ones.

The cliff face seemed to ripple nearly to the base, then tried to settle back into its former seating. Instead the big explosives went off with timed percussions designed not only for their force, but also for the conflicting vibrations that were set into motion. It sounded like the mountain range was being reforged by a thunderous hammer from hell.

Without warning, the cliff face came apart like smashed fine china. Sheets of stone, rock, snow and vegetation skidded off the mountain in layers that hit and broke apart in midair. Huge chunks of rock dropped into the Inge River.

To Manning it looked like the events were taking place in slow motion, but he knew in reality it was only a matter of seconds.

White stone dust and dark dirt clouds fogged the area. Parts of the mountain sides collapsed inward, helping to control the flow of the falling debris, raining it over the river and the sloped sides of the riverbank.

None of the falling rock landed more than a hundred yards on the other side of the river.

"Jesus," the pilot said in a stunned voice.

"Yeah," Manning said as the adrenaline sped through his system. "It's really something else, isn't it?" He put the now-useless remote-control detonator away in one of the rear seats. "Damn, would you just look at that?"

Where an eighth of a mile of the Sergiusz Mountains had been, there now existed an open gate carved in stone. The shattered remains of the cliff face served as an uneven but serviceable road across the river. And it served as a dam, as well.

Movement at the top of the mutilated ridge drew Manning's attention. He watched as the first of the South Haakovian armored divisions started down the long incline he'd created with the explosions. Fast Break was a definite go.

BOLAN WATCHED from the passenger seat of a Hummer as the first tanks crawled at low speed across the road of poured broken rock. Larkin kept the vehicle to the edge of the road but not so close that there was a danger of tumbling over on loose stones. The tanks and APCs had no trouble negotiating the incline, and each tread that rolled over the road only served to make it more firm for the next one.

The Executioner thumbed the transmit button on the headset. "Stone Hammer Leader to Phoenix One. Over."

"Go. You have Phoenix One." Katz's voice sounded sure and strong.

Bolan gripped the seat belt a little tighter as the Hummer's suspension rocked over the uneven terrain. "We are go at this end, Phoenix One. Your people will move out at your discretion."

"Understood, Stone Hammer Leader. Phoenix, out."

"See you in the hell zones," Bolan said, then cleared the channel. He glanced into the sky, saw the drifting clouds of stone dust and dirt clouds. They were on borrowed time. It wouldn't be long before the North Haakovian army noticed the movement.

The Hummer straightened out when it reached the opposite shore, and the ride got easier.

Bolan had Larkin halt the vehicle, and contacted the group leaders of each unit, verifying orders and troop movement. The tanks deployed in groups of three, working out of loose deuce formations. APCs followed them, flanked by roving bands of attack buggies and armed Hummers.

Above the ground, a layer of Apache gunships, A-10 Warthogs, F-15s and F-16s prevented North Haakovian air attack and provided a long-distance punch when needed. Fat-bodied CH-47 Chinook helicopters carried the infantry, ready to boot them out at a moment's notice.

The Inge River was already backing up, starting to flow around the pile of rock that had suddenly dammed it. It wouldn't be long before it overflowed its boundaries and turned the shoreline into mud. But by that time the South Haakovian armor would be on the right side of the river.

"Let's go," Bolan told Larkin.

The driver let out the clutch and gained speed, moving up alongside the slower-moving train of armored vehicles.

Bolan reached into his pocket, produced a handkerchief and tied it around his lower face. The utility compartment yielded a pair of goggles that kept the mud out of his face.

Twenty minutes passed. In that time, under medium speed since they didn't have to wait on infantry units that were on foot, the cav units were almost ten miles within the North Haakovian border.

"Stone Hammer Leader, this is G-Force. Over."

"Go, G-Force."

"We've got a MiG checking us out. Should I go ahead and announce us?"

Bolan pulled out his binoculars, shifted his goggles down around his neck and scanned the air until he found the North Haakovian aircraft. "That's affirmative, G-Force. Make sure they know they have an engraved invitation to the ball. Stone Hammer Leader, out."

A heartbeat later an F-15 cut out from the high-flying troops overhead, streaking for the enemy aircraft. The F-15 juked and flipped, dodged a pair of air to air missiles and came up firing. It looked like it was close enough to pass through the flames thrown out by the explosion of the MiG.

A howl of triumph went through the South Haakovian ranks that shattered the rumble of engines and clanking of tank treads. Some of the tank crews used their PA systems to play the South Haakovian liberation song. The music blared out, a heart-thumping marching tune that Bolan felt John Philip Sousa would have been proud of. Tank commanders took small South Haakovian flags from inside their vehicles and tied them to their radio antennas.

"Goddamn," Larkin said, gazing in awe at the line of tanks and APCs staggered out in loose formation behind them, "you'd think we're leading an army, Colonel, to listen to those goofs."

Bolan smiled, his own spirits buoyed by the quick victory Grimaldi had provided for the South Haakovian forces. "We *are* leading an army. Those people aren't just prepared to die for their country and their ideals anymore. Somewhere during the night they've decided to fight for it first."

"Next thing you know," Larkin said with a smile, "these guys are going to be thinking they're going to win this damn thing."

"Maybe we are," Bolan replied. But as they passed the flaming wreckage of the exploded MiG, he knew everyone would be reminded of the price some of them would have to pay.

Even as they passed, though, the strains of the liberation song never dimmed.

"WATER LEVEL'S definitely dropped," Calvin James said. He stood on the riverbank looking at the fresh mud that was being left by the receding water.

"But is it enough?" Katz asked. He glanced at his watch. Ten minutes had passed since Striker had radioed him regarding the fall of the mountain. The water hadn't drained away as quickly as they'd thought. Despite the dam caused by the destroyed mountain, there were evidently enough gaps in the rocks to provide much of the water egress through it.

James took a length of string from his pocket and unrolled it so the pebble tied to it spun free at the end. Leaning out over the river where the tanker trucks had been sunk, he dropped it into the water, marked the depth and pulled it back up. "Hell, Yakov, we're almost three feet below now. Let's go for it and see where it gets us."

Katz nodded, turned and clambered up on the outside of the first tank in line to cross. He banged the turret with his hand. "Driver," he ordered, "let's take it across."

"Yes, sir."

With a growl of power, the tank lurched forward, locking tracks for a moment as it came around to address the marked lane across the submerged tankers. Colored flags fluttered in the breeze from the guide wires.

"Ahead," Katz called. "Low gear. Let's take this easy."

"Yes, sir."

The tank nosed forward and dipped into the running water of the river. It wallowed for a moment in the mud, then found traction and continued on. When the treads made contact with the first tanker, there was a deep basso booming that echoed the length of the tanker. Metal crumpled, but it held.

Katz hung on to the turret with his hand, knowing every eye was on him, knowing he had to be a leader these men could respect if they were going to follow him into battle.

The submerged tankers continued to give way under the tank's weight, but they held. Water ran more than two inches deep across the main body of the M-1A1 Abrams, but climbed no higher, well within the vehicle's abilities to handle.

A long minute later, it climbed away from the last tanker and trundled its way to the top of the riverbank.

Katz stepped over the side and dropped down. He assumed a drill instructor's pose, hand on hip, as he surveyed the line of tanks waiting to pass over. The infantry units milled about, talking among themselves. "All right," the Israeli bellowed. "Next man through, let's go. We're burning daylight here."

James rode a Bradley M-2 APC through next, jumping off as it pulled by Katz. "Gee, Katz, you really going to stand there and yell John Wayne quotes at them till they get across?"

"It serves a purpose. Makes them remember they are fighting men, gives them a sense of pride in themselves and in what they're doing. And can you think of anyone better to quote right now?"

"No," James said agreeably, "but Wayne died in that one."

Katz looked at him for a moment, then clapped the ex-SEAL on the shoulder. "You know, Calvin, you're right. I've got better things to do. You stand here and cheer them on." He turned and walked away, taking his map case from his pocket.

Monitoring the advance recon provided by the front-runner of the South Haakovian's aerial arm, Katz made notations on his map. The North Haakovian armor knew the South Haakovian forces were in-country now, had somehow crossed an area of the Inge River that had been deemed impassable. Steps were being taken to reroute the North's cav units and build up an avenging wall that would splinter Striker's group. According to the numbers Striker was using, the initial heads-up confrontation would take place in just under an hour, no sooner than fifty minutes. The air forces would begin tangling up long before that. The way the Israeli had it figured, his group of tanks would be cutting the time frame very thin if they were to be effective.

CHAPTER SIXTEEN

Carl Lyons pulled the rest of his gear into place in the back of the unmarked van. He looked up at his teammates and J. D. Ethan. "You guys ready to do this?"

Schwarz pulled on a dark watch cap. "Hell, yes."

Blancanales nodded and took up the laser-sighted CAR-15 from one of the seats.

"Let's do it," Ethan said as he slipped a hideout gun into his boot.

Lyons hit the backdoor release and pushed through. They were parked in an alley three blocks from the crack house. He took the lead and they moved out at a jog. Thumbing the transmit button on his headset, he said, "Downtown, this is Night Ranger."

"Go, Night Ranger." Keller's voice was more subdued now, and Lyons could tell the big vice captain had slipped from petty bureaucrat to cop.

"We're on the move."

"Right. You people just let us know when."

Lyons cleared the freq and moved across the first street, slowing to a walk that didn't attact attention. Blancanales, Schwarz and Ethan came across behind him in a staggered fashion that wouldn't let anyone guess they were together. He paused on the other side until they pulled the ranks together, then went on through the trash-filled alleys.

The Springer Apartments were a big investment for the Colombian cartels, Lyons had found out. It had taken

Kurtzman's computers more than an hour to break through all the real-estate camouflage to find out who really owned the building. It was no surprise to find it linked to a Medellín investment firm, but it made the foundation a little firmer in the minds of the LAPD.

Lyons halted across the street from the buildings and studied the terrain.

The apartments were three stories tall, built in a typical O-configuration around a swimming pool and park area. According to the maps and blueprints the big Able Team warrior had seen, there were one hundred twelve units. Most of them were supposed to be rented out, but when the Bear's cybernetic sidekicks investigated, a number of those people either didn't exist or had been dead for a long time.

Lyons wiped perspiration from his grease-painted brow, cursed the humidity rolling in from the coast and moved into the attack path Able had chosen for their approach.

A breezeway on the second floor opened up to allow a southerly breeze to flow into the inner courtyard. When they'd reconned the area, Lyons had seen two guards with assault weapons lounging in the shadows.

"How close are you going to have to be with that thing?" Lyons asked as he squatted behind an overflowing Dumpster.

Schwarz unlimbered a high-powered air rifle. "Fifty feet. Seventy-five. These tranquilizer darts don't always fly true, and I didn't get any of the free lessons *Wild Kingdom* was giving."

Lyons measured the distance from the Dumpster to the breezeway opening by eye. "I make it sixty feet."

"So do I." Schwarz settled into position, pulled the butt stock into his shoulder and sighted through the StarTron scope. "The problem's going to be to get both those guys into the open at the same time. And this thing's a bolt-action, so the second shot's going to take some time to get off."

"I'll flush them out for you," Lyons said as he handed his Ithaca shotgun to Blancanales. "You just make sure you take them down." He stood and walked toward the breezeway, knowing immediately when the sentry picked him up because he could feel the guy's eyes on him. Putting a slight stagger into his walk, the Able Team warrior weaved close to the brick wall of the apartment building.

"Hey," a rough voice called out from above.

Lyons halted, kept his hands at his sides and gave the impression of peering up through the darkness blearily.

"This here's private property, man," the Hispanic said, stepping out into the moonlight.

"I'm looking to buy some private property," Lyons called back. "Or at least rent it real good for a while." He kept facing them so the word POLICE, which was stenciled across the back of his sweater, wouldn't show. "Somebody told me you got girls up there."

"You better just go on, man. Somebody done told you wrong."

"Wait," Lyons called out. "I got money right here." He reached into his jeans pocket, held his other hand palm-up to show that it was empty, then fished his money clip into view. It was thick enough to be impressive even at that distance. "Hey, I'm just one of those lonely guys tonight, you know, amigo? From outta town, outta luck and looking to get my ashes hauled."

The guard waved to someone behind him. The second man came forward, an orange coal of a cigarette dangling between his lips.

Lyons heard the cough of the air rifle and saw the first man stagger slightly when the dart hit him. The second guard whirled to look at his partner.

A heartbeat later a projectile imbedded itself in the guard's neck, sending him to the concrete floor on rubbery legs.

The big ex-cop stuck the money into his pocket and took a running start at the wall. His feet drummed hard, then he pressed his right foot against the wall and shoved himself upward, hands stretched out to grip anything that came within reach. His fingers curled around the wrought-iron railing that covered the lower third of the breezeway opening. His body slammed against the brick wall, scraping his chin, and he hauled himself up.

His .357 Magnum pistol was in his fist before he threw a leg over the railing.

Both of the guards were out, and the walkway surrounding the second floor was clear of interested observers. After giving his teammates the all clear, Lyons lifted the two guards and shoved them over the side out of the way. The drug in their system would keep them unconscious for most of an hour. They thumped and rolled when they hit the sidewalk, but neither appeared to be seriously injured.

Blancanales flipped the sling from the CAR-15 and Lyons grabbed it, helping the man climb the wall while Ethan and Schwarz tucked the unconscious guards out of sight. He handed Lyons the Ithaca as he came over the railing. Less than two minutes later, the four men stood in the breezeway.

"Any idea where we can find Vasquez and Osmundo?" Lyons asked Ethan.

"No."

"Then we'll have to stop and ask somebody." Lyons took the first set of stairs leading down.

"Where are you going to find anybody?" Schwarz asked. "This place is like a ghost town."

"Only for the moment," Ethan replied. "Word I get is that when Vasquez's people aren't preying on somebody else, they prey on each other. So it's not surprising that they aren't moving around in here tonight."

"That still doesn't tell me where you're going to find somebody to ask."

"You've been out of apartments for too long, buddy," Lyons said with a grin. "At an apartment complex, where's the one place you can plan on finding somebody at any time?"

"The laundry room," Ethan answered.

"Right." Lyons pointed at the building tucked between the empty swimming pool and the park area. Lighted windows covered by wax paper cut weak holes in the darkness.

Somebody had taken the lock out a long time ago, leaving chewed wood around the space it had occupied.

Lyons went through the door, followed by Ethan as Blancanales and Schwarz took the other door. Five people were inside the small room, huddled together at one end of two rows of ten washers. One of the three dryers hummed and tumbled. The smell of marijuana was thick in the room, cutting easily through the odors of detergents and bleach.

"Oh, shit," one of the men said.

One of the two women scrambled for the back door, but was stopped cold in her tracks as Blancanales walked through with the CAR-15 at waist-level.

"The first person who goes for a piece dies," Lyons said coldly. "I promise you that."

Nobody moved.

"Now, down on the floor," he ordered, "and nobody has to get hurt."

The five people dropped onto their stomachs and lay there, glaring up at him.

Lyons covered them with the shotgun while Ethan, Blancanales and Schwarz secured them with disposable plastic handcuffs.

"Are you police?" one of the men asked, rolling around to check the cuffs on his wrists.

"Yeah," Lyons replied. "And let me set something straight—I'm asking the questions here."

The big ex-cop walked over to stand above the man who'd talked. He kept the muzzle of the Ithaca only a couple inches from the man's nose, and gave the guy a soft, slow smile. "There's only one main question. Where's Osmundo and Vasquez?"

The man hesitated only briefly before telling him.

PRESIDENT Franzen Stensvik gripped the railing of the balcony overlooking the command-post screens and shouted orders at everyone who would listen to him.

There, on the center screen, in full color for everyone to see, was proof that the South Haakovian army had pulled off the impossible. The screen shifted between three different views presented by cameras mounted on aircraft positioned over different parts of the battlefield.

The North Haakovian cavalry had been caught off guard, attacked from a side where no attack should have come. And Stensvik wasn't sure how that had been accomplished.

Without the sound on, the scene looked eerie, surrealistic. Main guns on the Soviet- and American-made tanks rocked and spit forth gobs of gray smoke. As Stensvik watched, another T-55 took a direct hit that separated the turret from the main body. The tank lurched out of control for a moment, then came to a full stop. Flames broke free of the interior and wrapped themselves around the hull. A fiery body tried to scramble free, gave up suddenly and slumped halfway out of the tank.

"We've got to pull back," Colonel Petrov said.

"We're not pulling back," Stensvik replied harshly.

"Those men are getting massacred out there."

"Only the frontline troops. The dead are forming a wall that will stop the advance of the South Haakovian troops. Once that happens, we can turn the battlefield to our advantage again."

"You're sacrificing those men."

"They're acceptable losses." Stensvik glared at the colonel, daring him to speak further.

Colonel Petrov shut up.

Stensvik lifted the phone connecting him to the duty officer. "Tell those battalion officers that I expect them to show me a victory when this is over."

"But, sir," the duty officer said, "those commanders are requesting permission to fall back and regroup. The South Haakovian offensive has—"

"Tell them the answer is no. Any man who pulls back will be found guilty of desertion and shot as a coward. There will not be a foot of North Haakovian soil that doesn't cost those rat bastards blood. Tell them I said that, too."

"Yes, sir." The duty officer turned back to his post, obviously unhappy about his assignment.

"President," the colonel said, "I must ask you to reconsider this. It's madness. You can't expect—"

Without hesitation, Stensvik drew his side arm and shot the officer in the chest three times.

A shocked look filled the dying man's face as he dropped to his knees and fell forward. Blood dripped through his fingers, through the holes of the balcony grate and splattered across the computer-room floor.

The technicians turned around to stare at the dead man as the thunderous reports of the pistol echoed inside the room.

Stensvik leaned across the railing and shouted, "Get back to work! All of you! I will not let everything I have worked for go down in ashes simply because you don't have the guts to fight for yourselves!"

Everyone quickly returned their attention to their computers.

Stensvik holstered his weapon and waved at the two guards standing behind him.

They approached cautiously.

"You," he told the first one, "clean up this mess."

"Yes, sir."

"And you, go find me another colonel."

"Yes, President Stensvik."

Both men went into motion.

Stensvik stepped over the corpse and walked to the elevator. There would be a period, he knew, as the word spread throughout the army, that plans would be made against him by his officers, especially some of the KGB men who were used to such tactics. But he wouldn't give up his position of power. They knew that. As long as he had control of the nuclear missiles, he didn't have to. Those people would plot and scheme, but in the end they would realize he had the power to destroy them all at any moment if he chose.

He took the elevator up to the fifth floor, talked on the phone long enough to get an operator to route a call to the

President of the United States, then went to the office on the south side of the building.

Taking a pair of binoculars from the desk drawer, he scanned the terrain, thinking he could see the smoke of the battle in the distance. He used the remote control to switch on the television, then adjusted it to one of the security monitoring stations fed by video up-links from a spotter plane overlooking the conflict. The movement was dizzying.

Lifting the phone, he called the duty officer and commanded him to order the spotter-plane cameramen to be more steady as they worked. He hung up before the man could reply.

He crossed the room to a liquor cabinet and poured himself a drink, then resumed his watch over the window.

A few minutes later the phone rang. When he answered, he was told by the operator that the White House was on the line. He opened the video up-link and saw the interior of the Oval Office come into view with the President standing before his desk. To his immediate left was the man Stensvik had seen at that post for days, yet had been unable to attain any information on.

"You have refused to acknowledge my order to pull the American troops from South Haakovia," Stensvik said without preamble.

"Yes." There was no weakness in the President.

"You can live with the number of people that are going to die as a result of your decision?"

"If you had your way," the President replied, "you'd kill them anyway." He shoved his hands in his pockets. "And from what I've been told, you're in a position to get your ass kicked soundly. Maybe it's time you reconsidered *your* stance in these matters."

"Never. As long as I have those missiles and the biological weapons, you will never take North Haakovia."

"I'm not taking North Haakovia," the President pointed out. "The South Haakovian people are. Now I promise you, when they sack your ass, I'm going to have a good laugh."

"You're a fool," Stensvik shouted. "Before I let those people anywhere near the walls of Sturegorsk, I'll launch those missiles. And one of them is aimed at the White House. You and that city will die."

"I will not be threatened," the President said calmly.

The phone connection went dead, and the television blanked out.

Angrily, not believing what had just transpired, Stensvik jiggled the handset. The operator came on in a cautious voice. "Get me the President back. *Now!*" He waited, the receiver clasped to his ear.

A few minutes went by, then the operator came back on. "I'm sorry, President Stensvik. The White House isn't accepting any calls from North Haakovia."

With a curse of rage, Stensvik ripped the phone from the wall and threw it against the bulletproof glass of the window. The phone hit and broke, the pieces raining to the carpet.

Someone knocked at the door.

"Enter," Stensvik called, slumping into his seat behind the desk. He drained his drink in one swallow.

The security guard he'd assigned to find him another officer stepped into the room followed by Colonel Kalinin. "Your new officer, sir," the guard said by way of presentation.

"Thank you, Corporal. You're dismissed." Stensvik waved the colonel forward, but didn't offer him a seat. "You're aware of what happened to your predecessor, Colonel?"

"Yes, sir." The man kept his eyes forward, locked on the wall behind the desk.

Stensvik drew his pistol and placed it heavily on the desktop. "Then you know," he said, "that I am only entertaining positive views about the turn the war has taken this morning?"

The man managed to keep flinching to a minimum. "Yes, sir."

Stensvik smiled. "Then reassure me as to the outcome of what might happen. And be convincing."

MACK BOLAN SHOULDERED the M-16/M-203 combination, reached for the trigger of the grenade launcher as he sighted on his target and squeezed. The 40 mm warhead sped from the throat of the launcher and slammed into the tread of the North Haakovian T-62 tank. The warrior threw himself facedown as the machine gunner tried to follow him.

The grenade exploded, threw the gunner's aim off for a moment and blew the tread apart. It flapped mechanically and took control away from the driver, creating hollow booms that were quickly lost amid the noise of the rest of the battlefield.

Bolan flailed out with his free arm, pushing himself into a roll that brought him back to his feet in a crouched position. He lifted the M-16 into target acquisition and squeezed off a series of 3-round bursts that caught the tank's machine gunner across the chest and face. The dead man jerked back against the turret.

The ground trembled under the Executioner's driving legs as he sprinted for the disabled tank. He ripped a fragmentation grenade from his combat harness, tossed the lever and pulled the pin, counting down the numbers. With three seconds left, still on the run, he dropped the grenade down the hatch and backpedaled.

There was a double concussion. The first sounded muffled by the body of the T-62. The second seemed to make the world come apart around Bolan as the shells inside the Russian tank blew up. Moving in a solid sheet of force, the concussion lifted the big warrior from his feet and hurled him forward.

His breath exploded from his lungs when he hit the ground, and for a moment he thought he'd lost his assault rifle. Then he felt the pistol grip still snug between his fingers.

It hurt to sit up, but he forced himself to his feet, staggering a few steps before he regained his equilibrium. He reached up, made sure the headset had made the trip with him and adjusted the mouthpiece.

He reloaded the grenade launcher and the rifle, then began to advance again, moving within the perimeters charted for the South Haakovian infantry.

The armored divisions of the North and South had clashed slightly northeast of Tasenka Valley, about three more miles farther in than he'd thought. Though the North Haakovian forces had had earlier warning than he would have liked, they seemed to have trouble getting organized.

That wasn't the case with the South Haakovian armored cavalry. Those men had come to fight, stirred on by patriotic fervor and an edge they hadn't expected to carry into battle. Gary Manning's fireworks had built more of an impetus in the troops than Bolan had dared hope for.

He ran hard, aiming for an incline that would allow him a higher position to survey the battle. The ground was hard, carrying a light skim of mud and melting snow that occasionally made footing unsure.

A South Haakovian TOW team was headed for the same hill, slowed slightly by having to care for a wounded team member while carrying the equipment.

Without breaking stride, Bolan ran to the team, took the wounded man across his shoulders in a fireman's carry and said, "Move it." Even with the extra weight and the treacherous ground he made good time.

At the top he put down the wounded soldier, tied off the bullet hole in his leg and made him as comfortable as possible while the rest of the TOW team set up their weapon. The Executioner scanned the advancing line of tanks, still more than two hundred yards apart.

The assault buggies moved like scorpions, darting into open areas and launching attacks that either took tanks out of action or slowed them down. Moving a bit more cautiously, the Hummers cruised the outer edges of the battle, catching the North Haakovian tanks and infantry in vicious cross fires that left corpses in their wake. More than a dozen North Haakovian tanks were already burned-out shells in the middle of the battleground, becoming an uneven line of obstacles.

Bolan knew the South Haakovian attack was in danger of becoming bogged down by their own successes. And their attack on the rear and sides of the North Haakovian armor was boxing their opponents in, leaving them no choice but to stand and fight.

The South Haakovian infantry continued to operate from whatever cover it could find as the soldiers pushed in on North Haakovian positions and defended against enemy infantrymen.

The TOW team launched its first guided missile. The back blast drifted over the Executioner as he watched the 600 mm warhead strike its target. The initial impact made the tank shudder, then the plasma bolt continued to penetrate, driving all the way through the turret and exiting on the other side. Evidently out of control, the T-55 pushed over a tree, rolled up on it with one tread, then turned over on its side.

The TOW team was already setting up its next shot.

Bullets suddenly dug fist-size clods from the ridge of the hill and ripped bark from the trees.

Ducking, Bolan swept the terrain and spotted an advancing North Haakovian ground unit. He lifted the M-16 as he saw one of the enemy soldiers draw his arm back to throw a grenade.

The Executioner put a 5.56 mm tumbler through the man's shoulder, knocking him off balance. The grenade was dropped. Bolan put another soldier down as the rest of the unit scrambled for the dropped explosive. Then the bomb erupted and threw bodies in all directions.

The warrior thumbed the transmit button on his headset, called for the mortar unit and ordered it to get ready to lay down a layer of covering smoke.

"Stone Hammer Leader, this is Heavy Metal One. Over." Heavy Metal One was the code designation of the American officer in charge of the cohesive South Haakovian tanks units. Colonel Houston Dawes was old-line military with a flare for the new technological advances in tanks.

"Go," Bolan said.

"Why are we going to smoke, sir? We appear to have these bastards outgunned and outclassed."

"That's not just an appearance, Heavy Metal One. You people are doing your job too well. With every direct hit those tanks are scoring, you're creating your own roadblock up here. I want to give you some room to maneuver."

The thunder of the tank engines continued to vibrate through the forest, accompanied by the squeak of shifting treads, punctuated by the blasts of the main guns and the chatter of small arms.

"Understood, sir. When you give the signal for smoke, we'll pull back momentarily for a defensive posture and let the artillery earn its keep. Over."

Bolan cleared the channel, knowing that Dawes hated to give up the momentum the South Haakovian forces had built up. He hit the transmit button again and called for Footman Leader, the South Haakovian officer in charge of the infantry units.

"Go, Stone Hammer Leader. Over."

"When the smoke goes out, I want you to keep your people in the area. Seek-and-strike missions only, nothing deep. I want to keep as many of them intact as I can. What I'm looking for is a way around the mire and mess building up in front of our advance without losing ground."

"Acknowledged, sir. You can count on us. Footman Leader, out."

Another group of North Haakovian infantry tried to take the hill. Bolan leaned out with the M-16 and snapped off single shots, joined by the TOW team. Together they picked off most of the men before they were able to make it halfway. The Executioner put a 40 mm grenade in the defile where at least three enemy soldiers were hiding. No one was left alive when the smoke cleared.

He recharged his weapon, heard the crackle of static on his headset, then Yakov Katzenelenbogen's voice filled the freq.

"Stone Hammer Leader, this is Phoenix One. Over."

A grim smile cracked Bolan's dust-covered lips as he thumbed the transmit button. "I was beginning to wonder if everything had worked out."

"The terrain slowed us more than we'd thought," Katz said. "But we're here now."

"That," Bolan replied as he shoved himself to his feet, "is what I needed to hear, Phoenix One." He called for the smoke from the mortar teams, watching as the shells thumped down in the no-man's-land between the tanks.

Clouds of thick red smoke poured into the air, becoming a blood-colored fog that ran rampant through the trees and over the snow.

He checked with Grimaldi and McCarter, and found out the South Haakovian air forces were still dealing with the North Haakovia fighters high overhead, but would be available for rapid-strike runs as needed.

"Okay," Bolan said as he built the entire battlefield inside his mind in three dimensions, "let's hit this thing on the numbers. Kick it off, Phoenix One."

CHAPTER SEVENTEEN

Sitting in the passenger seat of the TOW-equipped Hummer, Yakov Katzenelenbogen surveyed the battlefield one final time.

His group of tanks was on a slope that topped out about two hundred yards above the North Haakovian forces and about eight hundred yards distant. A dense tree line hid most of them, but wouldn't prevent the main guns from being used when the time came.

The primary thrust of the battle was taking place left of Katz's position. While most of the North Haakovian forces were tied up trying to advance against Bolan's army, some were still busy trying to make the turn to get back into the action. The swooping dives of the A-10 Warthogs and the bombing runs of the F-15s made it hard for them to make it totally unscathed.

He watched as the dense red smoke hurled by the mortar brigade under Striker's orders filled the battle zone and obscured the South Haakovian tanks. The northern army started to advance again, thinking their opponents were pulling back.

It was, Katz knew, a rallying point for the northern commanders, a time when they thought the sacrifice of their troops and their equipment was not in vain. It was also his job to help them snatch defeat from the seeming jaws of victory.

The Israeli thumbed the trasmit button on his headset. "Okay, men, let's get our jobs done right the first time."

Six APCs charged through the trees and zipped down the incline to a position a little more than two hundred yards from the outer perimeter of the North Haakovian forces. Infantry deployed at once, securing cover behind natural formations and behind the shelled remains of Soviet tanks. The M-2 Bradleys formed a hard line facing the North Haakovian army, three turned southwest and three turned northwest. Armed with dual TOWs, the APCs began attacking the tanks immediately.

Only seconds after they were in place, the South Haakovian tanks crept forward, still taking cover along the ridge, and began to shell the North Haakovian positions.

"Take us down there," Katz told his driver.

The man nodded, hit the accelerator and let out the clutch.

Katz took out the Squad Automatic Weapon sitting behind his seat and slipped off the safety. He made sure the TOW was still operational, then keyed the headset. "Phoenix One to Stone Hammer Leader. Over."

"Go, Phoenix One."

"It appears your strategies are paying off."

"I see that," Bolan replied. "Keep the pressure on. While they're confused, we're making the end run to catch them in a cross fire again. Stone Hammer Leader out."

And it was true, Katz saw with grim satisfaction. The pincer movement Striker had called for was a simple military maneuver, but terribly efficient once it was working. Today it had worked because their opponents hadn't been expecting it, and because it was easy enough to coordinate even through the inexperienced South Haakovian troops.

The southernmost arm of the North Haakovian armor was stranded, mired between the tanks it had already lost, and the ones Katz's team were destroying right behind them. A MiG fell from the sky in flaming debris, scattering over a dozen of the North Haakovian tanks trying to figure out which way to go and how to get there. The fighter-jet wreckage killed at least three of the tank commanders as they surveyed the battle zones from the hatches of their vehicles.

Suddenly it felt like an earthquake erupted under the Hummer, nearly knocking it over on its side. The driver lost control for a moment, fought the steering wheel viciously and ground to a stop when the engine died.

A T-55 chewed up through the ridge, its treads tearing hunks of snow-covered soil loose and throwing them back down over the other tanks. It struggled onto level ground like a flailing turtle. With mechanical whining, the turret swiveled and leveled the main gun at the Hummer.

The driver ground the engine, but failed to get it started.

"Out," Katz ordered, hitting the driver with his shoulder. He forced the man out of the vehicle and into a run. "Move it, soldier, or you'll be dead in another heartbeat." Swinging around the SAW, Katz finished off the remainder of the clip as he followed his driver for cover.

The 5.56 mm rounds scattered over the tank like an angry horde of bees, managed no appreciable structural damage and did even less toward discouraging the attack.

Katz distinctly remembered hearing the whomp of the main gun, then the sizzling explosion of the sabot round striking the Hummer. The utility vehicle flipped over several times, crushed, bent and broken, and tumbled over the edge onto the retreating tanks.

By the time he had a fresh magazine clipped onto the SAW, the T-55 had turned its main gun on Katz.

"Yakov," McCarter's voice echoed in the headset, "grab some real estate and hang on to your bloody arse, mate."

Katz reached for his driver, bringing them both down in a sprawling dive as jet engines strained overhead. Looking up, he had a vague impression of an A-10 Warthog diving to the attack.

From a very close distance the Warthog started firing the seven-barrel revolving 30 mm cannon. Holes ripped in the ground, then chewed through the tank, slamming into it again and again as McCarter found the range.

It shuddered and quivered like a big cat, and was blown back over the edge of the incline it had climbed.

The Warthog screamed on through the sky unscathed.

Katz pushed himself to his feet and keyed the transmitter. "Thanks, David."

"We got lucky, mate. I just happened to see you were in a sticky bit on a pass through looking for targets. You take care of yourself down there."

"You do the same."

The Warthog dipped its wings and roared away.

Katz blew dirt and snow from the action of the SAW and made sure it was ready to be fired. He looked at the North Haakovian cavalry, saw that the split—though obviously not something they wanted—was definitely happening.

But much of the battle, he knew, remained yet to be fought. He moved forward to confront it head-on.

WITH AN INNATE SKILL that had one time embarrassed him as a rookie cop, Carl Lyons picked the lock on the third-floor apartment and opened the door. He held the Ithaca pumpgun in his right hand, the business end sweeping the small living room.

A man and a woman lay coiled together on a couch that hadn't seen a good day in a very long time. Moving wildly enough to let Lyons knew he was under the influence of either alcohol or drugs, the man shoved the woman off him and reached for the small pistol tucked under a cushion.

Lyons leaped forward and brought the butt stock of the shotgun smashing down. If either of them fired, the surprise they had planned would fall apart. The guy was hammered into unconsciousness at once.

"Not one scream," Lyons told the woman in a cold whisper as he swung the shotgun on her, "and you get to live."

She nodded her head, stayed on the floor and kept her arms across her breasts protectively. Ethan stepped forward, rolled her over, secured her arms with the disposable cuffs and gagged her with gray duct tape from a roll in his pocket.

Schwarz checked the kitchen while Blancanales covered the bedrooms. There were four people in the bedroom, but they didn't put up a fight when they found out what kind of firepower they were up against. Using the duct tape, Lyons and Ethan bound and gagged them, then stashed them in the kitchen under the table.

By the time they'd finished, Blancanales and Schwarz had started preparations for the second leg of the penetration.

According to their own intel as well as what they had picked up from the people in the laundry room, Rudy Vasquez was with Hector Osmundo in the suite of rooms carved from three of the regular apartments on the third floor. Two of the rooms fronted the north wall, and the third was along the east wall, forming an L. All of the doors had reinforced bars and bulletproof glass. The three rooms had become a fortress.

The room they were in now joined Vasquez's suite on the east side. Schwarz slipped the point of a heavy-bladed combat knife through the adjoining wall, cleaving the plaster easily. "You called it right, Ironman," he said as he withdrew the knife. "They didn't bother with any reinforcement along the walls. We can be through this PDQ."

"Get it done."

Blancanales pulled out the king size bed and pushed it against a wall away from the adjoining one. He shook it experimentally. "This thing's really not going to help contain much of the blast."

"With these walls," Schwarz said as he dug plastic explosive from his utility pack, "it's not going to take much. Hell, I bet Ironman could kick his way through. It's just with explosives, we make a more astounding entrance in a shorter amount of time." He retrieved a graphite pencil from his pocket and traced a rectangle along the wall roughly five feet by five feet. Taking a whitish block of C-4 from the pack, he tossed it to Blancanales. "Roll me out foot-long ropes about as wide as your finger. As many as you can get."

Satisfied that everything was going well, and feeling the need to move, Lyons went back through the apartment and peered through the window that looked onto the main entrance of Vasquez's suite. Ethan trailed him.

A man left the suite, dressed in a suit and wearing wraparound sunglasses even though it was pitch dark. His cigarette glowed for an instant, illuminating the pockmarks on his lean face. His hair was pulled back in a ponytail.

"Vasquez?" Lyons asked, figuring it would be about their luck now.

Ethan nodded his head.

From the brief glimpse allowed inside the suite, Lyons saw that it was well lighted and a number of people were still there. "I guess there's a party going on."

"Man's known for that," Ethan said. "Partying and Colombian neckties. That's why no one's been able to pin anything on him. If Vasquez can't buy you off, he kills you." He glanced at Lyons. "You sure you're going to know this Osmundo guy?"

Lyons nodded. Kurtzman's faxed intel had contained photos, as well as NCIC and Interpol information. Osmundo had taken care of his own violent work in his early days. He had the scars to prove it, and his body was still broad and blocky with muscle. The word the big Able Team warrior had was that Osmundo still liked to do his own killing when the chance presented itself. "Yeah. He'll be the guy who has a squared-off head like a railroad tie, and a face cut out with an ax by a blind man."

"Sounds lovely."

"Guy's a stone killer," Lyons said seriously. "Problem is, I need him alive and breathing."

"Ironman," Schwarz called softly.

Lyons moved to the back of the apartment, where Schwarz was working on a remote control. Fat C-4 worms clung to the wall around the rectangle that had been drawn, and three Xs of the same material filled out the center. Shiny moons that became electronic detonators as Lyons moved closer were imbedded in each line of plastic explosive.

"We're go here," Schwarz said.

Blancanales shoved the bedsprings over the mined wall.

"Okay," Lyons said, "let's ring in the first act." He moved back to the living room and gazed out the window. He tapped the headset's transmit button. "Downtown, this is Night Ranger. Over."

"Go, Night Ranger." Keller sounded tense.

"Let's rock and roll, guy. Night Ranger, out." Lyons peered through the glass intently, watching as two LAPD helicopters scooted into place over the apartment complex and suddenly switched on their spotlights. The harsh white beams slithered around the dark corners of the inner courtyard.

Doors started to open, and windows flew up. Men and women began to run for the exits from the courtyard, but found themselves cut off by uniformed policemen.

The PA system mounted under the bellies of the helicopters blared out even over the *wop-wop-wop* of the rotor blades. "This is the Los Angeles Police Department. We have a federal writ to search the premises. Failure to comply with this request will result in your arrest and subsequent criminal charges."

A few handguns cracked, the bullets throwing sparks off the sides of the helicopters. Police snipers in the open bays returned select fire. Three bodies dropped out of doorways and windows as the rounds hit their targets. Within seconds the apartment complex changed from a ghost town to an ant hill.

"Good to see so many concerned citizens willing to cooperate with their local police," Ethan said.

"I'm impressed," Blancanales replied. "The helicopters have *police* stamped all over them, and those guys still waited for the announcement before they started shooting."

"It's the illiterates," Ethan said. "Your average L.A. bad guy's intelligence quotient is dropping way below the national norm."

Ignoring the byplay, Lyons crossed the room and took up a position at the door to the bedroom. He pulled a gas mask from his kit, saw the others doing the same, then palmed two CS grenades. "Do the wall, Gadgets."

"Got it set up so the outer edges blow first," Schwarz said, "then the middle explosives punch it on through into the suite." He pressed the remote-control button.

Thunder filled the bedroom, rolled briefly, then the echoes started to die away.

Lyons was on the move, cutting the corner and pulling the pins on the grenades.

The explosives had blown a gaping hole in the wall. The torn and shattered bedsprings had been flung into the opposite wall, and broken boards jutted from the closet door.

Pitching underhanded, Lyons put both of the grenades through the opening, unslung the Ithaca and went through. The first room up was the kitchen galley. The grenades hissed white smoke and flooded the room.

Three cooks had been working over deep-fat fryers. One of them reached for a pistol in a drawer.

Lyons fired point-blank. The double-aught charge lifted the man from his feet and flipped him onto a grill. The scent of charring human flesh filtered through the big Able Team warrior's gas mask. Ethan shot the second man, spinning the body into the sink.

The third cook used the meat cleaver he had in his hand, swung it hard at Lyons, who was sliding on the tiles. The big ex-cop let it come as he regained his balance and felt it thud with bruising force against his Kevlar vest. He swung the butt stock of the Ithaca, wiping the surprised look off the cook's face. The unconscious body slumped to the floor.

A mustached face poked around the corner. "What the hell is going on, Alphonso?" Then he saw the armed men in the kitchen and brought up his gun hand.

Lyons shouldered the shotgun and pulled off two rounds. The face went away. Stripping two more CS grenades from his equipment pack, the Able Team leader heaved them into the next room. He paused at the doorway, splinters digging into his arm from where the buckshot had ripped away the wooden facing.

The setting at the formal dining room table was elegent, done in black on white. The six men inside the room looked out of place in the formal attire they wore. And the vicious little automatic pistols they had drawn, Lyons noted, didn't go with the cut of the suits at all.

He fired at two men bunched together, making the round perform double duty, and they went spinning away. Then he racked the slide and took out the closest guy with his last shell. The body slammed onto the table, destroying the glassware.

Whirling, Lyons confronted Blancanales, who had come behind him. As he thumbed more shells into the Ithaca, he said, "Six guys. One's down for good. Two others I shot up some. Three are unaccounted for." He racked the slide. "I got your back."

Blancanales nodded, brandished the MAC-10 he held, then charged into the room. The Ingram machine pistol chattered in Pol's hands as he threw himself into a slide. The thirty rounds of .45ACP cut a swath through the room, catching one of the wounded men and taking him permanently out of the play.

Swinging back around the doorway, Lyons leveled the shotgun and sought targets through the swirling CS gas and gunsmoke. As soon as he found one, he touched the trigger, racked the slide and searched for the next.

Blancanales reloaded on the fly and took out the last gunner before the man could get a bead on him.

From there the suite jogged left, heading west. Schwarz took the lead as Lyons reloaded, tossing more CS grenades ahead of them. The harsh crackling of automatic weapons sounded out in the courtyard, punctuated from time to time by bloodcurdling screams.

The living room took up two-thirds of the space available in the rest of the suite. It was open and spacious, with a lot of heavy furniture that provided plenty of cover.

A quick glance showed Lyons that at least a dozen people were in the room. Five of them were women, which left seven shooters. He looked back at his team and took out an M-429 grenade. "Thunderflash," he told Ethan. "I toss it in, there's going to be a hell of a lot of noise, a big flash that should blind most of the people in there and next to no damage."

Ethan nodded and took a two-handed grip on his 10 mm pistol.

Lyons slung the Ithaca and drew his .45. The laser sight splashed against the wall when he tested it. He popped the ring, counted down and tossed the M-429 into the room.

Startled exclamations rang out as some of the people inside realized what it was. The sound of smashing glass was drowned in the sudden roar of the grenade.

Even with his eyes squeezed shut tightly to prevent the flash from blinding him, Lyons sensed the light. Once it was gone, he cupped the Colt Government Model, swung around the doorway and moved into the room in a Weaver's stance.

A man moved to his left, raising an Uzi.

Lyons dropped the ruby dot of the laser sight over the man's forehead and triggered a round that yanked the man's face out of his line of sight. He heard the guns of his teammates firing around him as he swept the room, trying to compensate for the reduced peripheral vision through the gas mask.

The front door was secure. A body lay near it, a key still in the outstretched hand.

Then he saw Hector Osmundo's face in the doorway that led off to the bedrooms. The cartel man withdrew his head instantly and slammed the door shut.

Lyons tapped Schwarz's shoulder, said, "Osmundo," and ran for the bedroom door. He tried the knob but it was locked. Stepping back, he raised a leg and kicked, feeling his foot go almost numb with the impact. On the third try the lock gave, and the door banged into the wall.

A window along the side was open, draperies fluttering in the breeze.

"There's no fire escape," Schwarz said.

Lyons crossed the room at a run and poked his head out cautiously. "Drainpipe," he said in disgust as he saw the wide ribbon of metal that ran from the rooftop to the street below.

Hector Osmundo and another man, it took a second look to confirm that it was Rudy Vasquez, were legging it for a silver-gray BMW parked on the street below. Osmundo paused to fire a salvo of shots that tore brick chips from the walls around the window.

Lyons reached for the drainpipe, tested it with one hand and realized even if it held his weight, he'd be a sitting duck for Osmundo.

Vasquez opened the driver's side door and jumped inside. Osmundo paused at the passenger side to reload, then caught the door as it opened.

"Shit," Lyons said, knowing that if Osmundo got away Able Team had no chance of finding the second bacteriological agent before it was released. He pulled a collapsible grappling hook from his equipment pouch, flipped the arms out and shook out the knotted nylon cord. The fire escape was twenty feet away. He made the cast easily, settling the hook over the edge.

"Carl," Schwarz said, "you're not—"

"I wish," Lyons replied honestly, then flung himself out the window.

The BMW took off at once, heading in the same direction Lyons was swinging.

The Able Team warrior had to kick off the wall once as his downward swing neared full velocity, and he let another five feet of cord play through his hands. He felt the Ithaca slamming against his back. Then gravity neared zero as his swing reached its zenith. He twisted like a cat and saw the BMW coming directly below him.

He let go of the cord and dropped the fifteen feet onto the sports car's hard top. The impact was painful and knocked the wind out of him, but instinctively he gripped both sides of the roof with his hands.

The car swerved, jerked as it went up over a curb and shuddered when it slammed through a stack of trash cans.

Moving while he had his balance, aware of the marked police cars roaring down the street in hot pursuit, Lyons reached in through the open window and seized the steering wheel. He yanked hard, pulled it through Vasquez's hands, and aimed it at a Dumpster beside a fire hydrant.

Metal screeched and ripped when contact was made.

The vehicle slewed sideways, the front wheels locked in the Dumpster frame as the broken hydrant shot a geyser of water into the air.

Lyons lost his hold and fell from the sports car. He hit the street hard, felt his right cheek bruise and abrade. Even though he was unable to catch his breath immediately, he pushed himself upright on his knees and drew the .45.

Vasquez brought up an Uzi.

The ruby dot of Lyons's laser sight touched the man's cheek, and the big Able Team warrior dropped the hammer.

The .45 round snapped the dealer's head back as the short burst from the Uzi ripped through the BMW's roof.

"Don't," Lyons ordered as Osmundo began to stir, "even think about it. I need you alive, but I promise you I'll shoot off the big pieces."

Blood trickling down his forehead, Osmundo raised his hands and placed his palms against the windshield.

"I don't believe it," Blancanales said as he jogged up to Lyons. "There's no way you did what I just saw you do. No way."

"Wrong." Lyons pushed himself to his feet and pointed at Osmundo as the LAPD surrounded them. "Cuff that son of a bitch and haul his ass out of the car before it explodes or something. I'm not going to go to that kind of trouble only to lose him."

BROGNOLA STOOD near the coffee service in the Oval Office and allowed himself one more glazed doughnut. He didn't really want the damn thing, but it gave him something to do with his hands and it washed away the taste of the antacid tablets.

The President started an exhalation that rapidly turned into a jaw-creaking yawn. He took off his glasses and blinked blearily at the CNN footage of the battles taking place in North Haakovia as the South Haakovian forces pressed their assault. "It's still too soon to tell, isn't it?"

"Tell what?" Brognola asked.

"Whether the right decision was made."

Brognola poured himself a cup of coffee and approached the Man. "The right decision *was* made, sir. All that remains now is how clear-cut that decision's result will be."

The President steepled his fingers under his chin and continued to watch the television broadcast. "Striker's strategy in North Haakovia seems to be working well."

"Yes." Brognola sat in his chair and sipped the coffee. "But we planned on that when we sent him over there."

"I know. But, occasionally, I have to wonder if that was the right thing to do."

"That country would have gone down without us," Brognola replied, "and Stensvik would still have tried his blackmail games with the United States. No. If anything, maybe we moved a little too late on this thing."

"Perhaps."

Brognola knew what was worrying the President most was international response to South Haakovia's invasion of their aggressor. Before, South Haakovia had generated sympathy by being the underdog, but now—by reaching out so surely for the reins to their own manifest destiny—they had become a threat in their own right. It had to be making the Commonwealth nervous, as well as the Chinese. And the Japanese business interests Stony Man Farm had uncovered in their search wouldn't be happy, either.

But so far none of those people had contacted the White House.

The intercom buzzed and the big Fed thought maybe he'd figured that last part just a little too soon.

The President answered the intercom, found out it was Barbara Price and asked that she be put on. "Yes, Ms. Price."

"I've got an update from Able Team. They've cancelled the Los Angeles end of the plague, and local law-enforcement people there are working with the National Centers for Disease Control to track down as much of the tainted cocaine as possible. I've also been informed that a serum has been developed for infected victims that will cut down our losses out there."

"Did they get any information regarding other bacterial weapons in this country?" the President asked.

"There's only one," Price replied. "It's based in Niagara Falls, New York."

"How sure are you of the intel?" Brognola asked.

"We have Hector Osmundo. He's the cartel man who set up the shipments from North Haakovia to Cuba to the stateside ports. He's doing everything he can right now to save his own neck."

"Have we got someone out in New York we can rely on?" the President asked.

"Able Team is en route by military jet."

"Will they get there in time?"

"We believe so. We know the area where the Colombians are supposed to rendezvous with a North Haakovian liaison team almost five hours from now. Figure the three hours it takes to fly there and setup time, Able should be in place ahead of their schedule."

"And they don't know we know?" Brognola asked.

"No."

"If there's anything I can do from here..." the President said.

"I'll let you know, sir." Price broke the connection.

"That's a very efficient young woman you have there."

"Yeah," Brognola replied. "I know."

CNN continued to broadcast new footage from the battles, and the big Fed had to respect the guys behind the cameras. Whomever they were, they were in the middle of the hot spots with no way to claim neutrality.

The intercom buzzed again, and the secretary announced a phone connection with Niklai Tachek, the president of Russia. "Put it through."

"I trust everything is well with you?" Tachek said.

"As well as can be expected," the Man replied.

"I see you have not knuckled under to Stensvik's demands."

"Was there ever any question?"

"Some," Tachek admitted.

"And now that that question has been answered, what is your government prepared to do about it?"

Brognola waited for the reply. From the beginning of American involvement in South Haakovia there had been the possibility of Russian intervention on behalf of the North.

"For the moment," Tachek said, "nothing."

The President hesitated, leaning forward in his chair. "Why?"

Tachek's voice was dry and filled with a touch of mirth. "Because for the moment the South Haakovian forces appear to be winning. But should that change, you can expect our interests to push for intervention on the North Haakovian sector. Stensvik has the missiles."

"And if the South Haakovian forces should falter?"

"If you have a victory within your grasp," Tachek warned, "reach for it. If you delay, I might be forced to side with Stensvik anyway. I've talked to the Chinese government. They're more adamant about interfering in the outcome of the war between the Haakovias. If your win doesn't come soon, I'd expect some pressure from them."

"Thanks for the words of warning."

"I felt I owed them to you," Tachek said. "Fortune be with you, my friend." The phone connection clicked dead.

The President returned the receiver to the cradle slowly. "So now we know where we stand on those issues."

"It's where we figured," Brognola pointed out.

''Yeah, but we have no way to let Striker know how much is riding on him.''

''Political mud fights wouldn't interest that man,'' Brognola said. ''And you couldn't get him any more motivated about this war if you tried. He's fighting for freedom, and that's the one thing Striker has stood for all his life. When the smoke clears on this, I have no doubt that he'll still be standing.''

CHAPTER EIGHTEEN

Four hours after the initial rounds had been fired, Mack Bolan called a halt to the advancing South Haakovian armored units and had them dig into the last protective cover they had before they reached the capital city.

Less than twenty percent of the North Haakovian armor survived the encounter. They limped back toward the city across a muddy plain filled with low-slung hills.

Bruised and battered, mud and blood staining his uniform, Bolan stood at the highest point of the South Haakovian line amid a copse of trees and watched the tanks run. He took a pair of binoculars from his chest pocket and scanned the retreat.

The aerial battle was still going on, though the encounters had lessened drastically. Both sides were too evenly matched to allow the other side supremacy, and the costs were going up in machines and men as fatigue became a factor.

The war was, as Bolan had known from the beginning, going to be decided on the ground.

Yakov Katzenelenbogen came to a halt beside him, leaning out of the chill wind for a moment to light a Camel cigarette. When he spoke the breeze snatched the smoke from his lips and strung it out to nothing. "If we go any farther, we risk taking on a number of casualties."

"I know. So far we've been luckier than we had any right to be."

"It wasn't luck," the Israeli replied. "It was planning. Fast Break worked even better than we thought it would."

Bolan glanced back over his shoulder. "Those men back there fought their asses off. That's what made this whole operation."

"You gave them something to believe in," Katz said. "A soldier who believes he can defeat his enemy has a much better chance of doing that than a soldier who doesn't believe it."

"Yeah. Well, now we're going to have to give them something more." The Executioner took out his map case and selected the map he wanted. He unfolded it, laid it on the ground and secured it in place with rocks at all four corners. "Get your team together."

Katz waved Manning, Encizo and James over. McCarter was still in the air. The Phoenix Force members looked haggard and tired, their uniforms streaked with mud and torn by bullets and terrain. They hunkered down around the map.

Bolan took a penlight from his pocket, but left it off while he pointed out features on the map. It was a street map, complete with handwritten notations he'd added from surveys Aaron Kurtzman had run. "This is Sturegorsk's presidential buildings." He tapped the sheet, indicating the rectangles representing the structures. "There are seven stories, five above ground and two below. The walls are designed to withstand anything short of a low-yield nuclear attack. Machine-gun ports cover the inner courtyard in all directions. It's mined."

"I take it we're not going through the front door," Encizo said.

Bolan flashed him a grin. "No." He pulled a diagram from his chest pack, one he'd drawn to scale on the vocal information Kurtzman and Price had gleaned from their informant. He placed it on the map, securing it with another rock. "According to Barb and the Bear, the lowest floor in the presidential building has an Olympic-size pool in it. That pool—" he pointed to the diagram "—has a drain tunnel that locks into a main sewer system under Sturegorsk."

"We're going through the sewer," Calvin James stated.

"Yeah."

The ex-SEAL shook his head. "Man, I *knew* you were going to say that."

"That's the only weak spot I could find. Any other attack risks too many losses. We need to get Janyte Varkaus clear of the area if we can, and we need to knock out the intelligence center so we can roll our armored vehicles into the city. Without taking the intelligence center, we're going to risk heavy losses on the cav units when we try to take Sturegorsk."

"We're going to try to take the city?" Manning asked. He scraped his face, peeling away dried flecks of blood from a long scratch along his jaw.

"We've come this far," Katz said. "If we turn back now, this thing could drag on for months, or perhaps years."

"Right," Bolan agreed. "One way or another, we're going to finish this thing today. South Haakovia has staked everything they have in this battle. They know it's all or nothing at this point. We're going to shave the odds and see if we can make it all."

"I'm in," Manning said. Encizo and James quickly echoed their teammate's decision.

"What about the nuclear warheads Stensvik has?" Katz asked.

"We try to take him down before he can use them," the Executioner replied. "If not, Aaron's running backup for us."

James looked back at the diagram. "So the sewer system lets us into the pool drain. Where do we go from there?"

"I'm after Janyte Varkaus and Stensvik," Bolan told him. "They'll be on this floor. The intelligence center is on the fourth floor. Katz will be leading a group toward those people. Once their computer network is destroyed, we give the order for the cav units to roll. At the speed they should be able to maintain over the terrain from here to Sturegorsk, we're looking at being inside the building for forty, forty-five minutes before reinforcements arrive."

"Could be tough," Encizo said.

"No doubt about it," Bolan replied. "That building is a fortress, and you can bet security will be crawling all over it. Our only ace will be to create as much confusion and cause as much damage as we can in as short a time as possible."

"If we blow the power relays and knock out the generators," Manning said, "we'll buy some time."

Bolan nodded. "The power goes before we break out of the pool area." He pointed to the diagram. "Underground cables supplying electricity are outside these walls."

"How thick are they?" Manning asked.

The warrior consulted the notes he'd made in his war book. "Three feet."

"Made out of what?"

"Concrete."

"Reinforcing plates?"

"No. They were counting on the ground acting as the major buffer."

"Okay," Manning said. "I can take those out, no problem."

"I'll hold you to that," Bolan replied.

"Where are the generators?" Katz asked.

"Top floor. That will be your second objective after the mission-control station. As we've already seen from satellite pictures, the presidential buildings are buttoned up against attack. Steel shutters cover the windows, and the doors are airtight against gas attack. We take out the power, and those people are going to be in the dark. Our kits will contain NVGs. It should give us an edge while we're inside."

"If it goes down that way," Encizo stated, "we could be talking about a cakewalk once we're inside."

"'If,'" Bolan said, "at this stage is a big word."

"Yeah."

Bolan glanced at Katz. "Yakov, anything you'd like to add?"

"No. It seems straightforward enough to me. Nothing cute, no fancy extra moves. It's doable."

"Anybody else?"

The men of Phoenix Force shook their heads.

"Then let's get it done." Bolan gathered the map and the diagram and replaced them in his gear.

The North Haakovian shelling continued, but it was more of a show than a defense. The South's cav units weren't moving into their radius. But the frequent explosions and the earth-jarring impacts remained in the periphery of every man's senses.

Bolan hit the transmit button on the headset. "Colonel Antavas?"

"Yes."

"I need to speak to you."

"Yes, sir." Down at the front line of the tanks, Antavas jogged from the ranks of his officers toward Bolan and Phoenix Force. The South Haakovian military man was squat and stocky, as tanned as an old saddle. He fired Bolan a crisp salute.

The warrior returned it. "I'm giving control of the armored units over to you now, Colonel."

"Why?" Antavas appeared slightly confused.

Bolan gave him a reassuring grin. "Because I'm moving the front line ahead of the army." He quickly outlined the mission he and Phoenix were about to undertake. "If we're successful in knocking out the central command post, the city should be open to you and those men."

"And if you're not?"

"Then you stand and fight for as long as you can. If you can advance on the city without losing this army, do so. But remember that you and these men are the only things holding North Haakovia from your country. If you falter or fail, your nation might fall with you, and everything we've worked for last night and today will be for nothing."

"Yes, sir. You can rely on me."

"I already am, soldier." Bolan called McCarter and told him to come in to pick up Phoenix and him. Grimaldi would remain in command of the South Haakovian air defenses until the operation ended.

Antavas offered Bolan his hand and the warrior accepted it. "I want to wish you good luck, Colonel."

"If we do this right, maybe we won't need it." He clapped the man on the shoulder. "You take care of yourself, Colonel, and you get these boys home after this is over like we promised."

Antavas saluted him.

Bolan moved out at a jog, running for the UH-60A Blackhawk transport copter McCarter put down in a clearing behind the line of South Haakovian tanks. Two more Patriot missiles destroyed targets overhead, creating a double peal of thunder.

He went in through the cargo hatch, immediately moving forward to the passenger seat. Katz, Encizo, Manning and James were at his heels. Once inside, the Israeli took charge of handing out the counterterrorist gear they would be using. The team stripped off and began suiting up for the mission.

McCarter was already outfitted in a combat blacksuit and a Kevlar vest. A Nomex hood fitted securely under his combat harness. His Browning Hi-Power was belted at his hip, with an identical one in shoulder leather. The Heckler & Koch MP-5 he was using as his lead weapon was secured under his seat.

Bolan hit the transmit button on the headset and doffed the South Haakovian uniform. "Stone Hammer Leader to G-Force. Over."

"Go. You have G-Force."

McCarter lifted off.

"Roger, G-Force. Initiate Windfall. Clay Pigeon is en route."

"Acknowledged, Stone Hammer Leader. You have Windfall in progress. G-Force, out."

Bolan took the pack of clothing Katz handed to him and began to dress.

"Geez," Manning said, "there's fresh underwear in here." He held up a pack. "Did anybody in here really think we were that close to not making it?"

Bolan grinned as he pulled on the Nomex jumpsuit. "I wasn't thinking that at all, Gary. Just remembered that clothes make the man. Figured we'd all feel better going in fresh. There's socks in there too. You'll probably want to double them up. You won't stay dry long after we hit those tunnels.''

"Ah." Encizo sighed. "You offer us hope, only to yank it away."

Bolan pulled on two pairs of socks, working his feet into the dry pair of boots that came with his ready-kit. Then he added the rest of his gear, leathering the Desert Eagle at his hip and the Beretta in its shoulder harness. He slipped the Nomex hood into his chest pocket. The M-16/M-203 was going to remain his lead weapon, so he stocked up on clips and grenade rounds.

Glancing through the Plexiglas nose of the Blackhawk, he saw Grimaldi arc through the sky with four other F-15s trailing him in a staggered V shape.

McCarter swung out around the main part of the battlefield and resumed a course for the northeast section of Sturegorsk. Windfall was designed to focus the attention of the North Haakovian radar on the approaching F-15s and allow the Blackhawk to fly in at just above ground level. The top speed for the helicopter was 180 mph. At that rate they could reach their goal in just over ten minutes.

Less than a minute later antiaircraft fire filled the air around the five F-15s. The fighter jets kicked loose rockets and bombs, aiming at targets well away from the presidential buildings. None of the South Haakovian planes were touched.

Nine minutes after that, McCarter steered the Blackhawk to an older section of Sturegorsk that wasn't as well defended as the areas around the presidential buildings and the military outposts.

Still, it was too much to hope for that they would arrive unseen, even after Grimaldi and his team had done their best to attract hostile attention.

"We've been made," James called from the open cargo door. The wind plucked at the loose wrinkles of the Nomex suit.

The low, throaty roar of .50-caliber machine guns beat through the whirling rotor blades.

"Where?" Bolan asked as he studied the North Haakovian street map and compared it to the blasted rubble spread out below them.

"North, northeast of us," James replied.

"Two jeeps," Katz added.

Finding the landmark he was looking for, a park that obviously hadn't been used in years, Bolan pointed. "There, David."

McCarter nodded. "I see it, mate." He moved the stick, dropping the Blackhawk to the street. The wheels touched, rolled and stopped near the manhole they were going to use to enter the sewer system.

"Let's go," Bolan said, surging from the passenger seat.

James shoved open the cargo door and ran for the manhole cover, prying tool already in hand. The jeeps roared around the block at the end of a crumbled building where glass shards from broken windows lay like gleaming water pools. The Blackhawk kept the North Haakovian soldiers from having a clear view of everything that was going on. Machine-gun fire tapped the helicopter's body, sounding like frantic beats on a snare drum.

Encizo and Manning debarked, carrying the rest of the team's equipment packs, and moved at a dead run to the open manhole where James was already descending. McCarter reached under the pilot's seat and flipped a toggle switch on a black box. An LED flashed crimson numbers, starting with 30, 29, 28 . . .

Wheeling around the Blackhawk, Bolan reached for the trigger of the M-203 and fired a grenade at the lead jeep. The driver must have seen the 40 mm warhead coming, because he tried to make adjustments. But there was no time. The grenade impacted against the grillework, blew the metal in toward the engine and flipped the jeep sideways. It caught fire just before it slid into its companion.

"Come on," McCarter urged as he dropped through the manhole.

Bolan joined him, covering the rear for Katz as the Israeli dropped through next. The Executioner slung the M-16, slid his body through the hole and lowered himself. A few heartbeats after he dropped below street level, the Blackhawk blew up. Flames and metal rolled across the opening. He waited until they died down, then reached up and pulled the manhole cover back into place.

The warrior reached into his equipment pack, took out the NVGs and put them on. Most of the murk of the sewer tunnel faded away, leaving him enough light to work by. "Okay," he said to his companions, "that was the easy part. Let's get the rest of it done."

James took point and they moved out.

"WHERE ARE THEY NOW?" Franzen Stensvik said into the telephone.

"Still thirty miles out, President Stensvik," Gerik replied from the central command post. "They are holding their position just out of reach of our rockets. Every time we try to hit them with Scuds, they retaliate with the Patriots. We've gotten nothing through their defenses."

"Dammit!" Stensvik roared. "Find a way. If you allow them to set up there, they will simply roll their artillery up until they are shelling the city."

"Yes, sir."

"And what of the South Haakovian helicopter that was spotted in the northeast quadrant of the city?"

"It was destroyed in battle with some of our roving patrols."

"Destroyed?"

"Yes, sir."

Stensvik considered that. "How many men were aboard?"

"I didn't ask."

"Do it now, fool." He didn't like the thoughts that crowded into his mind. The waiting South Haakovian armor massed within his borders gave physical reality to the fog of his paranoia. There had to be some linchpin he could reach out for that would release him from the nightmare that had taken shape this morning. His stomach rolled with nausea. When the elevator cage arrived at the designated floor, he held the stop button with his palm, keeping the door open.

"There were no bodies discovered in the wreckage, sir," Gerik reported back.

Stensvik grunted. "So what should that tell you?"

"That the South Haakovians weren't killed."

"Find them," Stensvik roared. "They're somewhere in this city, setting about some kind of mission that can only bring more ruin to us. Find them and stop them."

"Yes, sir."

Stensvik slammed the phone into its cradle so hard that the plastic body cracked and showered parts onto the carpeted floor.

Two guardsmen fell into step just behind him as he marched to Janyte Varkaus's prison cell. He put the key in the lock and entered without knocking. He was disappointed that he didn't catch her unawares.

Instead the woman sat calmly on the sofa, her bare feet curled under her legs. The room was nearly dark, and he stood for a moment letting his eyes adjust. Then he walked toward her, a merciless smile twisting his lips.

"Madam President," he said, clicking his heels together and reaching for her hand as if to kiss it.

She didn't jerk it away as he'd anticipated, moving forward instead with considerable force and fury. Something shiny and sharp came at him, clenched tightly in her hand.

"Die, you pig!" she screamed vehemently.

Stensvik was so caught off guard that he couldn't move. The gleaming object struck him full in the chest, then snapped against the tight weave of his bulletproof vest under the military uniform jacket. He saw the sharp piece of mirror drop between his feet, felt the adrenaline kick into his system.

She was frozen for a moment, staring in mute surprise at the shattered stub of the mirror in her white-knuckled fist. Thin streamers of blood curled and twisted around her narrow wrist. Then she attacked him with renewed vigor, slashing at his eyes.

Stensvik backhanded her, slapping her again and again until she fell to the floor. He yelled for the guards, trying not to let the fear sound in his voice.

They arrived immediately, saw the woman crumpled on the floor, tears of silent rage streaming down her face.

"Clean up this cow as soon as you can," Stensvik ordered, "and bring her to the broadcasting room. She has a speech to make in the next few minutes, and I want her presentable." He headed for the door, and by the time he reached the hallway, he'd decided that once Janyte Varkaus had delivered her speech on television, she had outlived her usefulness. And he would take great pleasure in ending *all* the threats she posed to him once and for all.

CHAPTER NINETEEN

Carl Lyons trained the infrared binoculars on the one-hundred-sixty-seven-foot drop of the American Falls, then swept them from left to right, taking in the coastline of Goat Island. Dawn was beginning to streak the eastern skies, muddying them with the prophetic color of blood, warring with the colored searchlights that still turned Niagara Falls into a panoramic fantasy of changing hues.

A number of boats floated in the white-capped waters. Some of them, the big Able Team warrior knew, had been rented by honeymooners getting ready to start their lives together.

And he also was grimly aware that if Franzen Stensvik and his covert team were successful, Niagara Falls would be the spawning ground of a new disease that would spread throughout the American and Canadian sides of the Falls.

Dropping the binoculars to hang by their strap for a moment, Lyons ran a big hand over his face. After nearly an hour of staring through the lenses, he didn't feel like he had much left to give. His beard stubble crackled under his fingers, feeling pointed and sharp against his skin.

In another half hour, the black wet suit he was wearing would make him stand out on the deck of the cruiser the harbor patrol was letting Able Team use for the surveillance effort.

"Ironman."

Lyons glanced aft and saw Pol Blancanales standing near the cabin with his own binoculars raised. Like Lyons, Blancanales was outfitted in a black wet suit. "Yeah."

"I got it." Blancanales's delivery was calm and understated.

The big ex-cop shifted, which made his bruised ribs hurt with the movement. L.A. hadn't been an easy jaunt, and there had been no recovery time during the quick flight to New York. "Where?"

"Eleven o'clock," Blancanales replied. "The *Lazy Marie*'s just chugging past the Bridal Veil and Luna Island."

Lyons moved the field glasses to the direction his teammate pointed out. The Bridal Veil was the third set of falls making up Niagara Falls, and was set apart from the American Falls by the small island.

The *Lazy Marie* was a large sleek motor-sailer, and there was definitely more crew aboard than necessary.

Lyons raised his voice. "Gadgets."

"I see them." Schwarz was behind the wheel, monitoring random radio frequencies for anything out of the ordinary. He started the engine, moved the cruiser out into the mainstream of the Niagara River and started cutting in for the motor-sailer.

"Dag Vaino's aboard," Blancanales said.

"You're sure?" Lyons asked.

"Yeah. Caught a glimpse of him as he was going below deck."

Lyons's adrenaline level kicked up. Vaino had locked horns with Striker and Phoenix Force. The terrorist was good, there was no gainsaying that. He slipped on his headset, tuning it to the frequency used by the harbor police and patrol units coordinating the action with him. None of the commanders had appreciated being left in the dark concerning what they were doing there, nor did they like deferring to a group of men they couldn't identify. But Barbara Price's request from the Justice Department had carried a presidential signature. All bitching about chain of command went on behind closed doors from that point on. "Marlin Leader, this is Santiago. Over."

"Go, Santiago. You have Marlin Leader."

"We've confirmed the bogey."

"Roger. We have her, too."

"On our signal then, Marlin Leader, and not before. Santiago, out." Lyons reached down and unhooked the big flare gun he'd tied to the railing. He raised his voice so it would reach his teammates. "Where's Vaino?"

"Don't know," Schwarz replied.

"How long has he been down?"

"Ten minutes."

Lyons looked at the motor-sailer, which was less than two hundred yards away now.

"Son of a bitch," Blancanales said.

Lyons turned to look at him. "What?"

"Is it my imagination, or is that boat sitting higher in the water now?"

Snapping his head around and lifting the infrared binoculars to his eyes, Lyons looked at the waterline. "It's not your imagination, Pol."

"Pressurized deployment in the hull," Schwarz said in sudden understanding. "They're getting out under the water."

"Yeah," Lyons said. "Let's go." He ran for the back of the cruiser where three Jet Skis were tied up waiting. Reaching for their stacked gear, he took out an air tank, slipped on the face mask and a pair of fins, then slung a spear gun and extra shafts over his shoulder. The Colt

Government Model was in shoulder leather, protected by the holster, and the .357 wheelgun was at his hip.

Pausing at the aft railing, he aimed the flare gun skyward and pulled the trigger. The flare jetted from the muzzle, burning into a falling crimson star high overhead.

"We're made," Blancanales said.

The announcement came only heartbeats ahead of the sudden autofire that raked the side of the cruiser.

Lyons flung the flare gun to one side, threw himself out into the river and swam for the nearest Jet Ski. The ignition caught instantly and he revved the powerful engine, bringing the craft around in a tight arc as he aimed it for the American Falls. He was aware of Blancanales and Schwarz scant lengths behind him.

The Jet Ski took flight at times as he skimmed across the white breakers. It jarred him with bruising force when he hit the surface of the river, aggravating his aching ribs. Bullets zipped and spun around him. He lowered his head, staying heavy on the handlebars as he fought for control.

The flashing lights mounted on the harbor police and patrol boats came into view. The two police helicopters that had been waiting in secluded places on either shore were flying closer, searchlights waving across the water. Gunfire from the *Lazy Marie* quickly shifted from the three Jet Skis to the approaching officials as the helmsman of the motor-sailer tried to make his bid for freedom.

Lyons aimed the Jet Ski at Goat Island and arced out around the suction of the falls.

According to the information Osmundo had, the North Haakovian teams were going to release the bacteriological agent behind the American Falls in the Cave of the Winds, and use the river itself as the medium. On its way through the river the agent would also infect the wildlife in the area, which would keep the bacteria alive and viable for a much longer time.

At the base of the American Falls, Lyons flipped the Jet Ski over, released it and dived deep, stroking for the bottom of the falls so he wouldn't be pounded into unconsciousness. His ears throbbed with the pressure.

The water turned black in short order, making it hard to get his bearings. He slipped a luminous compass from his combat harness, followed the directions he and Schwarz had arrived at and swam as hard as he could.

Long minutes ticked by, lost in the soundless void trapped inside the rush of the water falling over the cliffs above him. There was a moment of confusion, his body was battered, then he was suddenly on the other side of the falls, feeling himself pushed forward instead of being pushed backward.

He angled up immediately. Within seconds he broke through to the surface, kicked to maintain his position and dropped the face mask and the air tank into the water. The misty breeze of the climate inside the Cave of the Winds broke over him, spraying him with water.

Taking the night-vision goggles from his combat harness, he slipped them into place, which turned the darkened cave into a landscape he could see. Blancanales and Schwarz popped into view beside him.

A line of autofire chopped into the water.

Lyons went under at once, mentally marking the area where the bullets had come from.

The cave was seventy-five feet by one hundred feet, with ledges cut out by the natural driving force of the falls. Dag Vaino and his group were scattered along a couple of them. Lyons wasn't sure how many men were there, but he knew at least two of them were on each of the three waterproof crates that rested on those ledges.

The big Able Team warrior kicked out strongly, unslung the spear gun and felt rock come up under his foot. He paused, found secure purchase under his tennis shoe and pushed up. The lenses of the NVGs were fogged over by the water, but they still allowed him to see his enemy.

He pointed his weapon at the nearest North Haakovian and pulled the trigger. The spear leaped across the distance, smashed into the guy's chest with a meaty thwack and sent him stumbling into two other men. His blood-curdling cry stopped when he hit the ground, dead.

As he cast the spear gun to one side, Lyons swept the .357 Magnum from his hip and thumbed the trigger back. A man tried to bring his assault rifle into play, but Lyons placed a bullet at the base of his throat, hammering the man backward and draping him over one of the crates. Lyons searched for Vaino. The last thing he wanted to do was to lose the terrorist in the dark.

Pol Blancanales came out at the water's edge, a compact MAC-10 clasped in his hand. He burned off a sustained burst, clearing the men from around another waterproof container without harming the crate.

Gadgets fired his Beretta as soon as he came free of the water. Five rounds staggered one gunner back from the crates, toppling him into another man. Another salvo of shots killed the second guy before he could get to his feet.

Finishing off the load in the wheelgun, Lyons reached for the .45, aware of movement coming at him from out of the shadows.

"Ironman!" Blancanales shouted. "Look out!"

Vaino's face swam into Lyons's vision for just a moment. Then the terrorist hit the big ex-cop in a full-body tackle that took both of them into the water.

Struggling to keep from breathing, caught off-guard and hurting for oxygen, Lyons dropped the .45, remembering the glimmer of steel in Vaino's hand that was the signature of a knife.

He kicked out at the terrorist and reached for his knife arm, wondering why the man had jumped him. Then his foot rebounded off Vaino's air tank, letting him know the former KGB agent was planning on making some type of getaway in the confusion.

The knife arm eluded Lyons.

Then he felt electric fire burn along his left bicep, knew he was cut, but wasn't sure how bad.

Working off the adrenaline rush, knowing he was building up an oxygen debt he wasn't going to be able to pay off without surfacing soon, Lyons trailed his fingers along Vaino's side, up to his arm and down to his hand. He wrapped his fingers around the man's wrist and hung on.

Vaino head-butted, which filled Lyons's mouth with the taste of blood.

Using his free hand, the Able Team leader reached down to his calf to free his Randall survival knife. Vaino fought against him, kicked out with his feet and gouged for Lyons's eyes with his other hand.

Unable to hang on to the man, Lyons felt the terrorist's wrist slip through his fingers, then felt him kick away. Without hesitation, even though his lungs were screaming for attention, he launched himself in pursuit.

Vaino dived deeper. Lyons caught the man around the ankle and pulled himself up behind the terrorist. Vaino tried to turn, but the undertow of the falls was beginning to suck at them, slowing his movement.

Lyons pulled himself up Vaino's body, locked his free arm around the terrorist's head, then slashed the Randall survival knife across his adversary's throat. He hung on until he felt all life jerk from the man's body.

When he let go, he knew he wasn't going to make it back to the surface. His lungs were burning, and black spots were starting to dance in the blindness created by the dark water. He stroked once, twice, then felt his arms and legs go rubbery as the undertow claimed him. Even if he made it through the falls relatively unharmed, he knew he wouldn't be able to hold his breath that long.

He stroked again, and a hand curled around his wrist. Someone thrust an air resuscitator between his teeth. He bit down, took a deep breath and let himself be guided toward the surface.

When they were out in the Cave of the Winds again, Lyons saw Blancanales sitting on one of the ledges with a flashlight in one hand and the MAC-10 in the other. The only North Haakovians in sight were dead ones. The crates remained unmoved.

"Look what I found," Schwarz said with mock pride as he helped Lyons toward the ledge.

"I see it," Blancanales replied as he played the flashlight beam over Lyons as the big warrior sat down and gulped fresh air. "You going to keep it, or are you going to throw it back?"

Lyons glanced at them seriously. "You try throwing me back, and I'm dragging both your asses with me." He glanced at the crates. "Did we get them?"

"Oh, yeah," Schwarz said. "Of course, while you were dancing around with Vaino, Pol and I had to do a little double duty to get the job done."

"What about yours?" Blancanales asked. "Is this going to be one of those big-one-got-away stories?"

"Not a chance. Vaino is fish food. Get hold of Stony Man and tell Barb we've got this end wrapped. The rest is up to Striker and Phoenix Force."

MACK BOLAN LED THE WAY through the drainage tunnel with his flashlight. The group was bone-tired from moving bent over at a fast clip, carrying full gear through three miles of tunnels and bad air.

Manning moved forward at the Executioner's wave and fixed a clump of plastic explosive to the circle of metal holding closed the large swimming pool drain on the lowest underground floor of the presidential building. "Twenty seconds," the Canadian said as he fell back with the others away from the shaft. "When that charge blows, it's going to release a real turd-floater."

Encizo gazed glumly into the central channel of the sewer. "You know," he said, "that's exactly what I'm afraid of."

The C-4 went off with a hollow bong that was lost immediately in the rush of water that cascaded into the central channel. The scent of chlorine and pool chemicals cut through the sweet smell of rot. The flow didn't quite raise the water level over the edge.

Once the water stopped running, Bolan walked under the shaft and looked up. Manning's charge had done its job, leaving the way clear up into the swimming pool. The warrior took his collapsible grappling hook from his kit, tossed it fifteen feet straight up and hooked it over the edge on the first cast. He went up hand over hand.

The bottom of the pool was still wet, its uneven surface covered with dozens of small puddles. Bolan got his feet under him and trotted for the shallow end. He unslung the M-16/M-203 as he ascended the steps.

No one was in the room. Electric lights mounted on the walls lighted the interior, giving a garish cast to the potted plastic ferns and chaise lounges. A number of the small, round wrought-iron patio tables had gaily colored umbrellas jutting from them.

Manning and James went to work on the walls.

Bolan looked at Katz. "McCarter and Encizo are with me. We're trying for Janyte Varkaus first, then make our attempt on Stensvik."

"Good hunting," Katz said, then exchanged glances with his teammates.

Encizo gave him a brief nod. McCarter flipped him a quick salute filled with jaunty enthusiasm.

"You, too," Bolan said.

Manning looked over his shoulder and continued to work. "Hey, guy, when I bring these walls down to disrupt the power supplies, everybody in this building's going to know it."

"That," Bolan said with a brief wintry smile, "can only work in our favor." He pulled the Nomex hood over his face and led the way out into the hallway, slipping the silenced 93-R into his hand.

A guard, intent on his cigarette almost twenty feet down the hall, spun around as they came out of the pool room. Evidently the room was soundproofed to an extent and he hadn't heard the muffled explosion that had drained the pool. He tried to bring up his AK-47.

Bolan dropped the Beretta into target acquisition and fired two rounds, which drilled into the gunner's face and punched him to the ground.

Encizo grabbed the corpse by the collar and dragged him into the pool room. McCarter crushed the cigarette underfoot and scuffed it up against the wall.

The stairwell was behind a plain white metal door and lighted by dim bulbs that were spaced too far apart. Voices, not very distant and coming closer, warned Bolan that they weren't alone. He waved his companions into hiding under the steps.

Noiselessly they slipped combat knives from their sheaths.

The pair of presidential security guards never knew what hit them as they walked toward the door. Encizo and McCarter stepped from the shadows in concert, clapped a hand over the mouth of each man and shoved the blades in textbook fashion between the third and fourth ribs.

The Executioner stepped over the bodies as the Phoenix Force members dragged them into hiding and started up the flight of stairs.

"Worse than bloody Hansel and Gretel," McCarter commented as he followed.

"They left bread crumbs, not corpses," Encizo pointed out.

Bolan halted at the landing, checked briefly through the small glass panel and opened the door.

Two men stood guard over one of the rooms he thought might hold Janyte Varkaus. Over his companion's shoulder, the most distant soldier spotted Bolan emerging from the stairwell. The guy shouted a warning and started to unsling his rifle.

Still moving forward at a walk, Bolan fired by point sighting. He put two bullets over the heart of the man facing him. As the other guard turned, he fired again, placing the round through the man's shoulder to knock him off balance. While the guy was still struggling to pull his weapon into play, the warrior fired again. The round hit him in the fleshy part of his thigh and slammed him from his feet. The AK-47 fell to the floor, and Encizo recovered the weapon before the man could reach for it again.

Kneeling beside the wounded man as he backed up tight against his dead comrade, Bolan said in a graveyard whisper, "I hope you now how to speak English." He raised the Beretta. "Otherwise you're no use to me at all."

McCarter worked on the door lock, had it open in seconds and passed through with the Browning Hi-Power leading the way.

Face gray with pain, both hands covering his wounds, the soldier nodded. "Yes. I know English."

"Good." Bolan looked up as McCarter reemerged from the prison cell.

The Briton shook his head. "Lady was definitely there, mate. But she's gone now. I found some blood in there, too. Still fresh." He held up a crimson-stained handkerchief.

"How much?"

"Not enough. Wherever she is, she's still alive. Or, at least she was when she left this room."

Returning his attention to the soldier, Bolan said, "You're going to tell me where Janyte Varkaus is."

"The TV room," the soldier said in a quavering voice. "The president took her to the TV room."

"Where?"

"Third floor above ground."

"Why?"

"The president is going to use her to make the South Haakovian army stop its advance on the city."

Working quickly, Bolan bound the man's wounds, then used a pair of disposable cuffs to bind his hands behind his back. Encizo helped carry the soldier into the prison cell, and McCarter relocked the door.

They returned to the stairwell and started climbing again. Before they reached the next landing, Bolan felt a quiver run through the building. The lights blinked, then came on a bit dimmer than they had been.

"Well," McCarter said dryly, "they surely know we're here now."

Bolan sheathed the Beretta, giving up any attempt at stealth as pandemonium erupted throughout the building. His boots rang on the metal steps as he unslung the M-16/M-203 and raced for the target landing, hoping he wasn't too late.

THE TELEVISION broadcasting room was small. The long desk behind Janyte Varkaus gleamed, looking expensive and officious. It was festooned with microphones. The background was a silvery screen that changed colors rapidly. For now it was a simple light green that one of the technicians said would make Janyte look even more pale and wan.

Her anger had overcome her fear as they'd worked to make her an object of pity designed to steal the courage from the hearts of the men who'd broken through the North Haakovian ranks and now stayed within striking distance of Sturegorsk. Twice she'd attempted to leave the television room. Twice Stensvik had assaulted her, and she'd had to be helped back to her feet.

In the end she'd decided there was only one way she could help her people.

She glanced down at her feet to make sure they were planted squarely on the masking-tape X that had been put down to mark her place. Wiping at her mouth with her unbandaged hand, she wasn't surprised to see blood come away on her fingers. The cuts on her injured hand burned and throbbed. The handkerchief the soldiers had used to bind it had become saturated with blood some time ago, and drops occasionally spilled to the carpet.

On the other side of the window walls, Stensvik was yelling at some of the technicians, slamming his fist on a piece of equipment that faced the television room.

Janyte was grimly reminded of how her husband had died and wondered whether he'd kill her in the same manner. Then she realized he wouldn't do that. The man wouldn't kill her on the air because she was too valuable to him as a hostage.

At least, he wouldn't kill her unless she forced him to.

A camera moved in at her and she almost flinched because it looked so alien. The cameraman made adjustments, then nodded at Stensvik.

The president stepped toward the glass and thumbed a button set into the wall. "Are you ready, Madam President?"

Janyte nodded without looking at the man. She took a final swipe at her bruised mouth, then composed herself as much as she could. Her heart beat frantically. She knew she had never said anything more important than what she was about to say.

A group of technicians pressed in behind Stensvik. Beyond them stood the dozen soldiers Stensvik had commanded to stay with him since a momentary power loss.

"Remember, Madam President," Stensvik warned, "you will deliver the presentation just the way you were instructed. Otherwise your people will get to see your public execution."

"I know what I have to do," she replied, squaring her shoulders.

"Okay. Start the transmission... now."

Janyte waited, thinking Stensvik might be testing her.

"Speak," Stensvik ordered.

Looking at the camera, Janyte said, "People of South Haakovia, I come into your homes today to bring you a message." She drew a deep, shuddering breath, then put every bit of passion into her words that she could muster. "Do not stop fighting! Live to be free!"

Out of her periphery she was aware of Stensvik raising his side arm and pointing it at her. She knew there was nowhere to run, and she turned to face her murderer, trying not to let her fear show.

CHAPTER TWENTY

"Damned elevator won't stop on the fourth floor," Calvin James said as the elevator coasted below the fourth floor for the second time.

Katz shifted inside the cage and gazed at the electronic card-key reader. "Evidently you need authorization to stop at that floor." The doors opened on the second floor, revealing a group of North Haakovian soldiers that waited to board. He reacted instantly, spraying the 32-round clip of his Uzi into the crowd and cutting them down like dandelions before a mower. Gunsmoke and the rattling thunder of the machine pistol filled the cage. "Get us to the third floor." He ducked to one side as the doors closed and slipped another magazine into the Uzi.

A scattered handful of bullets ripped through the metal elevator doors and tore into the back wall.

The cage jerked upward, then slid to a smooth stop at the third floor.

"I got the escape hatch," Manning said as he slung his CAR-15 and reached for the ceiling. He had to leap up to shove the emergency exit open, then jumped up again and started to pull himself through.

James hit the emergency stop button, then used a Swiss army knife to remove the control panel and cut one of the power supply wires. "It won't move again until we get ready to move it."

Reaching up, Katz accepted a hand from the big Canadian. Together they helped James through.

The doors over the fourth floor were tight and didn't give easily when Katz reached up and tested them.

"Want to bet whether they're wired for alarms?" James asked.

"No," Katz replied. It was a foregone conclusion that security would be heavy at the command post. The Israeli pulled himself up the side bars of the shaft, the Uzi hanging by its strap around his neck.

Manning and James scrambled up behind him.

Bracing himself on the narrow beam fronting the closed doors, Katz lifted the Uzi and nodded to James. "Open the doors."

Moving quickly, James balanced himself, fisted his Randall survival knife and thrust it into the seam between the doors. Klaxons went off immediately. He twisted the blade, created a gap that he could get the fingers of his free hand into and shoved.

The doors parted reluctantly, revealing a pair of soldiers.

James slashed the heavy blade of his survival knife across the throat of the closer one, released the haft of the knife and grabbed the man's shirt. He pulled, yanking the dying man off his feet and into the shaft.

Katz hammered the other soldier out of the way with a short burst of 9 mm Parabellums.

Striding into the command post, Katz leveled the Uzi as a group of officers and security personnel turned to face him. They clawed for their weapons. He cut them down in a blazing figure eight, dropped the machine pistol to hang by its strap when the clip emptied and drew his Beretta to finish off the survivors. At least two rounds had struck him in the Kevlar vest, and another had scraped along his right thigh. He felt the blood seeping through his pants.

Manning and James fanned out behind him, firing a burst that cleared the catwalks surrounding the computer workstations below. Three bodies rolled between the railings and tumbled onto desks, wiping out the computer and the furniture all at one time.

Return fire was starting to get on target, blazing from the metal flooring of the balcony.

Katz went to ground, exchanging the Beretta for the Uzi, and fed the machine pistol a fresh magazine. Lying on his back, out of easy reach for the North Haakovian guns, he yanked an M-451 Multi-Starflash grenade from his combat harness, pulled the pin and heaved the bomb over the side.

The explosive went off a few seconds later, throwing out white-hot sparks, multiple concussions and blinding flashes. It had been designed by Accuracy Systems to disorient and discourage hostile forces. Inside the command post, the effects were even more startling.

Katz rose from the railing with the Uzi on selective fire. He triggered round after round into North Haakovian soldiers struggling to recover their senses. "Gary?"

"Yeah."

"It's time we finished this."

"Right." Manning dropped into a kneeling position and reached into his pack for the specially prepared packages. They were about the size of LP albums, only two inches thicker. Tossing them like Frisbees, the big Canadian passed out two each to Katz and James and kept two for himself. "You throw 'em," he said, "and I'll blow 'em."

Katz glanced downward as he readied the first package.

Confusion reigned in the command post. The surviving technicians were busy running for cover, evidently unable to get through any of the exits. Smoke from electric fires was clogging the visibility, and the shrill keening of the warning Klaxons was deafening.

The Israeli threw the first package at a bank of Cray computers, saw it go spinning into place not five feet from where he'd aimed it. The second one followed, sliding under another cybernetic system stacked against the wall.

None of the North Haakovians seemed interested in retrieving the packages. Their aim was getting progressively better as they settled into cover.

Katz felt another round slam into the back of his right shoulder, deflected by the body armor. "Calvin?"

"Done."

"Gary?"

"Signed, sealed and delivered."

"Then I suggest we let those nasty little surprises of yours do their jobs." Katz pushed himself to his feet, staying low, and burned off the clip in short bursts as he covered their retreat to the elevator shaft.

Clambering down quickly, Katz watched Manning drop through the escape hatch and said, "Set them off, Gary."

Manning fumbled for the remote-control detonator in his combat harness, produced it and touched the button.

Thunder swelled in growing rumbles, then coughed out into the elevator shaft with a gigantic belch. A wall of heat and flame followed it.

Hanging on to the edge of the escape hatch, Katz pulled the door into place and dropped to the floor. He looked at James and said, "Take us up and let's finish this."

James nodded, then touched the severed wires behind the control panel together. The cage lurched into action, starting up when the ex-SEAL punched up the top floor.

The explosions inside the command post continued. Katz didn't even try to imagine what kind of hell it must be like inside there. Manning's talents with explosives was the stuff nightmares were made of. The Israeli tapped the transmit button on his headset. "Stonewall, this is Phoenix One. Over."

"Go, Phoenix One." Stonewall was Colonel Antavas's code name.

"You may begin your final assault. Phoenix One, out." As Katz inserted a fresh magazine into the Uzi, he visualized the line of South Haakovian tanks approaching Sturegorsk now that the missile launchers no longer had coordinates from the command post to guide them. It wouldn't be easy, but it was no longer impossible. He tapped the transmit button again. "Stone Hammer Leader, this is Phoenix One. Over."

"Roger, Phoenix One. You have Stone Hammer Leader."

"Did you copy the transmission to Stonewall?"

"Affirmative, Phoenix One. You people do good work. See you soon for the final walk-through. Stone Hammer Leader, out."

Katz checked his gear again as the elevator came to a stop at the top floor. James unhooked the spliced wire while Manning covered the doorway.

Bullets ripped into the elevator cage as Katz dived to one side. At least four soldiers stood in the hallway.

Manning ripped a grenade from his harness, armed it, counted down, then heaved it. The explosion cleared the hallway of opposition.

Katz stepped over the corpses, moving quickly, the Uzi tight and sure in his hands. The generators weren't going to be easy targets, either, but the Israeli knew they had to go down. Otherwise the entire covert team was going to be compromised.

MACK BOLAN HALTED at the third-floor landing and looked through the window, the last of Katz's transmission ringing in his ears. Four guards stood in front of one of the doors in the hallway, peering inside with obvious interest.

He signaled to McCarter and Encizo, letting them know about the four guards, then slipped through the doorway. He shifted the M-16 to his off hand, drew the Beretta and sighted on the first of his targets.

Encizo flanked him, his silenced H&K MP-5 in his fists.

"Now," Bolan said when they were less than fifteen feet from the soldiers. He squeezed the trigger of the 93-R, adjusted for the recoil and locked on his next target.

The H&K MP-5 stuttered in the Cuban's fists, and the combined firepower swept the North Haakovian soldiers away.

Bolan took up a position at the door and looked inside. He watched Janyte Varkaus make her impassioned plea to her country to continue the fight, then saw Stensvik raise his pistol to take her life.

Shouldering the M-16, Bolan shouted, "Stensvik!"

The North Haakovian dictator whirled in the Executioner's direction. His pistol went off, and the bullet plowed through the glass, bringing it down in gleaming shards. On the other side of the room, Janyte Varkaus dived for cover behind the big wooden desk.

Rather than going for the riskier head shot, Bolan punched two rounds into the big man's chest and saw him go down.

The crowd of officers and soldiers around Stensvik surged forward.

Bolan charged into the room, firing on the run. Encizo and McCarter were on his heels. The Phoenix Force members took up support positions behind desks and broadcasting equipment. They provided covering fire as the Executioner raced for the little room Janyte was hiding in.

"Get the woman!" Stensvik roared. "Kill her! Now!"

"Bloody bugger must have been wearing a vest," McCarter said over the headset. "I know you hit him."

Bolan knew it, too. He ran on, driving his feet hard against the carpet. He glanced to the side, saw a handful of men move forward in answer to Stensvik's orders. He emptied the M-16 in rapid 3-round bursts that put most of them down. On top of the wall of windows now, he swung the assault rifle in a short arc that shattered the glass. He smashed through like a halfback breaking through a defensive line, trusting the Kevlar and the Nomex hood to keep him from serious injury.

The impact staggered him. He went down in a sprawl, caught himself on his empty hand and pushed himself up hard enough to get traction. He launched into a roll as half a dozen bullets scored the carpet where he'd landed, then he was behind the big desk with Janyte.

She was waiting for him as he came around the corner, and swung at him hard with a microphone stand she'd obviously ripped from the cluster at the desk.

He reached up, barely managing to catch the steel length before it collided with his head. She fought to resist him. "We're on the same side," he said. "Save it for them."

She looked into his eyes, evidently seeing something she recognized despite the Nomex mask. "Oh," she said. "It's you."

"Yeah." Bolan reloaded the M-16 and passed the Beretta over as he took stock of her. "How are you doing?"

"I've been better." Her voice told him she didn't want to go into it.

And the big warrior knew there was no time. "You know how to use that?"

She nodded and took a two-handed grip on the 93-R. "As long as I keep this end of it from pointing at me, I'm dangerous to everybody but me."

"That'll do." Bolan leaned around the desk and fired a couple 3-round bursts that kept the more aggressive of Stensvik's soldiers and officers honest. "Phoenix Two."

"Yeah, mate."

Harsh blasts of gunfire made hearing difficult inside the room even with the earphone.

Bolan got his legs under him and found out he'd been cut more than he'd at first thought. But none of the cuts seemed to require immediate attention. "I've got a grenade coming out. Going to be a short fuse. You people keep your heads down."

"Affirmative."

Yanking the grenade from his combat harness, Bolan pulled the pin and counted down. Then he lobbed the bomb over the desk.

The gunfire suddenly quieted, and hysterical voices screamed words the Executioner couldn't understand. A heartbeat later the concussion of the grenade drowned out all other sounds. Flying glass rattled off the walls, raining over Bolan and Varkaus.

He glanced around the desk and saw a tangle of bodies strewed around the room. One man staggered to his feet and charged blindly at the television room. The Executioner put a 5.56 mm round through the man's heart.

Then the lights went out, and the silence of the building descended like a cloak.

"The other team got the generators," Encizo said.

Bolan slipped his NVGs from his kit and put them on. The darkness went away. He scanned the unmoving bodies, reached for Janyte's hand and felt it bloody and slick in his. "Your hand?" he asked.

"Will be fine until there is time to look at it," she replied.

He accepted her at her word and guided them out of the room.

McCarter and Encizo were already going through the confusion of corpses.

"Stensvik?" Bolan asked.

"Not among the dead, mate," McCarter replied. "Bastard slipped away."

The Executioner looked around the room and spotted another exit between rows of shelving for canned film and boxed videotape. Before he could move, Stensvik's voice issued electronically from somewhere overhead.

"You've failed, Colonel Pollock. The missiles have been launched, and by now the second bacterial agent has been released by your country. If I can't have these countries, no one can. The rest of the world can blame each other for everything that has happened here. And I hope you kill each other over it. This was none of your affair from the beginning."

Bolan didn't argue. He headed for the door. If it was true, and it was too late to save the world from Stensvik's machinations, he wasn't going to be too late to avenge it.

"IT'S CONFIRMED," Akira Tokaido said in a tense voice. "North Haakovia has just gone ballistic. Satellite up-link says there are eleven ICBMs spreading out over the globe."

"Aaron," Barbara Price said quietly at Kurtzman's side. She squeezed his shoulder in support.

Kurtzman knew the Stony Man Farm mission controller was aware that he'd hoped it wouldn't come to this. Even with his access to the Strategic Defense Initiative, the program he'd had to create was a monster. And it was totally untested because there had been no way to run it except through computer simulation.

"I've got it," Kurtzman replied in a voice that he knew sounded far away. All of his concentration and energies were locked on to the display screen in front of him.

The computer room grew quiet.

He was vaugely aware that Tokaido had put up the same monitor image that Kurtzman was studying.

Moving now, his brain locked totally with the efforts he could eke out of the computers at his fingertips, he keyed in the defensive program, stayed ready to adjust it as necessary.

Eleven digital representations of the ICBMs streaking through space arced over the atmosphere of the earth. Abruptly five of them winked out of existence.

Some of the tension eased in Kurtzman's chest, but he had a heightened perception of everything taking place on the screen. The one-shot nuclear-powered X-ray lasers had done their jobs as the first layer of the defense system.

Four more winked out as they encountered the satellite-based killer rockets that homed in on their targets and destroyed them.

Two ICBMs remained, starting their curving downward spiral toward the earth. One was coming for the American east coast, while the other was streaking for Russian airspace.

Kurtzman's throat got dry as the two missiles came within range of the magnetically powered rail guns. If they missed, the last layer involved was the group of dust-carrying rockets that would spread particles over the target area and hopefully deflect or destroy the warheads. He didn't want to go that far. As close to the earth as the

ICBMs would be at that point, there would have to be some damage caused from fallout.

Then the last two streaks winked out.

"Yes!" Tokaido screamed, vaulting up from his seat. He dropped to one knee and threw a triumphant fist into the air. "Take that, Space Cadet!" He gave a villainous laugh full of melodrama.

"Shit," Kurtzman said as he fell against the back of his wheelchair in complete exhaustion.

Price squeezed his shoulder.

"Hey, Aaron," Tokaido called out.

Kurtzman looked up at the younger man.

"Want to do it again? Maybe go for a free game while you're hot?"

"Hell," Kurtzman said, "I'm just happy with getting the extended play."

"TAKE CARE OF HER," Bolan told McCarter and Encizo as he bolted through the door, "and cover the stairway in case Stensvik tries to come back down."

The Briton reached out and took Janyte by the hand to guide her through the darkness.

On the other side of the door, a hallway ran for about twenty paces, then jogged right. Bolan covered the distance at a dead run, bouncing himself off the opposite wall with his empty palm.

Two men were waiting for him in the next hallway. Muzzle-flashes sparked in his NVGs, creating weird-shaped light patterns.

The Executioner went to ground in a baseball slide, feet forward. He squeezed the M-16's trigger, jolted the first man against the wall and dropped him into an unmoving heap on the floor while he slid into the second, who came down on him in a whirl of tangled limbs.

While the man was going for his knife, Bolan butt stroked him with the assault rifle and knocked him unconscious. The Executioner levered himself up and moved back into a run. He thumbed the transmit button on the headset. "Phoenix One, this is Stone Hammer Leader. Over."

"Go, Stone Hammer Leader."

"Stensvik's loose somewhere between the third and fifth aboveground floors. He has no way down except through Two and Four in the stairwell. Over."

The Executioner slipped the Desert Eagle .44 from its holster, preferring the heavier slug against the possibility of bulletproof vests on any of the men. At least if they were hit with the big 240-grain bullets, they would be taken down for a short time, allowing him a handful of seconds to readjust his combat reactions.

Two men were moving toward him, and he shot them both. Neither soldier had worn a Kevlar vest.

The warrior pressed on. If this many men were walking the halls searching for enemy targets, Stensvik couldn't be far away.

The hallway he was in widened out, booted into a wider corridor. He turned and followed it. Halfway down he saw the vague, blurred outlines of the North Haakovian flag hanging outside a suite of offices.

If Stensvik had any alternate escape routes open to him, the warrior reasoned that they possibly could be in his personal quarters or his offices.

The door was locked when he reached it. He jiggled the handle, positioning himself to one side so any exploratory rounds wouldn't find a home in him. The door didn't open, but nobody opened fire on him, either.

He stepped forward, lifted his foot and rammed it against the locking mechanism. Wood splintered. With a harsh, ringing bang, the door slammed against the wall.

The entry room was large and spacious, furnished to impress rather than to be functional. A row of desks pooled at the opposite wall forty feet away. The side walls were about the same distance. To the left was a sitting area with a trio of couches and a handful of chairs. A coffee table sat between them, littered with magazines. To the right was a line of false trees.

Movement picked up in the faulty peripheral vision provided by the NVGs drew Bolan's attention to the right. He thought he might have seen a manlike figure moving within the shadows between the trees, but he wasn't sure. As he turned to take a good look, a muzzle-flash stabbed into the darkness.

It felt like someone had dropped a red-hot anvil on the warrior's right shoulder. The incredible force slammed into him, jerked him around and knocked the M-16 from his grasp. Another round punched into the Kevlar vest and knocked him down. Before he even tried to suck his breath back into his lungs, he used his legs and good arm to slide back to the open doorway. The blood poured from his injured arm.

"Pollock!" Stensvik roared. "I know you're still alive! Answer me!"

Air came hurtfully into Bolan's lungs, but he made himself take it in anyway. He reached across his body and took out the Desert Eagle. The numbness was spreading down his right arm, and he couldn't feel his last two fingers. He flexed his hand, made himself test it just in case he needed it.

"Pollock!" Stensvik shouted. "Answer me!"

"I hear you," Bolan yelled back.

"You son of a bitch," Stensvik said. "I knew it would come down to me and you. And I knew when it did I would beat you. You're lucky to still be alive."

"So are you. If I'd known about that vest, I'd have put those rounds between your eyes back there."

"I'll let you live."

Bolan glanced around the corner and saw the North Haakovian president more clearly now, outlined against the trunk of the tree he stood beside. "You don't seem to be in the position to be offering anybody a deal like that. Your building has been infiltrated, and your city's about to fall."

"The building is wired," Stensvik said. He held up a metal box that gleamed from the emergency lights mounted on one of the walls. "Let me go, or I'll blow us all up."

Bolan tapped the transmit button on the headset. "Phoenix One."

"Go."

"I found him." He gave directions to where Stensvik's office was in the building.

"You don't sound like yourself," Katz said. "Is something wrong?"

"Stensvik found me, too," Bolan said, then explained the situation.

"We're on our way," Katz said and signed off.

Bolan exhaled, making himself relax and force the pain out of his mind. He tore off a section of his undershirt, ripped it into two smaller pieces and used it to fill the entrance and exit wounds the bullet had made.

"Pollock!" Stensvik yelled.

Bolan got his feet under him and forced himself into a standing position. "What?"

"I'm no fool. I know you have allies within this building. I'm waiting for your answer."

"I don't believe you," Bolan yelled back. He held the Desert Eagle in his fist. He knew he could shoot with his off hand, but targeting Stensvik in the gloom and getting the man before he triggered the remote control was definitely long odds. He needed a way to take out the man and the threat at one time. Glancing around, he saw the M-16/M-203 laying in the middle of the floor.

"The building *is* mined," Stensvik said.

"I don't believe you'll kill yourself," Bolan said. He sucked air into his lungs and flexed his injured arm, getting it ready.

"You leave me no choice. If I turn myself over to you, the South Haakovians will kill me. If I try to fight, I'll never be able to get away from all of you. Either way I'm a dead man. And if I'm going to be a dead man, I'll take everyone in this building with me."

"You're a coward," Bolan said, sheathing the Desert Eagle.

"You're wrong," Stensvik said, "I'll—"

Bolan broke cover without warning, pumping his legs as hard as he could, feeling the agony thrill through his arm and shoulder.

Bullets chipped the floor in front of the warrior, then the Executioner threw himself at the M-16. He slid and came up with the assault rifle clutched in his arms. Hearing the whine of bullets striking the floor around him, he rolled over into a prone position and braced on his elbows as he tucked the rifle to his shoulder.

The numbers fell fast through his mind as he lined the barrel up on Stensvik. He reached forward, the vision of the remote control in the North Haakovian president's hand emblazoned in his brain. He passed the trigger for the

M-16 and pulled the trigger of the grenade launcher instead. The assault rifle chugged against his shoulder.

The 40 mm warhead sped true, catching Stensvik in the face.

The explosion blinded the Executioner, and he ducked his head as flying debris settled over him. When he looked up again, Stensvik, the remote control and part of the wall behind them were missing.

The warrior pushed himself to his feet and walked over to the wall as Phoenix Force and Janyte Varkaus raced through the door with guns bristling. Standing at the edge of the ruins of the wall overlooking Sturegorsk, Bolan looked south and saw the first of the South Haakovian armored units plow through the blockades around the city. There wasn't much resistance. At street level the mangled remains of Franzen Stensvik lay atop a broken section of the wall that had been blown free.

"It's over," Janyte said as she came to stand beside him.

"Yeah, it's over," Bolan replied, "and we won."

Tears glittered in Janyte's eyes. "I don't feel like a winner."

Bolan looked at the men of Phoenix Force, seeing the grim lines on their tired and battered features. "It's too soon. It'll take some time before you realize that."

The South Haakovian tanks continued to pour into the city, cruising along the streets as their flags waved proudly.

"It came to this," Janyte said. "So many lives lost. I have to ask myself if it was worth it."

The Executioner didn't hesitated. "You're talking about freedom for your country. Freedom is something that's never come cheaply to anyone. It's something revolutionaries take for themselves at immense cost, then give to their children with great love." He looked deep into her eyes. "There's nothing else like it in the world."

THE FREEDOM TRILOGY

JOIN MACK BOLAN'S FIGHT FOR FREEDOM IN THE FREEDOM TRILOGY...

Beginning in June 1993, Gold Eagle presents a special three-book in-line continuity featuring Mack Bolan, the Executioner, along with ABLE TEAM and PHOENIX FORCE, as they face off against a communist dictator. A dictator with far-reaching plans to gain control of the troubled Baltic state area and whose ultimate goal is world supremacy. The fight for freedom starts in June with THE EXECUTIONER #174: BATTLE PLAN, continues in THE EXECUTIONER #175: BATTLE GROUND, and concludes in August with the longer 352-page Mack Bolan novel BATTLE FORCE.

Available at your favorite retail outlets in June through to August.

America's toughest agents target a Golden Triangle drug pipeline in the second installment of

SLAM

by DAN MATTHEWS

The scene has switched to the jungles of Southeast Asia as the SLAM team continues its never-ending battle against drugs in Book 2: **WHITE POWDER, BLACK DEATH.** SLAM takes fire in a deadly game of hide-and-seek and must play as hard and dirty as the enemy to destroy a well-crafted offensive from a drug lord playing for keeps.

Step into the future with the second installment of

by FRANK RICH

In Book 2: **THE DEVIL KNOCKS**, Jake Strait is the chosen hero of the hour as he tries to take control of an impregnable fortress called Denver.

Jake Strait is a licensed enforcer in a future world gone mad—a world where suburbs are guarded and farmlands are garrisoned around a city of evil.

JS2